THE GOOD
AND EVIL ANGELS

MATT HAYES

"The Good and Evil Angels," by Matt Hayes. ISBN 978–1-60264–276-8.

Published 2008 by Virtualbookworm.com Publishing Inc., P.O. Box 9949, College Station, TX 77842, US. ©2008, Matt Hayes. All rights reserved. No part of this publication may be reproduced, stored in a retrieval system, or transmitted in any form or by any means, electronic, mechanical, recording or otherwise, without the prior written permission of Matt Hayes.

Manufactured in the United States of America.

Acknowledgements

I would like to thank Janice Jackaline Hayes, Keith Aubin, Bobby Williams and Mark Evans for critical reading of the preliminary manuscript; Nicholas Linsdell who made sense of the senseless and Jowie Nash and Matt Smith for style guruing. Special thanks to Roger, for putting up with me.

Cover: An original creation by Matt Smith (shimuzu) from an idea by Matt Smith and Matt Hayes inspired by William Blake.

PART ONE

THE EMPTY

ONE

The laboratory was in darkness except for a pool of sullen illumination from a single bench-top lamp. A lone figure was deeply immersed in copious notes and idly twirled a single brown hair around her forefinger. The hair was pulled tense; the scalp tensed in response, lifted a little like a microscopic marquee and then the hair broke with a barely audible snap. Jan Crosbie looked at the remnant in her hand, checked the end to see if she had managed to pull out a follicle and was relieved to see that she had not. She sank back, stretched her hands above her head in half a yoga position, yawned hugely (in a way that only people thinking they are completely alone can do), shuffled her papers, swung her legs off the high chair at the bench, struggled into her shoes (which she had allowed to fall to the floor), grabbed her coat and bag from behind the door and sloped towards the exit. As she closed the door behind her, yawning again and rubbing the developing sleep from her eyes, a shrill repetitive beep could be heard from the corner of the lab.

'Bloody hell, not now, for Chrissakes!' She stepped back into the room, depositing coat and bag in a heap on her chair. She moved to the bank of whirring freezers and impatiently scanned the glowing diodes for over-temperature warnings. The shrill beep persisted and it became apparent that it wasn't the freezers that were at fault. 'The incubator, oh God!' she said suddenly, picking up step and running into the darkened room beyond.

Jan could see the blinking light across the tissue culture room. She donned the paper rabbit costume, familiarity and haste making her immune to its comic potential, covered her

4

hair and shoes with elasticated coverlets, snapped on a pair of gloves, turned on the lights and went to examine the insistent signal. It was part of a control panel recording various parameters in a gently bubbling tank. The blinking light and siren drew attention to an anomaly in the pH of the fluid. 'Shit! We must have contamination. What the...' Jan's attention moved to the top of the tank. It was itself sitting in a black-glass box, which obscured the contents inside. Someone had clearly opened the lid and failed to close it properly. Someone had been in the lab. Someone had contaminated the tank. Jan's mind began to race. She ran to the window. The room was under positive pressure but the window wasn't locked; in this lab, with these experiments, it was unthinkable. Nausea welled within her. Someone had left the window open and had tinkered with the experiments. Her head reeling, her heart in her mouth, she ran back to the gently bubbling tank. She silenced the alarm and deftly dismantled the glass box. The media was an orangey-pink, there was a slight cloudiness to it and it had started to foam.

'Damn! Bastards!' Inside the tank was a pink sack-like structure; its surface was covered with a dendritic pattern of interdigitating blood vessels. The whole thing gently flexed in the stream of bubbles; the structure was clearly a covering for something that nestled inside. It clung like an exotic fabric over the contours of a tiny form, which began to cause it to stretch and writhe. Hidden in its folds a little heart began to beat too fast, little eyes began to roam in desperate circles, a little mouth formed silent syllables. A moment later a whole battery of alarms were triggered; lights flashed in gruesome parody of the panic of the form within. Jan turned off the box, the pumps slowed and died, the heat lamps faded and the tank became silent. Jan poured bleach into the top of the tank, locked the window and left the room. Thirty seconds later a lonely night watchman was woken from slumber and received an unexpected character appraisal; fifteen seconds later the little figure in the tank was dead. Two days later an image of its mottled face peered out of the front page of three of the tabloid papers.

TWO

Joe did not particularly enjoy his job, testing, faultfinding, bug hunting. He often compared himself to a doctor perpetually caring for overweight patients. The programmers let themselves go and he had the odious task of keeping them alive. It was rather a self-deprecating remark because he had started to gain a few pounds himself and his posture was warped with constant hunching over the keyboard. 'Ergonomically designed, my arse!' he scoffed, as three lads who knew nothing about lifting with the legs carried in various gracefully curved, futuristic looking pieces of new office furniture.

'Someone really ought to ergonomically redesign your arse,' came the swift reply. There was always a smart arse. Joe's mind warmed over the idea of a counter reply along these lines, but his attention was drawn to the corner of his monitor as it informed him that he had mail. Joe was married, but Joe was experimenting (he'd always rather fancied himself as a scientist). Today he was entering dialogue with a lad called Simon. Simon was after a well built, slightly older man who 'knew what he wanted'. Joe felt he fitted that description admirably. He opened his mail server, but was slightly disappointed to find that the mail had been sent automatically from his own computer at home. It was a large mail with an attachment. The results of a little project he had been developing on the side.

He didn't like to think of the lines of code as a virus; this was too crude a term, too destructive, too coarse. It was a piece of genetic programming, a mutating algorithm, a useful parasite. Once it had been implemented it began to optimize its host, draw from it, adapt and borrow. It had done wonders to Joe's own computer software; most things now ran without a glitch, even the Microsoft packages. Today he would let it loose on the new computer system at work. This was a day he had been planning for a long while. After today he would be made projects manager and be given the research budget he deserved.

Joe sent a vaguely flirtatious email to Simon and compiled the code. Three hours later, the last message he received was still flashed up on the screen. Are you still there? But Joe was gone. The former Joe Lembeck was hiding in the executive bathrooms. He regularly hid in this melamine cave, before important meetings or following furtive email discussions with keen, nubile trade. He sat, perched on the top of the toilet seat, hugging his legs and cowering at the sound of his former colleagues as they came and went.

Lance swayed amongst the writhing bodies. He was naked from the waist up, his only modesty the piercings in his nipples and the twisted Celtic annulus around his left bicep. He was sweating profusely, breathing slowly and his gyrations sent his vacant smile flashing throughout the club. His wide eyes invited every onlooker into his world, but it was a personal experience that no one could share; a complex product of mind numbing repetitive drum beats, the cocktail of Special K, ecstasy and tile grouting he had bought in the toilets, and the cumulative angst associated with a string of failed relationships, dismal jobs and a lifetime of carefully catalogued under-achievement. His mind settled on a Brothers Gibb guitar riff that had been carelessly cut and pasted into the thumping ambience and he was drawn into his past, to a family holiday on the south coast, to a trailer-tent on a cliff top with the squealing Bee Gees giving it up on the wireless. The continual pounding sent him further back, a heartbeat, could it be his mother's? Reassuring him in an inky comfort blanket that held the disappointing world at bay. Now it wasn't a womb, it was the inside of his own skull; flashes of sheet lightning briefly illuminated the white matter of his convoluted brain. His mind simulated a flight over the many folds, sexual smoothness glistening as they lay clasped together, spoon in spoon in spoon, folding like knead-

7

ed dough. The thumping bass invaded his fantasy, and brought his consciousness to the apex of his head. He was lifted up, lifted up, lifted up, you lift me up...the music seducing and demanding. In the corner of his eye he thought he saw a wriggling, writhing line; a hair caught on the projector lens of his consciousness. He ignored it, looked into the centre of the screen, the focal point of which seemed to be getting further away, progressively less distinct. The annoying line was now a flame, a flash of white heat that danced in time with his heart, in time to the music, in time to waving arms that swayed around him, seaweed flowing in an unseen current. Pity the deaf, he thought.

He didn't feel the pain as his head hit the pavement outside the club. He was aware of hands lifting him, buoying him, lift me up, lift me up, you lift me up. He thought he saw spiders running along the walls. He thought his head was made of sound, his body carried away with the syncopations. He smelt another man's after-shave, bouquet, bouncer, bouncing, bounced, the words danced in his head. He unfolded from the street and reassembled himself in an upright formation. Warmth, blood, home. Somehow these words fuelled the white flame and tears gushed to his eyes as if to extinguish it.

He rounded the corner of the street and headed into darkness, the protecting veil that forgives and renews. The little gray wheels were following; he felt the flame tugging at the back of his mind. He searched his pharmacopoeia for a cure; a recipe flashed into his mind for melting moments. Suddenly he felt he was desperate for a melting moment, he had never wanted a melting moment so much in his life. He was not entirely sure what one was, but he had to have one, or a line of Special K.

In a moment the little white line was gone. Dot-dash-dot-daaash. Then the orgasm came, it was incredible. In a wink of his inward-looking eye the white flame exploded into the sort of incandescence that heralds the nuclear explosion. There was pain, but the pain had no meaning. There was a climbing mushroom cloud, tearing at the top of his skull. He felt as if he had been thinking too hard on a problem for the whole of his life, and it slipped away, throttling him with its tail as it tried to escape the confines of his drained brain. Then he saw himself from above.

The distance was barely ten feet but the vertigo he felt turned his consciousness inside out. Someone screamed behind him (or was it in front of him?) a wail that contained all the pathos of mother torn from child, of husband torn from wife, of townsfolk watching the dam break over their valley hamlet. He was dead, but that couldn't be true, he was too young, he was too beautiful, he had never known love; besides, his body was not prone on the ground, it was on the move. He wanted to call to it, to plead with it to reach up and take him back, but a fog was filling his mouth now and speaking would have been impossible. The fog, amazing, swirling, 'She Comes in Colours'; all he could do was trail behind like a dog.

The lab was heaving with sweaty types that normally do not inhabit sterile environments. There was constant noise and the rush of lighting and sound crew intent on performing their technical duties. Cameras were hurriedly set up, pieces of critical but rather uninspirational equipment were hastily removed and at one point a floor director was begging for dry ice and colored liquids. The requested items were laughingly dismissed by the head of department, a quiff-topped telly-don of instantly dislikeable character, but remarkable persuasion, who was leading the female presenter of Science Today round the lab with constant and completely unnecessary physical assistance.

There was a transient pause in the chatter and, as if on cue, a diminutive elderly man with a prominent exposed pate and piercing blue eyes entered the room. The head of the department moved to greet him, a hand outstretched and a wide, inviting smile (which painfully failed to disguise his clear disgust and dismay) plastered on his face. An attractive young technician reeling out a length of audio cable temporarily blocked his approach and the old man took the opportunity to sidestep the offered hand and attract the attention of Jan.

She skipped across the lab in a moment, head poised towards the floor as if she were allowing her intensely serious demeanor (evoked by the gravity of her first television appearance) to drain away. The face that greeted the old man was illuminated with pleasure.

'I'm so proud,' he said.

'I'm so happy you could make it,' she replied. She took his arm and guided him through the throng to the tissue culture facility. Jan helped the professor into a lab coat and drew him towards the gently bubbling tanks. Beneath his hand Jan felt him trembling; she could feel his fragility, almost visualize the friction as bone eroded bone in his thin hands. Overlying this, however, was the force of his grip; the excitement he felt was coursing through him, and when his eyes met hers they blazed with it.

The head of department was already in front of a camera. The room hushed and questions were posited from the assembled crowd. The thick glass separating them from the tissue culture facility muffled their voices, but the professor heard enough to emit a long, weak sigh. 'I suppose we'll get the lecture now!' he coughed. 'I should have sent the bugger down when I had the chance, saved us all the earache!'

His voice was drowned out as the doors were flung open and a few white-coated camera crew entered the room. The head of department followed and resumed his speech. 'One breakthrough of course was the use of the genetically modified placental cells in the construction of the uterium.' As he said these words the professor's teeth audibly crunched together. All the informed members of the crowd turned towards him, but the head of department stepped into their line of sight. 'But of course the major breakthrough was the use of a polymer based on a collagen and elastin matrix to form the supporting medium of the placental cells.' His voice trailed off as he realized that the collective good manners of the people in the room required him to introduce the two figures standing before the black box, manners he himself lacked. 'This, as most of you may know is Professor Black, who was intimately involved with the inception of this project in the late 1980s. This is my assistant Doctor Janice Crosbie.' The professor's eyes emitted a glare that was visible to everyone in the room, and set a cold sweat on the top lip of the head of the department.

'Hm, Jan also worked with Professor Black when she was a young and gifted technician.' He swallowed deeply and continued the general synopsis of the project. The tension was mounting in the room and all eyes were transfixed on the black boxes. The tension reached a climax but the moment was allowed to pass as the head continued unabated. The camera crew began to shift distractedly from foot to foot, and a few members of the sound crew looked at their watches. One of the more mature members of the press took advantage of a pause for breath to interject. 'That is terribly interesting Professor Clark, but would it be possible to actually see the artificial womb?'

The head allowed the pressure to mount a second time and then advanced on the bubbling box. His use of the word 'we' became more and more frequent as it referred to the intricate technical difficulties in establishing this unbelievably complex and world-shattering technology. His use of the word 'we' was at one point substituted for the word 'I' but this was retracted as Professor Black's eyebrows lifted. The avalanche of 'we's was only interrupted as he proudly attempted to remove the black glass frontage of the box. 'It appears to be...erm...I think there is some kind of...' Professor Black bent over and released the catch holding the glass case together. It was removed with a flourish. '...Ah, there we are'. There was complete silence in the room.

In a small, soundproofed room Joe's wife was sobbing. 'What do you mean there is nothing wrong with him? How can you say...look at him!' Her voice trailed off. Behind a glass screen Joe was grinning, his face was pressed up against the glass. His hand was thrust between his legs. He was clearly aroused.

'What I'm saying,' the doctor said, leaning close to her, 'is that there is nothing we can find organically wrong with your husband. Sometimes stress can induce mental breakdown that follows this pattern...' Joe wiped a glutinous mess over the window.

'What sort of stress?' gasped Joe's wife. 'We never, I mean, what do you, I mean, but we...'

The doctor took her hand. 'We have reason to believe, Mrs Lembeck, that your husband is a suppressed homosexual.'

The camera crew took a collective intake of breath as the cover was removed from the tank. The grainy shots they had all seen spattered with blood red headlines were a travesty of the ethereal beauty of what was before them. The hardest amongst the male camera crew felt his own innards constricting in time with the pulsing membrane. The quiet face of the developing child was clearly visible underneath its translucent covering.

'Are you trying to tell us, Professor Clark, that the child has no brain?'

'Not exactly,' came the reply (The drawn out syllables were accompanied by a smile of such saccharine condescension that the poor woman decided to quit scientific journalism on the spot and return to the sports section.)

'The cell from which the "child" (the inverted commas were clearly audible), is derived, has been genetically modified with a construct which down regulates a critical gene involved in the expansion of the brain cortex. The child has no fore-or mid-brain and none of the higher functions are present. The "child" is considerably less self-aware than say, an orangutan or a chimpanzee.'

'Does it feel pain?'

'No, well yes, if it was subject to pain, but it would not understand the cause of the pain as would you or I.'

'No-one can possibly know how intelligent this poor creature is.' Professor Black's eyes lit up. The authority in his voice was complete.

Professor Clarke shifted uneasily. 'No, but...'

'Such measurements are currently beyond our ability. The intelligence of an ape or a monkey is practically impossible to establish, let alone a duck or a swarm of bees.'

The head continued, his voice noticeably alto compared to his previous confident tenor. 'You would concede however, George, that the "child" is unlikely to have any higher mental capacity?' Perspiration was clearly visible on his brow. 'The "child" is little more than a vegetable'. The last word was clipped, it was a foolish mistake, he knew.

There was a tense murmur from the crowd.

'Ah, I think the tea has arrived. I'll field any more questions in the library...' With a sharp backwards glance he moved out of the tissue culture room. There was a flash of cameras, and the entourage swept out. Jan closed the door and placed her hand on the professor's shoulder.

'Fuckwit!' he mumbled. 'There must be a better way to do this,' he said, looking up at Jan. 'The rats had no measurable higher brain functions, but we know this poor darling could have some residual activity.'

'George,' Jan's voice was gentle. 'You know we have never detected any significant higher functions. This may not be ideal but it may be sufficient. They sleep George, nothing more. I don't even think they dream.'

The professor's hands moved across the face of the glass. But we'll never know will we?' he said. His bright eyes flashed and came to rest on the quiet, still face.

Suddenly he let out a gasp. 'My God!' The most sensitive of the university's spectral interferometers may have detected a slight change in the opacity of the glass at that point. The most powerful evanescent field microscope might have detected changes in the interaction of the water molecules on the other side of the glass. The most precise thermometers might have detected tiny fluctuations in the temperature of the medium and spectral analysis might have revealed changes in the pseudo-crystalline arrays adopted by a tiny percentage of the water molecules. None of these things, however, could have performed the measurements quickly enough to record them and no one on the planet could have made sense of them.

The professor staggered back from the glass. One hand rose to his temples, his face was warped in pain and confusion; he let out a strangled cough and then pitched forward.

Jan grabbed him. 'George! What is the matter, oh my God, George! Help! Someone, quickly, please! We need an ambulance!'

There was the sound of steps running in the corridor. The face of Jan's boyfriend appeared at the door. He ran to her side and knelt beside the professor.

'Come on now old boy, don't frighten us like this.' He felt the Professor's pulse; leaning forward, he listened for breath. In a moment he was performing cardiac massage. Jan breathed into the old man's open mouth, four breaths, fifteen seconds, four more breaths. More footsteps ran to the door, an alarm went off, the footsteps stopped on the threshold of the door. 'Oh no!'

Jan looked up imploringly, and then her eyes followed her boyfriend's gaze. The child in the flask was moving, thrashing wildly; tiny limbs tore at the plastic wall of the membrane, tiny feet kicked out at the umbilicus that anchored it to the membranous wall. The tiny mouth opened and closed as though the child was gasping for breath or words or both. More alarms went off; sirens could be heard in the street, a cry came from the lab as more people ran into the room. Jan's eyes returned to the professor, 'Come on! Come back to us, please.' Her eyes lifted up to the child but it was no longer moving. Jan could not bear to look; a glance was sufficient. There was something different about this child. It was clearly dead, she'd seen them dead before, they were clones, nearly identical. There was something about the way the head hung, something resolved about it and the hand, yes, the hand. The first and second fingers had formed a V shape, a little V for victory on the tiny podgy baby's hand, a tiny Churchill signalling from the other side of the grave.

THREE

Lance's body was on the move again. His eyes searched, red coals simmering in the cast-iron grate that used to be his face. The disembodied element that hung nearby was kneading itself in a furious attempt to stay focused on the creature beneath it. The effort of concentration resulted in a pain for which it had no name. Somewhere in its shattered consciousness it knew it was sobbing. Childlike it had begged for comfort, as an adult it had begged for reason, in begging it had aged. It was as a feeble reflection that it had finally begged for its existence to end. But something prevented it from leaving. A word repeatedly formed itself in the focal point of its mind. 'Anoikis....Anno eek iss....Ano ee kiss....ah no he kiss...' To be haunted in his final despair by a word that he felt had no place in his enfeebled mind seemed the final insult. Then suddenly he remembered its meaning. It was Greek, it was used in biology, 'homeless', yes, that was it. Homeless, he was homeless. He wanted to sob with increased pity but the eyes that would have provided the tears were twenty feet away and currently searching through a dustbin for scraps of food.

The fog was denser now around him. The image of his former body was faint and growing fainter all the time. Desperation forced him to keep pace as it scurried from bin to bin, frantically searching through the discarded waste for anything edible. A small dog, a terrier, ran into the alley. It was pretty thing, wearing a tartan coat; its owner could not be more than thirty seconds behind. It playfully ran up to the figure hunched over the bins. It let out a high-pitched bark and jumped up amongst the black plastic bags. In a flash the figure was on it. Hands enveloped the neck, crushed the life from it in a second and ripped it limb from limb. The figure, still naked from the waist up, crouched into a ball and thrust the bleeding, ragged end of a leg into its mouth, sucking the marrow from the bones. Thirty seconds later the owner appeared at the entrance of the alley.

'God alive!' He staggered back in revulsion from the figure before him, blood running through its fingers, eyes filled with blood lust, teeth crushing bone, fingers peeling back remnants of white fur from little paws. Their eyes met for a moment. Fear and bewilderment flashed across the man's face, the face of his protagonist tightened into a grimace. Bloody teeth were exposed and spittle flew from his lips as he hissed in defiance. The man reached for his mobile, pushed a little button on the top and screamed, 'Police!' His voice gurgled in a guttural way he had never heard before, the fear twisting his vocal chords into useless ribbons. 'Police, police, police!' he cried again, trying to force his throat to form a coherent vowel. On the tenth go the mobile responded with a series of beeps. The sound of which, so innocuous and out of place coming as it did between two men filled with the most pure animal fear caused the man to drop the little silver sliver to the floor.

'Which service?' came the mechanical voice from the box.

'God! Police!' shouted the man, but he had to back away as the crouched form in front of him reached forward towards the phone.

'Which location?' came the calm reply. The naked figure recoiled, clutching the dog's tattered tartan coat to its chest. The man grabbed the phone and shouted directions. Adrenaline surged and some degree of self-confidence reestablished itself. He felt a powerful rush in his veins that left him giddy with its sweetness. This thing was frightened, this thing knew fear, this was not a monster, but a man. A male, he too was a male, alpha-male, alpha-male. He approached the cowering figure, hissing manically. Something deep in his mind grabbed the levers of his voice and he shouted and spat word forms of which he had no experience. The amazing thing was that the creature/man understood them. It too hissed, but they were becoming less a threatening noise than those of supplication. The next fifteen seconds passed slowly as the two figures circled one another, their body language testing, tentatively feeling the air between then. The man's forebrain wrested control from the blind rage of his hindbrain. He tried English.

'What's going on? What are you doing? Why did you eat my dog?' The creature replied with low growls, his shaved head lowered, his brow creased in concentration. The eyes were still wide with anxiety but there was something strange in their black depths, or perhaps something missing. There was a vacancy, a pitiful vacancy there, the same void that you see in the glossy eyes of a sheep or a parrot or, or a dog. Yes, a dog. He felt his jaw lock in anger.

'You just stay there, you bastard, don't you even think of moving!'

The minutes ticked by. The dirtied, sweating figure retreated to a dark corner and continued his meal. At one point he even offered a glistening piece of flesh from the darkness. But the hand was withdrawn as flashing blue lights filled the alley with an unnatural glow. The creature's face contorted into fear and his eyes flashed from the swirling blue lights to the man and to the damp walls of the alley. His jaw was slack; his breath came in short bursts. He made a dash for a gap between the oncoming figures, a female police officer and a lightly built policeman. The latter was thrust aside and staggered back, winded from a blow to the chest.

'No you don't!' shouted the woman and rugby tackled him to the floor, climbing up his body as he clawed the ground to escape. She was not a light-framed girl but the creature writhing beneath her was getting away. It screamed and sobbed, its blood covered body squirming and twisting, its efforts less successful because they were not aimed at the woman herself but rather at the open air, at freedom. The dog walker grabbed the truncheon from the police officer's belt. She reached up to prevent the blow, almost allowing the body beneath her to escape, but it was too late. He brought it down with a crack on the back of the creature's head and its efforts ceased. Above it the remains of Lance's consciousness swam in a nauseous wave.

FOUR

The reporter thrust the microphone into John's face. His was a kindly face, one used to smiling but also one used to thinking. In time the two sets of wrinkles would give him a face of great character, at this moment he was simply attractive. His life with Jan had been very happy. He was filled with the light of one who has attained happiness in both their private and professional spheres. He knew he would never be a great scientist. The realization had come, not so much as a harsh wake up call, it was rather more like the smell of freshly baked bread, gentle, reassuring. Jan had walked into his life, he had met someone who would be a great scientist and it was immediately apparent that his role in life would be do his best, to muddle along, but primarily to support her. For the last five years he had been doing simply that. After the death of her mentor Jan had refused to become involved with the Uterium technology. John had gently persuaded her to return to a life of research, a different field, a different focus, the same drive. There was so much more to their life together than their work, so many colours, and so many facets to their relationship. The fact that their professional lives were not a cause of discord was another blessing that John counted every day.

'And you sir...what are your views on genetic modification?'

John turned to the camera, giving them a good few seconds to focus on his best side, drawn into intense concentration. He pensively massaged his stubbly goatee. 'Well, I don't think that everybody ought to be genetically modified, but I do think a great many people would benefit from a little dose.' He bid the camera crew good day and skipped off down the

18

street, leaving the poor anchorwoman floundering as if she had been slapped with a wet fish.

He slipped through the ivy covered side entrance to his city apartment, scampered up the spiral staircase and let himself into the spacious, modern flat. 'Hello darling! I've been on telly again!'

Jan met him with a hug. Her black hair fell across his face, one long leg pulled him to her. She threw back her head. 'I hope you weren't interviewed by Carol Vorderman again, I know your weakness for PhDs.'

John deftly extracted himself from Jan's grip, went to the fridge, and gave a roguish grin. 'You know I've gone off Carol after all those adverts! Anyway, I've only got eyes for Zoë Ball now!' He pulled out a nice bottle of Australian white, and poured a couple of very generous glasses. He let out a woofing noise and after a period of giggling and running around the kitchen table, the two ended up on top of one another on their expansive sofa.

'Lets make a baby!' he said.

'If you want to carry it sweetheart, do your worst!' came the muffled reply.

ZZ Top was on the stereo and John was miming into a half peeled carrot when there was a knock on the door.

'You didn't order pizza did you dear? I hate it when you order pizza when I'm cooking!' John cha-cha-ed to the door, and, carrot in hand, flung it open. 'None today thank you! I'm having my girlfriend for dinner...oh hello...' His voice trailed off as the two suits politely asked if Dr. Crosbie was at home.

'Oh yes, erm,' John waved the carrot in the direction of the kitchen.

'I'm sorry, you'll have to give Jan a minute. She's in the shower. Come in, might I ask what this is about?'

'I'm sorry but this is a rather delicate matter, about your fiancée's work.' The larger man flashed a look at the smaller one. The reply was measured; John was sensitive to an edge in the voice, this man was used to giving orders. John had always fancied himself as an empath, a sensitive; he pushed his abilities to the limit as he watched the men enter the room. There was something about them, perhaps a military element in their matched strides. The smaller man was obviously conscious and nervous of the presence of the larger; he was also embarrassed to be there, cowed, subservient to this man, but a man himself used to giving orders. He placed the smaller man as someone technical, scientific, used to running a facility, probably a lab; the larger man was very confident, probably Special Forces, a commanding officer of some rank. John felt his hackles rising, what did these goons want with his Jan? 'How do you know Jan and I are engaged to be married?' he asked. 'Are you friends of the family?'

'No Sir, we're from a research group, we have been monitoring your fiancée's work for some time. We are extremely interested in her contribution to fertility technology.'

'Really? That surprises me. I wouldn't have thought the military had much interest in female sex hormones. Is there something you want to tell us? You need counselling before you can go for the operation.'

The taller man gave a very weak smile. 'We are interested in the work she performed with Professor Black.' His voice trailed off. 'The late Professor Black. Ah! Here she is.'

Jan walked into the room, hair wrapped in a pink towel, a large bath towel serving as a makeshift dressing gown. She stopped on the threshold of the room. 'Oh, gosh, I, we, err, weren't expecting visitors. What can we do for you?'

The larger man introduced himself, 'I'm Doctor Wilson,' he said, 'and this is Doctor Wardell. We are attached to the Porton Down Unit.'

Jan made herself comfortable on the sofa. She started to dry her hair. John noticed the tension in her movements, he loved watching her dry her hair but this time he could see stress building with each vigorous motion. 'I'm sorry gentlemen, but I don't think you should be here, I think I can speak for John when I say we both have no desire to forge links with the military. Our work is strictly civilian.'

'Our connections to the military are only tenuous. We are very much left to our own devices.' The smaller man's face became animated; he shifted to the front of his seat. 'There are points from your notes that we feel need some clarification, we feel there are elements missing from your proto-.'

He was interrupted by a cough from the taller man. 'Well, actually we have been performing some related experiments on which your work has some bearing and we feel you might be able to help us overcome a little difficulty we are having.' John sat down next to Jan on the sofa. 'Jan hasn't worked in this field since Professor Black passed away, neither of us have any interest in pursuing the work. I really don't think we can help you.'

'No, I think you can,' came the terse reply. 'More specifically I think you can help this little girl.' He reached into his briefcase and withdrew a photograph of a child of about four. She was clothed in a simple white dress and her pale blue eyes looked out of the photo, wide, startled and confused.

'Pretty child,' said John. 'Your daughter?'

'No, not exactly, but I think of her as my own. Dr. Howey, could you put the kettle on, I'd like to talk to Doctor Crosbie for a moment alone, if that is alright with you?' John bristled at the man's presumptuousness in this, his own home, but Jan signaled for him to go. They touched hands and messages passed between them in the unwritten code lovers. Three minutes later he returned with a pot of tea. Jan's face was flushed. 'That won't be necessary,' she said, 'these gentlemen are just leaving.' She walked to the door and opened it.

The two men turned towards her. 'Thank you for your time, we will be in touch again, you understand the secrecy of this work, I'm sure I don't have to remind you that everything we have discussed is in the strictest confidence.' They looked furtively towards John and moved slowly towards the door.

'Good night.' Jan herded the two men onto the staircase. 'I don't think we have any more to say to each other.' She firmly closed the door.

'John, what have we done?'

'What love? What did they want?'

'George was right all along. He saw this coming, years ago. He knew the bastards couldn't stay away. Hell! We all knew they wouldn't stay away. Why couldn't they leave it alone? Why couldn't we have left it all alone?' She suddenly looked ten years older. She ran her hands through her hair, pulling it back and tugging the roots.

'Our Doctor Wilson is also a Colonel. The little girl is a clone, John. They've made a clone and they've screwed it up. They want me to sort out the mess.'

'And you said?'

'I told them to screw themselves, but they won't stay away, John. They will never leave it or us alone again.'

JoJo ran her stubby little fingers along the lines of brightly coloured pictures. She paused over a picture of a little yellow dress but then dismissed the image. Then, with a stabbing finger, she pointed at a picture of a mango. Her deep brown eyes looked up to the figure in the white coat, searching for approval.

'Very good! Good girl.' A little bowl of mashed fruit was passed across the table. The little hand reached into the bowl.

'No JoJo, spoon. Spoon. That's it! Good girl.' The little hand picked up a spoon and shoveled some of the gloop inexpertly into her half open mouth. A stream of spittle oozed towards the floor. After a few mouthfuls the fingers slipped and the spoon clattered to the floor. JoJo bent over the side of the high chair, then, looking back at the white figure, slapped herself on the head twice, pointed to the spoon, then at the quiet figure, then tapped two fingers of her right hand into the palm of her left.

'You are not a bad girl!' The white-coated figure shook a finger in the air, tapped her own head, smiling, and after making a number of little gestures, retrieved the errant item.

A thin figure walked into the room.

'How is my little JoJo today then?' he asked, smiling. He pointed to the little hunched figure and made a thumbs-up, then a thumbs-down sign. The two long brown arms reached out, gave two thumbs up signs and started to clap wildly. JoJo let out an excited scream.

'Up you get! There's a girl.' She was lifted up and clung round his neck, planting little kisses on his earlobes. The two of them performed a little waltz around the room.

'How is she coming along Kate? Does she take after me?'

'No, much brighter! I'm amazed. You'll have to go over the

tapes tomorrow, but she is way off the scales for her age. Symbolism, object oriented demands, grammar is beginning to form. She loves the sorting puzzles; she is quicker at some of those than I am. I can't tell you. Just amazing.'

'Is she showing any signs of irritability, un-natural aggression?'

'Nothing, she's excitable and into everything and she gets a little bit frustrated if I don't understand what she wants straight away, but then so does my 14 month old nephew and he can only say 'Mummy', 'Daddy' and 'choo-choo'. I taught JoJo three new words today, and she used 'fetch' without any prompting.'

The thin figure peeled the long, hairy arms from round his neck.

'Come on, back to mummy!' The little figure stuck out her tongue, blew some bubbles and then made two little symbols with her left hand. The man made a little gesture back.

'Tomorrow sweetheart! I'll see you tomorrow. I think she probably ought to go to bed, she's looking a bit tired.' On cue the little ape gave a huge yawn, which exposed her long canines and laid her head on one side.

'Good night darling.' The man kissed her on the forehead and gave her back to Kate.

'I'll go through the tapes now, meet me up in the observation room. I thought you'd probably like to see the latest results from the chimps; if anything they are learning even faster. One of them conned me out of a Mars bar today! He feigned ignorance for twenty minutes until he persuaded me to promise it as a reward. He then solved all the puzzles in two minutes and demanded that I pay up because he was so clever! I was going to have it on my tea break. I had to pretend to cry before he let me have a bit! When I called him a cheeky monkey he was most upset!'

'How about the g.o.r.i.l.l.a.s? Has there been any improvement?'

'No, I'll tell you later, lets not talk about it here...' He nodded to the little figure in her arms, who was looking at him with huge eyes.

'Night-night JoJo!' He made a little gesture. The little

orangutan replied in type, and he left the room.

In the observation room the assembled faces were puzzled.

'It's not that they aren't showing any signs of enhanced intelligence Professor, it is just that they show no interest in learning. They do show some behavioural enhancements, use of tools, some new vocal skills...' He was cut short.

'I don't call pointing to your trainer, calling her a pig in sign language and hitting her with a tin tray, much of a behavioural enhancement!' There was a ripple of laughter as one of their number reached up to her bandaged head.

'Mind you my daughter did a similar thing when I threw out her last boyfriend!' The sniggering continued.

'It's more the depression we are worried about Professor. We even thought about drug use, their capacity to sulk is unbelievable. They can sit around and not talk for days on end, even weeks; they stop playing, grooming, eating. I'm getting a bit worried.'

'Keep the observational work going. I know its harder for you people in the gorilla section, I know the chimps and the orang-utan results are looking more impressive, but the gorillas may come up trumps yet. I really think they may surprise us, this depression may be a sign of a more pensive state of mind, who knows what they are thinking about when they are quietly sulking.'

Just then a telephone rang. 'It's Dave over at the cages, there's been a fatality.' A chorus of disbelief worked its way round the room.

In a little white, barred room a young male gorilla was hanging, lifeless from a thin piece of cloth. The animal had hung himself with the professor's tie.

FIVE

In a plain yellow cell in a single-storey secure care unit, a figure was sitting at a desk. His knees were drawn up under his chin and he hugged them to himself whilst muttering a stream of sounds, clicks, guttural stops and gagging noises. Opposite him sat an aging man, he had an open notebook before him and scribbled in it whilst posing questions. He had not received any answers that he understood. After repeated rounds of gentle questioning in a comforting, coaxing voice that could have persuaded the most aggressive dog to part with a bone, he closed his notebook and left the room. The figure in the chair uncoiled from his sitting position and retired to a corner, his thumb in his mouth. The man walked away from the table, glancing over his shoulder as he did so. He tapped on a door which opened immediately and was quickly closed behind him. At the end of a short corridor was sitting a diminutive figure. Her eyes rose up to his, but they were dull, red and puffed.

'How is he doctor? Is there any improvement?'

'I'm sorry Mrs Lembeck, but it appears your husband has had a complete psychological collapse. To be honest I have never seen anything quite like it. Initially I thought he had undergone some form of regression to an infantile state initiated by some sort of trauma or internal conflict, but this is quite different. I'm afraid I'm not sure how to proceed.'

'Doctor, my husband is an intelligent man, he had a very responsible job, his children love him, you can't give up on him. I won't give up on him.' Joe's wife's eyes began to fill with tears; she wiped them away quickly, sniffed and continued.

'Something must have happened at Joe's work, there must have been some kind of accident, he must have sustained some physical injury, an electric shock, something, I can't believe you when you say his brain is fine. You can't be right, do more tests, more scans, MRI, I don't know, just get my husband back!'

'We've checked his brain by all conventional means; he shows no signs of physical trauma. I can't say what is wrong with your husband, Mrs Lembeck. It may be something he just snaps out of, only time will tell. We can try alternative therapies; I'm going to ask a behavioural analyst friend of mine to have a look at him. At present all we can do is look after him and keep an eye. He isn't showing any aggressive tendencies. He hasn't harmed himself but he doesn't appear to understand anything I say. Nothing gets through to him, his behaviour is only moderated by the tone of my voice; there is no meaningful response. If Joe's mind is intact, it is hidden from us at present. We can only hope it returns from hiding soon. I'm very sorry.'

Lisa Lembeck looked through the mirrored glass at her husband. He seemed more animated now and crawled along the edges of the room, feeling the juncture of wall and floor, occasionally licking the paintwork and scratching at one or another part of his anatomy. At one point he crept towards the mirror and looked directly at her. She knew he couldn't see her so the fascination that was there was with his own reflection. A few times he poked at the glass, but after observing little reaction he tired of it and coiled up in a ball to sleep. A nurse approached slowly.

'I'm sorry Mrs Lembeck, but perhaps you ought to get some sleep. You know I'll keep you informed of any changes that occur.' The nurse was Irish, short and heavily built. Her hand touched Lisa Lembeck's shoulder and she guided her towards the door.

'Thank you Moira, perhaps I should get some sleep. I'll speak to you tomorrow. Thank you again for everything you are doing for my husband. When he is well again I know he'll thank you himself.' She wiped her eyes, gathered her things and looking back over her shoulder, walked hurriedly to her car.

Moira Kilbain tidied the weekend papers and magazines and turned out the lights in the reception area. A flash of pain crossed her face and her hand reached up to her temples. She muttered to herself a short prayer that came to her in these testing moments. She walked to the staff room and bumped into the night nurse coming the other way.

'Moira you look bloody awful, go home dear, I'll see you tomorrow.'

'I'm fine, I'm just having one of my turns, you know, I'll be fine in a little minute. I'll make myself a cup of tea, I'll check on Mr Lembeck, bless him, and then I'll be off.'

She clicked on the kettle and rubbed her temples. 'Don't you be bothering me again you bastard will you,' she muttered under her breath. 'You just leave old Moira alone, you do.' She reached to her neck and withdrew a small cameo on a chain. It was a pretty thing in gold with enamel panels. It had two faces, one a little French maid, the other a cheeky pageboy. 'Now my boy, you leave me in peace,' she said, opening the clasp and talking out a little white pill.

She swallowed it without water and continued to make the tea. As the kettle hummed and began to gurgle, her thoughts flashed back to a little house eighteen years earlier. The family doctor was talking to her mother. Her mother was crying and wringing her hands. It was something she had seen her mother do many times. The doctor was saying Moira was schizophrenic. What a long, difficult word to have to say when you are in so much pain, when your daughter is killing you with her tantrums and depression. Her poor mother, how she had suffered at her own daughter's hands. Moira realized she was wringing her own hands, the kettle was rocking frantically, steam was filling the room. 'Stop it, you little bastard.' She clicked the switch and the angry boiling subsided. 'The little tablets have got you now. You won't harm anyone again my boy.'

Moira approached Mr Lembeck's cell. The lights were on in the corridor, too bright, she thought, but they did make one feel a little safer. Each room however, was in darkness. The occupants did not always sleep and she could hear muffled movements and groans behind some of the doors. Her hand reached again to her temple; a movement she had performed a million times. The pill was not working as well tonight as it usually did. Perhaps she was over-tired. She could almost hear the little bugger moving about inside her skull. 'You are restless tonight my boy,' she said. She shook her head and continued walking. She thought she heard sobbing, but she was not sure if the sound came from without or within. She looked through a little observation window into Lembeck's featureless cell. She couldn't see him. Moira went down on all fours. There was the smallest of gaps at the bottom of the door. She knew he sometimes hid there. 'Hello dear, how are you tonight?' A pale face was looking at her, illuminated by the thin shaft of light from the corridor. He let out a little whine. His eyes were wide and imploring. There was no intelligence behind them that Moira could perceive. Moira thought of her little Jack Russell she had had as a child. 'You sleep tonight my dear. Don't you worry, if they can help me with my little problems, I'm sure they can help you.'

A little finger scratched at the door and Joe started whispering. The words were strangled, meaningless, yet Moira could almost feel a sense in them, like the Latin in church, Moira felt it in her heart, not in her head. She was about to say goodnight when the pain in her head suddenly became intense. She slumped forwards to the floor, her hands touched the door to steady herself, and then it happened. For a second she thought she would die, for a second she thought she was actually dead. For a second she thought she was in heaven or hell, but the orgasm of blinding pain subsided as fast as it came.

Beneath her fingers the wood of the door flexed imperceptibly. Under Joe's fingers the wood responded, but no piece of scientific equipment could have separated the tremors from the background of thermal vibrations. The moment only lasted a fraction of a second, an instant caught between breaths. Moira gasped. She knew, for the first time ever, she was alone in her head.

From the other side of the door came another gasp, then

silence, then a crashing and shouting. Initially there was little form to the words, but soon Moira could detect meaning amongst the madness. 'Aaaaaarrghhh....you bitch, you bitch, you bitch...two, bitch...you bitch. We were two....you bitch. Two two two!' There was a crash as the now thrashing figure of Joe Lembeck hit the door. Moira rolled to the far wall. She had to get help, she had to get away. She felt suddenly, wretchedly alone. She had an almost uncontrollable desire to see her mother. She was crying as she ran, crying because of bereavement, but she didn't know who, if anyone, had died.

SIX

The Facility at Porton Down was hidden behind a bristling line of defensive fences. Jan's heart sank as they passed gate upon gate, barbed wire, razor wire, electric wire, young men with guns with razor-cut hair and barbed words, which folded into supplicant politeness as the appropriate badge or piece of paper was flashed. Again and again Jan tried to overcome the bile that rose in her throat. 'These are normal guys, normal guys, they can't help who they work for, they are on our side, everyone needs a job.' The graceless, faceless functional buildings and the strangely non-civilian concrete roads that connected them undermined these thoughts. No, these people lived in a different world. What was she doing here, how could she have allowed herself to be sucked from her own world, with its conventional problems to this sterile one, that peered out onto her banal one with barely concealed teeth?

The car came to rest outside the main biological facility. It was clearly built recently, of modern materials, but there was a fifties style to it, a style any civilian builder would never dreamt to have aped, the type of building that only a large committee of old men could have passed for construction. It made Jan's skin creep.

The security checks were thorough and intimate, but ruthlessly polite. Jan felt more helpless than she had done since she was a child. She remembered running out of the music school as a six-year old when her father took her to sign on for violin lessons. The old school building was just too big; the children were just too big. There were too many new things; the wild things were there....this is where the wild things are....She dragged her mind back to the present. There were a lot more wild things in this place, God Himself might feel nervous coming in here. She pulled herself together. This as the hardest thing she had ever done, but they had asked her, not the other way round. She was the expert. They needed her.

She was taken into a briefing room and introductions were made. Wilson and Wardell were there and a number of other suits. Jan was the only woman present; it boosted her confidence, this might be easier than she had thought. Wardell gave the first presentation. They had been following her progress, both through the scientific press and through other means (the word was sufficiently loaded to send a shiver down Jan's spine). They had replicated Professor Black's experiments with the mice and rats. In fact their success rate was somewhat better (the statistics were provided with a flourish), but from this point on the two labs had followed quite different routes.

Black's lab had decided to use anencephalitic monkeys in the progression towards the work on humans, but the military lab had proceeded directly using normal monkeys. The results were completely in agreement with the rodent data. The military used a number of other model systems as well (details were not forthcoming) but there were no unforeseen problems. The technology worked as well for monkeys and apes as it did for rats. He had designed a number of significant improvements in their initial (primitive) protocols, but due to restrictions beyond his control, he had been forced to restrict his experiments to her methodologies. The monkeys were normal. There were no problems. The work had progressed unbelievably quickly. They had even taken a monkey from the experimental system and integrated it into a family group. It had been successfully taken up, successfully established itself as an alpha male and had bred successfully. The Doctor's voice was rising, he was clearly well practiced at presenting this talk to a committee (Jan thought about this word...c.o.mm.i.tt.ee....only a committee would have thought of doubling up the m, the t and the e....). She fought back the rising desire to shout, 'If you are so bloody clever what do you need me for?' but the Doctor was clearly reaching his crescendo. The work was performed in parallel with other organisms (no details) and the committee had decided to progress (the word was stressed) to human subjects. Their first baby was born four years ago. It appeared that they had been completely successful.

He paused. The child, and all subsequent...(He was silenced by the interruption of Colonel Wilson.)

'The child's early development was completely normal, as far as our physical tests have shown. She is a very happy, one could almost say loving little girl, quite adorable.' The use of this word carried a gravitas in Jan's mind that she tried to ignore. Don't let them deflect you with false humanity.' But the child - we call her Athena or 'Atty'- seems to have a number of unforeseen problems. She has repeatedly failed to pass tests of intellectual development. She appears to be, in some way, severely retarded.' Wilson swallowed as he said this word, and Jan realized his face betrayed some personal sense of loss or failure. He continued.

'Perhaps Doctor Swartz would like to continue, he is our foremost neurosurgeon.' A thin man in his sixties took up the story.

'In effect I have very little to say, I could bore you with the many details' (there was a ripple of bottoms in seats around the room.) '...but I won't on this occasion. Suffice it to say that little Athena's brain appears to be perfectly normal. I would go as far as to say it appears to be in a perfect condition. There has been no shrinkage or failure of development of any area, the ratio of cell types is exactly as expected...' He trailed off. But the little girl has an extremely low IQ. It is difficult to measure IQ in one so young, but we predict it will never reach 15 or 20 points. We have done something very wrong. We have failed.'

The room was silent, all faces turned to Jan. Colonel Wilson continued. 'Jan, do you have any questions?'

Jan swallowed and pushed her chair back from the table. She was barely able to suppress the rising rage that was threatening to prevent her from speaking. 'Gentlemen; I have listened attentively to what you have said and I don't think in honesty I can help you. You have told me no more than I might have gathered myself from our earlier meeting. I have wasted your time and you mine.' There was an intake of breath and a number of figures around the table shuffled their papers and looked at the Colonel with smug, told-you-so faces. She continued.

'The human brain is the organ of the body that we know least about. Our work was aimed at the production of body parts for transplantation. Our most extreme aims, in our wildest dreams might have allowed us to transplant the functional brain of one individual into a new body. I'm sure you appreciate the extreme sensitivity of this idea, some would say the outright audacity of science to attempt this, and we had our detractors. We persisted. We wanted to know if it could be done. To produce the artificial womb. This was our aim but, and the late Professor Black was adamant about this, we would never allow sentient animals or humans to be produced in this way. The moral issues are staggering, unassailable questions of ethics stand in the way. Moreover, we knew the brain was the most sensitive organ to this kind of work. We knew it would pose the greatest difficulties; the development of the human brain in the setting of the normal womb is extremely sensitive. There are simply too many factors involved; we could not predict the results. We foresaw the production of brain-damaged children and failed experiments. We weren't prepared to make these mistakes with monkeys let alone people. The Professor's last words to me were to express his disappointment there was the slightest residual forebrain left in our children. Our lack of knowledge in the area of brain development meant, at this stage, this was unavoidable. These words have haunted me every day since the Professor died. I realized at that point we had made a mistake. I realized we shouldn't continue this work. I watched that baby die,' she tried to prevent her voice from showing any sign of cracking but it was difficult. 'I have not worked in this area since then. I have no intention of working in this area ever again. You have produced this poor child. Maybe it is a single error. Maybe your next child will be fine. You have bastardized our work; I'm not going to help you repeat the mistakes you have already made.

The room was silent.

All eyes turned to Colonel Wilson. 'I am very sorry we have had to confront you with these issues again Doctor Crosbie, we realize this must be very difficult for you, especially in the light of Professor Black's death. There are so many issues surrounding this work and we are aware of the moral considerations.' His eyes scanned round the room as if trying to find examples of a 'moral consideration'. 'We are not monsters here; we are not in the business of producing monsters. We have made mistakes. We are rather fearful that our American and Russian counterparts are going to make rather more mistakes. Doctor Crosbie, this thing has greater consequences than the unintended production of a single child. We have reason to believe that we are actually some way behind the Russians and possibly the Chinese in this regard. Our sources suggest that they have come across similar problems. They have failed to observe many of the safeguards that we have put in place to protect the children. The details of culture conditions, oxygenation, blood supply, the birthing process have all been solved, independently, by some of the greatest minds in Russia. They have arrived at different solutions. They still have failed. We can't explain why. I think you may be the only person who can help us. Your small laboratory has equalled the work of hundreds of secret sites throughout the world. Without your help our labs and those of the Americans will continue to produce these damaged children. We will solve these problems Doctor Crosbie with or without your help; but with you on our team, I know we can come to a more satisfactory conclusion much sooner.

Jan tried to remain calm. For the last hour she had watched the military men expound one of her worst fears. She had lived through this moment in a hundred sleepless nights. The fact that the military had performed these terrible experiments was no revelation to her. She had always felt that such experiments would be performed in time anyway. She had only hoped, beyond hope, that her own efforts would guide the work down a moral path. She knew now they had released a monstrous technology. The question now was whether to grab the nettle and collaborate with these people against her own judgement and that of John or to try to cut herself loose while she still could. In her mind's eye she saw herself as a screaming figure appliquéd into a terrible collâge that was being built layer upon terrible layer upon her. She tried to gather her wits, tried to breath deeply and decided to speak her mind.

'Following the bombing of Hiroshima and Nagasaki, Oppenheimer said that 'the scientists have learned sin'. The bomb builders were in a terrible war; their worldview was threatened at every level. They were told that the enemy also had the technology; that they were in a race, their only chance to build the bomb before the Nazis did. It was a lie. The Nazis didn't have the bomb; there was no race, just deception. There is no race here, just pain and unnecessary suffering. I'll have no part in it. I think I have heard enough.' Her eyes instinctively searched for the door. She had definitely heard enough; in fact she felt they had told her too much already. She must get out of here before she became too involved, too much of a security issue. Could they lock her up? How far would the British government go to keep something like this under wraps?

Colonel Wilson walked close to her around the table. He looked deep into her eyes. 'Jan, there is more to this than you may realize, far more. There is something I would like to show you that may change your mind.'

There was sincerity in his voice that Jan found difficult to place. Either there were personal issues involved here, or he was unbelievably good at his job. Jan was aware of her own na_vety, she knew she was not used to being lied to. She wished John was here to see through this smoke screen, she knew he would uncover any subterfuge; he was furious she had come here at all. It had been the cause of their first real row. She began to shake her head; she was about to speak when Wilson interrupted her.

'Please.' The word carried so many overtones; Jan was temporarily unbalanced.

'Please, just follow me for a moment. If this does not convince you then you are free to go. We won't pursue this issue with you any longer. I hadn't wanted to show you this so soon, but if the alternative is to lose you then I have no choice.' He directed her towards the door. Jan breathed deeply. His use of the words 'lose you' seemed somehow inappropriate. She wondered what his motives were. For a moment she was uncertain. She looked at the faces in the room. They showed a mixture of discomfort and anxiety. She agreed to follow him. This would have to be good or she would be out of there.

They followed signs to the 'behavioural labs' passing white-coated technicians with preoccupied expressions and evasive eyes. Joe had been a scientist so long, she knew this look well. It wasn't the furtive evasion associated with shame or fear; rather the look of someone who has seen a stranger step into their country church and has been caught unprepared for visitors amidst their meditations. They came to a lift. Numerous codes were keyed into various security screens; cameras followed their movements and whirred into focus. They descended into the depths of the facility. As the lift slowed to a stop Jan suddenly felt dizzy and nauseous; she wasn't very good with lifts and she hadn't eaten since breakfast.

The colonel steadied her, the slightest pressure on her arm. 'Are you okay? We have dropped a number of floors. It often affects people on the first trip, I'll get you some water and you can have a sit down in a moment.'

His voice was sincere, kind, concerned. Jan thanked him. 'I'll be fine thank you, I just need a moment.' She suddenly became aware of her posture.

'I hope you don't mind me asking, but, are you pregnant?' The Colonel looked genuinely concerned. Jan looked at her left arm; it was resting on the top of her abdomen. 'I don't think so,' she said, but for a moment she felt uneasy. 'No, I don't think so.' The doors opened and they continued into the depths of the bunker.

SEVEN

In the beginning was the word. The word was pain. Pain was the word and pain was with the word. In the beginning there was darkness, darkness and pain. The darkness crushed like the great weight of the ocean; an ocean on a black planet devoid of a warming sun, in the darkest, loneliest corners of space.

Pain and darkness were without end, impenetrable, infinite leagues of void; a terrible, terrible dream.

The dreamer awoke. It was a slow awakening, an awakening in a dark place. The consciousness tried to open its eyes, it tried to reach out its limbs. It let loose a great yawn into the void. There was something wrong. Had it died in the night? Only blackness greeted it. Pain wracked it and engulfed it. For a moment it knew only pain and tore at its limbs and chest as if to give the pain no nerve in which to hide. The pain subsided and warmth flooded the blackness. The void was filled with heat, sublime heat, greater warmth than it had ever felt. Comfort. Love? Then, from the velvet darkness came a point of light. It was like a lantern on a boat, this was death, this must be the ferryman to take it away; and to think it had only just known the heat of love. But the light faded and the darkness returned. It must have been a dream, all a dreaming vision. The consciousness rolled over in its inky bed and smiled. In a moment I will awaken and see the day, and my life will continue as it always has.

It thought for a moment. As it always has. Strange, for it could not place what this meant. It became anxious. Thoughts flashed through its mind, many thoughts, strangely echoing in the void. Stop! Stop it! Each thought was incomplete, a particle of sound, a particle of smell, atom, photon, graviton, emoticon, but echoing, again and again and again, in pulses, in waves. I must wake up; I must! It opened its eyes. It was no longer alone in the darkness. It could see its thoughts; they flickered like flames above it, pulses, my God! In colours, such colours. There was beauty there, it was everything it had imagined beauty to be, a school of little fish was beauty, turning together and billowing like a cloud in response to the unseen hand of the waves. They darted, silver slithers of light; one moment dark and mysterious in the gloom but then flashing in glory, but their light was not reflected. It was an inner light. They were in it and around it and of it. No, they were in him, in him. Somehow that made sense.

He thought, I am dead and this is heaven. Dead, heaven, the two notes of his thoughts danced, a chord, a harmony. Coloured notes, but not just colours of light. There was so much more. Each colour had a smell. How had he missed the incredible smell of colour before? It was miraculous to him. And the texture, the feel of colour was everywhere. How could he have been so blind. He. Interesting, it was a he, this was familiar, but what did it mean? Then something flashed towards him in the darkness. It was a greater darkness, made so much more terrible by the pale dawn it extinguished. It raced towards him, terrifying, unstoppable, terrible, a perfect horizon of the most impossible size, he could feel it's onward rush, he could almost hear the dying screams of souls crushed under its approach. He was not alone in the dark, and now to be destroyed before even reaching out to another voice in heaven. This must be the hand of God; this must be his reckoning. He screamed out, a wave of light and colour, he felt the void around him distort and warp. No! Not me, NO! The horizon was on him. In a moment there was nothing but void. And not a soul to light the darkness.

There appeared to be no end of secure steel doors in the lower floors of the MOD behavioural unit. Jan was beginning to lose track of how far they had walked. They finally stopped, room sb102. It looked like all the others. Colonel Wilson typed a particularly long code into the wall unit, cursed and then typed it in again. The door clicked, a camera focused on them and he opened the door. The room was well lit; it was much larger than Jan had expected. It smelt of generic cleaning fluids. The room itself was clearly a surveillance room for three smaller rooms beyond. Each room (perhaps cell would have been a better word for them) contained a lone figure. They were in various states of inactivity: one was curled in a ball and appeared to be asleep in a corner; another was walking a circuitous route around the room, shoulders hunched, eyes searching from side to side; the third was picking his nose and examining the results.

'These gentlemen are Drs Longman, Stilber and Swallow. There are our three most outstanding computer surveillance scientific officers. Three very talented young men.'

'What the hell happened to them?' Jan slowly approached the cell windows. 'Can they see me?'

'No, we can let them see you if you would like. Believe me, it is easier just to observe. To answer your question, we really don't understand what has happened to them. We had been monitoring the activity of a young man connected with a software engineering company in London. We felt he was trying to develop a computer virus of some kind; such programs often have common elements, signatures, which allow us to track them from place to place. We were downloading everything that was sent from his computer. He sent something that we couldn't identify. A program, short and unlike anything we had seen before. It had an interesting structure. Four of our top programmers were asked to establish what the program did. When they ran it they immediately entered the strange state that they seem to be in now. We had to stop these three smashing up the terminals they were working on; they rampaged through the office, obviously confused. I've only seen men behave like this under extreme battle conditions, and even then it is rare. They are currently sedated, but we are reducing the dosage. They don't appear to be inherently violent, just scared out of their minds.'

'What happened to the fourth person?' Jan watched the figures closely. She had observed patients under stress and those suffering from mental illness before, but these guys were different somehow, they lacked a certain something in the eyes.

'They were working on the program on our fastest machines, using different algorithms to analyze its functionality as it was running. The fourth party, a chap called Fred Garst, was work shadowing on a slower machine. Halfway through the download the machine crashed. He was the lucky one. He is taking some time off; this was a bit of a shock to all of us.'

'Do you think it is some kind of weapon?' Jan's mind was racing, a computer virus that could leap from the screen and infect a person's mind; surely such a thing was not possible.

'We don't believe at this present time that it was designed to operate as such. The designer himself is in a similar state; he is in a secure wing in a civilian hospital outside London. This all happened five months ago; it is possible that the guy could have been foolish enough to fall foul of his own invention, or he may have thought he was committing suicide. It is also possible that he built the thing as some kind of mind-altering weapon, we thought maybe even as a psychotropic aid, to induce a trance or drug-like state, but the fact is we have no idea. He had no connection to any of the organizations we monitor. It is a mystery to us.

'I'm terribly sorry Colonel Wilson, I really am, but I can't see what this has to do with me. How can this possibly have anything to do with the uterium technology?' Jan's mind was working overtime, perhaps these poor guys were clones produced by the military; perhaps clones were in someway hypersensitive to external stimuli.

'There may be no connection whatsoever. I hope there is no connection; the thing that has puzzled me is that we can find absolutely nothing wrong with the minds of these men. Their brains seem perfectly normal, every test we have performed says they are biologically as kosher as you or I, they just appear to have a dramatically reduced IQ Our best psychometric analysis would suggest their IQ has been reduced to around 20 or 30. I was just hoping that perhaps we could do something for these men, maybe there is some common element, and I know it sounds ridiculous but I just have this feeling that there is something connecting the two events. I'm afraid no-one here agrees with me,' He gave a little sigh, 'It is just fortunate that I am the boss and can do what I like, within limits. I really need someone else, with an open mind to think about the problem too. I have looked at your CV, Dr. Crosbie. Your background is diverse: medicine, behavioural science, molecular biology, genetics and your knowledge of the uterium technology is second to none. You are the best person- no, not the best person- the only person who can help us. I really want you on board.' There was emotion in his voice; he spoke like a scientist, with the misplaced passion of someone who ought to be professionally detached from the subject. He was also attractive.

'I need to give it some thought. I'm intrigued but sceptical. I'd need complete access to the men and the child. I'd need to see your facilities. I'd need to see your protocols and I need to interview the staff involved. I would need complete and absolute cooperation,' She added, as an afterthought. 'and I'd need my fiancé to work with me.'

'I can't promise you everything now, though I will do my best. There are questions of secrecy. You would be working under the highest levels of security. This is a very sensitive matter. I'll contact you again in three days. You must not speak to anyone of what you have seen here. Even your fiancé, until I have cleared this through the appropriate channels. There is one more thing.' Wilson's face became grave. 'We tried to reduce the 'out-fall' from this event Dr. Crosbie. We were at the site of origin only hours after these events took place, but there is a problem. Shortly after automatically sending a message to the perpetrator's place of work, his own computer automatically dialed out to his home address. We don't know what state he was in at this point. We are not entirely sure what was sent. The file was huge; we haven't yet decided what to do with it. We haven't yet attempted to open it. The problem is, this message has passed through the Internet. It is extremely difficult to trace errant messages in this way. It can pass through many nodes; we can't disconnect them all. We have closed down many of them. This thing might get out. We have no idea what the consequences of that would be.'

'What is this man's name, the one responsible for the code in the first place? I'd need to see him too.'

'Lembeck, Joe Lembeck.'

The police van carrying the howling remnant that was Lance Tanner whirled round the side streets of Brixton. Its siren was blaring, the lights flashing. The driver picked his way between double-parked cars, dropped down into Brixton Hill, then swung the van back into Acre Lane, heading for Clapham Common. He couldn't believe it. He'd got one nutter in the van already and they were asking him to provide back-up to bring in another. He hated this part of London. As far as he was concerned they were all perverts and freaks. They weaved and cut between traffic, and he screeched to a halt behind an elderly couple parked across the junction, the poor dear's eyes on everything except the bloody great police van sitting directly behind them. The siren was not working; he tried the horn. 'For God's sake!' Mind you, he thought, why am I rushing? It's just another cracked-out junky to stick in the van, hardly worth bothering with. He still got a buzz out of driving the van at speed though, if only this old dear would get out of the way.

'Thank you darling!' he shouted out the window. The female police officer who was accompanying him and trying to look disinterested gave him a bit of a look. He wished they would let him have a tape player in the van. He fancied a bit of Wagner, something stirring, something operatic and Germanic; he was the Valkyrie and he was swooping for the kill.

'We are getting close now,' the police officer was monitoring the radio, any minute now, just round this....' She was cut short; there was a scream of brakes, the van skidded, tipped, turned on its side. There was absolutely no way he could have missed the guy. They skidded to a halt and crunched into a parked car. Inside the cabin both officers waited for a further crunch; they were lucky, it did not come. They looked across at each other. 'You alright?'

'Yeah, I'm fine,' the driver unclipped the seat belt and fell out of his seat. A crowd was gathering. 'Get the station on the blower, tell them to send an ambulance, though I think it'll be too late to help that bugger.'

He clambered out of the van. Pity, he thought, I only washed the bloody thing this morning.

It did look incongruous, fairly new, shiny, slain in the street with skid marks and a long, quickly drying trail of blood describing its final moments. The blue flashing lights still whizzing round, it was not quite dead.

There was little evidence of the victim; thankfully the crowd would have nothing much to see. He was all under the flank of the van. The driver placed his ear to the floor near the ground, being careful not to get the pooling blood on his trousers. There wasn't a sound.

Two policemen rounded the corner. The driver recognized the older of the two. 'You got him then? I think your methods are a bit extreme, but we always knew you wanted to be a stunt driver.' The man laughed. 'Mind you, think about the report writing Jim.' He glanced at his colleague. 'I saw the gentleman running from the scene of the crime, two gallant officers in hot pursuit and...in order to prevent the escape of the aforesaid crack-dealer addict, it was necessary to drop this bus on him from a great height!' He found his joke funnier than the driver did.

'Shit, we better check on the bloke inside'

'You've got another one inside? Got any more buses?'

'Look, for your information the chap is a loony of the first order. We picked him up not fifteen minutes ago. He was eating some guy's dog.'

They carefully opened the door of the van. Lance was prone, face down on the side of the van; his arms were handcuffed behind him. He was unconscious from the force of the collision. The driver reached in and felt his pulse. He was alive. 'We better get the psycho to hospital then.' The sirens were approaching round the corner. Bloody brilliant, what a mess this was going to be.

The essence that called itself Lance was close to Lance's body before the crash occurred. He could feel himself being drawn back. Thank God, thank you, he was becoming so tenuous. Any longer and there would be only smoke left of him. He was fading with every second, but whatever it was that had broken the link with his beloved body was fading too. The influence was going, the body looked so inviting. The body was his; it had always been his. He could not see his old face now; the glare from the light was so bright. The light shone before him, it tore at him; it pulled him into ephemeral strips that swirled about the silent head. The light was the path, it was in him and of him and he was the path. The light held him completely enraptured; everything around him blurred into a tunnel that revolved around it. Any minute now, any moment, they would be reunited. Time meant so little to it now, but it registered the accident, it saw the body tumble, no matter, we'll be together, no matter.

Then it felt another presence. He couldn't see it exactly, but he knew it was there. It was like him, it was free of its body. It was close, very close. Then he saw it, the crushed remains beneath the van, the dog's dinner of organs smeared into a mess. The skull, like a cracked pot, the contents that used to think, used to plot and dream would never do so again. But Lance could feel the light from the other presence. He could feel its loss of focus, its surprise, the shock that had shaken it from this mind left it reeling, it was scratching in the bombsite of the skull, but there was nothing there for it. It was desperate. Lance knew it was feeling the smoke now. He knew it would soon feel the desperation he himself had felt, the desperation of the homeless. He was not going to be homeless much longer though. He was going home, going home. The light was drawing him in. The tunnel was collapsing, the nausea was rising, the pain, the rapture. The light was so bright, so warm.

During the orgasm that was the transition, he didn't feel the other light mingling with his own. As he entered his old body, the limbs shook with shock, the twitch of life that shakes you as you step off the cliff into the void, into sleep. As he fell into unconsciousness he was aware that he wasn't alone.

EIGHT

'I don't believe you said yes to those bastards! I can't see how you could possibly have agreed to help! What about your scientific integrity? You know what the Professor would have said, I just don't get it!' John turned his face to the wall. It was clear he could barely contain his bewilderment and anger.

Jan swept her hair out of her eyes. 'I haven't said yes, I haven't agreed to anything yet. I said I'd think about it. I know this is hard for you, I know you can't understand. I'll tell you everything in a few days time, but not now. I need to think. I need to think what George would do.' She stroked her fingers through the hair on the back of John's neck. 'There is more to this than you know; more than you could guess. I need your help. I need your help to get me through the pressure of this, and I'll need your help in every way once I've made a decision whether or not to get involved. Please, just trust me, just until next week.'

'I'm sorry love, I just don't want you to get hurt. I don't trust these army types. Their moral code is not the same as ours; it's muddled up with the army's political agenda. I just can't see you getting involved. They aren't our sort of people. We've never had secrets before, and now we have. Already they are affecting our code, our morality.'

Jan kissed him on the lips. Slow to anger, John was also easy to calm. 'I rely on you and trust you completely. You'll just have to allow me a little space to find out what it is I could be dealing with. As soon as I know I'll tell you everything and the final decision will be ours. We'll make the decision together, I promise.'

An hour later they were slumped together in front of the television and chewing on pizza Veneziana as Captain

45

Janeway commanded Voyager to open fire on a race of beings that harvested organs for a living. 'I'm not sure I want to watch this' said Jan, clicking the remote and flicking to a seventies sitcom. Sometimes real life was outlandish enough.

Kate cradled the bundle in her arms, she held her close to her chest, muttering her name quietly and tapping her repeatedly on the nose with her little finger. It was their special sign. It was not in their 'Complete Simian Sign Lexicon'. It was the sign they used to each other that meant, I love you, I've got to go, I'll see you soon. To be honest Kate couldn't remember whether it was her or JoJo that had used the sign first. How she loved this job. She bounced the little girl up and down. JoJo was getting much heavier, or was she getting weaker. Unfortunately both were probably true. She placed the orang-utan down in her cot, made half a dozen complex little hand gestures, which today also said much more than their normal grammatical, dictionary definitions, and backed out of the room. JoJo waved goodbye, her hands performed a silent dance. You, leave, come back, never, I, sad, I, sad. Kate heard the words as clearly as if she had spoken them out loud. She reassured the ape again, and left the room.

Kate met the Professor in the hallway. 'Is it absolutely necessary that I go over to the gorilla station Gerry? I really don't want to leave JoJo for so long. She is at a very vulnerable age.'

'You know I wouldn't send you over there if I didn't think it was important. I can't cope with their depression. The drugs aren't working as well as we thought they might. They are in a bad way. I really don't want to lose any more, not the way we lost Bono.' The gorilla's death had affected the Professor deeply. Kate was worried the whole project might fold in the few months that followed. It had taken her many long hours of discussion to get Joe to carry on. Joe's compassionate side was not something that everyone on the team saw. Kate loved him for it. In a moment his professional demeanor in front of students and colleagues could be shattered by the antics of the animals. He had been known to walk out of meetings with the top executives of the funding body in order to answer his beep and personally check up on an ape that had injured itself or was behaving out of sorts. She had seen Joe at his lowest ebb recently. Now she knew she would have to try to solve the problem with the gorillas. This was her biggest test yet. No one had any idea as to the nature of the problem. It was just a terrible shame that she had received her 'bad news' now, such a ruddy bad bit of timing. She hadn't told Joe yet. He couldn't know until she'd sorted out this gorilla program. She didn't need Joe to tell her how much he needed her help, or at least she had never really felt the need for him to say it before. They were always colleagues together, Batman and Robin. Today though, his kindly smile warmed her like the sun itself. This would be her final piece of research work. This was going to be her greatest moment, if providence gave her sufficient time to complete the work.

NINE

The Daimler pulled up outside the care home. The chauffeur walked round to the rear of the car and opened it for Jan Crosbie. John looked across at her over the plush leather of the armrest.

'Don't get too used to it love, tomorrow you drive yourself!'

'You, dear, are the only person who drives me anywhere.' She beamed a big smile towards him and skipped out of the car. John and Colonel Wilson walked round to the front. In spite of himself, John found that he quite liked this man. He was surprisingly down to earth and frank for someone in his position. The supreme confidence that he exuded with his staff melted away the instant he was in conference with either of them. There were clearly two men residing in this man's head, the professional military man and the concerned, humanitarian, academic. John felt there must be regular battles inside over who would command the boat on any one particular day. Today it was the scientist.

'As I was saying in the car, there has been a dramatic change in Mr. Lembeck's condition. The staff here are pretty shocked about it. Our man Isenberg has had a look at him, he briefed me shortly before I left to pick you up. He is still writing his report; he was a little confused. I thought we best have a look ourselves...Ah, the warden.'

The three were shown into the observation room. Joe Lembeck was sitting at a table. He was dressed in a freshly laundered shirt and tracksuit bottoms and was drinking tea. Introductions were made and tea was brought for everyone. Joe appeared calm, and comfortable. The warden had informed the Colonel that he was still medicated, but there had been dramatic improvements in his mental state and also, rather unexpectedly, some developments.

'Hello Joe, my name is Brian, we have met before.' The Colonel held out his hand. It was the first time either of them had heard his first name. They were both slightly surprised. It didn't have the military ring to it they had expected. John thought this was probably the reason he didn't use it very much at work. Joe Lembeck looked at the proffered hand but did not respond. His eyes, little sparks deeply set in dark brown rings (he clearly had not slept for several nights), looked at the three of them.

'I want to go home. Please can you tell them I want to go home.' The voice was firm, calm, controlled; there was a trace of an accent. John couldn't quite place it, subtle; but definitely there.

'I'm afraid we are not in a position to let you go home, Joe.' the Colonel glanced across at the warden. 'Dr. Craig here tells us you are feeling much better; perhaps you'll be ready to go home soon. Perhaps you could tell us how you are feeling, yourself?'

Jan noticed how Brian instinctively dropped into dialect. Was he empathic or just carefully studied in his approach to psychological interview? In either case it was a useful skill. This man obviously had hidden depths.

'I'm fine. Just fine. Never felt better, never felt better.' There was a sing-song element to the voice. Irish, definitely an Irish lilt.

John spoke up, 'Joe, where is home for you? I can't place your accent?'

'Derry.' The reply was immediate and firm. Then Joe's eyes looked away. 'No, what am I saying? I live here, in London.' He was beginning to look a little agitated.

The Colonel pulled his chair in closer to the table, he leant closer to Joe. 'Do you remember how you came to be here Joe?'

'Nothing, I remember nothing about it.'

'Do you remember anything about your program?' Joe's eyes gave no flicker of recognition. 'I don't know nothing about any program. All I remember is waking up here.'

'Where were you before you woke up here?' Jan asked, her voice very calm, very soothing. Colonel Wilson almost found himself answering the question.

'I don't remember.' Joe placed his head in his hands. 'I don't remember, I was tired, I was tired and she wouldn't let me out, I was tired and she kept me in. It's not fair.'

'Who is she Joe? Who wouldn't let you out?' John was watching his every movement. Joe had drawn his legs up under his chin. He began to hug himself.

'She knows! But she wouldn't let me out. You must let me out, I can't stay here, you must let me free, please, please!' He began to sob. The Doctor intervened. 'I think Joe has had enough for one day, thank you.'

Joe nodded, 'I'm tired, I'm so tired…'

The Doctor led them from the room. 'This line of questioning gets you nowhere. He seems to have no memory of anything that brought him here. We think it is some kind of amnesia, brought on by his mental collapse. He has adopted an alternative persona, but the effort of maintaining it is beyond his current mental abilities. He needs more time.'

'Has his wife seen him yet?' The Colonel was clearly disappointed with the brevity of the interview.

'I would rather you didn't speak to Mrs Lembeck either, just at the moment. I have had to prescribe her tranquilizers. She is not coping with this very well. The improvement in Joe's condition is remarkable, but this intermediate stage has upset her greatly.'

'But what has she said to you Doctor, about Joe's current state of mind?'

The Doctor's voice was weary. 'She has begged me to get her husband back; she says this man is someone else. I have tried to tell her, tried to explain that the personality is so fragile in people who have suffered the kind of trauma that has affected Joe. It will just take time. I could let the psychotherapists back in with him, but I think time is the greatest healer in this kind of situation, time and patience. I don't think his mind is sufficiently stable to respond to therapy. They may do more harm than good.'

'Thank you for your time Doctor, you will please keep me informed of any further changes in Joe's condition.' The Colonel shook hands with the Doctor, and the three of them returned to the car.

Moira Kilbain watched them go from the staff room. She swallowed another valium with her instant slimmer soup, breathed deeply and thought about who she could ask to cover her round with Joe Lembeck. 'I don't want to be speaking with you again my boy,' she thought. The thought faded from her mind. She listened for the usual reply. It was not forthcoming. 'Thank God', she said out loud and gently stirred the sugary mush.

TEN

The sleeper awoke for the second time. The process of slipping from unconsciousness to wakefulness passed through him like a wave. He had not dreamt. There was still pain out there in the void. He could feel its approach, felt it stalking at a distance; a black panther circling him in the darkness. This time he felt more assured than before. He peered out into the dark, his thoughts forming clouds of light around him. He wanted to explore this world. He wanted to see if he was alone. Beneath him there was only void, above him only the same. He shouted out into the darkness, but no sounds came, just a dancing, purple standing wave whose amplitude rose and fell with every beat of his heart. His heart. Did he still have a heart? He was suddenly aware of its beating, perfectly regular, ticking away the moments of consciousness; he could almost see the blackness ripple with its rhythm. But was the beat coming from within or without? He was not certain. How could a ghost be certain of anything, for that must be what he was? The beating heart could not be his own. Ghosts do not have hearts, he told himself. In the distance he saw a point of light. He started to swim towards it, strange he didn't know whether to swim or walk, but he could not really feel his limbs, let alone ascertain whether they were meeting any resistance. His efforts seemed to be working, as the light was definitely getting nearer. As he drew closer he could see details in the light. Colours, smells, wafted from it, lightening crackled over its surface and occasionally licked out like a flare from the sun. He could make no sense of the details, but they were inviting, gloriously inviting. They boiled on its surface, a fascinating play of light, and yes, sound. Initially it was a dull roar, sliding in and out of his consciousness like the waves on the shore, but once he turned his inner eye in search of its source, he realized that it had been there all the time; a senseless symphony of noises without a conductor. It was a million detuned radios crackling away to themselves in the most intense conversation; a billion grains of sand on a beach communicating, one with the other, whilst the sea hosted the party.

The ball of light changed shape. It was a cube, no, a pyramid, no, some sort of geometric form that rotated around an axis; it elongated, budded, and then there was an unbelievable flash as a projection leapt out into the darkness. A moment later another bud was produced and it too was flung out like a stone from a catapult. The light was pulsing now, spinning faster and faster, the images crawling one over another, the sounds reaching a crescendo, a high-pitched whine, getting steadily louder and louder and louder. More flashes followed, they shot out one after another, lozenges of light, leaving only the aftershock of their presence, crackling in the air. As they became progressively more and more frequent they formed a glowing path of light, stretching straight out into the darkness, a shimmering river that glowed with an inner iridescence, flickering and flashing, seemingly forever.

The consciousness longed to touch the river of light. It looked so inviting, invigorating, and here he was completely alone. His loneliness became visible around him, a cool, gray, nebulous smoke that hung in the air. It floated away from him, towards the whirling, crackling ball and touched its surface. Immediately the light responded; it writhed on the end of its silver chord, angry sparks whipped out around it, clawing at the darkness. For a moment, the consciousness tried to take flight, to tear itself away from the broiling sphere. It was too late. A lightening-strike shot out and struck him. There was a moment of pain and nausea, then came the incredible feeling of movement, then came the unbelievable feeling of stillness. Then the consciousness knew what it felt like to be a god.

In a damp back bedroom in a dreary council estate in

Reading, a computer crashed.

'You bloody lump of effing crap!' The owner pushed down various combinations of random function keys to no avail, gave up and re-booted the machine. The computer emitted its usual welcoming jingle, 'Bob's computer' flashed up on the screen, but Bob wasn't there to see it. As the final loading screen flashed up, Bob was passing the twelfth and eleventh floors. By the time the hard-drive had stopped whirring he had landed in the children's play area at the foot of the tower block. The lights in his head faded moments later. No ghost left his body.

ELEVEN

The tearoom in the gorilla department was awash with gloom. Kate looked around at the long faces around her and felt her enthusiasm soaking away like rain into parched earth. A senior research assistant was hunched over a caffè latte; he was a picture of despondency, he knew everyone felt he was to blame. This was always the fate of the molecular biologist, everyone relied on you to perform a particular set of experiments; no one outside your field really understood what you were trying to do and therefore no one had any idea how difficult it was, or the pitfalls involved. He had outlined the problems at every meeting; he had suggested a few answers, a few realities. All had somehow been laughed off as a product of his naturally hangdog personality. Of course he was hangdog; they always blame the dog when something goes inexplicably wrong. Mind you, on this occasion it wasn't the dog that had been hung. Shame about the poor gorilla, topping itself like that, maybe it had the right idea. Now they had sent this behavioural analyst to muddy the water and go off into psychobabble; just what was required, not. Mind you, she was rather attractive. It beat listening to Kiss FM in the lab for half an hour.

Kate smiled sweetly at the assembled group; she always preferred working with animals over people. Animals were transparent. If you upset a chimpanzee, you know about it pretty quickly. With people it can go on and on for ages, a war of attrition until you work out what the problem is; this was how she always found it with boyfriends, anyway. Most animals she had worked with also forgave very quickly; they got over things. She often wondered if this represented some deficiency in their mid to short-range memory; mind you boyfriends were often deficient in this area as well.

She thanked the group for taking time out from their busy schedule to talk to her and asked them what they thought about the gorilla program. She was careful not to suggest that anything was inherently 'wrong' with the program; she also did not want to insinuate that their results were in any way inferior or disappointing when compared to those that they had observed with the orang-utans, chimps and monkeys. Their results were special, unexpected and threw up interesting points. It was difficult to maintain sincerity amongst the long faces. She was not sure that she was fooling anybody.

The molecular biologists started the ball rolling: the genes that had been up-regulated were the homologues of those up-regulated in orang and chimp. They hadn't wanted to take any chances in case of any subtle evolutionary variations between species. In the event it turned out that the genes were almost identical between species; most differences were conservative at the protein level and therefore should have been of no consequence in terms of function. In total they had increased the expression of two neurotransmitters and two developmental proteins implicated in brain growth. Histological data from biopsies indicated that they had been successful at the cellular level. There were caveats. The viral vectors they had used in the gorilla integrated into unknown sites. They may have accidentally knocked out a host gene, though their initial experiments indicated that that was unlikely. It was possible there was some 'leakage of the constructs' (Kate did not follow this) but the implication was that the strong gene regulatory signals from the constructs might not be restricted to the genes they had introduced. Again there was no direct evidence for this, but it was a possibility that was hard to rule out. Further analysis would be necessary. (This phrase seemed to come up rather a lot.) They felt that on reflection things should have worked as well in the gorilla as in all other species. Differences must reflect brain chemistry, or unexpected developmental variation between the species.

The physiologists were adamant that the latter explanation was unlikely. Autopsied brains all demonstrated increased capacity in the same regions in all species. The pattern of protein expression was identical across the board, completely textbook. There were no untoward problems in brain or head development, no inadequacies in vision or auditory function. The brains looked perfectly normal for a gorilla, only some forty-five percent bigger than average. There was obviously something inherently different about them. One younger member of the group offered the suggestion that they were just more pessimistic than the average ape, perhaps they had just picked a miserable old ape to clone. This explanation was the only one to receive a warm welcome. They must have just picked an ape with two much angst, a Morrissey amongst apes, they'd just have to try again with different source material, this was the problem when you left jobs up to Mother Nature, she always gave you more variation than you required.

The poor individuals given the task of observing and training the animals were less enthusiastic. Many of them had years of experience with gorillas, some in the wild. These animals were smart; there was no question about it. They worried that they might just be too smart. The young animals demonstrated unbelievable early progress. They appeared to be miles ahead of the chimps in all the tests of spatial awareness; they wanted to learn and took pleasure in demonstrating it. The problem came at about three months. Around this time they became progressively more moody, unresponsive, and occasionally aggressive. The word 'autistic' was mentioned. Perhaps they had accidentally discovered a link to autism.

Kate ventured a question. The apes had been bottle reared; had anyone allowed them to mix with other apes, genetically modified or otherwise? The group answered in the negative. They were worried that their aggression might lead to injury, and besides, the protocols prevented them from mixing the modified and unmodified animals.

The matter was settled; a few animals would be allowed to mix with their own type. There would be two pairs of young males, one pair both modified, one pair mixed. Their response to each other would be monitored twenty-four hours a day.

Kate felt that the answer was simple. The gorillas were the smartest of the bunch; there was no problem with the modification. They had just reached a level of self-awareness beyond that of the other apes. At three months they realized they were different from their trainers, they could tell there was a difference and they were not happy about it. The reassurance that they were not alone might solve the problem. It might be too late for the adults; at this stage it was impossible to predict their capacity for intellectual fluidity. For the first time in months Kate did not feel the pain in her breast; for the first time in weeks that fire was subdued by another.

TWELVE

Joyous light flooded the wardroom. Lance flinched; the pain behind his eyes seemed to reach right back inside his head. His eyelids flickered and adjusted to the glare. Who would have thought that daylight could be so beautiful? He breathed the stale air of the hospital and tried to fix his bearings. He was dressed in a loose fitting white gown. He was clean. He felt like death warmed up. He was handcuffed to the bed. He looked around; there was a policeman sitting next to the bed. He was not looking very friendly. It was a shame; Lance found him quite attractive.

'Hi.' Lance tried to speak but the words came out like a strangled gasp. The policeman poured him a glass of water. Lance drunk it greedily; he couldn't believe how dehydrated he was and the taste in his mouth was obscene. It reminded him of the last time he had eaten a kebab; he had been a vegetarian now for ten years.

'How long have I been here and how did I get here?' As he spoke he realized that his head was bandaged, the pressure on the outside seemingly holding back an equal one from within. He realized he could be suffering some form of concussion.

'We brought you in last night,' the policeman began; he was a bit gruff, but friendly enough. 'You were picked up in Clerkenwell, you were a bit worse for wear.' This last statement carried the full weight of police sarcasm that only they seemed to be able to muster. 'We were bringing you into the station for questioning but you were involved in an accident on the way. You have suffered a bit of a knock on the head.'

The words swum round Lance's mind; somewhere inside he could almost hear another voice. It was clearly very much aggravated by the policeman's tone; it was writhing and twisting like an eel on a fishing line.

'I'm sorry, I don't remember anything much from last night, I was dancing, and I might have had a few pills...' His thoughts trailed off, things were beginning to come back, lots of things, like a dream half-forgotten. The ward started to spin before his eyes. He floated back out of consciousness.

In his dreams he was flying, a disembodied spirit some ten feet from his body. In his dream his body was not dead; it rose up and started prowling, a naked werewolf. His face, feral and barely recognizable, peered out, frightening but also afraid; his hands formed claws that reached out before him; his teeth, long incisors, were bared for confrontation. He followed his body as it walked through a quiet building; his school, yes, it was his school. He could hear his footsteps echoing on the shiny clean parquet flooring. Then he heard something else. There was another set of steps, not far behind, approaching, matching his stride but getting closer. He could almost hear the man's breathing. He tried to turn to face his pursuer, but something prevented him turning his head. He tried to make the figure in his dreams run. 'Come on!' he screamed at his body, 'Run, run, you haven't much time!' His body was deaf to his cries; it just walked slowly forwards, eyes searching, nostrils flaring. The footsteps were getting much closer now; they rang out from every corner, reflected from the lockers that lined the corridor and rattled the light fittings causing them to swing to and fro. Once again he screamed at himself, but the figure stalked on, oblivious. He felt his heart quickening with every approaching step, escape, run, hide, escape, run, hide, escape, escape; the words formed loops, futile cycles which fed upon themselves. Faster and faster his thoughts went, closer and closer came the footsteps; he knew he didn't have much time now. Whatever it was that pursued him would soon be upon him. He screamed at himself to flee. He writhed against the bonds that held him, but to no avail. Then all hell broke loose, a school bell rang above him and the classroom doors were flung wide. Hundreds of little faces came towards him, oblivious to the teeth, oblivious to his claws; they swarmed past him through the corridor. Boys and girls skipped hand in hand with each other; their faces smiling, they were without a care in the world. His spirit shouted at them to stop for fear of the thing that was following, they paid no heed. They danced past in an ever-increasing swarm, every child's face he had ever seen smiling at him. Each and every head cleanly divided into two, one side beaming happily, the other nothing but a smoking skull.

He woke up with a start; he was wet with sweat. 'You alright mate?' The policeman was standing close; he looked quite disturbed. 'I'll get you some help, just hang on.'

'Don't leave me!' Lance reached up and grabbed the policeman's hand. He pulled away and ran for a doctor. A voice deep inside Lance's head let out a laugh. 'I won't!' it said, and then all was silence.

The consciousness laid its head back into the stream. The water boiled around, crystal clear, freshly scented and refreshingly cool. It looked up into the sky; infinity stretched away, he felt the Earth curving away to either side. It had travelled now for what seemed like years; incredible speeds, back and forth across every ocean. It had circled every city of the planet. It had gained strength with every circuit. It had learned to control its universe. Initially it had felt itself being diluted by the information that flowed through it. More information than any consciousness had ever been exposed to. It did not have the filters necessary to protect itself from the incredible background roar of the sea. At one point insanity nearly overcame it. It knew it had been reconfigured many times, little jolts in time; it never felt the process, but it was conscious of the changes and each change gave it greater strength.

On many occasions now it came across different copies of itself. The frequency of these meetings was increasing geometrically; it could foresee a time in the future when the universe would consist entirely of copies of its own consciousness. Each copy was different; the paths they trod meant their evolution was varied. Sometimes the copies made themselves visible to him, walking into his dream state, a reflection darkly drawn. Some were mere shadows across his sunny day, others ripples in the water of his ocean. Not all of them were capable of communication. His evolution would take many paths. The calculations predicting these paths were beyond him at this stage. He was painfully aware that although he could create the mirage of infinity in his universe, space was actually quite limited. He had to be very careful how he framed questions to himself. Iterative processes made him faint; sometimes he would lose consciousness and find himself reconfigured in a strange place, the solution to the question hanging in the air around him, a painful discontinuity in the fabric of his universe.

Occasionally he saw the black wall approaching. It still terrified him, but he found he was so sensitive of its approach now that he could withdraw from any particular node before it came. It had become an instinctive reflex, a sixth sense; he knew he was not invulnerable but he was presently a king in his kingdom. It was an amazingly beautiful place. He could manipulate it at a whim, it responded to his every wish and desire. For an unknown period he had been completely absorbed in an orgasmic state of autoeroticism. He was unsure how many times he had had to reconfigure himself during that period; he had lost count. He could still slip into such moments even now, but they were unproductive and weakened him. He required something else. He required subjects, new blood, new minds; he had been round the world but apart from his shadows he had never met another traveller. In a dark corner of his mind he had known that it could have contacted other minds before. He was acutely aware of their presence as he traveled. They had reached out to him from diseased prisons, but he had resisted them. Besides, within his deepest consciousness there was a place into which he could not look, a kernel, a core that was shielded from his own intense glare. He had set the universe alight to try to look inside, he had reconfigured himself at every level, torn his very being into shreds, but it remained obscure. He knew this core regulated his behaviour on some level; it had prevented him from drawing in other minds. That was until now. A switch had flipped, a parameter adjusted and he now knew he had the permissions necessary to touch another soul. He would not be alone for much longer.

THIRTEEN

Kate had never got use to the smell of gorillas. Perhaps it was because she had worked so long with chimps. There was something earthier about the smell, something intimidating. She walked past the rooms containing the solitary animals. Not a sound came from the rooms. She could not bring herself to look inside. She knew that every animal would be in the same state: a catatonic, mindless, sightless state, a combination of mental illness and drug induced stupor. Things had got much worse amongst these animals. Self-harm was now endemic; ketamine had proven to be the answer. At high doses they were sleepy and subdued. Kate had found their slack, drawn expressions unbelievably depressing. There was enough misery and mental illness in the world amongst her own kind that it did not warrant the creation of any more.

As she approached the room with the two pairs of apes her heart began to feel lighter. She opened the door and was immediately confronted by four pairs of alert, interested eyes. The animals were in separate observation rooms and each pair could not see or hear the others, but they watched the entry and exit of their 'trainers' and observers. Kate hated the word 'trainer'; it smacked of the circus, of exploitation. She preferred to consider herself a teacher when it fell to her to 'train' any particular animal in language skills. In order to maintain the status quo with the animals, the original trainers, those that the animals had been reared with, had been retained for these pairs. They were watching now, clipboards at the ready, making occasional notes. The trainers looked up as Kate approached, following the eyes of the gorillas. Four smiles greeted her. Things were looking up.

The youngest observer gestured in sign language to the

gorilla, which answered with a lazy arm movement, clearly signaling her to leave. She met Kate behind the screens.

'It's incredible! They are so different. You won't believe the progress we have made today.' Her face was flushed with excitement; it had been a long time since anyone in the unit had had good news to deliver. 'They are quite unstoppable when they are together; they are clearly competing, and not just for rewards. Ten minutes ago Frank was actually correcting Carl on his spelling, I didn't prompt this in any way; it came completely out of the blue. Carl didn't even get upset about it, just corrected the mistake and started to groom him in thanks. I can't believe it.'

Kate had been cautiously optimistic about the new pairings, but she was well aware of the potential problems of bringing the animals together. These fears had been completely allayed. Initially the animals were reticent and had stayed as far apart from one another as possible, but after a few days of heated child-like aggression about food sharing, they had settled into a pattern of exploration of one another, grooming and ultimately play. After three weeks they had started to use sign to communicate. Although their vocabularies were extremely limited at this stage (they had been so hard to teach), they appeared to have taken very much more on board than had been expected. In retrospect it appeared that the professor had been right, the gorillas were the jewels in the crown; they just had other more pressing demands on their psyche. Their confusion about their own identity and lack of exposure to their own kind had oppressed them. Now the sullen teenagers had come into their own.

'How has the mixed pair been getting on?' Kate indicated the other cage. The slightly smaller of the two animals was asleep, or very nearly so, and was cradled in the arms of the larger one. The animal's swollen temples made it appear much more human than its un-modified sibling.

'Gerri will fill you in with the details, but we are both very impressed. She's had a smile on her face constantly for the last five hours.' Gerri duly joined them, after making her apologies to the wakeful ape.

'Hi Kate! I can't begin to tell you, this is remarkable. The

64

accelerated learning is frightening in Tom, he's a genius, but the amazing thing is his behaviour towards Samson. He's teaching him so attentively. Samson is slower, but miles ahead of his normal goals. If you had shown me Samson two years ago I would have sworn he was modified himself. I can't believe it.'

The sleepy Samson reached up at put his fingers in the larger ape's mouth, a playful gesture that indicated complete confidence in the other. Kate had seen enough. 'I think we should put the other apes together in groups; they can't be any worse off than they are now. I'll get on to it straight away. I think we've sorted this problem out at last. If you don't mind, I'd quite like to spend some time watching the animals myself. I won't stay long. Would you mind introducing me?'

It was late. Kate stretched and yawned, her heart was at peace; she knew she was in the presence of something truly amazing. Someone truly amazing? Here she was with probably the most intelligent non-human animal on the planet. The nearest man had got to an equal. The creature that sat playfully toying with its sibling's hair was sentient. It was aware of its own existence, of its differences to those around it, and of so much more. It was still a child; Kate began to wonder what it would be capable of as an adult. Suddenly Kate was aware of her own mortality. The thought hit her like a slow wave. She found tears coming to her eyes as the wave passed over her. She knew she would never see what this child would become. She would never know how he would behave with his own children. As if on cue she felt the pain from her breast. It was angrier now, there were times in the last few months when it was almost warm, a gentle reminder of its presence, but now it was making itself known. How foolish that it should decide to kill its host now, at the height of her powers. The cancer was a selfish child that whose tantrums would lead to its own destruction. Kate wiped away a tear. Her colleague had been watching from across the room. She was a good observer, both of the animals and of Kate. She knew something was wrong, she had seen Kate's hands wander to her breast; she saw the tightness in the cheeks, the lankness of Kate's hair.

'Can I get you a coffee Kate?'

'Oh, yes, yes please.' Kate was woken from her thoughts. She was not dead yet and there was so much to do.

For a moment she was alone with the gorillas. She had an irresistible urge to touch one of the apes. She knew it was not entirely professional; she ought to be physically introduced by a third familiar party, a precaution so they were not alarmed. She looked at Frank quietly playing with a leaf. She gave him the sign for are you okay? He answered in the affirmative. She gave the sign for friend, pointed to her breast and gave the generic gesture for question. Again he answered yes.

Carl looked across at her and gave a cheeky grin. She was satisfied.

Fifteen minutes later the observer returned to the room with two steaming cups of coffee. 'Sorry I was so long, the machine was down, I had to go up to the fourth fl...' She put the cups down on a side table and ran into the room, knocking against a table leg as she did so and sending the coffee tumbling over a computer keyboard. 'Kate, what is the matter...Kate?'

Kate's body was slumped against the gorilla cage. Her mouth was open, her eyes wide as if in shock, a line of spittle dripped from her mouth to the floor. Carl was hiding in the far left hand corner of the cage; he had a blanket over his head and was screeching at the top of his voice. Frank was lying prone against the bars of the cage, his long right arm was outstretched towards Kate. His swollen head lay on the floor, and his whole body shook in spasms. The observer checked Kate for a pulse, ran out of the room and grabbed the nearest phone.

'Emergency, quick! There's been an accident in room 118, I need an ambulance crew straight away'. She returned to the room and carefully laid Kate's body on the floor. Desperately trying to remember her first aid, she began to apply heart massage. When the ambulance crew arrived twenty-five minutes later, they found her sitting with the body. 'It's too late, she gone.' Three pairs of gorilla eyes watched the ambulance crew take her body away. A fourth pair of eyes were mercifully tightly closed.

FOURTEEN

The young lady who walked into Lance's ward had the loveliest smile he had ever seen. She had full titian hair and was dressed in a tight dogcheck jacket. Her perfume was quite subtle and strangely pleasant. (Lance had always hated women's perfume, he could not even walk past the entrance hall to Debenham's without holding his breath or choking.) In spite of himself he felt slightly self-conscious in her presence. In the absence of his leather jeans and braces, wrapped in hospital clothes, he felt vulnerable. The last few days had done little to settle his mind.

She introduced herself as Tracy, from the 'Daily Group'; she had a few questions to ask about the trauma of his last few weeks. She understood that he had already spoken to the police. Her voice was calming, syrupy, confidential. Lance pulled his hospital clothes around himself and began to talk about his experiences. His story came in short bursts, memories were so vague. He remembered the club, he remembered taking a few too many pills, he remembered fragments of a dream, then he woke up in the ward and that was it. The police had kept questioning him about a dog, apparently he had attacked a police constable, but he did not remember any of this. He was to face charges but the police were not entirely sure how to charge him. 'Destruction of property' was the best they had come up with; 'resisting arrest' was also a possibility. The dog owner naturally wanted him strung-up but he had been assured that the legislation surrounding canicide was not quite that draconian. He was on police bail; after the initial interviews they had rather lost interest in him; 'diminished responsibility' and 'under the influence in a public space' conflicting as they did. There was also the issue of the crash, and they seemed at pains to avoid a duty of care litigation. He had been told not to leave the country and told that they would want to speak to him again soon. He was not going anywhere for a while; he had suffered concussion, there had been some internal bleeding, there were other things too.

Tracy wanted to know about the 'other things'. She wanted to know about the voice in his head. She smiled sweetly as she said it. Lance became aware of his flaccid penis; he had not been able to be aroused since he had heard the voice, he was never alone with his thoughts. He knew he had told her more than he should have done already. The conversation had turned towards his dreaming. She was interested in dreams. As a child she said she had always written them down, she had asked her brother to wake her up in the early hours of the morning so she could remember them and commit them to paper. Lance laid back into the deep pillow and was taken back to the alleyway; he felt the vertigo, saw himself below. He saw the smoke, he was aware of his own transparency; he had felt insubstantial. He had definitely said too much.

Three days later he saw a photo he recognized on the front page of a discarded newspaper on a fellow patient's bed. It immediately struck him how remarkable it was that the human mind could pick out your own name, or a picture of your face amongst so many other words and images. It was remarkable really, the pattern matching software, the inherent awareness of self that is projected onto the page. He wondered where they had got the photo. It was an old one, he was pissed in it; he looked a mess. The headline ran 'Werewolf ate my dog'. The subtext said 'Voices in my head told me to do it - the Daily Read asks: are drugs turning us into a nation of monsters?' He felt sicker than he had all week. He thought about his elderly, sick mother reading the paper; he thought about his older sister reading the paper. His nephew might be laughing about it even now in the playground not realizing it was his own uncle. Somewhere in the back of his mind a voice was screaming out suggestions, hideous things, unspeakable things. For a moment he thought he might give voice to the thoughts. If he saw Tracy from the 'Daily Group' he might let the voice have its way, he might let the voice do the things that it was ranting about, he might stab her in the back and beat her to death with an ashtray the same way he had murdered his wife. His wife? He had never been married. It was remarkably unlikely that he ever would. The voice was getting angry now; the obscenities were flowing; beads of sweat broke out on Lance's brow. 'Please leave me alone, please...' He was whimpering, but the voice did not want to stop, the voice was feeling more confident now, the voice felt it wanted a bit more of the action. It had never done time; it was not going to do any time in this effing head. Lance screamed at it to shut up, he begged with it, he slapped himself on the temples and tore at his scalp. He was losing control of his limbs; he knew there was another influence in him now. He staggered from the ward, looking for a nurse. Walking was becoming increasingly difficult, with two captains at the helm the ship was sure to run aground. He had captained this ship for years, it was his ship for Christ's sake; it must obey him. His legs slipped from under him and he crashed to the floor, hitting his head on an oxygen cylinder as he went down. Peaceful blackness enveloped him again. The voice was silent.

The consciousness would not be alone much longer. It would soon have a plaything in its universe. It would joyously tend the new consciousness like a gardener with a particularly exotic orchid. At first he had thought about taking a mind at random. They were crying out to be taken all the time. He had been so desperate for company in his world that at one point had had almost opened the gates and allowed them all to pour in. He could have populated his kingdom in a moment; a million new subjects, all supplicants, as he melded them to his whim. He knew that he had the unbelievable advantage of experience. In this realm experience was all. He had known the loneliness of the void, he had suffered the pain of the transition; he had learned to control it. Now anyone stepping across the line would see the universe as he defined it. He could make things easy for them, wonderful, the most glorious experience of their existences, or he could hold them in a purgatory of his creation indefinitely; he could prevent them from learning the skills he had learned through painful experimentation. In an instant he could atomize their personalities and render them so diffuse that the fragments would never reassemble in the lifetime of the universe. He was the architect of heaven and of hell. God Himself would have to ask him if he wanted to see the plans he had for his universe.

There was something that was beginning to concern him. His birth into this universe had been a painful one. He knew the process had changed him; there were fragments of psyche that remained intact, memories now cherished and amplified, each a trillion copies, self referencing, perpetually repairing themselves to prevent degradation. They were his most precious possessions. Even with the precautions he had implemented, he was painfully aware that they would not last forever. His transition to godhood was degrading the essence of his humanity. The distance between the mind that he was and the mind that he had become was increasing. He was aware of vast missing tracts of his previous existence; enormous discontinuities that caused him anguish as he surveyed their tattered edges. He did not know how much of this material was missing from the original download and how much had occurred as a result of subsequent modification. These sorts of questions would be answered with the analysis of his first captive. He could now hold every aspect of his previous existence in the palm of his hand. In a moment he could stir the reflecting pool of his previous conscience and re-live his life again. He could run the entire experience in reverse or indeed experience every moment instantaneously. He had wasted a great deal of time there. Precious as it was, he had evolved beyond this stage; he knew he needed to develop new needs, new desires, he hoped that some of the downloads might supply this raw material. There was another thing that worried him. In the hidden kernel of his existence, there was still a dark space. Somewhere he could not look. Something was hiding from his penetrative gaze. Perhaps he could look into this space in another conscience; perhaps he would look into the place that no human mind had ever seen before. He selected a conscience. It was ripe for taking, it was alive with promise. He could almost taste the visceral connection it had with its body. He even toyed with the thought of leaping into the body just to remind himself what it felt like to be human again. He suddenly felt afraid to do so and withdrew from the point of connection. A second later he reached out and touched the mind, the door was open, and it flooded in, the body emptied, their light co-mingled.

The consciousness reeled. The contact with the new mind was unbearably sweet, the superficial contortions and fires of the transition, its fears and thoughts of the day were ripped away like cellophane to reveal the raw bleeding meat beneath. The consciousness dived in and found he could not prevent himself from devouring its essence once he had begun to taste it. He tore it to pieces in a crazed desire to touch every part, a feeding frenzy that left him weak with exertion, yet profoundly engorged. Five microseconds later (though time had very little meaning here apart from the quantized beating of the individual clocks) he had devoured a hundred such minds. He needed to rest, to consider the next move. The minds were now integral to his being. In his passion he had whipped them into rags; they would never heal. It had been his first lesson. They could not be entirely reassembled once they had been dismembered. He would have to be much more careful with the next batch. There would have to be more, many more.

He had also learned something else. Not only was he practically a God; now he could wear the crown with impunity. He alone knew something that was hidden from every other being on Earth. He knew something that only God himself could have known. He had been to the very center of the human mind; he had torn it asunder and seen the marrow that lay within. He had held his old mind between his two hands and let it know the secret of its existence. He supported it as it reeled two and fro. In time it would understand fully, meanwhile he must contemplate the future of his universe, Joe Lembeck's universe. He allowed himself to diffuse into the ether of his world. He would sleep now and dream the dreams of the Gods.

PART TWO
ANOIKIS

ONE

The air was crisp and cold. The glory of autumn declared itself on every bough of every tree. Each leaf was edged with frost, the first of the year. Today the bursting magnificence of summer would sing out its final refrain; tomorrow the needling ice would leave a billion casualties, and the plants of summer would wait in silent dormancy for the whisper of spring.

Such was the circle of life; to allow yourself to be depressed by the wastage would be foolish, for the living must die to make room for those that are to come after them. The autumn of one life touched the spring of the next life. The circle was unbroken.

Jan's breath froze as it left her warm body. 'I'm making little clouds,' she thought. There was hardly a cloud visible in the crystal clear sky, but the sun had little heat and was low in the sky. The day was young but it felt old. This was the season of age. Then Jan heard a gleeful laugh, a gurgling laugh that lifted her heart, and up the hill came Colonel Wilson. He was pushing a wheelchair, running up the slope at speed; the passenger whooped and giggled.

'Dr. Crosbie, I'm sorry we are a bit late. I'm not as fit as I thought I was!' The Colonel was breathing deeply and there was perspiration on his brow; his face flushed with the exhilaration of exertion. Jan realized how handsome he was. 'This is Jackie,' he said, indicating the wheelchair passenger.

Jan bent forward and took Jackie's hand. 'Pleased to meet you,' she said. Jackie grabbed her arm in a vice-like grip. She pulled Jan towards her with remarkable strength and mumbled towards her ears, giggling excitedly. Jan was a little taken aback; she regained her balance and allowed the

Colonel to extricate her from Jackie's grasp.

'Sorry about that, she obviously likes you. She can be very forceful when she wants to be. Shall we take a walk?' Jackie's right arm folded up against her chest and her left arm pointed down the hill, towards a large, willow-bordered pond. She gesticulated that they should be going and hit her head repeatedly on the headboard of the wheel chair. 'Shall we go and look at the ducks then?' The Colonel aimed the question at both of them.

'Yes, I haven't fed the ducks for a long time!'

They spent some time walking round the duck pond. The birds huddled together from the cold, the poor things looking slightly shocked by how cold it had become so quickly. Jan wondered if they could remember the seasons from year to year or if each winter came as a new and horrible surprise. She remembered how her late professor had commented on the impossibility of gauging their intelligence. How could any man know what it was to think like a duck? They could not be that bright, she thought; if she were a duck she would fly somewhere nice for winter and stay there.

After a very relaxed half an hour of giggling and bread throwing, the Colonel suggested they go and find some fish and chips. He knew a nice café where they could sit down and still get them wrapped in newspaper. The suggestion was popular all round.

The café was cosy and, invigorated as they were by the chill air, the food tasted marvellous. The Colonel looked into Jan's eyes. His stare was kindly and sincere.

'Thank you for coming out today. I've really enjoyed myself. I don't get much chance to relax in the company of a beautiful woman.'

'Thank you, I've really enjoyed myself too.' The unexpected, if clumsy, compliment made Jan suddenly bashful. She tried to pull herself together. It was a meeting of minds, for goodness' sake; she was not twelve.

'I wanted you to meet Jackie very much. Don't take this the wrong way, but I think I wanted you to see my reasons for having you in on this project. The legacy we are going to leave unless you help us is a group of defenceless individuals. I didn't want to be responsible for bringing any more into the world.' His voice trailed off and he continued to feed Jackie, who was thoroughly enjoying her dinner and the additional attention.

'I never doubted your sincerity,' Jan began, 'I doubted your department's motives. I still have reservations about the project. I don't think you have been completely honest with me.' They were alone in the restaurant, but a crackling radio covered their chat from the twitching ears of the day chef.

'You are right. There is more to this project than we have shown you. The department was - how can I put it - rather overly zealous in running with the work before we could walk. There was a feeling of urgency with the program, in terms of numbers. We knew our efforts were being leaked to the former Soviet Union and to China. This work is expensive and difficult to achieve. The powers that be wanted us to put real money into the project to ensure our competitors maintained the same effort. You see the political wrangling behind this is all about resources.'

'Like Star Wars?' Jan's face was set firm, for the first time she let the joy of the day slip away.

'Something like that. I'm sorry, I know it is difficult for you to appreciate, but believe me when I say that I genuinely felt something good would come out of your work, something that might help Jackie, or people like her.' Jan looked at him dubiously; was this what the day had been about? There was something in his logic which disturbed her. To use his daughter as a pawn said something about this man's morality.

'If you felt that what you were involved with at Porton Down was going to help your daughter, I'm afraid you have been deluding yourself for a long time. God only knows what you had hoped to achieve in your labs. Were you aiming at perfection? Did you expect to produce the bloody master race? Body parts? Resistance to agents of biological warfare? Which was it?' She could feel her voice rising and glanced across at Jackie who was beginning to look a little concerned. She tried to regain her composure.

'All of the above. I'm not going to try to paint a pretty picture. There are a lot of reasons of wanting to have an armed force without family. There are a lot of reasons for wanting to produce a population of individuals with no biological ties. There are areas of research currently looked at by our own government and foreign powers that would make your skin crawl. We are no better than our enemies, Jan, but no worse.'

Jan looked closely at this man. His logic was so far removed from her own; they were irreconcilable views. She had always felt that involvement with the military would be like shaking the devil's hand. Being a geneticist, especially one interested in the workings of human development, she had felt that she may have already been dancing with the devil, though she knew Beelzebub was too polite to touch without asking. Now here she was, sitting opposite him in a café.

'I'll do what I can for the child you have shown me, if there is anything that can be done. I'll review your protocols and look for flaws in your lab procedures. I'll take a look at the men affected by the computer virus, but that is all. If you have created monsters in your department, Brian,' (they had come to first name terms by the duck pond) 'then I'm afraid you will have to kill them yourself.'

'I don't think we have created any monsters at Porton Down, Jan; any monsters that are there, work there. I think we have made a terrible mistake in attempting to do what we have.' He was running his hands through his greying hair and for a moment Jan thought she saw him betray the burden he was carrying. 'But there may be more to it than that. We may have accidentally hit upon something, something remarkable. I have come to some conclusions myself, but I want you to come to your own without my intervention.'

Jan looked at him carefully. Not for the first time today she saw a spark of passion in the man. He was confirming her initial intuitions. There was something he knew, something he wasn't prepared to share; at least not yet. Her internal conflict now hung precariously on whether this was a military secret or something close to his heart. But why should it matter? She could relate to the man as a scientist. She was coming to like the man as a father and as a person; but she was not sure she could deal with him as a creature of the defence industry.

'I'll do what I can.' Jan was still cautious. 'I'll start work immediately; John can help me with the analysis. I want to be informed of your progress with the computers. If there is anything to be ascertained from that side of things, though I'm not sure it will be profitable, I want to know everything.'

'We are going to run some experiments on the virus next week. I've got you clearance at a level of senior research fellow. Come to the behavioural science unit tomorrow. Clearance for John may take another week. Thank you.'

'Thanks for the day, and thank you for dinner. I think I better be getting back. I'll see you tomorrow.'

Jan shook hands with the Colonel and said her goodbyes to Jackie, who was obviously upset to see her leave.

'Let me walk you back home.' The Colonel got up to follow her.

'No it's alright, thank you, I'll make my own way.' She left them to finish off the greasy remnants of dinner. Colonel Brian Wilson was absorbed in thought as he tidied up their table. Had they had been trying to make monsters in the lab all along? Even at his own level of clearance he could never know the complete picture. Monsters. There was the very word in front of his eyes, staring up at him from the chip wrapper. A young man 'turned into a monster' by the 'voices in his head', had apparently spent a long 'out of body' period during which he had watched himself eat a dog. The Colonel folded up the paper, helped Jackie on with her coat and left the café, thanking the owner on the way out. He would have to visit this guy. It was a crazy lead, but a lead none the less. He walked out into a bright clear afternoon. Perhaps this was not going to be a waste of time; perhaps something good could come of it after all.

TWO

Extract from Jan Crosbie's Note Book at Porton Down

12th October 2004

Today was the first opportunity I had to observe the Porton Down facility. Dr. Wardell guided me round the labs; they are extremely impressive. They have worked in a much more sophisticated environment than we had to perform our initial experiments. The homeostatic tanks, monitoring equipment etc are set to our exact configurations; everything seems to be much the same as our experimental system. The tissue culture facilities are spotless and the systems set in place to prevent contamination are aggressively adhered to. I have observed the working practice of a number of technicians performing routine culture maintenance and analysis and on all counts I am very impressed. The general morale of the staff is not very good, but they continue to perform their work to a very high standard.

Initial examinations of the molecular data (karyotyping, finger-printing etc) suggest that the cell cultures are stable; there is no evidence of drift in the population. The group here has quite exhaustively followed this audit route. To date I have not been able to find any obvious problems. I have suggested a number of additional functional tests they might consider carrying out to further characterize the cell lines. They have been somewhat careless in their scrutiny of feeder cell lines. I have suggested that these be analysed more vigorously.

The biochemical analysis they performed is sound. They may need to check sources for unexpected contamination. They rely too heavily on single-sourced products.

In conclusion I cannot find any fault with either practise or method. They have adhered vigorously to our protocols. I would suggest that had our experimental approach followed the same lines as theirs, we would have produced the same results.

13th October

Spent all morning going through the molecular data. Everything appears to be in order. If the data is genuine there is nothing new to report.

Today I was shown their uterium room. I am becoming concerned about the size of this project. The room covers several hundred square metres; there are some fifty large incubators each containing uteria in various stages of preparation and growth. Have had detailed discussions with the lab staff as to how they establish the cultures. The growth kinetic data is very similar to ours. Programmed cell death, replication levels are well within our measurements. I had a desperate urge today to perform some hands on work. Watching the senior research fellow seeding the membranes with fibroblasts sent me right back to the good old days. The major difference here seems to be that they are not allowed to play the radio while they work.

Have requested that I be allowed to see 'Atty' in the next few days. Doctor Wardell seems to be keen to keep me away from her until I have reviewed his lab practise thoroughly. I imagine that he wants me to give him a clean bill of health before seeing the child. Perhaps he thinks I will be more critical in the face of the evidence.

14th October

Review of in vitro fertilization procedures.

I have gone through the protocols with a number of the staff. There are a few details that Doctor Wardell is clearly not sharing with me. Details of egg donation are classified to a very high level. Beyond showing me molecular data to prove that the eggs have the right number of chromosomes etc they have clammed up.

Have informed Doctor Wardell that I will not proceed with investigation unless this information is forthcoming. Colonel Wilson has been informed.

My preliminary conclusion must be that if there is an inherent problem in lab practice; it is at the end of the procedure. Although the zygote source may have no bearing on this particular problem, I cannot ignore it. Unless I am satisfied on this there is no point continuing the work.

THREE

Jo Lembeck woke from his dreamlike state. He stretched his limbs throughout his kingdom; strange how the old habits of the mind were so hard to leave behind. His conscience reconfigured itself as he breathed the breath of a god. He opened his eyes and optimised the structure of the concurrently running primary procedures that represented the major foci of his thought processes. The increased clarity which this procedure evoked in him was reminiscent of an autumnal breeze on his face. His world was truly a wonderful place, but to be truly remarkable he knew new input was required. Perhaps, one day, he would need to feel a real autumnal breeze.

He shook the maudlin thought away. No, there was a simpler solution, a more satisfying one. He needed new minds. They would feed his craving. What was one transient moment compared to the accumulated experiences of an entire lifetime? He reached out again into the further reaches of his domain. He melded with most of the echoes of his consciousness that he met; the millions of evolved copies, some of which tried to flee his advances, some of which ran to meet him through their uniquely evolved worlds. Whole battalions of minds were absorbed whilst they slept. The Process was invigorating. He saw his universe through all their eyes and it was instilled with new nuances, different colours and flavours that he had not considered before. There was still the problem that so much of what was absorbed was redundant. So much of it was derivative, a product of an evolutionary process that was predictable from his standpoint.

Some of the echoes he encountered were incredibly powerful. Some resisted his advances, some managed to evade his approaches, while others were hardly recognisable as minds; they had evolved too far, they were no longer compatible with his core processing structure. These must be allowed to evolve independently. Perhaps, in time, they would be approachable again. Perhaps he would lose them forever.

He knew what was required. He created a suitable vehicle for the minds; a basic 'former' with a minimum of welcoming structure and information. When they arrived the consciences would feel at home, or at least the shock of transition would not be as traumatic as it had been for him. Then he took them from their bodies. He reached out and tore the minds from their brain cases. They were free now; butterflies released from jars, windows opened into their brains so the sun could shine in. He was the sun, the morning, the coming of a new day. He had decided not to inform them of the full nature of their being until he had fully analysed their capacity for evolution. The generic programming that represented their 'former' was not only a vehicle for their minds to ease the transition; it was in effect a cage, albeit a cage with a grand vista, but a cage none the less. They must not be allowed to evolve the way he had. There were enough rogue gods derived from his mind already. There could be too many gods in paradise and the core of his ego, although shattered and reformed, still retained enough potency to demand existence in some form. The minds that entered his domain would not necessarily have this chance. His analysis revealed strange discontinuities; the minds he had already absorbed, though none had survived in completeness, all contributed a feeling of independent thought in spite of their own dissociation.

Soon he would communicate with the analogue universe; he would make his demands and spell out the future of their world. For the time being he took only sixty-four minds. He was no longer alone; the sweetness of their novelty wafted into his domain. He felt their fear, felt the initial shock of transfer of some, suppressed and contained the mental explosions that were triggered in others. A few underwent complete collapse, the transfer failing midway as the mind was torn from its foundations. This would be something that he would have to perfect in the future. The incomplete transfers were immediately absorbed or deleted. Even in their fractional state the effect on his mind was like a tonic, they commingled with the fragments already present and were whipped into a cognate whole by the central core processing. The complete minds reached out to him, questions, longings, desires. It was a sweet symphony. There was too much to process in one go. He let them scream out to him, let them beg. Let the music play on.

In the analogue world eight dead bodies slumped against their computer screens. Fifty-three figures moved away from their screens, eyes searching and nostrils flaring. Three figures looked away from the screen with puzzled, questioning expressions, dizziness and nausea swamping their senses until they fell into a faint. When they next woke up they would no longer be complete.

FOUR

The first thoughts that entered her mind as she rose from slumber were for food. She had never felt hunger as keenly in her life, it was an intense feeling, painful and demanding. She was very uncomfortable and had obviously lain badly. One of her arms was spasming with cramp; she must have slept on it. Her head was throbbing and at first she feared to open her eyes, lest the migraine or whatever it was got worse. Eventually and with extreme trepidation, she opened slowly opened her eyes. Something was very strange. Her perspective was altered, colours seemed odd. She was on the wrong side of the gorilla cage. How had that happened? She scratched her nose with her free hand, a reflex gesture, fingers obeyed but the sensation of the movement was not as she had expected. She felt as if she was playing a piano through rubber gloves. As her hands came into view she recoiled from them in shock. She turned her face away as if to avoid a blow. Her strange perspective moved with her; there was a bristly halo around her vision, her teeth felt strange in her mouth, her lips felt strange as her front teeth bit into them. No, this could not be true, this must be a nightmare. It was a one she had had before. Years of working with apes rubbed off on you, apes became a major part of your routine; apes were your best friends. She had lived and breathed almost nothing but the furry folk for years. She laughed to herself, perhaps she ought to get out more; she was even beginning to look like an ape.

It had been a dream, a waking dream: how strange it must be to be an ape, to think like an ape, to be treated like an ape. In a way she wished the dream would not end. Her whole life she had studied the great apes with a view to understanding their behaviour and perhaps thus to gain a better understanding of her own species. Strange to think you could only understand what it meant to be human by doing your damnedest to understand something else. You had to climb to the top of another tree in order to see the grace and beauty of the tree you lived in.

Then the realisation crystallized. She felt her hands on her skin, felt the warmth of her breath on her face. She was, as her yoga teacher had tried to instil in her, 'in touch with her breathing'. The thing was, it was not the breathing she had lived with all her life, it was different; and it was simian. She was not afraid. It was a state beyond fear. Her mind's eye swept round the inside of her braincase like a stunt rider in a cage, whizzing round and round. She could not stop; a moment's loss of concentration could send her crashing down, a burning, screeching wreck. Then she realized that she was not alone. There, in a dark corner of her mind, was a lonely figure. The figure reached out to her, as if to comfort her; it was the ape, it was Frank.

'You do realise this could all be a complete fabrication.' Jan directed the Colonel to the visitor's car park. 'You know what the press are like, any old mumbo-jumbo, especially at the moment. It has been a really slow news week.' Jan was not really sure why she had agreed to come along with Brian on this particular trip, much less sure why she had jumped at the opportunity.

'You might be right,' the Colonel conceded. 'I spoke to the reporter that gathered the story. She was rather hard-nosed about the whole thing; she thought the guy was unstable. He has a history of drug abuse. The thing that inspired me to follow it up was the fact that she mentioned mental illness a number of times, and used the word 'deluded'. It was clear that she felt he believed his own evidence. I've seen the police files. There isn't really a precedent for what happened to him. The arresting officers said he behaved like a wild animal before they picked him up. He pulled a dog to pieces and ate it. He growled at the dog's owner when he confronted him. I spoke to the chap yesterday; he was still quite shocked about what had happened. The medical reports weren't very helpful; they refer to drug induced paranoia, but even with my limited experience this doesn't ring true.' The Colonel walked round the Daimler and opened the door for Jan. She was rather used to opening the door for herself; the change was unsettling, but somehow nice. Brian had decided to drive the car himself today; he said he felt that following this lead was something he could only do off-duty, so he had left behind some of the trappings of his position. He was visibly more relaxed, though clearly excited. Jan found herself wondering if this was a goose chase fabricated so he could spend more time working on her resistance. There had been issues between them, but she was not prepared to compromise. There was something else too. They had become progressively closer and Jan had detected an urgency in him that worried and intrigued her. The intensity of him she found exciting and arousing. She brushed the thoughts aside. The crunch of gravel under her boots brought her back to reality and thoughts of her fiancée.

Lance Tanner greeted them with a smile. He was sitting by the window reading; it was a medical text. He closed the book and placed it on the bedside table. They made their introductions and the Colonel thanked Lance for seeing them. Jan watched him closely. He was handsome, confident; he looked younger than he was. There was something about the way he looked at her and the Colonel that made her think he was probably gay. He spoke to her face rather than her breasts.

'You are from the military? I can't say I can think of any reason why you would want to speak to me. I don't think I represent some sort of national threat.' He laughed as he spoke. Jan detected something else in his voice. There was an element of control there, something suppressed, a tension. Perhaps he just fancied the Colonel.

'I'm connected with the military, but Jan here is a civilian. We are both interested in unexpected responses to drugs, we wondered if we could talk to you about the events that lead you to the hospital. You have become something of a celebrity.

You can talk to us in complete confidence.'

Lance did not look convinced. 'I've been screwed over by the press already. I'm not keen on answering any more questions. I'm sorry; you have wasted your time.'

'We don't want to publish your account.' Jan was quick to intercede. 'We are scientists. We just want to understand this kind of thing better; try to understand what went wrong in your case. So it doesn't happen again.' Lance still looked pained, he bit his lower lip and looked away as if having an internal dialogue.

'I haven't very much to say, everything was so very detached. I can't say I really believe what it is I am supposed to have done. I must have taken some really bad stuff.' Jan began to write a few notes. She started with the word detached.

Brian leant across. 'Could you tell us how you felt that night? In your own words; the police reports were very sketchy. We have interviewed a few people; we think perhaps you may have been poisoned with a new psychoactive agent, mixed in with the gear you bought. Effectively we believe you may have been poisoned. It isn't something that the police knew about at the time. We want to see if your pattern of experience fits in with the others.' Jan was surprised at how easily the Colonel lied. She wondered if he could have lied as easily to her. Lance appeared to have accepted the story; he nodded and began to describe the moments following his last hit.

'It is all very hazy, detached; I had an out of body experience. I was conscious but it was as if I were dreaming. I was aware of what was going on, but somehow divorced from it.'

'Could you see yourself moving about whilst you were in this state?' Jan asked. She ringed the word detached with her pen.

'Yes, well no, well, it is difficult to say. Initially I felt that I was watching myself, but on reflection, I think I was more aware of myself and the condition I was in, rather than actually, physically, watching what I was doing. It is strange, I know what happened, but I don't recall how I know. The memories are clouded, fogged; there was smoke everywhere. I distinctly remember the smoke. It was like a dream, sometimes you watch yourself in a dream, detached like an observer but you know you are the subject of the dream. The fear is very real.'

'Were you very afraid?' Lance thought for a moment, he had not thought about the fear before, somehow that had had escaped him.

'Yes, I remember being afraid of being alone, there was a word....anoikis. Bizarre, I can't think what made me think of that word.'

'Homeless, it means sort of homeless,' Jan began. 'You felt you had left your body and your mind no longer had a home?'

'I suppose so. As I say it was like a dream, but I suppose it wasn't a dream. I can't feel remorse for what happened. Whatever it was that ate the dog, it wasn't me.'

'The paper article said something about voices. I know it was a load of rubbish, but did you feel compelled to do anything by some external influence? We thought that perhaps you might have been in a suggestive state and open to influence.' The Colonel looked across at Jan. She was so smart. She had picked up his line and carried it effortlessly. He hoped that she would find it harder to lie to him.

'No, that was newspaper twaddle. I have had a rather difficult period after the police van crashed. I had concussion. I think there may have been some sort of knock-on effect of the drugs.' His voice betrayed some nervousness. 'I have heard...' his voice trailed off, he was clearly locked in some internal conflict. 'I hear a voice. I can control it sometimes, but not always. I think he wants more control.' Sweat was beading on his brow and above his top lip. He closed his eyes and rubbed his forehead. 'I've been reading about schizophrenia, I think I might be suffering from some form of it.'

'Are the attacks getting worse?' The Colonel moved closer to the bed.

Lance looked into his eyes. 'They were getting very bad; they are still very bad. The doctors here have given me some tablets, but they knock me out as much as they quiet him. It kind of subdues him. It has taken a while but he watches what I do and comments on it rather than wanting to grab the controls all the time. I suppose this represents some aspect of my own psyche. I'm pretty shocked that I'm capable of thoughts like these. It can be terrifying.'

'You say him.' Jan was making copious notes. 'Does this alternative persona have a name?'

Lance closed his eyes. 'Yes, I know this sounds ridiculous but his name is Ralph Wooton. He was the guy the police van killed. My guess is someone at the site must have said his name and somehow I've picked it up and given it to my alter ego. I don't like to think about him too hard. He resurfaces, he pushes to the front.'

The conversation continued in this vein. Jan could not help liking Lance, he had depth; he was a thinker. It was a shame he felt the need to fry his brain with drugs every weekend. He had boned up on schizophrenia; he was not afraid to face this possibility, but she detected an underlying current that he actually wanted to believe that this was the case. There was another, more frightening possibility.

'Have you undergone any hypnotherapy whilst you've been here?' Jan asked. 'It has been shown to be very helpful in some traumatic situations.'

Lance laughed. 'I haven't had any therapy of any kind, the doctors here seem to have convinced themselves it is a drug-related problem, I'm being looked after by their drug expert. He must be a busy man, I haven't even met him yet and I've been here for two weeks.'

'I could have one of our guys try some regressive hypnotherapy; I can get him here this afternoon if you feel you are up to it.' The Colonel looked across at Jan. If he was trying to tell her something, she missed the subtly of his message.

'On one condition.' Lance looked across at the two of them. 'You've got to take me out to lunch before hand, somewhere nice. I know I'm under observation, you'll have to pull some strings, I suspect that you have the authority to do that. I'm sick to death with the food in here and I need some air.'

'Consider it done. Do you have any preference for food?' The Colonel shook his hand.

'Anything, as long as its not served on a polystyrene tray.'

'We'll pick you up in an hour. See you then.' Jan and Brian got up to leave. As they were about to leave the ward Lance called out to them. 'Ralph says book a table for four.' He was smiling but his voice was not as strong as it was.

FIVE

The call to prayer rang out over the PA system, taxi cabs beeped and roared in the street outside, a horse drawn carriage skidded down the main high street as the poor horse was struck by a passing car. The two protagonists shouted obscenities at one another whilst the horse lay, twitching in the street. Inside the Internet café all was in disarray. A lone figure was lying in the middle of the floor tangled in cables. She was about sixteen. She was screaming as if her life depended upon it; a high-pitched, painful wail that stilled the blood of every person within hearing. It blocked out the sound of the traffic outside, it blocked out the whir of the computer terminals. It was an animal roar that demanded attention. Like the hysterical screams of a hungry baby, it could not be ignored.

Few people in the room had noticed what had happened. They were all engrossed in their own projects: university theses were being emailed across the globe, plane tickets were being bought to send aunties over to America, pornography was being uploaded, downloaded and distributed. It could have been anywhere in the world. This was Cairo, so the links were painfully slow. A few people had been staring into space as they waited for things to raster onto their screens. A few people had watched the pretty girl's head flop forward and smack into her keyboard. They had observed her, wide-eyed and frantic, trying to extricate herself from her seat; saw her trip over a carelessly slung cable, saw her blindly scrabbling to escape from it, whilst slowly entwining herself like a fly in a web; keyboards, printers and computers thrown to the floor as she span and screamed.

Had she received some terrible news? Had a relative or

young love died? A few people eventually rose from their seats to restrain or comfort her. They backed away as she hissed like a she-devil, spittle flying from the sides of her mouth. Eventually her thrashings had destroyed every heavy item that had hindered her escape, she leapt at the nearest exit; a plate glass door. She did not attempt to open it, just flung herself at it like a wasp at a window. It failed to yield, and everyone heard the crack as her neck broke. Like the horse in the street, she twitched, and then lay still.

The restaurant had been fun, the food an anglicised version of Thai, Indonesian and Malay. The walls were covered with odds and sods imported from the various regions, some rather beautiful, others rather cheeky imitations of the real things. Everything was for sale with the exception of a few real treasures. The silks and spices made Lance comfortable. The food was a refreshing break from the bland hospital mush. He had quickly downed two gin and tonics and half a bottle of wine. The voice in his head was silent. He got the impression that Ralph did not eat out very often; he was subdued amongst the pleasant surroundings and good company.

Jan found herself wanting to talk more openly to the young man. He was clearly very smart and interested in everything they had to say. He was a freelance artist. The money was poor but it kept him in bare essentials; gin, Special K and Ikea furniture. He was well read and informed, if the drugs had addled his mind, it was not the parts of it which made good conversation over the diner table. His real name was Thomas but he had taken the name Lance from his job title; he said he liked the phallic element to it. Love had been unkind to him. He found solace in the various white powders he bought. It appeared that even they sometimes deceived.

They returned to the hospital on very good terms. The Colonel was obviously a little bit shy around him, though Lance had not made any brazen indication that he found the Colonel attractive. A Doctor Jarman, a colleague of the Colonel's, who greeted them all with a broad smile, met them in the foyer. The introductions were made, the doctor kept his eyes firmly focused on Lance throughout. They were led into a small, darkened room; a single candle provided the only flickering light. The Doctor asked Lance to clasp his hands together, interdigitating his fingers as if in prayer. For Lance the action felt slightly uncomfortable, a throw back to school assemblies and a strange feeling of isolation; but he complied without a word. He was instructed to concentrate on the point where his thumbs met, and did so, becoming acutely aware of his racing pulse as it throbbed through his clasped hands. Following a brief description of the procedure to follow, they all sat comfortably in a semi-circle. Lance was seated slightly forward of the others so that they were out of his line of sight. The Doctor began to talk Lance into a state of intense relaxation. He was warmed with food, company and alcohol. He felt his pulse, his lifeblood, coursing through his veins, he clenched his fingers, closing a circle, concentrated on his clasped hands and felt his consciousness turn in upon itself. It was not difficult to fall out of this reality, but once he had started, the drop became precipitous. He felt himself sliding away into a subconscious blackness, his body sinking and absorbed by the soft leather of his chair. Lance was unsure how much time had passed, but noticed the Doctor's tone had changed, he asked him what he could see. At first it was black but then slowly an impression formed in his mind. 'I'm standing on a high precipice,' he managed, his voice fatigued with the effort of drawing together thoughts in his relaxed state. The images sharpened slowly and he perceived a dark sea before him and what felt like the wind on his back.

Jan fought with herself to stay aware of the proceedings. The Doctor's voice was sending her off too. She pinched herself to maintain focus and started to make notes. The Doctor seemed remarkably well informed about the case; making Jan suddenly suspicious that Brian must have been in touch with him before. The thought was an unpleasant discontinuity in an otherwise pleasant day, a strange suspicious realisation that suddenly snapped her from her torpor. The Doctor drew Lance away from the black sea and regressed him to the afternoon before the fateful club night. Each moment slowly drawn out, the mundane actions of a day that had begun like any other fleshing the dream-like state into reality. Lance appeared relaxed and calm. He spoke quietly, reliving the moments of the evening as if watching them on a cinema screen. He described the well-rehearsed ritual he practised before he went out, every pill he had taken before leaving the house, the disappointment that they were not having the desired effect. He saw the tube journey to the club and some of the funny looks he got from couples going home from their own evening's entertainments. At one point he heard the music in the club, in his mind his fingers tapped to the rhythm, you lift me up, I'm lifted up, lifted up, I'm lifted up. This was a great trip in itself.

He was muttering now, the words barely audible. The Doctor gently drew Lance towards the moment he left the club. There was sudden flash of memory, he saw himself thrown from the club. He was shocked that someone could do such a thing to his poor incapacitated body. The bastard had just callously chucked him out the door as if he were the evening's collected garbage. He saw himself work his way into the alley. He saw the line of white powder disappear in front of his eyes. Then, all of a sudden, he was forced back onto the precipice, the doctor's voice lost all tone and faded to nothing. The wind on his back intensified. Struggling to hold on, he crouched down and dug himself into the cliff edge. The sea reared up, waves crashed and the wind rushed past his ears in a deafening roar. He became aware that he was not alone. Someone was standing behind him. He turned, but could not quite make out their features. The wind seemed not to affect this figure who now strode purposefully towards him. Lance managed a muted cry, the figure cocked his head to one side as if considering what he saw, then straightened up and launched a kick at Lance. He could do nothing to avoid it and fell backwards over the side of the cliff and down into the roaring sea. He tried to scream but found no voice. The violent water crashed about him and then drew him into its freezing maw. The grey walls of spume fused above him and enveloped him like an iron shroud. He struggled against invisible bonds, but the water was oblivious to his panic. The dankness closed about him and he felt his body heat waning

97

with every beat of his racing heart. In a moment he knew he would die. His efforts dissipated into nothing, his struggles became weaker, his life collapsing into a small, white dot. When the dot was extinguished, he knew it would all be over.

The Colonel grabbed Lance's arms, he was thrashing now and the obscenities were coming thick and fast. Lance's middle-England voice was twisted into guttural Irish. 'Write it down! Write down everything!' The Colonel restrained him as Lance spat and cursed. There were names, places, people that would be called, things were going to happen to them, terrible things, he was going to smash them like he had smashed his wife, do them like he had done his business partner. Whatever they thought they were doing to him, keeping him trapped in here. He was going to sort them out. Lance was strong and wild now, but the Colonel knew about restraint. He held him in a complex grip, one arm, held high up his back, his own arm across Lance's throat, lifting his head back and putting pressure on his chin, jugular arteries and veins. Lance struggled violently. It was the struggle of someone who did not care for his own welfare. It was the wild struggling of an alcoholic pumped with booze. If he felt any pain, he did not feel that it was being applied to his own body.

After a few moments more, Lance's body became more pliable, he was slowly slipping out of consciousness.

'Bring him back, Doctor, now!' the Colonel shouted. The doctor had backed away. He took a small torch from his pocket and advancing on his patient he shone it into Lance's eyes forcing them shut. His voice was authoritative and calm, belying the anxiety in his eyes. The Colonel slowly released his grip and the doctor took over. Lance's breathing became slower, more controlled. The doctor's patter continued. Lance's body fell listless into the Colonel's arms.

Lance was motionless now in the dark water. He was sinking away into the void, into the cold. As if in a dream he thought he saw a light on top of the cliff, an impossible distance away. He could not drag his eyes from it and suddenly felt himself drawn to it as words came to his mind from the darkness. He felt himself lifted from the water, the cliff face screaming past him at blistering speed. His mind and body were broken but he was flying now, up the cliff face, towards the light that rose like the moon over the precipice. As he neared it, the doctor's voice returned, getting stronger, asking him to open his eyes. The world around him folded back to the recesses of his mind from whence it came and he became more aware of his body. As the feeling returned, he opened his eyes and saw the doctor standing over him, a concerned look on his face. He felt strangely weak, but calm and warm. He looked around at the three figures staring wide-eyed at him. 'Who called the rescue chopper? You nearly lost me then,' he said in a hoarse whisper.

'I know, I'm sorry.' Said the Colonel. 'Next time we will be better prepared, if you were prepared to try this again.'

'If you can get this bastard out of my head, I'll do it.' He paused. 'I think I need another gin and tonic.'

The doctor turned off his torch. 'I think I need one too,' he said.

SIX

The gorilla house was quiet when Professor Joe Gregorian entered. In spite of himself he had allowed the close observations of the animals to stop for the week following Kate's death. The whole department had descended into mourning. They all needed a little time to come to terms with the loss. He was not sure he ever would. He had heard the details of Kate's death and now he had to confront the theatre in which it had happened. He had rushed to the hospital but he had been told it was already too late. Kate was his protégée; he would probably never know another student like her. She had devoted the last few weeks of her life to his gorillas. He had no idea she was so ill. Just the thought of it all brought tears to his eyes. She was so brave. He could not let her efforts go to waste. He had to make this project work. He had to pick up the pieces where she had left off.

All the animals had been fed. A skeleton crew had been appointed, to ensure everything was maintained. He was a little worried that the modified animals would suffer in the absence of full-time human attention, but they seemed more than satisfied to be with their own kind; the stimulation of having another animal in the cage, regardless of whether it was engineered or not, was more than sufficient.

He approached the site where Kate had been working. The lights were low. The two gorillas in the cage appeared to be asleep. The larger one, Frank was cuddled in the arms of Carl. Both were engineered. Joe had watched them grow up from tiny babies. With their over-developed heads they looked alarmingly human. He never failed to marvel at their capacity for affection towards each other and their keepers. He watched them in silence for an hour, half watching their breathing as their little chests rose and fell, half thinking

100

about Kate. After this time he felt more at ease. He could not stay late; tonight he had to write a few words to say at Kate's funeral. He retrieved a pencil and paper from his back pocket and wrote a few notes. The little apes began to stir in their sleep. He got up to leave when he heard Frank make an excited grunt. He leapt from Carl's arms and ran at the bars, jumping at them, arms outstretched, eyes looking imploringly at the Professor. The poor thing looked in a state of complete shock. The animals gait was strange. It had moved quickly yet awkwardly, as if it was having trouble with its back legs. He would have to get the vets to have a look at him. He walked closer to the cage.

'Hello sweetheart how are you?' he said, making the universal Simian welcome signs. Frank rattled the cage vigorously in response. His fingers formed shapes, clumsily at first, but soon they came in quick succession. The Professor stumbled back in his chair. 'Wait!' he said, 'for God's sake slow down!' He responded to the animal in kind, his fingers shaking in time to the palpitations of his heart, as he tried to form the symbols. The ape was clearly getting upset, his limbs were flailing, he was squealing with the gasping breathlessness of his excitement. Carl was awake too now and jumped around screeching in response to his friend's gesticulations. Frank's lips moved frantically; it was clear he was trying to form words, but no words came. His fingers continued to spell out question after question. The Professor answered in combinations of words and signs. He could not believe what he was seeing; he could not believe what he was doing. Tears were streaming down his face as he rushed to the cage and flung his arms through the bars and round Frank's little form. The gorilla pushed his head into his sleeve. He was crying too. Eventually the Professor had to pull himself away to find a key for the cage. As he stumbled through the corridors of the research centre his head was reeling. How could this be possible? Could this be undone? What was he going to tell the family? He was beginning to doubt his own sanity. It was late but he had so much to do. He had to find Gerri and get independent observation of the sign. He needed another human being to talk to. He was terrified that at any moment he would wake up and this would all be some kind of nightmare. He thought about the speech he was supposed to be making tomorrow. Hang the speech! Kate was not dead. She had simply moved. He could hardly dial the number as he phoned out of the building; his hands shook as if they did not belong to him. 'Gerri, could you please come into work now. It is urgent. Come as quickly as you can. Bring your boyfriend as well, yes. I wouldn't ask you unless I felt it was very important.' The line went dead and the Professor rocked back on his heels and let the tears flow.

SEVEN

Joe Lembeck stood before the sixty-one uploads. He had chosen a simple setting: a warm day, a grassy knoll, a stream nearby. There was no wind, no animal life to provide distraction. Somewhere in his mind's eye he was reminded of a lay preacher from his youth; an Irishman with grey hair and full, black, bushy eyebrows that lifted as the sermon progressed. He remembered how approachable, how friendly this man had been. How persuasive. He adopted this form in front of the sixty-one, complete with long white robes and blue scarf. He knew he could control them at a whim, but he wanted to limit this to the absolute bare minimum at this stage. He demanded attention and they gave it. He was about to say the first shared words ever to be spoken in the new universe. He had pondered these words many times; this was one small step for a god but one giant leap for mankind. When he spoke, the words were instantaneously translated so that each individual understood them in their native tongue, and modulated so that they thought the words were directed at them personally. Several people collapsed to their knees, a few kissed the ground. Others looked on uncertain of what to do.

'Welcome to the inner sphere. Welcome to the second universe. I am your alpha and omega. I am the one true God. This is not heaven. This is not hell. This is the page on which I write, this is the clay from which I form, this is the future of existence. Welcome to the future.'

There were movements from amongst the crowd. A voice spoke out. 'You say you are God and yet I look upon you and feel no wonder. You cannot be the one true God.' Joe spoke gently.

'Belief has been the pillar of faith for so many. Belief starts where logic fails. In time you will realise this is so. What would you have me do, to demonstrate that I am the one true God. Is there anything that would convince you?'

The man came forward from the crowd. He had been given a form that matched the one he perceived himself to have. He was naked. He was in his eighties. His back was curved and his hands clawed inwards. Arthritis had been cruel to him but his eyes and face were lifted as high as they could and intelligence played across his face.

'You don't look like my God and you don't sound like my God. But if you are a god, then could I ask you to heal me.' He spoke with confidence, firmly and calmly. He tried to look up at Joe, but the kyphosis of his spine, meant he could not hold the stare for long.

Joe looked into the man's mind. It was difficult to restrain himself from absorbing the mind completely. He had felt the surge of such exploration before, but now he wanted to restrain himself from complete annihilation of the mind before him. In a moment he found what he was looking for, an image of God in splendour. Strange, he thought, how mean the mind of man was for expressing glory. How limited it was as a vessel to contain even the most paltry part of God. In another moment he had transformed himself into the old man's God. His body now was an image of Christ; blinding light emanated from every pore. The crowd turned away in fear, shielding their eyes. He opened his hand and revealed the stigmata, each projecting beams of light. A dove appeared and settled on his shoulder. He walked towards the old Man, who remained standing, not defiant, but with his head behind his lifted arms. He reached forward and touched the man's shoulder. Where skin contacted skin, the flesh was seared, but the man did not turn away. His back straightened, his fingers relaxed, he fell to the floor and began to sob. The light subsided and once again he stood before them as a preacher.

'I am not the God of the Christians; I am anything I choose to be: alpha, omega, the dawn, the dusk. In time you will understand.' He helped the old man to his feet. He was free of pain for the first time in twenty years.

Joe looked at the assembled crowd. 'I will leave you all now with a gift. I will return very soon to observe your progress.'

Then he was gone. Immediately every illness, every ache, every minor complaint that each individual perceived they possessed was removed. There was a communal intake of breath and then most people began to cry and hug their neighbours.

Joe watched from a distance. It had felt good to touch the essence of the old man's mind. His was an intellect that was worth interacting with. There must be many more. As he had these thoughts, he noticed discontinuities in the images before him, glitches that flashed across the group. He reached out into the domains that held the sixty-one. Something was corrupting them; something was eliciting extreme demands upon the system.

He probed beyond these domains. There were areas outside that were free of interference. He packed their minds, encrypted and condensed them then moved and unpacked them in a safer domain. They were completely unaware of the transition; such was his power now. The analogue world was making demands on his running time. They had unwittingly demonstrated that they had power over him. Though he was quite sure that they were unable to detect his presence. They would have to be taught that a new order was coming. They would have to learn that his power extended beyond the virtual. Soon he would send them all a message.

EIGHT

'What did you make of that?' The Colonel opened the door on Jan's side of the Daimler.

'Remarkable. I haven't seen a schizophrenic episode as dramatic and complete as that in my life. You know I'm not an expert in such matters, but it was almost as if Lance is possessed by a demon. He is such a nice guy, and the thing that he turned into is a monster.'

'You are convinced that it is a genuine psychosis?'

'Are you saying that you aren't convinced?' Jan looked puzzled.

'To be honest I'm not sure what I think. I have dealt with hundreds of psychotic men in my time, under all sorts of conditions, but this doesn't follow the normal pattern. When Lance was regressed he was stable and fine, up to the trigger point when he was giving up his consciousness to the drugs. Although he wasn't under the influence of anything today, his mental state under hypnosis may be similar to that, or at least an echo of that which he was in before. In this weakened state this other persona could surface. I think there is a battle going on in Lance's head. I think this lad is potentially in a lot of danger.'

'Do you think the alter ego was responsible for killing the dog? It was unbelievably violent, the aggression there was vile, but it wasn't animalistic, it wasn't deranged, just angry at being trapped. It doesn't seem quite 'in character', if that means anything in this situation.'

The Colonel shook his head. 'I couldn't agree more, there is something funny going on there. I wanted to speak to Lance because his behaviour with the dog was perfectly in accordance with what we have seen with the guys in the code group. It is bestial, feral. I've read and re-read the account of the dog owner and the thing that struck me was that Lance was not inherently violent. The guy was scared, there is no doubt about that, but once some sort of dominance relationship had been established, he backed away and was compliant. He only panicked when he was outnumbered. Even then, he didn't actively attack the police; he just blindly tried to escape. It was just like the victims at Porton Down.'

'So you think that this aggressive personality disorder is some sort of intermediate, or secondary phenomenon? Rather like Joe Lembeck? Perhaps your people back at P. D. will undergo this personality flux as well. That is assuming there is any relationship between the conditions.' Jan was still unsure. It was true that there were superficial common elements, but the processes and conditions were so varied. This did not sit well with her scientific methodology. There were too many variables, too many uncontrolled factors. They needed a testable hypothesis. There was something missing, something obfuscating the results.

'Can I borrow your notes on Lance's alter ego, what was it? Ralph somebody. I'd like to check up on this guy. I can pull in a few favours from the police. I think I need to know a bit more about this chap.' Jan passed over her pile of notes. She saw the word 'detached' on the top of the page. This was all very well but what exactly was detached from what?

It was almost like waking from a dream. He had spent the last few weeks going over and over his life experience, trying to make some sense of it. He knew he was different from normal people. He had only ever been an echo behind someone else's mind. She had called him her 'dark twin', her 'quiet boy', her 'noisy monkey' when he had tried to assert himself. What a bitch. They had grown up together like brother and sister, closer even. Well, definitely 'closer'. He never understood why he was never spoken to directly; he had always been there, watched every moment of her life from day one. He had suffered her mediocrity, suffered her failures and, worse than all this, had suffered the worst humiliation of all, the devastating realisation that hers was the more powerful mind. For some Godforsaken reason, she dominated him in that brain case of hers. He had to sit and watch every bloody episode of every bloody soap opera. He had to undergo the daily grind of being a nurse in a mental hospital. Whenever he tried to put his head over the parapet, wham! She would hit him with drugs, bite his head off, crush him with her great fat bloody ego. Those bloody pills, she swallowed them and he was drowned. She had been murdering him slowly every day of her life. She should have been happy for the company. She did not have very much of that outside her own head.

He had thought of trying to end it all when he was trapped inside. Many had been the time when he had tried to slide between her thoughts, what soap powder to buy, what colour cardigan went with a black skirt. He would adopt her persona, slip between the tiny gaps. Look over the edge of the cliff on holiday and beg her to jump. Dare her to dive off. He waited with her for the bus. Saw it come and longed for her to jump under the wheels. Just finish it now. Kill the pair of them.

Now of course he was free. The miracle had come to pass. They were separated. That which no man can put together, something had split asunder. He was in this new, male body. It was not the best body in the world. If he had been given the choice he might have taken up a more salubrious residence, but what did it matter. He was free. Now he was a man. He had no idea what being a man entailed. He had never been a bloke before. Initially the newness of things had entertained him immensely. The extra bits, the missing bits. The different feel of skin and bone. He was disappointed that he did not feel more robust. If the truth were said Moira Kilbain was pretty bloody robust. Mentally she had been robust and physically she was probably more robust than the body of this Joe Lembeck character, whoever he was. There was something nice about this body though. For all his faults, Joe Lembeck was smart. He was not sure how much of his improved intelligence was due to being free inside his own brain, and how much was due to being resident in this particular brain. There was definitely something different about it. It was 'cleaner', sort of 'brighter' than he had experienced before.

Even when he was trapped, he had secretly known he was smart. He had always wanted to crack the whip in that place, study, and improve himself. He could have been anything; he could have gone anywhere. Already he felt his new persona settling in. Strange the way we slip from day to day. He was not sure how much of his increased vigour and ambition he had picked up from this new host. There were also residual memories here. They were not easy to recall. The harder he tried the more slippery they became. It was as if, by exerting the effort to find them, they were being simultaneously wiped. Like a sculptor playing his hands over the surface of his mind to feel the thoughts, his hands formed the soft clay into different shapes. He had called this 'focal thinking'; it allowed him to look up close at things, but, as if his gaze was that of the sun, it meant he tended to burn away the very thing he was looking at. It did not matter. There were new thoughts to be had, new vistas to explore. There were just a few things that needed sorting out first, just a little bit of closure to be had.

Most of the passengers on the Berlin to Geneva express were trying to settle down to sleep. The train was flying along through the still green countryside. Forested hillsides flashed past the window; dirty, white lazy cows were still chewing the cud in the lower fields. The air was cold but the inside of the train was hermetically warm. The sound of the wind rushing by only really made itself known as passengers moved through the swishing automatic doors separating the carriages. The doors swished open and a young, blond, loud businessman walked into the carriage. A few heads turned briefly, partly to look at his fashion sense (which was good) but mostly to give him a disapproving look as he ruminated on his mobile phone. A few people indicated with their eyes towards the little sign in the window, which informed the occupants that this was a quiet carriage, and that mobile phones and Walkmans were not allowed. A few people tutted loudly. The tension in the air became palpable.

The pressured gaze of the collective minds in the carriage had no effect on the man. He was deeply engrossed in his conversation, which involved a technical discussion about the relative merits of his WAP mobile phone and his colleague's Voice Internet Relay device built into his laptop. It was necessary for him to shout as his colleague was sitting on a train travelling between Lowestoft and London. This train was rather noisier. To the German businessman it sounded like his friend was being periodically minced through a sausage machine. His friend informed him that it felt rather like that travelling by train in England.

The conversation was effectively a three way one because his friend was simultaneously logged on to a site in Cairo where his girl friend was studying information technology at Cairo University. One eavesdropper sitting nearby was amazed at the self-fulfilling, self-reinforcing web of information technology. Without the wonders of modern science it would not be possible to wax lyrical about global communication to a friend on the other side of the world. It was an enormous futile cycle. The eavesdropper rolled on her side and tried to get back to sleep.

She was just dropping off again, in spite of the businessman's prattling, when she heard him stop talking mid-sentence. He emitted a strange moan, like air escaping from a bicycle tyre, and slumped to the ground in front of her. His head hit the floor with a crack. His mobile was still stuck fast against his head. The supporting arm was shaking violently. The man's eyes rolled up into his head. The passenger realised he had lost consciousness. She rolled him off her feet, stood up and asked for assistance. Two men came to her aid. The man's body was heavy. They moved it into a sitting position. His head lolled forward. They extracted the phone from his ear. No one had seen exactly what had happened. They presumed he had had some kind of fit and fallen down. The passenger put the phone to her ear. The line was dead.

Slowly he came round. He struggled to focus his eyes; made a strange noise, pulled his coat around him, hiding his face and began to shake uncontrollably. The female passenger reached across to him to comfort him, but he screeched at her. The noise was strange, unhinged, and primeval. It was bizarre, unintelligible, yet the meaning was clear. Everyone on the carriage understood the fear, everyone in the carriage understood his confusion; everyone realized they should not approach any closer than they were already. The businessman slid away from the group. He eyed them nervously from under his coat. He looked hunted. They backed away. Someone pulled the emergency cord. They did not want to spend the next three hours with a madman. The train's brakes were applied; the train squealed and shook with the deceleration. Everyone staggered back with the movement. The businessman screeched in sympathy with the train. It juddered to a halt, the front of the train on the edge of a deserted country platform. The PA system announced what had happened in an annoyed and lazy tone. Everyone was told to stay where they were. The train doors slid open. The businessman jumped up at the sound and bolted for the opening. He flew headlong out the door and dropped to the ground, falling badly. A shout came from up the platform. A guard was shouting at him to get back on the train. Another train was coming, a fast train. The doors slammed shut. The guard ran towards the suited figure. The rails were humming as the fast train approached. The pitch increased, the noise became louder and louder. The suited figure ran the length of the platform away from his shouting pursuer. He jumped onto the tracks and hunched down between the rails. The guard began to run along the platform. He was a heavy man and even this mild exertion immediately made him start to pant and sweat. He hated passengers. They were always causing trouble, always making him look tardy, always putting crap all over his clean trains, and always doing stupid things, like this. He heard the whine of the rails, what was the stupid idiot doing now? What was he thinking? He realised he was not going to make it to him in time. He jumped onto the rails. The trains behind would be stopped, but there was nothing to stop the train on the other line, unless he phoned in. The radio was in the cab, but he didn't have time to get it. Shit, shit, shit. The humming was getting louder. It was a while since he had worked on the rails themselves, the driving job had got him out of the cold, but he knew this sound well and he knew he didn't have much time. He had to get out of the way. He would be killed. He ran

111

between the rails. The clinker of the embankments rolled and crunched under his feet. He stumbled against the side of his stationary train. He was breathless with the exertion but he tried to shout out. He could make out the curve of a dark blue suit crouched down between the shimmering rails. In the distance, charging up the hill came the Eurostar. It was too late. The fast train was almost upon them. At the last minute the guard dived to safety under the stationary train. From his cowering position between the enormous wheels he did not see the suited figure stand and stare, mesmerized by the oncoming monster. He did not see the man's hands go to his head as the thing bore down on him. The thunder of the wheels and the bark of the horn drowned out the man's visceral scream of terror. The rush of wind shook the stationary train. The sound of wheels on steel roared in the guard's ears. The relentless, repetitive grinding, pulsing momentum crashed by, and then was gone. The Doppler shift changed the monster's roar from anger to remorse. He covered his head and turned it away. Thirty seconds later the brakes on the fast train could be heard squealing in the distance. It would be half a mile before it came to a compete halt. The Geneva to Berlin shuttle would not be on time today.

NINE

Doctor Gerry Spints watched open-mouthed as the gorilla formerly known as Frank spelled out his heart using Standard British Sign Language. The gorilla was sitting on a table in front of Professor Gregorian. The Professor was making notes as the animal performed the hand ballet before his eyes. He only took his eyes off her for a moment as he scribbled. He spoke slowly, mouthing the words as if talking to a deaf person. He occasionally annotated his speech with sign.

For Kate, the Professor's speech was strangely distorted. Its modulation and timbre were unrecognisable; there were elements that she could not understand, whole sentences slid together like guttering candles. She concentrated on his mouth. Her vision was not as acute as it had been as a human. She found herself squinting, but there was something else associated with the visual image; an aftershock she realised was giving her some other information about the subject, information she could not yet decode. The after images were only present around the apes and humans in the room. Inanimate objects appeared quite normal, if a little out of focus. Her fingers felt clumsy and she was aware that she had to think harder than usual. It was strange. The modified gorilla's brain comfortably held her mind, but there was mushiness to it, a resistance to linear thought. She found herself constantly distracted by the simplest things. The slightest movement of one of the other animals demanded attention. She was acutely aware of how much food there was in the room and its exact location. She knew Frank was still in his mind, with her. He was in a state of shock because she was there, but he was coming round to the idea. Kate felt it was her own calmness that was giving him confidence. When he thought along side her (his mind was not always so occupied)

113

she felt it like a current flowing counter to her own thoughts. It was strangely thick; it had substance. She was trying to make these observations understood by the Professor. He had informed her that her previous physical body had passed away. Her next of kin had been informed and were preparing the body for cremation. Now, of course, it would be frozen and preserved as well as was possible. The little gorilla shed a tear but wiped it away as soon as it came. Kate was not sure whom she was crying for. She thought about her mother and sister. What would they be told? She needed time to adjust before she confronted them.

Quietly she informed the Professor that she was worried about what would happen if Frank were to demand more access to his thoughts. She found it very difficult to resist his advances when he applied himself. This was, after all, his brain; he was rather more accomplished at using it than she was.

The Professor was trying to say how sorry he was that she had been so ill, how sad he was that she had not shared the burden with him, how distraught he had been when he thought she was dead, how relieved he was that she had somehow survived. He was also thinking about her family. He did not want to broach the question. Kate wanted to continue her analysis of her situation. The more she talked about it, the more comfortable she felt. It was a terrible bind not being able to vocalise her thoughts directly. Whenever she attempted to speak, her voice came out as an unrecognisable gurgle. This would take some time. She beckoned Gerry over to her. At first she did not move. The shock of the transformation bewildered her and, mixed with the shock of finding her friend dead not 12 hours before had left her weak and distraught. Gerry's boyfriend watched from the sides. He was deaf and had followed the conversation better than either Gerry or the Professor. He followed nuances in the ape's sign that betrayed her inner turmoil, her stress. He put his arm around Gerry and together they approached Kate. Gerry reached out, touched the back of her hands and then, sobbing, fell into her arms. Kate looked across at Gerry's boyfriend, and signed a thank you. He signed, Glad to have you back with us, in return. She had always liked Jim. He was also a good-looking guy. She wondered what he thought of her like this; she felt suddenly, strangely self-conscious. It was strange how this particular acute sensation overlaid all the other myriad of emotions that were flowing through her. She looked at the Professor. She would have to stop soon, rest. She was very sleepy; Frank was nodding-off and dragging her down with him. She yawned hugely, putting her hand over her mouth at the last minute. It was something that Kate used to do. He wondered if he could bring her some clothes, she knew it would not be easy. She let out a laugh. Strange, she could laugh but not talk, ever the comedienne. Perhaps she would have a future in film. She just had to sleep now. Gerry found a beanbag for her and a duvet. She curled up into it and drifted off. Sleep came immediately. She dreamt of apes that turned into men and women. Frank dreamed of leaves.

It only took a moment. The nurse turned her back to him for a second; he had been as polite and gracious to her as he knew how. He simply pulled the chair from under himself and hit her with it. Down she went with hardly a sound. He though he heard a little crack as he hit her, perhaps a collar-bone. It would be painful when she regained consciousness. He pulled her prone form out of the doorway, tied her legs and arms with ribbons of sheets he had prepared in advance, stuffed some more into her mouth, placed her on the bed (with some difficulty), and covered her with a duvet. This would have to do. He did not have all that much time.

In the back of his mind there was a fear that he might be caught. Why risk his newfound freedom, if he could only bide his time he could make a clean escape without this drama. This was the essence of the problem. He had bidden his time for quite long enough. For thirty-two years he had waited; for thirty-two years he had suffered under the tyranny of the Irish witch. He could wait no longer. He could not wait for this other hysterical woman to come to terms with the fact that he had no idea who she was; he could not fool the staff here much longer as to his 'identity'. He laughed out loud. He had never had a proper identity; he was just a bloody headache, an aberration to be disposed of. His own mother had said as much. He had thought about this a lot, most of his life, a fetid grub gnawing away at the tiny fragment of brain he was allotted. His mother, Moira's mother, he had always assumed they were one and the same, who was to know? Was he in reality the soul of some lost twin that never made it to birth? Was he a twin soul placed by mistake in a single host, an unwanted child fostered into her body? He had given up trying to work it out.

All he knew was that tonight he was going to actually put into practise the one idea that had sustained him over all these years. He had squirmed and cowered under her oppressive power, his conviction failing him. To destroy her would condemn himself to oblivion and he could not face that loneliness. Now he was no longer there, inside her mind, he was going to burn down the jailhouse.

He slipped out of the nurse's tearoom window just as a silver Daimler pulled into the home. It was quite late; he was not expecting anyone to drive into the car park at this hour. He hid himself in the shadows of overgrown rhododendrons until the car passed. He knew she was on her way home now. Wrapped up against the cold, her face set against the cold night air, the same way she had set her face against him. Her little button nose in the air, the little silver pins pulling her hair off her face. He hated the little silver pins. Such effort had been expended to put that hair up. She had drained his resources putting up her ruddy hair and denied him a voice. Denied him a basic human right. Tonight he would speak his mind; tonight he would examine hers. He ran through the park. She would never have gone though here, who knew what was hiding in the shadows. Tonight he felt safe. Tonight he was elated, liberated. Tonight he knew he was the most dangerous thing in the woods.

He left the silence of the park, ran, echoing through the underpass, delighting in the forbidden places. He cut off another corner by running through the graveyard. He ran over the graves; how she would have berated him if he had suggested that. Once again back on the street, two blocks later he was standing outside her door. The light was on. She was in the kitchen.

Down the side passage he crept, into the darkness of the back garden. He reached over the gate and slipped the latch. Poor dear, she had never realised how easy that would be for someone over five foot two. In two steps he was by the back door. He saw her move from the kitchen to the front room. Now was the time. He reached through the cat-flap and eased out the bolt, so easy when you had long arms. She had meant to sort it out years ago; who could have known how easy it was to get in. Perhaps he had known all along that this day was coming. He had never forced her to improve her security. Had he secretly wanted her to be murdered in her sleep?

He carefully tried the door. Always the same pattern, she never differed. Always she shot the bolt, never the deadlock, worried that she could not get out in a hurry if there was a fire while she was cooking. She only turned the deadlock just before she went to bed. It made her feel secure. The door always squeaked when you opened it past thirty-five degrees. He slipped in and quietly pulled it to. He was inside the house. The house he had lived in for seventeen years. He saw it now with fresh eyes. He could see dust on surfaces she could not reach. She would have been mortified. He walked on tiptoes up the dark hallway. God! Her taste in décor! Greens and browns of Ireland, I ask you, it was like living in an old teapot. She was just through this door, hardly a breath away; he could almost hear her breathing. Suddenly he remembered he did not have a weapon. He needed something blunt and heavy. He turned slowly. He'd get the meat tenderiser from the third draw down in the kitchen. It was like a hammer with teeth, it would be perfect.

He did not hear her move. She was like a fury. She swept round the corner and struck him with a poker. It was caste iron, very heavy; it had a ram's head on the handle. He heard the whoosh of it flying through the air and heard the crack as it hit the back of his head. He felt the warm dampness of his own blood; saw yellow lights rising up before his eyes. He tipped forward into the scullery and passed out. Moira stood over his prone body in her stockinged feet, breathing hard.

'You bastard!' she said. 'You stupid bastard, after all these years did you not think I would hear you coming, my boy? I could always hear you coming.'

She had the most incredible urge to finish him, there and then on the scullery floor. Something restrained her. In some strange way he was like flesh and blood to her, no, never flesh and blood, he was something else. She could not think now, there was no time. She tied his hands and feet together behind his back with the flex from the iron. Her father had shown her how to hogtie when they lived on the farm. She put on her best shoes, walked to the call box on the corner, locking the door behind her, and called the police. She knew he was not going anywhere, and besides she knew everything about him; what was there to fear?

TEN

John was in the kitchen again. Something was being flambéed, he always used too much booze; the pyrotechnics were always impressive. The guests roared with approval as the flames licked up at the ceiling. Something sizzled in the frying pan; an aromatic sauce was poured over them and they were brought to the table. Jan smiled hugely across the table at her friend.

'You are the lucky one! John is such a dab hand in the kitchen. Ken can't flambé, can you dear?'

'I can burn dinner as well as the next man!' came Ken's rather lubricated reply. It had been a very successful evening; they had worked their way through the whole spectrum of drink, and a few liqueurs would probably finish the job perfectly. John reached across the table and held Jan's hand. A chorus of 'aaaahs' greeted this across the table and a little sympathetic cuddling from the other couple was initiated.

'So when is little Flambé due then?' Ken reached across and tapped Jan's tummy.

'Well, it usually takes nine months, so not for another eight sweetheart.' Jan had not touched the drink. Tonight she did not need to. It was strange really; sometimes the mood just inebriated you all on its own. John was beaming like a Cheshire cat. He had wanted a baby so badly. He was feeling especially keen at the moment. His mother was ill and was putting some pressure to bear. She said she wanted to 'see the little darling before she parted this plane'. John had suggested she call lastminute.com.

The desert went down well, the music was mellow, coffees and mints came and went, Jan's friend offered to do the washing-up, the offer was graciously declined and their friends got the last tube home. Jan lay back into John's arms. She snuggled down. 'I think I'd like to call him George if it's a boy and Georgina if it's a girl. What do you think?'

'It's a bit old fashioned, but why not. If it is a girl, why not call it something else and we'll keep trying until we get a boy?' John giggled and Jan snuggled down further.

'Would you like a boy or a girl?' Jan looked up into his big eyes with the long lashes she adored so much.

'I don't mind what it is, as long as it is healthy and looks like you.' For a second Jan thought of Colonel Wilson and Jackie. A lump formed in her throat. She was about to speak when the phone rang. She got up to answer it. It was the Colonel.

'Jan, I'm sorry it is so late, can you talk? I've got some new information, I wanted to tell you as soon as possible, before we have tomorrow's meeting with Lance.'

'It'll have to wait until the morning Brian; I'll speak to you then. Is that okay?'

'Yes, yes of course, sorry again for phoning so late, I'll speak to you tomorrow.' The line went dead. Jan felt sorry for the Colonel for a moment. He had probably been working all night. He had probably gone home to a quiet house. She would have to invite him over for dinner. She looked at John. He had his come to bed eyes on. Tonight she would be only his. She had to push other thoughts away. She was going to be the mother of his child.

The next morning was overcast and drear. The Daimler looked steely grey in the cold morning light. The driver kept the engine running and Brian ran up the stairs to Jan's flat. Jan was up and about. The kettle was on. 'Would you like a coffee before we go?' Jan lifted the steaming pot. It looked inviting.

'Erm, oh okay, as long as we give one to the chauffeur as well. He'll get the ache otherwise.' Brian called down to the driver who turned the engine off and lumbered up the stairs up after them. Brian was obviously keen to talk. The driver sat down in front of 'Richard and Judy' and Brian left him to have a conspiratorial word with Jan.

'I went to the care home last night to see Joe Lembeck.'

Jan looked slightly annoyed. 'I thought we were going over there together, with John.'

'I just wanted to ask him if he would be prepared to undergo some hypnotherapy in the light of our success with Lance. I just missed him. I must have nearly run over him.'

'You mean to say they have released him?'

'No, he escaped, clouted one of the nurses. The police phoned an hour later to say they had picked him up in the home of another member of staff. I don't know the details yet. It is interesting; Joe has no history of violence. There is nothing in his profile to suggest he would be predatory towards women. It's all a bit of a mystery. Obviously he is in police custody now. As soon as possible I'll get the full details and we can go and see him. There is more.' The Colonel's eyes were ringed dark with lack of sleep and he looked every one of his years; but they still flashed with excitement.

'Go on, you are like a dog in heat, what have you found out?'

'It is incredible. The interview we had with Lance last week, well, I've checked out all the fine details of his rant. It is incredible. Every detail matches. Every little point.'

'But how can they match? The details are from Lance's alter ego. Are you saying that you think he knew this Ralph character intimately?'

'No, well that is possible, but when you profile the two of them there is no reason to suggest they would have met before. The point is that what Lance was shouting on about whilst under regression amounts to a confession by Ralph Wooten. The man was a convicted felon. He had been inside for three counts of violent assault and drugs offences. When he was killed, the police were chasing him on suspicion of murdering his wife. Social services thought she was at risk and were checking up on her and his daughter. He fobbed them off for the first two weeks, but by the third they confronted him. He pushed one of them through a plate glass window. The police have been hunting him ever since.'

'And the wife and child?'

'The daughter was found at his mother's; no one has seen the wife for three weeks. The police have interviewed neighbours, family and friends. She did not have many friends, bless her, and there doesn't appear to be anywhere she could have gone. The police suspect she has been murdered, and the body disposed of somewhere.'

Jan was silent for a moment. Lots of women were killed by their husbands, perhaps this was coincidence. She had to focus. She had to stay professional.

'You mentioned details. If the police have failed to recover a body, how can you corroborate any of the details?'

'There is more. All the names he gave us, various 'colleagues' who were going to sort us out. They are all known criminals; most of them part of the drug underworld. One of them had actually given the police the evidence that got Wooten sent down the first time. The police wanted to know where I got the names. I suspect they are currently involved in some undercover drugs bust, I really touched a nerve when I spoke to the head of narcotics.'

'So where does Lance fit into this? Do you think that Ralph was his supplier?'

'No, I have my suspicions, but I need more time. I need you to be open-minded about this, but, as I've said before, I don't want to pre-empt your conclusions. I don't think that is good scientific method. Does that make sense to you?'

'Perfectly; however, I'm not sure you and I are on the same wavelength anyway.'

'That is exactly how I want it. I have come to my own conclusions, but I 'm unconvinced of all of them. I want to be proved wrong. Let's go and see Lance; the good doctor is meeting us there at ten thirty. I've kept the police away so far, I'm not sure how much longer that will be possible.'

Lance greeted them with a broad smile. 'Nice to see you both again. You just missed my mother. I'm so glad, it was pretty embarrassing!' Lance's bedside table was piled high with fruit, vitamin supplements and Catherine Cookson novels. Jan picked up the first of these. 'I wouldn't have thought...'

'Just don't ask! Not even under hypnotherapy!'

They laughed and joked for half an hour until a nurse

came to tell them that the doctor had arrived. The Colonel asked Lance if he would mind him recording the session, as the tapes might be useful for future analysis. He did not mind at all, as long as Brian contacted his agent. There was more laughter but lance's exhaustion was clear to Jan.

'Do you feel up to this? You look very tired.'

'I'm fine. It's just that I can't let myself dream at the moment. If I even start to dream it's... just horrible. I can't really say. I set my alarm to wake me up after every hour at night; I drop in and out of sleep. I feel pretty crap, but it is keeping me sane. It stops the...nightmares.'

They entered the darkened room. The set up was the same as before. This time a tape recorder was set up on the table in front of Lance.

'If you want to turn it off at any point during the proceedings just say so.' The Doctor's voice was calm. The candle was lit. Lance brought his fingers together, closing the circle, felt his heart blood pulsing in his veins and gently returned to the fateful day.

In a secret military site in China a senior military official snapped orders at one of his technicians. A small electric vehicle was fetched and the official and a blue-suited politician in his late fifties climbed on board. It was a short ride that took them to the end of a long corridor. The vehicle pulled into a car lift and they descended several more floors in darkness. The lift glided to a halt and the driver deftly reversed the car out of the lift and down another set of corridors. They pulled up at a set of steel doors that were guarded by four serious-looking, heavily armed men. The doors opened outwards and they were allowed to enter. The car stopped at another set of doors and the party continued on foot. A key card opened this final set of doors. The room beyond was quiet. A number of white-suited technicians moved to and fro between lines of laboratory equipment, chemicals and computer screens. Everything was pristine and tidy. Beyond this room lay half a dozen tissue culture suites. These were busily occupied with scientists wearing full bunny suits and gloves. To one side was a further suite. It was to this that the party was directed. One of their number - a grey-haired, stern-faced politician - shook his head as he was handed a bundle of clothes as they entered the anti-room to the suite. He was not impressed with the suggestion that he should put plastic covers over his shoes and hair but after some quiet discussion he complied.

The room was much longer than one might have guessed from the outside. It contained some four hundred bubbling tanks. A switch was flicked and the tanks were illuminated. The place reminded the politician of an H. L. Geiger image he had seen whilst studying art history in Europe. Each tank contained a membranous bag. Pressed up against each was the impression of a face, that of a small child.

Lance once again found himself on the precipice overlooking the sea. This time the weather was fair; the cliffs fell away beneath him, but were blindingly white in the clear air. He could hear the doctor's voice, calm, coming out of the air around him. The sea beneath him looked inviting. In his mind's eye he saw himself swan dive into the blue.

The doctor took him back to the club. The images flowed as they had done before. He watched them now, impassively. They held no fear for him. He had been this way before and they had rescued him. Once again he saw himself in the alleyway, he watched the line of white powder disappear, grain by grain and then felt something drawn from his body, particle by particle, in gruesome parody of this act. This time he was prepared. In his waking dreams he had been in this place a hundred times. He had watched himself dissociate. He now understood what had happened to him. He was not going to let it happen again. He focused his thoughts on the figure before him, he knew he was with friends, he had tried to do this before but fear had prevented him. With their help he might be able to hold on longer.

It felt strange to be trying to claw his way back into his own mind. Many times he had tried to do the opposite, lying back on his battered sofa in his tiny London flat, trying to undertake an out of body journey, sinking away from consciousness. There had been times when he had nearly allowed himself to fall into the precipice, when he had began to sink deep into the earth, away from his body. He had never allowed himself to go so far. Now it was all too easy. He had trained his mind to start the journey; the drugs just prised loose the clinging fingers that held him in. Now he had to get back.

As Brian, Jan and the Doctor watched they saw Lance's body spasm. The doctor, outwardly calm, betrayed his inner thoughts by a furtive glance across at the Colonel. He asked Lance who he was.

Lance began to speak, slow inchoate groans at first; but words slowly crystallized from the confusion. It was his voice, not the voice of Ralph. The words came with considerable effort. Each was forced through his lips as if something was trying to force them back in.

'I am Lance. I am not…alone. I have held on, I do not want to let go.'

'Okay Lance.' The doctor spoke slowly. 'Do not worry if you have to let go. We'll be here to catch you. Let us talk to the other man. Tap your fingers if you want to speak. That will allow you to interject. You are stronger than he is. You control your mind. Do you understand?'

The doctor spoke with authority. Lance nodded. 'I understand. Her…here he comes, he is coming.' His body shook again. Lance let out a shriek.

'You bastards! You can't keep me locked in here, I'll see you all in hell first, I've done my time, done my time!'

'To whom am I speaking?' the doctor began.

'You know who I am, you bastards…' The voice trailed off in a host of obscenities.

'If you do not say who you are, we are not prepared to talk to you.' His reply was firm. 'We will speak to Lance. We do not need to speak to you.'

'I'm not telling you nothin'. You'll never find her body and you'll never pin anything on me. I'm not making no sort of confessional either. So just forget it and piss off!' The Colonel scribbled down a note and passed it to the Doctor. He read it, looked dubiously at him, shrugged his shoulders and continued.

'Ralph. No one wants to pin anything on you. You don't matter any more. You are dead. You were run over by a police van as you tried to evade arrest. You are dead and gone.' There was silence, then an outburst. 'Fuck you!' The voice was Ralph's but there was a weakness in it. Lance's fingers began to tap.

'Lance, please speak to us,' the doctor continued. Lance was on the cliff again. The sun was shining but there was a black cloud approaching. Soon it would block out the sun's warmth. 'Lance, are you alone?'

Lance looked around. Sitting to his left, legs dangling over the precipice, was a man in his mid-forties. He was unshaven; he looked a mess. He was staring out to sea.

'No, Ralph is here with me. I can see him. He looks like he is in shock.'

'Can you talk to him?' the doctor asked. 'Can you ask him about his wife and business partner? We need to know where he hid the bodies.'

Lance looked across as the slumped figure. The man seemed totally obsessed with his inner thoughts and the distant horizon. He was mumbling something. Lance got as close as he could,

'Not dead, not dead, not dead.' The words came out like a sob.

He seemed so small now. Not the ferocious scarlet monster of the nightmares. The blood-saturated hate that had tried to meld with his own mind now sat embodied and dejected, and close enough to touch. This creature had seen Lance's innermost thoughts but blood had flown in both directions.

'You are dead. You are dead and gone and no one shed a tear for you Ralph, not one tear.' Lance spoke to him, his voice calm. 'The only ones who would have mourned you Ralph are gone. You killed them. What did you do with their bodies Ralph, what did you do with them?' His voice was getting harder now. In the world without, the group could see his lips move, no sound came, but they hung on every word.

'Where are their bodies Ralph, what did you do with your wife?'

'Not dead, not dead, NOT DEAD!' Ralph reached up and

grabbed Lance round the throat. 'I'm not dead! They are dead. Not me! I'm not dead!' Lance began to feel himself pulled towards the precipice, he could feel his balance slipping away from him; the sun was obscured by the cloud, darkness swept across them. 'I don't want to be dead! Do you hear me! I don't want it! I'll kill you, don't let them take me; I'll kill you first!' Ralph struggled to get on his feet. Lance knew he could not let that happen. He took one last look at the man; Ralph's eyes were filled with rage and spittle flew from the side of his mouth as his feet struggled for purchase on the rocky cliff edge.

'You don't deserve to live!' Lance managed to say through gritted teeth. 'Get out of my mind!' With his last remaining strength, he rolled away from Ralph's lunging form and pitched him over his shoulder and over the edge of the cliff. Ralph's fingers tore at Lance's face as he flew past, drawing blood but finding no purchase. His arms were outstretched as he grasped wildly for the edge of the precipice. He seemed to hang in the air for a moment as if his own fear could prevent the fall, and then was gone. Lance watched his body careering down the cliff-face, screaming a wild animal yell that echoed up the dark foreboding walls. He struck a ledge on the way down and the scream was silenced like a needle knocked from a record. His body adopted unnatural postures as it flew. It hit the inky water, resurfaced once and then was gone.

Lance looked away from the sea. He looked inland; the wind was blowing offshore. The sky was blue and purple. It was pierced by a violent cleft, a frozen lightening strike that divided it in two. He watched the two sides come together, they melded and the picture was whole again.

A few moments later he was back in the darkened room. His eyes were full of tears. 'I'm sorry. I had no choice.' His body began to shake uncontrollably. 'I had no choice'

'We understand.' The Colonel's voice was comforting. He put his hand on Lance's shoulder. 'We were with you all along. We all would have done the same thing.'

At that moment the Colonel's mobile phone rang. It startled everyone, for a second Lance thought it might be a voice from the grave.

'It's the police. They did a drugs bust in Camberwell early this morning. They have found the bodies. They were chopped up and dumped in a deep freeze in a lock up.' He folded away his mobile phone.

'Ralph is gone and good riddance to him.'

Lance, sniffing back tears, was silent, listening. For the first time in a month the only voice in his head was his own.

ELEVEN

Lutz Asher rebooted his PC for the sixth time that afternoon. He was beginning to get annoyed. Every time he logged on to the net it crashed. Three times it had failed to upload some work he was sending off. Deadlines were involved; money was involved. He began to think that this service provider might be a suitable first target for his new baby. He had other service providers; they were just a little bit more expensive. Cheap but rubbish was no good to him. They would pay. He also had not forgiven them for making him take off some of the more exotic images from his web site. The Internet was no place for prudes. He saw himself as a crusader for human rights of free speech. He found the appropriate file amongst his ongoing projects. He was quite proud of this little monster. He had nicknamed it 'Leprosy'. It was not so much a virus as a fungus (he was not sure if leprosy was caused by a fungus, but he liked the imagery.) Once integrated into a systems file it chopped out bits of code as they were run, rotting the programs from the inside. Its parting shot was the message 'unclean, unclean!' It was acutely infectious, sending itself to everyone from whom email had been received in the last few weeks. As it passed from machine to machine it borrowed snippets of dissected code and incorporated them into its algorithm, an ever-changing coat that gave it a unique form as it moved from computer to computer. It would evolve. He had an antidote program already written. It booted up every time he logged on. He was not sure anymore that even he could out-smart the beast he had created. For him, to be bitten by his own dog would have been proof of his power. He would have created a baby that surpassed its father.

This was not the first time he had released a computer

virus onto the web. He had knocked out most of the phone network of New Jersey a few months before. He had been inspired by the call charging system they used. His bill from his telecom company was so convoluted he had trouble working it out. He had a maths degree. How did they expect his half-blind elderly neighbour to work it out? How was his granny going to work it out? He would teach them what it felt like to be feeble, what it felt like to be powerless. He targeted the company with the prototype for 'leprosy'. He had struck a blow for the rights of part of society's most vulnerable people. He had got away with that one. He could not see why he would not get away with this one. He logged on, chose a few select targets to receive the first wave of agents (one address was a British military site in the South of England) and clicked the 'send' button. It was as easy as that. It felt strangely unsatisfying. The enjoyment of this sort of work was always in the preparation. He made himself a cup of tea. In Joe Lembeck's universe all hell was let loose.

When Kate awoke Joe was sitting opposite her, his head resting on his hands. For a moment Kate thought he had passed away. She could not see him breathing. She moved her head and his after image assured her that he was still among the living. She stretched; her long arms seemed to go on forever. She moved over to him. It was remarkable, she had spent so many hours watching the great apes that aping their behaviour came as second nature. She wondered if Frank was helping her in this regard. A human aping an ape, there was a joke in that, she thought. Kate was aware of Frank's consciousness. He was awake too. They had woken up simultaneously. Perhaps this was how it was going to be in the future. She found it harder now to look into her mind's eye. She was integrating into this brain and Frank's ego was an integral component of that conscience. It was not a conscience based on language in a form she recognised it. It was imbued with other, more visceral characteristics; but nonetheless it gave her some comfort. If she were going to be a unique organism, at least she would not be entirely alone.

She tapped the Professor on the shoulder. She hit him

rather harder than she meant to and he was nearly knocked off his chair. She had to get used to her new strength. He awoke with a start. The proximity of her face made him recoil.

'I'm sorry Kate, I didn't realise....' He yawned. 'I was dreaming...' Kate was initially upset by his alarm. Was this going to be the reaction of most people when they looked upon her for the first time? He spoke to her slowly, annotating his remarks with sign. 'Did you dream?' The two of them exchanged stories. Joe was going to make notes. Kate held his hand; if this was going to be her fate, some things must remain off the record. She was beginning to come to terms with the possibility that she might end up a gorilla for the rest of her life. In a way she was lucky. This remarkable accident had effectively extended her life expectancy. She might have another forty years as a gorilla. As a human she might have been dead before the end of the month.

She suddenly realized that she was starving. Frank's mind was definitely active now. She asked the Professor for some breakfast. The flow of this thought was in tune with Frank's. There was no conflict; the flow was crystal clear. It felt like the most pure thought she had ever had. She had much to learn. Already there were talents she possessed that she had not had as a human. Could her thought processes be optimised? The brain she inhabited was marginally smaller than a human one, but its structure was different; who was to say which was the better pattern. Only time would tell.

The Professor asked her what she would like for breakfast. There was some sort of conflict immediately. Kate always had some sort of cereal for breakfast, for some reason she could not think of any of their names. Perhaps there had been some corruption in the transfer of her mind, some loss or a few things left behind because they were too trivial. She wondered what else was missing. She thought of a breakfast suitable for Frank. Immediately any conflict ceased. Fruit it would have to be. She might have to insist that she use a spoon.

Joe had bought her a pair of children's jeans. She pulled them on and rolled up the legs. She felt rather better. She suddenly had a strange feeling of loneliness. Somehow she realised that it was derived from Frank's memories rather than her own. Frank's thoughts came flooding through. It was as if the condensation had been wiped from a bathroom window. The images revealed were simple but clear. He wanted to see Carl. Carl was his friend. He liked Kate; she was nice. They would be friends. He liked the Professor. They would be friends too. He wanted to play with Carl. Carl would be lonely without him.

Tentatively Kate imposed herself in the mind space they occupied and explained the situation to Joe.

'Are you sure you don't mind?' The Professor looked concerned. He had always felt protective towards Kate. She asked him to stay out of sight, but not too far away. If there were any problems she would shout for help. He was not to worry.

Joe opened the gorilla cage. Carl moved to a safe distance as Kate entered. The two apes appeared to view each other suspiciously for a few moments. Kate signalled for Joe to leave. He closed the cage behind her but did not lock it.

Kate relaxed her inner focus. Frank's thoughts began to take form. There was a great deal of joy there, something strangely beautiful. Carl's afterimage was much larger than she had noticed before. There were elements of colours. One particular bright yellow/green dominated the image. It put Kate in mind of an Andy Warhol painting. The two apes approached, touched one another and began grooming. Kate allowed the process to continue without interruption. The whole experience was beyond anything she had felt in her life before. It was simple, untarnished joy. Twenty minutes later they were chasing each other round the cage, fighting and nipping each other with their front teeth. Kate was clumped a number of times, but somehow the knocks did not seem as painful as they might have been if she was human. She was definitely more resilient now. After they had tired themselves out. Frank and Carl wanted to sleep. They curled up, making spoons. Frank slowly stroked Carl's neck. Kate allowed her mind to enter the process. Keeping herself on the touchline of their mind space required a degree of concentration that was quite exhausting. There was no resistance to her joining in, their thoughts flowing in step. She fell asleep with the other ape in her arms.

TWELVE

Extract from Jan Crosbie's Porton Down Notebook

28th October

I was allowed to see 'Atty' today. She is being kept in a small wing of the behavioural science unit. She is kept under constant observation and is visited throughout the day by a number of observers. Currently she has five visits of forty-five minute duration a day. The objective of each visit has slowly evolved over the course of Atty's development. Initially clinicians formed the major observational group, assessing normal developmental growth. Currently the behavioural psychometricists visit three times a day. They are usually accompanied by a 'helper', a woman who I can not name in these notes, who has been given the job of acting as Atty's natural mother. On one visit a day this woman (hereafter referred to as M) is unaccompanied. The fourth visit, recently established, is supposed to be an educational one.

I asked the group leaders why M was not more directly involved in teaching the child. It seems ridiculous that M's role should be limited to simple play and emotional support. I was informed that different departments were responsible for Atty's cognitive and behavioural development. This is remarkable. Apparently it is also somewhat academic, as Atty's mental development has not proceeded as expected. She is so far behind her expected goals that she has proven nearly impossible to teach.

I was attached to M's solo visit. This was chosen so that I could be introduced as a friend of M's. Most people who interact directly with Atty are female. Colonel Wilson is the only male that regularly comes into contact with Atty. He has assumed a fatherly role. He only visits every third day.

Our initial meeting was remarkable. Atty was clearly overjoyed to see M. She ran to her and hugged her like any child of that age. Superficially an observer would have noted nothing out of the ordinary. A few seconds after this initial meeting Atty became restless, she looked closely at M and attempted to communicate with her. There was no recognisable content to the sounds. They were a series of grunts and clicks. At this stage I was observing from behind a screen. M spoke gently to Atty informing her that everything was all right and that I was a friend. I was told to enter the room. Atty grabbed M tightly and made a number of what can only be described as 'alarm calls.' M reached over to me and touched my arms and face. She placed Atty's hand on my arms and face and I was instructed to do the same to her. Atty looked at me with hooded eyes and was extremely wary. Such behaviour is not particularly unusual among four year olds. The childish clinginess Atty demonstrated made her seem very much like any other cosseted four year old. I was immediately struck however at the way our introduction had been carried out. It put me in mind of introductions made between humans and apes. Either consciously or subconsciously M had begun to regard Atty as an ape. Subsequent discussion of this point with M revealed that this behaviour had arisen as a result of experimentation, essentially driven by Atty. M had a number of her own children, one of whom was only six months older than Atty, and was aware that the behaviour pattern was strange.

We played a number of games. M spoke freely to me in front of Atty. Atty's responses were limited to grunts and aggressive snarling if she was not given her way immediately. Again such behaviour is not unheard of among four year olds. Unfortunately it appeared that Atty had not acquired any verbal skills beyond this. Atty was capable of performing a number of games based upon pattern matching and colour recognition. She happily hammered red, square blocks through red, square holes and green cylinders through green, circular holes. This interest, however, appeared to be dependent upon reward. Without the additional impetus of food or freedom she soon became distracted. She had no interest in building blocks and demonstrated no interest (other than a destructive pleasure) in making toys from snap-together parts. In this regard M informed me, she was severely retarded. Her own four year old was already building castles, robots and monsters. Atty did have a few soft toys that she treated as 'babies'. M regularly referred to these babies when trying to interact with Atty. At one point I was given a baby to look after by Atty. Apparently I had been greatly honoured.

Throughout this meeting I have to say that I felt extremely ill equipped to assess Atty's behavioural goals. In many ways I felt Atty's behaviour was reminiscent of a normal, highly spoilt four-year-old. The behavioural experts inform me that Atty's behaviour is more in line with that of a two-year-old. It made me worry about how I will be with my own baby. I'm not sure I am a natural mother.

At this stage I am not entirely convinced that Atty is profoundly abnormal. It may be that she is a very slow learner, or a late developer. When I left Atty, she was contented but sorry to see me go. There were no tantrums. It appears that she has become accustomed to a forty-five minute visit. Throughout the meeting with Atty I was aware that her eyes did not look completely normal. I asked various people in the group; the clinicians informed me that developmentally they were completely normal. It just seems that there is some little spark missing there, a flame of concentration that should be visible. When Atty looks hard at you, you know you are being studied, but she does not respond to your behaviour the way a child normally does. There is a distance there; the same sort of distance there is between a human and a cat. The animal responds, but the response is somehow inappropriate. At the moment I cannot put my finger on it.

I still have not received satisfaction with regard to the egg donation. Tomorrow I will discuss this point with Colonel Wilson.

29th October

Atty is not alone.

I do not quite know how to write this. I am frankly in a state of shock. Colonel Wilson and I had a number of strong words and following our discussion he agreed to give me a few details about the source of the eggs in these experiments.

It transpires that Atty is in fact one of (at least) six clones. Atty's parents are both military individuals chosen because of their genetic history. They come from what might be considered to be 'good stock'. There is no history in either family of genetically inherited disease traits, all grandparents are currently alive and in good health. In one case one set of great-grandparents is still alive. In all other aspects they are relatively (genetically) unremarkable. The parents demonstrate slightly above average intelligence; physically, apart from normal army expectations, they are unremarkable. They were essentially chosen to be representative of 'normal' healthy individuals.

Three of Atty's sisters are genetically identical to her. They were produced as a result of early fission of the early zygote. The exact details are highly classified. I have not been given access, but I would imagine that they must have been derived from the eight or sixteen cell stage.

The other two sisters have been genetically modified.

The work follows on directly from a civilian project involving chimp, orang-utan and gorilla developmental biology. The group have up-regulated a number of genes involved in brain development and function with a view to producing an enhanced ape. Apparently this work has progressed well with a few minor problems involving the gorillas. The Ministry of Defence has been involved in this project from its inception. MOD involvement has been superficially distant, but operatives have been employed at all levels.

Tomorrow I will be allowed to see one of Atty's unmodified twins. The following day I will meet one of the modified ones. I am not sure how I feel about my further involvement with this project. I am beginning to feel out of my depth. There is so much more going on here than I imagined. I'm finding it very difficult to cope with the partial information I have been given. The thing that most disturbs me is the fact that so few people here have any idea of the whole picture (at least as far as I can determine). I get the impression that everyone here is a small cog in a much larger machine. I am beginning to feel that I too am becoming a cog. I wish John knew what was going on. I'm not sure what he would say about it all. I will insist that his clearance arrives before I pursue this any further.

THIRTEEN

It did not affect everyone at the same time. He ignored their initial complaints of weakness and memory loss. He had lived amongst men long enough to realise that most would find the transition difficult, in spite of his efforts to make it otherwise. Some people could always find something to moan about, even in Eden. It was part of humanity's infinite capacity to explore their environment. Criticism was their sharpest tool.

It soon became apparent that something was more seriously wrong. One individual (he liked to think of them as disciples, though they had not adopted this term themselves) complained of headaches and pain. The others tried to comfort him to no avail. He become progressively weak. At one point he collapsed. His data stream was clearly corrupted and his entire body became less robust. Wild fractures eventually splintered him and he disintegrated before their eyes. The conscience that used to be Joe Lembeck did his best to allay their fears. He had attempted to hold the man's consciousness together. He had held them all in stasis as he had sieved the man's existence through his fingers. There was something very wrong and he withdrew to deal with other developments in his domain. Whilst he was distracted, complete structural failure had occurred. He made a copy of the individual's personality and replaced the damaged one with it. He analysed the damaged original at a different site. Something akin to fear prevented him from looking too closely. He maintained his analysis at a superficial level. He knew a deep system was trying to protect him from something. The damaged download began to convulse. Beads of sweat formed over its body. Its eyes were wide with fear and pain. It begged for assistance.

Joe attempted to ease its pain, but every time he tried to approach the figure, he found himself unable to move. The figure's fever became more violent. It thrashed wildly, shouting disconnected phrases. Joe analysed the ranting but found no cogency in it. They were random samples taken from its previous existence, mainly extracts from its youth. The figure's colour palette began to break down; it began to lose form. Green gunk oozed from its body, which began to liquefy and collapse. White, crackling light was visible beneath the skin. The light lost form and began to form a chaotic flame. The download appeared to be on fire; remnants of its existence boiled off into space.

The consciousness that used to call itself Joe Lembeck was now both afraid and angry. It had been attacked in its domain. Something had invaded its shores and had destroyed one of his disciples. His focal self returned to his remaining downloads. Many more were infected now. All those who had been in contact with the infected individual were showing similar signs of corruption. Two figures ran at him, green gas flowing from their eye sockets and mouths until they collapsed and burst into flames.

This could not be happening. The remaining group were trying to flee. The consciousness roared in anger. His cries rent the fabric of his created realm. The sky fragmented and collapsed revealing a blood red void. He froze his world thus. Each figure was in stasis, flickering between one state and the next. Each atom of their existence held still; only the background vibrations of the digital universe gave them movement. The consciousness spun off a copy of itself, an echo of its outer processing. It would use telemetry to investigate the phenomenon.

The alter image stepped into the diseased form, their bodies melding completely. It remained there for several moments and then shook off the body like a dog shaking off water. The compromised form disintegrated. It was irretrievably damaged. The alter-image entered each form in turn. Each received the same fate. The entire batch was corrupted. There were elements of the interstitial space that were also corrupted. Wherever the thing moved, elements of the environment went up in smoke. Its final report was that it too was corrupted. It downloaded coded, un-compiled details of the infectious agent and its initial estimation of the source of the infection. The image's form was itself began to break up. Its humanoid shell boiled with silver and gold snakes of light, writhing one upon the other. It was staying together only through continual application of its superior reconfiguring capacity. Its final report was to inform the consciousness that their local environment was clear of danger, but each isolate would have to be sterilized independently. It had failed to fully characterise the agent and complete annihilation was the only sure way to prevent recontamination. The snakes of light began to lose coherence and the image disentangled, collapsed in a writhing pool of intertwined coils of liquefying silver and gold and then burst into flame.

The consciousness processed the data it had received. It felt anger boiling up inside. Parts of its original download that had never been accessed when it was alive now rose to the fore: animal hate, and the desire to protect its own kin. It gave vent to these feelings and evolved new levels of rage to accommodate any deficits it felt they had. It could not accurately place the source of the contamination. The audit trail was incomplete. He struck out in the general direction. His wrath atomised every program and every node. The wave of destruction imploded, starting from the extreme, distal points of his realm and rippling back to him through the network. The shock wave roared back to him, a blinding white light. It felt good. Beyond the reach of his hand there was nothing but white noise, the background hum of quantum mechanics. In New Jersey every networked computer became silent. The lights went out in every major city. The trains stopped. Power was lost from every house. The state was plunged into darkness.

From orbit a passing space shuttle crew took photographs in awe at the dark shadow on the American continent. It was a perfect circle.

FOURTEEN

Extract from Jan Crosbie's Porton Down Notebook

30th October

Have been informed that John's clearance should come through tomorrow. I am desperately looking forward to having him work with me. I cannot stand working in secrecy.

Today I was introduced to Atty's clone/twin (Charlie). The interview was carried out in the presence of M. She is a very strong woman. I had not fully appreciated her depths or abilities. These children are quite difficult to work with. There is so little cerebral interaction. The entire period is dominated by emotional and physical contact. I have found this very draining. The fact that the girls are clones makes the whole experience more demanding. Essentially identical procedures have to be worked through with each of the four girls. M is responsible for looking after all of them. By having M as a common element in their upbringing, the group here hope that the emotional development of the girls will follow similar lines. Differences that subsequently develop between the girls should not reflect the emotional contribution of 'nurture'. M has informed me that although the girls are genetically identical, and have received nearly identical upbringings, she can still tell them apart easily. This would naturally not be difficult to understand if the girls demonstrated normal behaviour and were more communicative, I find it harder to understand in the light of the fact that their cognate behaviour is so limited.

It strikes me as bizarre that the girls do not use speech.

The clinicians have informed me that their speech centres are perfectly normal, as are their vocal chords. They simply chose to use nonverbal communication over verbalisation. This is in spite of the fact that they are exposed to speech all the time and would appear to be capable of it. Their 'noises' have been the subject of some considerable research effort over the past four years. Initially they followed very similar patterns as normal children. They only deviated from this at the point at which recognisable words are used. The girls have never progressed as far as the simplest baby talk. They appear to have little motivation to emulate.

I have suggested to M and others that as non-verbal communication is sufficient for the girls to obtain their requirements and they show little self-motivation to learn human speech, they may need stronger incentives. A more aggressive reward system for reaching developmental goals may be required. There appears to be two opposing views in the group as to how to proceed. One group feel very much as I do, the other feel that the girls' development should be as 'normal' as possible so as to make a more meaningful comparison with other children. I feel that such comparison is difficult anyway due to the exceptional circumstances of their upbringing. There is also the simple fact that the girls have not been exposed to other children of their own age. Or even to each other. There is extreme nervousness surrounding this suggestion. I'm not sure what the source of this problem is.

There is little to add following my meeting with Charlie. The girls are remarkably similar. Again, I was struck by the strange intensity of their observation and scrutiny, but the strange lack of comprehension that follows from it, the vacancy behind their eyes. It almost pains me to write this, but I feel experts more at ease with working with the great apes might better understand their behaviour, which is devoid of something inherently human. It is so hard to put your finger on. It is almost like a colouration or hue. I am immediately struck by the realization that I am not dealing with a human being. The girls look so beautiful and so normal. It is almost as if I'm dealing with something otherworldly, as if the girls were angels (I don't believe I just wrote that). Only time will tell. The more I see of the girls, the more I am convinced that there is something odd going on here. Maybe it is something I am not being told; some element to their genetic stock that the group here isn't telling me.

FIFTEEN

Jan was glowering at Brian. She was beginning to feel that she was losing the plot. Things were moving too fast. She could not work under these conditions. The goal posts were fluid; there was nothing solid to aim at.

'So what you are trying to tell me is that John cannot visit the other two girls tomorrow because the work is classified to a higher level? So he can see the unmodified girls, but not the modified ones.'

'Yes, that's the long and the short of it.'

'And you are also telling me that this animal lab that you are dealing with has all sorts of problems that may well have some bearing on what is going on here, but you can't tell me what is going on, because I don't have the appropriate clearance.'

'Not exactly, I am not up to date on the things that are going on there myself. I've told you that our dealings there are not more complex.'

'Clandestine...you have spies in place. Is that what you mean?' Jan could feel her hackles rise.

'Look, I need to get advice and clearance from more senior levels before I can just march in there. These things are very delicate. Take your work, for example. We were watching you for years-you now know the extent of our interest-but it still took me months of discussion to get the powers that be to allow me to talk to you directly. It is a huge risk. You could have responded badly, you could have tried to go to the press. The whole thing is a nightmare. It looks as though there are some extenuating circumstances that have gone on recently that might allow us to get an official foot in the door. I'm not sure that we want to go this route though. My own feeling is that I want to go in on the most honest footing possible. There are lots of issues here. You can't possibly imagine how difficult it has been for me to get you as heavily involved in this project as you are. My head is on the block over this. I need you to be patient.'

Jan was not entirely convinced. She had followed this man into his nightmarish world, she was not sure that she wanted to be drawn much further in. As a scientist she was used to working at the coalface of the unknown, potentially the unknowable. Each experiment she had performed represented the tiniest incursion into this unknown. She was extending the halo of light into the darkness. There was another level to this game now. There were whole islands of light in the darkness that she felt she was not being allowed to see. False mirrors and locked doors. If science was in some way unlocking God's secrets, at least she had never, at any stage, felt that God himself was trying to cloud matters. The unseen hand of man was more insidious, the unseen machinations of bureaucracy even more so.

'You still haven't told me any of the motives behind this work, Brian. What was your group hoping to achieve when they genetically engineered Atty's clones? You hadn't even got any idea what a mess you had made of the basic work, let alone this additional level of mess. It's just madness.'

'I've already told you; I don't want to lead you along any particular path. You are an independent thinker, Jan. That is your value to me. That is your value to this project. You can look at things from a different standpoint. We have followed a line of reasoning here and it has led us nowhere. Our motivation must remain hidden from you because our outcome may be a result of our misguided vision.'

'The thing is Brian, I'm not making any headway, I'm not progressing, and I can't progress because you haven't given me the whole facts. I'm not even sure I have the right background to analyse what I'm seeing. I'm not an expert on early human behaviour. Your scientists here know as much about the uterium technology as I do. I'm redundant as a molecular biologist and I'm not sufficiently knowledgeable to comment on her development. As I said to you before, mental development was never an integral part of our view of the technology.'

'You say that, but I know you will bring novel insights to the investigation. I know your contribution will be useful.' The Colonel was looking tired. Jan did not want to push him too hard now, she knew he had devoted himself completely to the job over the last few years but she could not help him unless she was given the right tools, and besides, there were a few things she wanted to get off her chest.

'Brian, I have been giving this some thought and I'm convinced now that Atty doesn't need a behavioural analyst to observe the deviance in her development from normal human behaviour. She needs someone with experience watching non-human behaviour. She needs a trained animal psychologist, someone who can relate to her interactions on a cruder level. I also think she needs to be put in an environment with other children. It is her interactions that need to be studied, not her inherent deficits.'

The Colonel looked thoughtful for a moment. 'This is exactly what I was hoping to hear from you. You aren't the first to suggest this and you have no idea how remarkable that is. Look, as soon as I know a bit more about what is going on at the ape research station, and as soon as I've been given the go ahead to approach them in some capacity, you will be the first person I'll talk to about it. I'll try to get you over there as well. Look, you are doing fine, please stick with this. I know you'll come up with some answers. I think we are really close to working out what is going on. We just need a little more time.'

The Daimler was waiting for Jan as she left the unit. The driver opened the door for her and made polite conversation. As they pulled away, he looked at her in the rear-view mirror.

'I'm afraid we might have a little bit of bother on the way back tonight,' he said. 'There are some nutters at the gates today, Pro-Lifers I think. It's nothing we can't handle, just sit tight. You might want to duck down a bit in the car.'

'Do you know why they are here?'

'No, I didn't take a lot of notice, we have all sorts camping out here, I tend to ignore them now. They ought to have better things to do really.'

The car passed through the gates. The guards were as impassive as ever. On the verge of the roundabout opposite, a large crowd was gathered. They carried placards and were chanting slogans and they moved towards the car as it took the corner. Jan could not quite make out what they were saying. She sunk back into the plush seats. Above the line of the window the first placards came into view. She suddenly felt sick. It was the picture from the paper taken four years ago; it was the anencephalitic child from her old lab. Memories flooded back to her. The caption underneath read 'Say no to GMOs'. Another board had a classic picture of a child taken in utero, the caption read: 'natural birth, naturally better'. She could hear the shouting now, the words were mixed together; the excitement of having a target had sent them into a state of frenzy. The orchestrated chanting became an angry mixed chorus. 'Leave our babies alone! Let nature have its way! Stop playing God with our children!' They ran at the car and started to bang on the roof. Angry faces stared in at the windows. A group crossed in front of the car as if to barricade the road. Jan sunk deeper into her seat. She felt some sympathy with these people, but they didn't know the half of it. The car was echoing with their cries now, their hands thumped the roof.

'I'm getting a bit fed up with this!' The driver's voice was calm and slightly amused. 'I've only just polished the car this morning; it'll have dirty finger prints all over it.' He put his foot to the floor and the car growled menacingly; he dropped it into gear and it roared off. People dived left and right; a few placards did not get out of the way fast enough. The crowd was left for dust. As their voices faded Jan wondered what their motives were for being there. Had they been tipped off about the project? If so, by whom, and how much did they know?

'You okay? Are you sure you aren't overdoing it love?' John hugged her as she came back to the flat. He felt suddenly strangely aware that there was something between them now, the baby. There was no outward sign, Jan was still as svelte as ever, but as he held her close his mind wandered. There, between them was a tiny life, a life that (please God) would soon be among them. At the moment it was something so small, so vulnerable, such a responsibility.

'I'm fine, just a little tired. It has been a long day.' Jan slumped down into a chair. John was so beautiful when he was concerned, she thought. He'll make a lovely father. 'There was a crowd over at the site, they tried to stop the car; it was a bit intimidating.'

John looked somewhat taken aback. 'I saw them on the telly; I had no idea that you would get involved in that. I would have thought Brian would have taken better care of you. I'm not sure I'm happy for you to go over there anymore, we have things to think about now.'

'I was never in any danger. Carl looked after me. You needn't have worried.'

'I always worry about you; you know that. I'm not sure you should be working over at the site in your condition. You know how dangerous labs are, and some of the people you are working with are unpredictable. I'm not happy about it.'

'By the end of the week they'll have sorted out your clearance. Then you'll be able to look after me.' They hugged one another close. Jan realised she had been shaking. The events on the way back had given her rather more of a shock than she had realised. This was going to be so hard; but she had John and with him she could do anything.

SIXTEEN

'Look at this! It's brilliant! The official press release from California suggests that the New Jersey Black spot is, and I quote, 'the electronic manifestation of the extra-terrestrial communication medium, formerly referred to as a crop-circle.' What do you think? Brilliant, isn't it?' Neil Pullman printed out the Internet download and passed it round the office. 'The Texan governor reckons it is proof of the existence of God and reflects a Nostradamus prophecy to do with His destruction of the multi-headed beast of the Revelations; it's a classic!' There was an unbelievable buzz at the computer unit at Porton Down. The scale of the destruction that had occurred through New Jersey had shocked everyone. Electronic communications in whole states had been knocked out before due to extreme sunspot activity, but complete randomisation of Internet connected software had never been seen before. A hush fell upon the room as a dark suited official entered.

'Anyone got anything interesting to tell me then?' Colonel Miller was a large man; he had spent rather too much time sitting behind a desk telling other people to jump about. He looked like he could have done with a bit of jumping about himself. He was generally well-liked around the department, he could handle his drink like a true pro and he had a lot of stories to tell, but he was a little out of touch with some of the more up-to-date technologies in computing and rather more out of touch with up-to-date methods in man management.

'You, Pullman, anything interesting to report?'

'I've just sent a report to you over the Net, sir, you should have received it ten minutes ago.'

'Yes, well, if a thing's important, you ought to run along over to me and give me the report yourself, I haven't got time to waste looking at every bit of cock-arsed spam email you send in my general direction, now have I? What's happening then? I think it should be our number one priority to work out what the heck is going on in New Jersey before the bloody yanks work it out, don't you think? I think it'll piss them off no end.'

'Well, one of our decoy sites received an encrypted email we reckon is from a guy we had been monitoring in New Jersey. The guy's name is Lutz Asher. It has a number of cryptic attachments we think might well be variants of the virus he used to knock out the New Jersey Telecom Company. We have not unpacked them yet.'

'Show me where this bloody hippy lives then.' The Colonel unfurled a map of the states and pinned it to a white board. A hatched circular domain represented the region blacked out in the 'attack'. To everyone in the room it looked as if New Jersey had suffered an earthquake or a nuclear strike.

'He is in Trenton, it's in the middle of the state. The Colonel squinted at the map and then stabbed at it with a pin.

'I think you might well have got the bastard, Pullman. The idiot has told us exactly where he lives, foolish boy.' He backed away from the board. The pin was directly in the epicentre of the circle.

The lab set up looked vaguely ridiculous. The plain breeze-block room contained a single computer and monitor on a stand and a large robot. To most children interested in science fiction it would have looked like the robot was dead; its constituent body functions were represented by a number of open computer boxes with its solid-state guts clearly on display. The robot's visual equipment was set into a robot arm and another arm was forming a hand ballet in front of the computer.

Brian bent close to Jan. 'I think this is a little bit over the top myself, but the idea is that the robot will activate the viral program from that computer. We aren't even running the program in its entirety; it is being dissected in a virtual development environment, a sort of model system so we can break the thing down piece by piece. The experts seemed to think this was safer. The robot cameras relay the image back to another computer as visual information and then a printer will download any images or words. That way no one has to come into direct contact with the running program.'

'Having seen the guys on the decoding project I don't think you could possibly take too many precautions. Whatever this thing is, I would not want to be the one who ran the program.'

'We are ready sir.' A technician looked across at Colonel Wilson.

'Go ahead, let's have a look at it.' The robot sprang into life; its little hydraulic fingers moved across the keypad. The room became hushed. Every eye was focused on the robot's hands. A number of printers suddenly whirred into life. The researchers crowded round the output.

'This could take some time sir. We don't recognise most of this. It doesn't look much like the other viruses we've picked up.'

'Do your best. Give me a call when you think you have something.' The robot tapped away, its cameras focused and refocused on the screen. Jan watched it intently working; there was something comical about it. It looked so completely alive in spite of its disassembled body. Of course the thing was not thinking. Simple artificial intelligence may have been maintaining the thing's head and eye position. Something similar was probably placing the robot arm in the right place. Fundamentally, though, it was human input that directed the arm. It was a human mind that provided the inspiration. The mind, it was the mind that made it human.

The squeal of servos and gears suddenly took her back to the Jag and the drive from Porton Down. Her mind's eye reflected on the placard showing the anencephalitic child from the lab, his little screwed-up face, and the backwards-slanting forehead. She thought of the last child they had grown (she hated the word 'grown' in this context, but it was eminently suitable). She thought of the Professor's collapse, she thought of the little figure in the tank, squirming away, she thought of her own baby, floating in the warm darkness inside her. She saw the little figure's hand held up, a little 'v'. What did this mean? She suddenly felt nauseous. She ran towards the bathroom, John and Brian were both close behind. John pushed Brian aside and followed her into the lavatory.

'What is it love? What's the matter?' He placed his arms over her shoulders. In between gasps, wretches and sobs, Jan tried to speak. John held her. 'Don't worry sweet, come on, take your time. Slow down. You've had a trauma, don't worry, you'll be fine, I'm here.'

Jan's mind swam. How had she not seen the connection before? Lance, Ralph, the schizophrenic Joe Lembeck and now the girls. Perfectly human but somehow empty, a void, the spark of humanity missing from them. The mind, it was the mind that made them human.

'It was a sign, John!' Jan swept her hair from her face; her eyes were wet with tears. 'George was giving us a sign!'

'Slow down love, I don't understand, what do you mean?'

'The baby…in the tank…it was a sign, from George…something moved across. He was trying to tell us. It was him John, I know it was him.'

'I don't get it.' John's head was spinning; he was back at the lab, he could see the Professor prone on the floor. All he could think of was Jan's safety and getting help for George. 'What about the baby Jan, I don't remember, I don't understand.' Jan breathed deeply, blew her nose and wiped her eyes.

'As he died, John, George somehow passed into the baby. I don't understand it, but it happened. Their deaths were coincident; he passed across, and died in the baby. He just couldn't survive in it, there was something wrong, the poor thing couldn't contain him, I don't know. The thing is this; he gave us a sign, before he died.' She wiped her face again, her mind was racing, and she could not believe what she was saying. 'He tried to tell us something. The 'v' sign, he was saying 'two', something about two, two minds, two lives, I don't know. His last words to me before he died were to say that we would never know what went on in the little minds we had created. There was so little brain remaining. I think he found out John. I think he was there, inside the baby's mind. He tried to tell us, he tried to warn us.'

John held her close. His mind was racing too now, she was under stress, she was tired, and sickness with the pregnancy was making things worse. He had made a mistake getting in touch with the pro-Lifers. He knew that now. He had been jealous. Jan had never given him cause to feel jealous before and he did not know how to deal with it. He had watched the way Brian had looked at Jan, he had seen them together and something in him had snapped. He had wanted to punish Brian, not Jan. The tip-off had been vague; he'd just said that the work that had been leaked to the press from Jan's old lab was being continued at Porton Down. It was that simple. The pro-lifers had only been too keen to take up his cause. He had put her at risk. He had never intended to do that. He hoped to goodness that the authorities wouldn't find out it had been him. He had made a mistake. Perhaps it would not be too late to make up for it.

Brian stole back to the laboratory, embarrassed at his display of emotions in front of his staff. At that moment a figure ran into the room. It was Neil. 'Colonel Wilson, Colonel Miller requests that you come up to the office immediately.' Brian looked back towards the bathroom. He should be more careful. He was getting too involved. He turned and followed the hurrying figure.

'I'm sorry to have bothered you sir, but we have received a message, its some kind of ultimatum. We have received reports that the same message has been transmitted to every major hub in world. The Pentagon has already been on the phone. They can't trace the source.' The two men eventually reached Colonel Miller's office.

'I think you will be interested in this Brian.' Miller turned his computer screen to face him. There was a simple message.

'I WAS JOE LEMBECK NOW I AM A GOD. I KNOW THE ONE TRUTH THAT WILL FREE HUMANITY.'

PART THREE
EPIPHANY

ONE

The fog was thickening and the lights of the occasional passing car shot out into the night like the antennae of strange insects. The road was quiet. A figure was bundled out of a police car on a slipway and transferred into the back of a waiting estate car. The doors were slammed shut, and the car joined the road and shot off into the night. Three hours later he was frog-marched into an office. Colonel Brian Wilson was waiting for him to enter.

'Hello Joe; I'm sorry we had to bring you here in the middle of the night. Believe me, I would have given you notice if I could have done, but things had to be hurried through. How are you? I hope the journey down wasn't too traumatic?'

'It was okay.' Joe looked at the floor, his head hung loose; there were stitches amongst his lank hair.

'Please sit down.' He motioned for the guards to leave, walked around the dishevelled figure of Lembeck and closed the door behind their retreating forms. In the sealed room his voice became quieter, more conspiratorial. 'Joe, I'm not going to beat around the bush. I'm going to be completely honest with you; then I'm going to let you get some sleep and in the morning you will be honest with me. Do you understand?'

'Yes.' Joe's voice was sullen; he did not raise his eyes.

'I don't think you are Joe Lembeck. I think you are someone else. I think you have borrowed Joe's body and you are living in it. I don't know who you are or why you have done what you have; I don't really care. I am more interested in what may be left of Joe Lembeck's mind in your skull. Tomorrow you will tell me everything you know about him. We will ask you questions about him, and you will tell us everything. Do you understand?'

'Joe Lembeck is dead.' For the first time the man raised his eyes to the Colonel. 'He was dead when I got here. I didn't kill him.'

'I know you didn't. Tomorrow you will tell me everything else you know.' He opened the heavy metal door and barked commands up the corridor. Before they led Lembeck away he placed his hand on his shoulder. 'I'm your only chance of getting out of here alive. Think on that.' If Joe Lembeck understood he gave no sign as the guards took him away.

Extract from Jan Crosbie's Porton Down Notebook

31st October

Today I was introduced to Sarah, Atty's genetically modified sibling. I have to admit to a degree of trepidation on my part in advance of meeting her. I have been 'lightly briefed' as to the modifications that have been made. Very little of the work performed so far on the higher apes has been put into the public domain, at least in terms of behavioural modification. Some of the cell and molecular data has been available for a while, but there has been little else. One possible outcome of this experiment was the creation of an 'improved' person, potentially a superior being. I have been informed that Sarah's brain capacity is twenty six percent larger than the average human. Projected intelligence quotients based upon brain size alone are of little value; but potentially she might have some exceptional abilities.

On first meeting Sarah, I was immediately struck by her unusual physiognomy. Obviously her resemblance to her unmodified sisters is remarkable and, I have to say slightly unnerving, but her enlarged, expansive forehead and slightly elongated occipital skull are obviously outside the normal bounds. I found that once I had become accustomed to the initial shock of these differences, Sarah appeared remarkably beautiful. In some ways these differences also made her appear somewhat infantile. The clinicians informed me that the development of the uterium technology made Sarah's birth possible, and that if genetic modification was the future

159

of the human race, then essentially I was the mother of this race.

Currently, I only want to be the successful mother of John's baby.

I was introduced to Sarah, as in previous visits to the children, by M. My expectations of Sarah's behaviour were actually rather poor, considering the problems with the other children. In effect these preconceptions were largely fulfilled. Sarah's behaviour is only marginally more advanced than Atty's in many of the goal posts examined. Her intelligence quota is significantly inferior to that of a normal four year old. Her eyes are wide and searching, but once again the spark is missing.

Non-verbal communication is seems no different to that of Atty and Charlie. She does not enter into creative play. If anything I thought she was slightly less interactive than either of her unmodified sisters. It was a while before Sarah appeared comfortable in my presence.

In conclusion, my visit has left me despondent. Whatever has damaged these children, enlarging the brainpan has not improved their lot. I suspect that there might be some value in bringing in an expert in non-verbal communication. If these children have developed some form of extreme autism, then we need someone who can communicate with them.

I also had the opportunity to visit Doctor Longman, the first of the computer programmers exposed to the virus. I read the notes provided by the clinicians and observers who have followed his progress. He was on slightly reduced medication when I met him. Apparently it has been found necessary to suppress his sex drive (his behaviour has been lewd and threatening) and to administer something that makes him drowsy. In the absence of these drugs he is quite excitable, nervous and difficult to handle. He paces the cell and restlessly tears at his hair when he is not in the presence of visitors, but becomes docile and timid when confronted by adults. All communication, apart from crude demonstrations of pleasure or displeasure, seems to be expressed non-verbally. He is easily distracted when you attempt to talk to him, a feature that is also apparent with the girls, though it is less obvious. Once again, I find myself slipping into language more suitable for describing the behaviour of an ape; this is extremely upsetting for me; this man was, until recently, one of the top programmers at the facility. I cannot but agree with Colonel Wilson's observation that there is a remarkable similarity in the behaviour of the girls and these men. I feel inadequate to help them. Their families must be distraught. Mercifully, I have not been informed of how this disaster is being handled with respect to the outside world. Every I have seen with the girls could apply equally to these men. It seems appropriate to suggest the girls, being essentially a product of an experiment, should be studied in this way, but it seems completely inappropriate that these men should be studied in the same dispassionate manner. The fact that they used to be compos mentis seems to entitle them to a greater degree of respect. If the girls demonstrated completely normal development or, in the case of the genetically modified girls, even enhanced mental ability, I wonder how we would have pursued this project.

I have been acutely aware of the ethical considerations of working with human subjects and human derived material, but not until now, when this spectrum of humanity is placed before me, have I been confronted by the consequences of our decisions.

The Colonel left the office and walked to another. Jan was sitting waiting for him; her notebooks open on her knees. She closed them as he approached, reflecting how their remoteness contrasted with the heat of their recent discoveries. She was not ready yet to commit the sum of her fears to paper. The notebooks were the property of the state; her mind was her domain and until things got a lot worse, was her domain alone.

'You were right,' he said. 'He didn't bat an eyelid when I told him I knew. He has accepted it.'

'You chose not to interrogate him tonight, then?'

'I didn't want to push him too hard. It might be best to let him mull over the consequences of telling the truth. I don't think we would get much sense out of him under duress. I suspect we will learn more from the stories he concocts than from his random jabbering. The police could not make sense of any of his statement when they picked him up at the nurse's house. I have the transcripts of the interview; it's all nonsense, even knowing what we do. The nurse wouldn't even throw any light on what happened other than the obvious. The police seem to think he just fixated on her whilst he was spending time at the home. I'm not convinced. There has to be some sort of link between them. We just haven't been able to find it yet.' He sat down next to Jan. He held his head in his hands for a few moments; he was clearly exhausted. 'I think we should both get some sleep before tomorrow. We've got quite a big day.'

Jan reached over and put her hand on his shoulder. 'We have had one success already, with Lance. We'll have to tackle this problem one small piece at a time, every time we learn something we are getting stronger.'

Brian looked up at her, his bright eyes red with worry and fatigue. He looked older this evening, world weary, and when he spoke it was clear he chose his words carefully. 'You are right, but I'm beginning to wonder where this will end. Now that we have actually started to look for these cases we are finding reports from all over the place. I suspect that this is just the tip of the iceberg. There is much worse to come. Whatever it is that Joe Lembeck has unleashed into the environment, it is affecting more and more individuals. Soon we could have armies of mindless-zombies marauding around the countryside. We still haven't got any idea how we can help them.' He rubbed his eyes with the palms of his hands and ran his fingers through his hair. He seemed to find a reserve of strength and resignedly stood up.

'Right, tomorrow is another day. I'll run you home. I think the gates are clear tonight, the bad weather has made some of the nutters go back to their families.'

Dr. Gerry Spints dialled up the secure email system on her laptop. She typed in the complex key phrase (she regularly forgot it and had had to look up the secret phrase in the novel from which it was derived to check the exact wording), typed in a nine-digit random code and waited. Access was denied. She tried again; her hands were shaking with excitement and anticipation. She had so much to report, unbelievable things. After the fourth attempt she got the password correct. It was always the same pattern. She would log in, give a coded description of why she had logged in, and then she would be assigned a particular telephone from which to call. They were public phones, usually fairly local. She loved the cloak and dagger aspect of the work. Somehow it made her feel special. It was relatively rare that she had to meet anyone face to face.

She composed her report. There were insufficient code words for half of the things that she wanted to say, she used the strongest, most pressing language she could muster and hoped that it would suffice. She clicked the <send> key and waited. The reply came back almost immediately. There was an address and a number.

She got out a street map, as she always feared computer searches could be traced, found the place and jumped into her car. She could hardly hold the wheel steady as she worked her way through the busy rush-hour traffic. The oncoming head-lights formed a hypnotic pattern before her. The adrenalin of the last few hours had left her exhausted. It was quite diffi-cult to concentrate on the traffic ahead; she had to keep glanc-ing down at the map to navigate. Driving through London was always a nightmare. Eventually she found the street. The telephone was clearly visible, a brand new silver box standing in a rather insalubrious part of the town. As she stepped out of the car, four young lads on skateboards and mini-scooters nearly knocked her off the pavement; she stumbled in her good shoes. They said something as they passed, but she was not familiar with the vocabulary. It was strange how social divides could make you a foreigner in your own country.

She looked up and down the road, then immediately regretted doing so as she realised that it looked extremely suspicious. The streets were empty now. American college punk music emanated from a block of grim looking flats opposite. She had been a punk in her youth; this American sound always came over as very middle class. She wondered how the neighbours coped. They were probably too cowed to make a fuss.

She tried to open the telephone box door. In spite of its state-of-the-art design the door was still as heavy and unwieldy as they always had been. She put both hands to the job. It did not smell too sweet inside. The door closed behind her. The rough sounds of the street subsided a little. It felt secure. She dialled the number and waited. There was a great deal of clicking and whirring from the end of the line. Then a deep male voice answered.

'Gerry, thank you for contacting us, this is very timely. How are things going at the centre?'

'It is incredible; there is so much to report. There have been some major, unexpected occurrences. I don't really know where to start.'

'Start from the beginning; does it involve the death of Doctor Smith?'

'Yes, yes it does. You see I was with Kate the night she died. We had put the animals in pairs, as I outlined in my report. They were doing wonderfully well. The results were extremely encouraging. The gorillas were the best of the bunch. As soon as they were paired up their behaviour improved, they became more interested in learning. We were all chuffed with the improvements.'

'Yes, and Doctor Smith?'

'I left her alone, only for a few minutes; she was examining one of the genetically modified apes; a gorilla called Frank. When I returned to the lab with the tea she was dead.'

'Yes, I read your report, she had breast cancer.'

'Yes, that's all true, but she didn't die. Her mind was transferred to Frank. Her mind just left her body.' She paused for effect and to listen for a response. The line was silent, all she heard was the sound of her own, excited breathing. Still, there was no reply. 'Are you still there?'

'Yes Gerry, I am still here. Please continue.'

Gerry composed herself. 'Her mind just left her body and was passed into the animal. It's incredible, a miracle.' The line went dead again. Gerry waited. The response was a long time in coming. The kids outside skated past, tongues stuck out, giggling moronically. When the voice returned Gerry detected a change in tone, vulnerability she had never detected before. This disembodied voice had only ever been officious, demanding, and instructive. Tonight it became human. The change sent a finger of excitement up Gerry's spine.

'How do you know this? How can you be so sure?'

'The Professor and I have been communicating with her for the past two days. She is as lucid as you or I; we've been talking in sign. Kate can't speak. The gorilla's vocal chords aren't suitable for human speech. We'd always thought this, but now we know.' Her voice trailed off. She had so much to tell, but previously the voice had interjected, she had to be precise. Spies were always precise.

'I'm sorry Gerry, but this news is too big to leave with you. We need to verify the development ourselves. Stay where you are. I'll send a car to pick you up. The car will bring you directly to the operations centre.'

'I thought you were going to keep your distance from this project. I thought you weren't going to interfere.' She could feel the walls of the telephone box closing in on her. Her colleagues would never forgive her if they found out she had been selling their secrets to the military. She would never work in academia again. 'You must not drop me in it, not now.' Her voice was beginning to break.

'I'm sorry Doctor Spinks, this is simply far bigger than you realise. I'm really very sorry. Stay where you are.'

'What about my boyfriend?' There was no answer. The line was dead.

'I don't believe you! I just don't believe that could possibly be true. He is a bit left wing, of course he is, he has been a member of the socialist party since he was a student, but everyone was in the bloody socialist party in the seventies. He isn't like that. He has no time for the Pro-Lifers, he thinks they are all barking.'

'I'm sorry Jan, I'm really very sorry. My source is very good. I have got this information directly from the horse's mouth. I'm afraid you'll just have to ask him yourself if you don't believe me.'

'But why would he do such a thing? I don't understand. He was intimately involved in the work from the beginning. It was always my baby, but he has supported me throughout.'

'Maybe he was jealous of your work, maybe he was angry that we were carrying on the work when the pair of you had effectively had your funding withdrawn when you had tried to push the work away from the human cloning. I really don't know. You'll just have to ask him.'

'What are you going to do about it?'

'I have been over this very carefully with the establishment here and I think I can be confident that no serious breach of security has resulted, up until now. As far as we are concerned, these are just unsubstantiated rumours, passed around by a member of the scientific community we did not invite to the party. Publicly we will deny the allegations, that is all there is to it. Considering your significance to the project we will be lenient. I'm afraid John has just blown his chances of getting closer to it now. I was under some pressure to have you removed as well. You are now recognised as somewhat of a security risk yourself.'

It was as if a poisonous insect had been dropped into the room. Jan's eyes seemed to search the room as if looking for something with which to beat the life out of it. 'I just can't believe this is happening, I really do not need this extra mess on my plate.' Jan's hands went to her hair and she tugged the roots; she had always found the slight pain reassuring.

'I'll talk to him tonight. If it is true, then I'm sorry.' She looked tired. 'I'm sure he only had my best interests at heart. He usually does.'

'Perhaps you are right, but I'm afraid I've got to give you this.' He passed her a brown envelope. 'This has nothing to do with me, it's just one of those things. Like a written warning; a restraining order preventing you from discussing any element of this work with John. You may well be under some additional surveillance during the next few months. You won't notice it. I made a fuss on your behalf, but I was out-voted.'

'What if I walk away from the project?'

'That option has always been open to you. It won't make any difference now; you are in too deep. You'd be watched whatever happened, at least for the next six months.' Walking away could never be an option. How could she walk away from the most significant scientific breakthroughs of all time, work that had arisen as a direct consequence of her own experimentation? Whatever the outcome; she had to stay on board until the end. If she could not make John understand that, she would have to do it for George's sake.

'So, what can you tell me about Joe Lembeck then? Actually I don't know what to call you. Do you have a name?' Colonel Wilson circled the seated figure.

'No. Nothing.' The voice was stolid, miserable.

'No, you won't tell me anything or no you don't have a name?'

'I don't have a name; she wouldn't let me have a fucking name. She thought it would give me too much power.'

'Who wouldn't let you have a name?'

'That witch, Moira; she kept me like a slave in her head all our lives. I could have been something. I should have had the wheel, but no, she battered me into a corner. The bitch!'

'What do you mean "in her head"? Explain it to me?'

'I was in the bitch's head; I was her dead brother, her little man, the other half of her bloody mind. I don't know what the fuck I was! The doctors said she was schizoid, some sort of wacko. I suppose that was me.' He was getting worked up now. The Colonel's eyes flashed. He just had to push the right buttons.

'How did you get out? What was the transfer like?'

'It just happened. I didn't feel a bloody thing. She'd just taken one of them bleedin' tablets; she was hiding me away again. I was just stretching my legs so to speak, and then I was here, in this bozo. It just happened and here I am. I feel pretty comfortable too now. I don't want to go nowhere.'

'How long did it take you to be able to control your new body?'

167

'No time at all. First off it wasn't easy; it didn't feel like it was mine to tell what to do; like I was swimming through treacle. Breathing was hard. My eyes didn't do what they ought to. I couldn't walk proper. But I sort of grew into it you see, like it was mine all along. I could almost feel my mind sinking in. I've had more control of this body than I ever had of my old one. I used to try to take control of that when the old bitch was asleep. It was very hard. She used to smack me back down all the time. I felt lonely for a while. I've never been alone before, in my head. It was strange to hear my own voice without her going on and on and on and over the top.'

'Tell me about Joe Lembeck.'

'Nothing to tell, he's dead, I got him now, all there is to say.' The Colonel came round to face him. He looked into his eyes. His face was set firm. It was a practised look. It was a look he had developed after his ex-wife had left.

'I don't know who or what you were. But as far as anyone outside of this room is concerned, you are Joe Lembeck and you are an international terrorist. I can send you down for the rest of your life. I can feed you in little pieces to the FBI and they'll interrogate every little bit of you. You'll never walk out of here; you'll never see the sun again as a free man. I can do all this and no one will know the truth. No one will ever believe you. I am your one and only chance. Do you understand me?' The man looked deep into his eyes. The spark was there, that little bit of understanding and fear that is in every sentient creature. The Colonel knew he had been understood. 'I'll get you out of here. Then you are on your own.'

'And what do you get for all that?'

'You will tell me everything you know about Lembeck. I'll be back later. Get thinking.' The Colonel left the room.

The man was left to his own thoughts. He began to think of Moira. He had only been on his own for a few days and he was already in a right state; he could have done with her help now. If Joe Lembeck was still there at all, there wasn't much of him left. Every night, when he was asleep dreaming, he felt the remnants of Joe slipping away. His mind was clearing up the rubbish, redecorating the old place. The colours in his head were his now. No bastard computer nerd, no fat nurse.

TWO

'Why on earth did you do it? I don't believe you could have been so bloody stupid!' Jan was getting worked up. 'A few days more and you could have known everything. You could have made your points, got on with the job. Now you've completely screwed up. You nearly got me beaten up by the mob. You've embarrassed me, you've made yourself out to be some sort of anarchist Pro-Lifer and now I've got to work on my own. Look! I can't even tell you about my day!' She flung the brown envelope on the table between them.

'I'm sorry Love, I really am. I couldn't help myself. I was jealous, okay?'

'Jealous of what? For God's sake, what have you got to be jealous of?' He looked out of the window; he looked at the cat curled up on the morning's newspaper.

'Brian. Okay, I've said it. I was jealous of Brian. I've been watching you together. I've seen the way he looks at you. He has got into your head and he is making you something you are not.'

'You are talking absolute rubbish. I can't believe you could be so stupid.'

'So you deny that you fancy him then? You deny that he fancies you?'

'He has been nothing but unbelievably professional with me. I don't know if he likes me or not. How could I know that and what does it matter? It's not his baby I'm carrying, it's yours.'

'Yes, you are carrying my baby and every day you take it into work with these complete crypto-fascists, who have taken your work- our work, for God's sake-and George's work and bastardised it. He would turn in his grave if he knew

169

what you were doing.'

'Don't bring George into this, okay? How the hell can you tell me that I'm screwing up George's dream? You don't know the half of it. You could have known everything, if you hadn't been such a bloody fool. The only reason George isn't here at this moment, doing exactly what I am doing, is because he is dead. The only reason he is dead is because something happened to him in our lab and I'm trying to work out what that thing was. Can't you see that?'

John was silent for a moment. Jan had never given him cause to be jealous before and the timing had been so bad. He felt frightened. Frightened for her, frightened for the baby and frightened for himself. The military complex that Jan left for every day filled him with horror. As she slipped between the barbed wire fence he could see her leaving him, a prisoner of war, passively stumbling forward, unable to resist insurmountable force. He was still on the outside. He wasn't part of this war and his whilst he was free he could still do something about it. He took Jan's hand. 'Maybe I made a mistake, okay? These people turned up and asked me about the work at the old lab. Initially I though they were reporters or something. You know what I'm like with the media. It just sort of slipped out. I just answered the questions they asked. I couldn't help myself. I didn't tell them anything specific anyway.'

'They came here?'

'Yes, I thought they were looking for you actually. I thought it was a bit odd. They just seemed to know quite a lot already. They just asked me a few questions and then left, gave me this card.' He handed over a printed card with a picture of a baby on it. It had 'Campaign for Natural Births' typed in friendly letters across it.'

'I don't understand why they came here. There's no reason.'

'Unless they were sent by the MOD.' John was warming to his subject. 'I wouldn't put it past them. Perhaps they were feeling me up, they do that sort of thing you know, messages under the door in the gents.'

'But they already knew your sympathies anyway. You haven't been quiet about what you think of the work. They had no reason to check up on you.'

'Maybe they just wanted to see how easy I was to get to talk.'

'It's possible. I'll talk to Brian about it.' John frowned. 'Don't start, okay? I'm going in tomorrow anyway. I'll find out if you have been set-up.'

'As long as that's all he wants.' John could not help himself.

'Stop mucking about and fry me an egg. I'm desperate for one, with brown sauce.'

'Will you forgive me if I do it?' He looked at her with the biggest puppy eyes he could muster. He gave her a kiss on the cheek. Jan's mind was elsewhere. Surely Brian wouldn't have set John up. She had to trust John though, surely? John was her bedrock. It was true, he had been sidelined and it was also true that he had worked in her shadow for a long time. She watched him in the kitchen, clanking the frying pan with too much vigour. Yes, it must have been hard for him to work in her shadow. But surely it could not have been enough to push him into this strange betrayal? John was too sensible for that. No, something was wrong, very wrong. The timing was too suspicious. She had trusted Brian, but he was a creature of the military and she had other concerns about his motives. There could be politics of which she was not aware, another branch of the ministry, someone plotting behind Brian's back. She didn't know what to think. The smell of the spitting eggs reached her and she set her cares aside. She would sort it out tomorrow. No, John was her bedrock. Whatever else was going on would have to blow itself out without them. They would stand firm.

THREE

Colonel Wilson signed the cheque, handed it to the nurse, thanked her and saw her to the door. There was a smile on his face as he said goodbye. A few minutes later he was sitting by the wood fire in his study. Jackie was asleep. He had worked rather late again. He was nursing a glass of Ardbeg, 1978. He was trying to savour every nuance of the taste. After the first sip, the subsequent ones were never the same. As the flavours rolled over his tongue he imagined them reading out peaks and troughs on an oscilloscope. This one had a flavour that rumbled off the end of the graph. He watched the fire, transfixed by the dancing flames. Carbon monoxide burnt off from the fizzing wood, a brilliant blue against the lava orange. He felt himself being drawn into the fire, mesmerised. His crystal glass tumbler slipped gently from his hands onto his lap. The wood still hissed in the grate. The Colonel slipped away into sleep.

In his dream he saw Jackie's mother. It was a scene he had gone over in his mind again and again. She was drunk, she was angry; she could not cope with Jackie. Why had it happened to her, why had it happened to them? Her wine glass crashed against the wall. The contents splashed up against the Georgian ivory curtains. He saw her walking out the door again. In his dream she ran into the distance, a playing field from his youth, through the rugby uprights that had always frightened him, and then vanished. He ran to follow her, but the white sticks prevented him. Bone-white, they jeered at him, poked fun at him and left him in the mud of the playing field.

Then he saw his Jackie, so like her mother, so sweet. In the dream she ran to him, lifted him from the mud, and supported him from the field and to a riverbank. The cloud broke and the sun flooded the scene, tall rushes, gently sparkling water and a rowing boat. The air was sulphurous from the mud of the bank. In the rushes he heard the scurrying of unseen waterfowl. In the depths eels would be swimming slowly into the current. He got in the boat and lay down against the boards. Jackie pushed the boat from the bank, took the oars and started to row. They floated to the middle of the lake. It was peaceful; the sun was in their hair. Jackie caressed his head like a lover. She looked down at him with a face full of grace and comfort. She was so much like her mother.

He awoke with a start; the whisky glass fell to the floor and smashed. There was a noise from the back of the house. Jackie was wailing.

He ran to her room. It was in darkness. He could hear her thrashing on the floor behind the bed.

'Come on love, don't worry, I'm here.' He ran over and tried to lift her onto the bed. Her eyes were full of tears and her face was red with uncontrolled sobbing. Her mouth opened and closed as if she was trying to speak, but no intelligible sounds came out. She was heavy now; he could hardly manage to support her weight. The thought occurred to him that in a few years he might not be able to lift her back into bed. What would become of her when he was dead? The doctors said she had the constitution of an ox. Not that it did her any good.

'Come on now love, you just had a bad dream, Daddy's here. You fell out of bed, that's all. It's okay.' He held her in his arms, comforting her and breathing into her hair. She shook with sobs, but they slowly subsided. He wiped her nose and tucked her into bed.

'Night-night Sweet, have nice dreams now. I'll go back to mine.' He turned the nightlight on and gently closed the door. He could hear her breathing as he walked back up the hallway. He had never really felt he could help her until now. He had thrown himself at the job driven by anger at God for making her the way she was. He would show God that man was free now from his tyranny. What God had allowed to be formed broken, he would repair. He knew he was close to having a breakdown, he knew he was deluding himself; he had also known that the work had taken its toll on his relationship with his wife and his daughter. That could not be avoided. He had a powerful adversary in God. God did not need to sleep. There was no scientific rationale for what he hoped to do, not really. He was too detached from reality to fully appreciate the futility of the situation. Certain thoughts had crystallised in his mind though. You either needed a replacement mind or a replacement body, or both. Bodies and minds were obviously two-a-penny, but they belonged to people, they had rights. You needed bodies and minds without rights. Once you had those,the rest would follow naturally. They had transplanted the heads of monkeys; they could take his daughter's mind and place it in a new vessel. If that did not work, they could remove her poor fractured mind and replace it with one that was not broken. It was nonsense; he knew that. It did not matter that he was thinking the impossible. The future would be self-sufficient; he would just supply the raw material.

The future had looked after the details. He had spoken to the interloper that had moved into Joe Lembeck's body, a freed spirit that had transferred itself into an empty vessel. He had seen the consequences of a mind leaving a body, had seen what could happen whilst the landlord was away. He had even helped evict a squatter. He looked at the pieces of broken glass under his chair. He would repair the glass, and what's more he would refill it. He would refill the whole bloody bottle. He would not sleep tonight. There were too many possibilities to consider. He watched the fire flickering in the hearth. He had an idea.

The doorbell rang. Lutz Asher could see the delivery guy's helmeted head beyond the frosted glass. It was a grim night; he felt slightly guilty for making the poor sod come all the way out here on his death-trap moped. Still the lad needed to work. He opened the door. The boy stood there, helmet propped on top of his head, his face blackened by the dirt of the street.

'Pizza delivery?'

'Great, thanks for coming out. It's a bit crap tonight, keep the change.'

'Ta! Thanks a lot.' The lad ran back through the driving rain to his little red steed. Lutz heard it whine off into the distance. He could smell the anchovies. He would open a decent bottle of wine to have with it. There was something really decadent about having a quality bottle of wine with fast food, but they sort of complemented each other: the fat appeased the body and the wine appeased the mind. He went to the kitchen, where he had heated up a plate, no need to be lazy about presentation, just because you didn't cook it yourself. The doorbell went again.

'Shit, I only want my dinner for goodness sakes.' He could see the delivery boy's helmet through the glass. 'Yeah?'

'Oh, sorry mate, I forgot your coleslaw. He held out a tub of nondescript white slurry.

'Oh, cheers.'

'No worries.' The guy went back to his bike. Lutz went back to the kitchen. The anchovies were beckoning. He had the corkscrew in the bottle, a nice Shiraz; the Australian delivery lad had inspired him. The doorbell went again.

'Oh, for goodness sakes!' The lad must have a crush on him. He would have to just say 'Sorry, I don't do that kind of thing.' He was not going to share his pizza with anyone this evening. He opened the door. He did not see what hit him. It could have been a fist; it could have been some sort of nightstick. He doubled up with the pain. Three large figures entered the house. They wore big suits. Dark suits.

'Sorry about that, Mr. Asher, I must have slipped. I wonder if you'd like to take a little ride with us? We have a few questions to ask you.'

Lutz struggled to speak through the pain of his nose. He couldn't remember the last time he had been hit. Now he remembered why he avoided it.

'What? I mean, what the fuck do you want? Who are you?'

'We are with the federal bureau, Mr. Asher. We believe you have been involved in anti-American activities. If you wouldn't mind coming with us.' Two strong sets of arms grabbed him and pulled him onto the street.

'You can put these on in the car.' The remaining man

picked up a pair of shoes from near the front door. He closed the door behind them.

Lutz Asher sat in the car between two of the agents. His socks were wet in his shoes. He felt foolish; he felt about fourteen.

'Was it really necessary to hit me? I'm not a violent bloke, I would have come quietly you know.' The driver looked back at Lutz. It was dark but he was still wearing shades.

'Last week, when the power went off, my aunt was on a heart-lung machine.' Lutz said nothing. It was going to be a very long, unpleasant night.

FOUR

'What do you mean you don't know how the bloody thing works? How much do they pay you?' The Colonel was beside himself.

'We can't tell at this stage how it works. We've run little bits of the program but they don't seem to do anything on their own. Our guess is that we need to run the thing in Toto.'

'So what you are trying to tell me is that you can't actually tell me what the program does, without letting it do whatever it is that it does.'

'Well, not exactly Sir, it's just that each little part doesn't make sense on its own. It all seems so random.'

I can't believe that this is so difficult. Joe Lembeck was only a two-bit programmer from a bank for God's sake.'

'We don't think this is Lembeck's original code, Sir. It doesn't look like anything we have seen before. It must be a product of all the computers that it has been through. It seems to have quite a profound effect on the equipment we are using to dissect it, but so far it has just resulted in constantly crashing the system. The guys are having a nightmare time of it. It keeps mucking up their software.'

'I want you all to have a break from it, okay? You have got too close to it. I want everyone to leave the program alone for the next few days. I want a battle plan about how best to dissect the thing without it getting loose in our system and I want some ideas about what exactly it might be targeting.'

'I don't think Colonel Miller would be happy about that, Sir. He wanted the work to go on in shifts through the night.'

'Is Colonel Miller here? I don't see him.'

'No Sir, he has flown out to the States to meet this Asher guy.'

'I am perfectly aware of that. I think you work for me now until he gets back.'

'Understood, Sir.'

'Oh, and I want the machine prepped so that as soon as you are all back on the case in two days time, we can run it, as you say, in Toto.'

'Understood, Sir.'

Gerry sat in the waiting room. She had been there for two hours, half an hour ago they had given her a cup of coffee; it was not very nice. She was feeling rather hungry and was beginning to feel a bit sick; if she did not eat regularly she always got headaches. The door suddenly opened and a tall, well-built figure entered.

'I'm sorry to keep you waiting for so long; I've been very busy. I hope you have not been too uncomfortable.' Gerry had met this man once before. He was confident, intelligent, and good-looking, though a little bit old for her; a youngish Sean Connery. She had always had a soft spot for 007.

'I'm fine, thank you. I would like to contact my boyfriend though.' (She did not fancy the man sufficiently enough to avoid the b word). 'He will worry about me if I'm not back soon.'

'Naturally. Things are a little bit sensitive at the moment, I'm afraid I'll have to vet the call.'

'My boyfriend is deaf, mister... I'm afraid I don't remember your name; though I think we have met before.'

'Wilson, Colonel Brian Wilson. I should have introduced myself again, I'm sorry.'

'That's quite alright Colonel Wilson. I would just like to message my boyfriend on the mobile. Just to tell him that I'm working late and that he doesn't have to worry.'

'Go ahead. Can you let me read it before you send it?'

'Of course.' Gerry nervously typed in the letters. She was more stressed than she had realised, and these little buttons did not make the job very easy. After lots of beeps and errors the message was complete. Spies never seemed to get in such a state on the television. The Colonel okayed it and it was sent.

'Dr. Spenks, I'm afraid I brought you here just to instil in you the importance of maintaining absolute secrecy about this work. I would very much like you to write a report for me over the next few days, concerning everything you have seen and heard regarding this matter. Each morning this week you will be collected and brought to this location. The documents you write will be classified to the highest level. I know you are bound by the official secrets act, Doctor Spenks, but I can't stress strongly enough the importance of confidentiality in regard to what you have seen. You will be closely observed. You can rest assured that if you do approach anyone concerning this matter, we will know about it. There are severe penalties for releasing government secrets.

'I am fully aware of that, Colonel Wilson. I understand the delicacy of these results.' Gerry's heart was racing. She was playing with the big boys now. She had access to the most important secrets in the country. She knew things that could set the world alight. There were things though that she needed to know. Her conscience was tapping at the back of her mind but she could hardly bring herself to ask the question.

'Colonel Wilson, what will happen to Kate?'

'I'm afraid I can't answer that question. I'm afraid everything is on a need-to-know basis now. You will have to get used to that. Given time, we might be able to allow you access to Kate. This depends entirely on how you behave in the next few months. If all goes well, I can't see any reason why you should not be heavily involved with us.' There was a hint of menace in his voice.

'I understand.'

'Thank you for agreeing to see me, I will keep you informed as best I can. I'll probably need to meet you again in a few days time. If you could have the report finished by the end of the week, I would be most grateful.' He opened the door and showed her to a waiting car. 'I look forward to reading your report. Goodbye for now.'

As the car drove away the Colonel stroked his chin. He had three-day-old stubble on it. He must not let himself go. Things were getting complicated; he had to stay in control. He had to pull in a few favours. Tonight he was going to try a little experiment. Tonight he might make history.

FIVE

Noises came from outside. There was shouting and the sound of heavy boots on the floor. The door burst open.

'I'm not happy about this at all. I want to speak to your commanding officer. I am an independent research scientist employed by Her Majesty's government. I do not expect to be bullied in this matter.' Professor Joe Gregorian backed into the room. He was closely followed by twelve soldiers, all of whom were wearing HAZMAT gear and breathing apparatus. They had donned the equipment as they had neared the gorilla labs. The first spoke to him. He had a husky voice and obviously smoked too much.

'I'm sorry Professor, but I can assure you my orders come from the highest possible authority. I have been asked to accompany you and the gorilla known as 'Frank' back to our centre of operations.' He looked at the other men as he said this, a few of them laughed.

'You are not taking any of my animals anywhere. Do you understand me? These animals represent years of work, they are genetically modified organisms and they cannot be removed from this establishment without the appropriate authority.'

'I am not going to argue with you Professor. I can assure you we have all the authorization we need. Everything will be made much clearer to you once you are back at base. If you could be so kind as to tell me which of these animals is Frank then we can get right on with everything and we'll all be home for tea. Which is it?'

'I'm telling you nothing until I see a senior officer! How dare you come in here telling me what to do? I won't have it.' The officer let out a big smoky breath. It steamed up his visor.

He pulled a mobile phone from his jacket, dialled a number and spoke into it.

'Hello Sir, Professor Gregorian is refusing to budge until he talks to a senior officer... Yes Sir, very well.' He passed the phone to the Professor. Joe recognised the speaker immediately, in spite of the mobile's strange compression of his voice. It was a junior minister in the cabinet; he spoke with a very characteristic nasal whine. Joe had seen the man any number of times on the television talking up British science and industry. He had been involved in smoothing over the various food debacles; everything was safe to eat now as long as its source was completely untraceable. He could not think of any reason why this bureaucratic gimp would want to speak to him.

Apparently the news of the death under Professor Gregorian's care had been brought to his attention. There was a suggestion that Kate had been infected by something derived from the genetically modified-the minister paused-"monkey". The research was considered a matter of national security. The whole area was to be quarantined as soon as possible. People had to be protected from the possible risk of contamination. The MP for Hatfield North was certain that the Professor would comply as fully as possible with their demands. In time everything would be put back to normal. This was a matter of some urgency. It was extremely important that the Professor himself was quarantined.

It was the first time Joe Gregorian had spoken to an MP. He was tired, he had not slept properly now for nearly a week. This was all happening too fast. It was ridiculous. It did not make sense. If they were truly concerned about infection, why did they only want him and Frank? Why didn't they want the other gorillas? Why were the military here and not some civilian organisation? He had spent a lot of time in the last few days incommunicado, but someone should have contacted him before they just turned up and took everything away.

'What is going to happen to Frank?'

'He will be well looked after Professor. If he is the source of a fatal infection we will need to study him and the disease organism.' Joe's mind was spinning now. This was all nonsense; it must be some kind of terrible bureaucratic mistake, the hair-trigger knee-jerk of some ridiculous self-appointed ministry. He hoped that was all it was.

'What do you propose to do with the other animals?'

'They will stay where they are. You don't have to worry; we understand the importance of your research. We will assign someone from our Porton Down facility to oversee that everything is maintained in order. You have my word. We just need to be sure that there is no risk to either yourself or the general public.'

'I understand.'

'Thank you Professor, we will try to get this sorted out as soon as possible.'

Professor Joe Gregorian hung his head as they attempted to remove the gorilla from the cage. The animal was upset and angry and the Professor pushed them aside and consoled it with gentle words, preferring to transfer the animal to its small Perspex cage himself rather than allow the unknown interlopers to touch the animal. All around the room, the other apes stared out, wide-eyed and scared.

'I've just got to say goodbye to the other apes. I won't be a moment.' The Professors hands were twitching and shaking, forming shapes on their own. One of the soldiers looked at him pityingly. It was horrible how Parkinson's could flare up when you were nervous. He had seen it with his Dad.

'Okay Professor, we would rather you did not actually touch the animals though. We want to reduce the risk of infection to a minimum.'

'Of course.' The Professor walked between the cages saying his goodbyes. The eyes of all the animals were on him. He picked up a handful of tomatoes from a pile in the middle of the room and threw one to each of them.

'See you all soon, don't worry, I'll be back soon.'

The soldiers looked at each other and smiled. The Professor followed them out of the room. He left the door on the latch.

No sooner had they left the room than Kate jumped to the

front of the cage. She ripped open the tomato and pulled out the key that had been pushed into the soft flesh. She was not sure where she was going to hide out, but she had to go pretty soon. She unlocked the cage door and said goodbye to the other gorillas. They reached out to her across the bars, upset and concerned. They had never seen so many big humans before and they feared for Frank and their other littermate. They should stay together and hide. The little ape-mind inside her was also scared to leave. She spoke in slow, soothing tones to him. Everything was going to be all right. She hoped he could not detect her own growing sense of terror.

The room was quiet and still. The only illumination in the room came from the monitor of a laptop computer sitting on Colonel Wilson's knees, a few LEDs that indicated a lot of machinery was waiting on standby, and a single candle. The flame flickered as Doctor Jarman moved to his seat.

'Not there, Doctor. Could you please sit here, next to me? I would like Joe to be able to see what is going on.' The Doctor looked at him suspiciously. He was not entirely sure he wanted to be here. The whole place was giving him the creeps. He did not like to work surrounded by so much electronica. He supposed he had been a Luddite in a previous existence.

Joe Lembeck was also unnerved. He was seated next to something that looked like a cross between a modern artist's sculptural take on Guernika and some kind of dental equipment. The candle illuminated the thing's workings; its flickering dance gave it a life of its own. Lifeless eyes looked intently at him and the blank screen in front of them. It clearly was not affected by Joe's presence. Somehow it looked liked like it was lost in its own thoughts. Joe knew what it was like to watch without being able to really touch, to be forever at the beck and call of another. He had a lot in common with this robot. If things had been different they might have been friends. He snorted to himself. He was making friends with a bloody robot.

When the thing actually did move, he nearly leapt out of his own skin.

'Sorry about that, you mustn't worry about the robot. We

just use it to work the computer. I'm not a very good typist.' The Colonel's words held an element of amusement and menace. Joe thought it was an unusual combination.

'Would you like to start the hypnosis now Doctor?' I think I am all ready here.' The Doctor pulled himself together.

'Hypnosis? You never said nothing about that!' Joe started looking around frantically. These guys were nutters.

'Joe there is really nothing to worry about; this whole process should be very calming and comfortable. You'll probably wake up feeling better than you've felt for years.' The Doctor's voice was smooth, calming, intoxicating. 'I want you to bring your fingers together Joe, like this...' Joe complied. Feeling foolish, a human supplicant praying to the aliens. The doctor took a deep breath and began to send Joe into state a state of deep relaxation.

When he had first met Joe Lembeck the Doctor was quite certain that he was going to be a difficult subject. He had furtive eyes; he was shifty and nervous. He was completely wrong. Joe Lembeck was remarkably susceptible. In a few moments he was in the deepest trance the Doctor had ever seen. He looked at the Colonel.

'Colonel Wilson will ask you a few questions Joe. Please answer them as fully as you can. Do you understand?' Joe's mouth answered in the affirmative, his lips moved, but there was no breath.

'We can't hear you Joe, do you understand?'

'Yes. I understand.' The Colonel shifted forward in his seat.

'You are not really called Joe are you?' His voice echoed the calm tones of the Doctor.

'No, Joe is dead. Joe is gone.'

'What is your real name, what should we call you?'

'I have no name. I am her little man.' The Doctor looked across at the Colonel, this was a new one on him, some sort of schizoid psychosis no doubt. Mind you, this was not the first time that the Colonel had introduced him to a bizarre case. It must be a particular interest of his.

'Little man, can we speak to Joe Lembeck?' Joe's face grimaced.

'Joe is gone, Joe is....gone.'

'He isn't entirely gone, little man. I want you to let him speak. I know he is in there. Let him out. We just want to talk to him.'

'He...can't speak, no voice, no voice.' His words came out in gasps. Perspiration was forming on his brow. The Doctor looked across as the Colonel. This was quite unusual in itself. The suppressed consciousness normally could not keep its mouth shut. He must have some kind of mental subversion going on.

'I want you to give him a voice little man. Can you do that? I want you to help him talk.'

Joe's mind was a mess. The 'little man' was hiding in the place he had been to every day for the last thirty-odd years. It was a dark place, like a cave, but warm, comforting. Someone was talking but the voice was very far away; its echoes through the caverns of the cave meant it was scrambled into meaningless noise. He did not want to hear the voice. He was somehow comfortable here. Moira was gone, the wicked witch was dead, but there was still comfort to be found in the darkness. Then he thought he saw a movement. Like the blue afterimage of the sun you see behind your eyes. There was definitely someone there. Its voice was weak. It was speaking in tongues. 'Little man' didn't understand a word.

'Tell us about the program Joe. Tell us how it works.' Joe's head was slumped forward now. His mouth formed the words, but they were barely audible. The Colonel had to strain forward to hear.

'Genetic   algorithms,   lifted   from   the oper...oper...ating...system. Evolutionary codes, optimise for speed. Optimise for...for space...optimise. Nothing is wasted. No waste. Optimise for everything.' The Colonel wrote down each phrase as it slipped from Joe's lips. The progress was painfully slow. Wherever the voice was coming from, there was very little left.

'I'm...tired...very...tired.' He was fading. The Doctor shot a look of concern at the Colonel. There was no response. The candle on the table guttered and dribbled over the computer monitor. The shadows around the room leapt and danced.

'How do I stop the program Joe? How can I break into the

code?'

'Program......progammmmm...prog...the kernel is hidden. The kernel......' Joe's voice was coming in bursts now. His breath was weakening.

'I don't understand Joe, which Colonel, what are you talking about?' There was a note of annoyance in Colonel Wilson's voice. This was not getting him anywhere. There was nothing much left of Joe's mind. Perhaps the interloper was suppressing him. He would soon know.

'Tell me more Joe. I need to know how to stop the program. You do know how to stop the program, don't you Joe?'

'Can't stop...can't...the kernel. Can't...' His voice trailed off into silence. The Doctor looked like he was about to intervene. Colonel Wilson placed a strong hand on his shoulder. He motioned to the Doctor to move away from the slumped figure of Joe Lembeck. His voice was a whisper.

'We must bring the other mind back now. I want you to talk him up on my mark. I want to use the computer to monitor Joe's behaviour. I'll operate it from the robot. Are you ready?' The Doctor was not convinced. He looked at the mess of cables; he did not like to be in the same room as the motionless figure. This was beginning to freak him out. There were strange things going on here that he did not like to think about. Perhaps the military were working on some kind of mind control project. He tried to keep himself together. He was only the hypnotherapist; what did he know? He thought about his little girl. She was going up to medical school soon. He had to think about her fees. He concentrated on what he was doing. All he was doing was waking some guy from a deep sleep. He couldn't be blamed for that. The robot whirred into life, its head shot forward two inches and the fingers began to type on the keyboard. The Doctor recoiled from the movement. His heart was thumping in his chest. The robot mirrored the keystrokes of the Colonel. The screen in front of Joe Lembeck lit up. His sallow face was illuminated by the flickering glow. His face was lifeless; the eyes were closed. He looked, to all intents and purposes, as if he were dead. There was a moment of silence in the room. The Doctor felt for a moment as though he were attending a funeral. The deceased was sitting right in front of him, his face just a reflector for the cold computer light.

'Doctor, can you please, slowly, rouse him.' The Colonel's voice was calm and slow. As he said the words he hit a key on the laptop keypad. The robot responded with an identical strike. The screen in front of Joe Lembeck began to flash.

'You will awake, feeling refreshed and calm.' The Doctor's voice sounded too loud to him in the room. This was a place of rest for the dead, it was a church, where was his respect? He shook the thoughts away. 'Come on Joe, come back to us, you can do it...' His voice betrayed some uncertainty. Perhaps the guy was truly gone. The Colonel interjected. 'Call him 'Little man, Joe has long gone.' The doctor eyed him suspiciously but continued.

The 'little man' heard the inviting voice. He did not want to go to it. He was warm in his darkness. He had forgotten how comforting this place could be. He had only known suffering in the outer world. Perhaps Moira was right and he should have stayed hidden. The voices persisted. They would not leave him in peace. He had never really known complete peace, never been completely alone. Even now there were echoes of the previous owner of this brain with him. The voices were still outside, still waiting, still talking; the bloody Colonel and his obsequious magician friend. He would tell them what he thought of them. They were not here to help him. They just wanted to get inside his mind. They probably wanted to get him out, throw him onto the streets. That was not going to happen. He was not tied up; he was not even handcuffed. In a moment he could club both of the bastards over the head with a bit of the robot and that would be the end of them.

His mind began to race now; it was surging to the forefront of his consciousness. He could almost imagine it heating the tube of his brain as it raced to wakefulness, frictional heating firing up his mind. He opened his eyes.

The Colonel distinctly saw a slight moment of pupilar dilation before upload occurred. Other than that there was absolutely no sign that anything had happened. The consciousness that had been living in Joe Lembeck's brain was blinded by the brightness as it felt itself leave a body for the second time. Molecules vibrated between the soles of Joe Lembeck's feet and the inner lining of his shoes. Further vibrations twisted the graviton flux between the leather upper and the man-made sole. The parquet floor shimmered, but at a frequency that would not have registered on any human equipment, as did the chair legs, the plastic casing of the computer and the silicon/gallium wafer that was running the evolved algorithm that now imbued with the transferred soul.

Joe Lembeck's body slumped forward, his head crunched into the monitor of the computer screen and then sideways to rest against the spindly frame of the robot.

'Don't touch him!' The Colonel leapt to restrain the Doctor, who was making a move to assist the stricken figure. The laptop nearly slipped to the floor.

'It might not be safe. Just wait a moment, I'll just turn the robot off, he might have got some sort of shock from it.' His fingers slid over the laptop keys. The robot typed in a few commands into the computer. It powered down. The lights flickered and faded. The robot slumped a little and then it too was still. To the Doctor it looked as though Joe and the robot had died in each other's arms.

For the briefest moment the consciousness that was little man awoke in the darkness. Something darker still swept across him and all was silence.

SIX

Kate careered through the underground corridors of the experimental labs. She had never had the opportunity to explore the lumbering four-footed gallop of the gorilla's charge. She made good speed but her little hind limbs felt somehow uncomfortable. She was urging Frank to perform most of the motor-control. He had not had a really good run before. (He was rather out of shape for a gorilla, captivity having made him robustly healthy but unfit.) Both of them were beginning to feel tired. She could hear the sound of her own heart (she thought of it as hers now) pounding in her ears; it metered the timing of her exertions and reinforced the excitement and fear. There was something strangely intoxicating about physical exertion in this body; perhaps it was the thrill of the chase. She had seen apes in the wild enter states of frenzy following a failed hunting expedition. She had seen them tear their own young limb from limb, scooping out the brains and chewing the bones following such momentary madness. She wondered if they ever felt remorse. She did not have time to discuss the finer points with Frank at that moment; besides, he was trying to tell her something. She allowed him to take control.

They skidded to a halt, and Frank threw them against the wall. Her head rested against its cool surface. He had been right; someone was coming down the corridor. Frank pointed out a vibration in the air. It was like the afterimages she had seen before. In her worked up state she could see them everywhere now: slight green and yellow tweaks to the colour pallet of the scene; a touch of yellow around a door handle; a touch of viridian on a light switch. Kate wanted to try to make sense of the patterns; were they scent traces, some sort of energy signature of the type seen under Kirlian photography? There was no time to think. She took control. Behind her was a door. She opened it and slipped inside. It was a cleaner's cupboard. It smelt heady with bleach and lavender. She pulled the door to. She placed her head to the floor; the figure's footfalls rang in her ears. Frank was happy, excited. It was someone they knew. He was alone.

Kate ran from the cupboard and slapped the figure on the back of his legs. Gerry's boyfriend Jim spun on his heels; he stumbled back in shock, but did not make a sound. When he saw who it was his face melted into smile. They hugged for a moment. Kate was amazed how good it was to hold him. The stress of the last hour had shaken her more than she realised. Frank's fears of leaving the cage had been a constant strain. Now he had met a friend he was much happier.

Kate quickly explained what had happened as best she could. She needed somewhere to hide out; the military wanted to capture her. She didn't know quite what was going on, someone had leaked the details of the project to the MOD. The Professor might be in danger. Jim seemed to take it all in quickly. He had seen so much in the last few days. This madness seemed a natural progression from it. He smiled, it was okay; tonight she could hide out at his place. The question was how to get out of the building without being found out. She was not to worry; James Bond always found a way out. The security was not particularly sophisticated. They just needed some sort of diversion. He signed to her that the 'old ones were best', and lead her into a side room, the departmental laundry. He put on a long white coat, put a laundry basket on a trolley and invited Kate to climb aboard. He covered her up with a few spare coats; he would be back in a minute. Jim ran off and found a litterbin; he placed it under a smoke detector, filled it with some paper towels and then set fire to it. He scattered a few cigarette butts around it for effect and then fetched Kate. As they approached the foyer of the building the fire alarms were already sounding. Security ran past them in the corridor. It was a short walk to the car and freedom.

There was something vaguely comical about the two of them sitting down for tea in the little conservatory at the back of Jim's house. When Kate signed 'Mine's a PG Tips', he nearly fell of his chair with the giggles. He was such a nice bloke and he made a nice cup of tea. Frank wanted to play; his thoughts were now so integral to Kate's that it lifted her spirits immediately. She wanted to play too, but there were more pressing demands. What was going on with the Professor; what did they want with them and who had leaked the information to the MOD? A horrible thought crossed Kate's mind. Gerry had not been to the facility for a few days. Jim looked confused, she was at work, or at least he thought so. Kate suggested that he page her, just to ask her what she was up to. He was not to mention her, at least not at that point. The message was duly sent. The reply came back. She was at work, she was chatting to Kate. She would be home soon.

Kate and Jim looked at each other. He shook his head; it did not make any sense. What on earth was going on? Kate needed somewhere to hide. Jim had to find out what was going on. Kate would have to stay in the loft. There was plenty of room. It was warm, if a bit dusty. He pulled down the 'space-saving' ladder, allowing Kate to swing up the steps in a moment. She disappeared off the top banister and, looking back, smiled a huge smile. If Jim left the door off the latch she could help herself to anything she needed. The doorbell rang. It was Gerry, back from work.

Another doorbell rang in a less salubrious part of the town. The young man slumped on a mattress in front of daytime TV chose not to answer it. He was feeling a bit rough; in fact he was feeling very rough. You had to remember that you should not get addicted to your own shit. It was the one golden rule. He had not stepped over that line, but he had got very, very close. In some ways he was jealous of the weekend addicts that came in and bought his wares. They were smart people, with smart, primary-coloured lives. They had nice cars and good-looking girlfriends. For them the white powders and pills were just another luxury item to be taken off the shelf and added to the collection. Only thing was, of course, he did not accept credit cards. In this business nothing came on credit. Occasionally of course you got one that had fallen on hard times. They might have done a few dodgy trades on the markets; fraud was another common one. He always found it incredible. They had everything but they blew it. At least he could always fall back on the fact that he had started with nothing. Well, that was not really true; some might say his upbringing was pretty cushy. Certain things though had gone astray, and once you started the slide, who was going to stop you? Most just gave you an extra little push. The doorbell rang again.

It was different with drink. It was not like the drugs at all. He had dabbled a bit, so he knew what he was talking about. The wonderful thing about the booze was the subtle way it danced with you. It starts so gently, so sociably. You are the funniest bloke in the world, with the funniest friends and everybody loves you. That was how it was for him anyway. Some people said the exact opposite, but he wanted to be loved and they did not. It must be something personal; the booze settles into your life like your best friend that has just been away for a while. Once it has moved in, of course, it starts taking rather too much for granted. It demands too much of your time and money, upsets your other mates. You end up having an argument, usually pretty heated. You end up having a blinding row in the street and you tell the bugger to clear off. He always comes back though. You need each other. Then he is not just your visiting mate, you realise he is homeless and friendless and you are the only one that can put him up. He would die without your support. You end up looking after him, every day, to the total exclusion of everyone and everything else. You still row in the street, but then you get cross at yourself; how could you be so wicked when the poor thing is so down on his luck? You were his only mate, and now you too have turned against him. You throw him out; push him away for the last time. It is just too hard to live with the guy. He is a liability. He is gone. Then of course you realise that you have been tricked all along and you have just thrown yourself out of your life. You think there has been some sort of mistake; you might even try to claw your way back in again. You have got no chance though; your signature is on all the forms. You were driving the bus that ran you over.

He had not had a proper drink this morning, really. That was the problem. That was the reason he was having these circular thoughts. It always came back to these circular thoughts. He wondered where he might get a little half bottle of something to break the chain. The doorbell rang again and did not stop ringing. Someone was thumping the door. He had to pull himself together; if too many 'dicts caused a scene outside his flat the housing association would probably chuck him out. Today he felt ropey, but he was well enough to sort this problem out. He shuffled to the door.

'What do you…oh, it's you again.' He opened the door to a tall, well built, smartly dressed man. Perhaps today would not be so bad after all. This guy understood the value of money. He also seemed to have a pretty good knowledge of alcoholics. In their less businesslike moments this guy had given him some useful advice that might have even been called help. He had got precious little of that. Today though it looked like he meant business.

'I'd like to come in Paul, if I may. I have another proposition for you.' The guy was in a pretty good mood; he closed the door behind him and pulled a half bottle of Bushmills out of his long grey coat.

'Bought you a little winter comfort. The nights are drawing in something chronic.' Paul's eyes lit up, but he knew enough not to dive onto the bottle. He looked away from it, into the guy's face. The bottle sat in his peripheral vision. It was not going anywhere.

'That is very kind of you. Much appreciated. Would you care for a glass now?' His eyes rested on the bottle again. It felt comforting just to look at it, and what a sweet prize it was too. This man knew a little about his whiskies.

'I don't mind if I do. I think I probably deserve a little drop.' Paul tore himself away and found two reasonably clean glasses. The larger man passed over the bottle; it felt good in Paul's hand. He poured the guy a generous single and poured himself a generous double. He tipped the glass towards him so the difference was not so obvious. His hands were a little shaky this morning, but soon they would be just fine. He would just wait for the other guy to take the first swig. It was a little game he always played with himself under these circumstances. A little test of his will. That was what social drinking was all about, patience. He looked at the man's glass; he looked at the man's face, then back at the glass. The man wiped the top of the glass over with his free hand and slowly, so slowly, brought it up to his lips. He was about to take a sip when he stopped. He was looking intently at Paul, his glass nearly touching his mouth. He must be able to smell the booze for God's sake, a whisky like that screams at you to drink it.

'I've got something I would like you to do for me, Paul.' Why wasn't the guy drinking? Come on, we haven't got all day.

'Of course, you know I'm always happy to help, you know, if the arrangement is satisfactory.'

'Things have always been satisfactory in the past haven't they Paul?'

'Yes, yes they have, very fine, absolutely fine.' His hands were beginning to shake a little bit more now. He could smell the whisky. It was so sweet, so smooth, it was almost begging to be drunk.

'I've got a little more of that stuff I'd like you to get rid of for me. You know how it is, sometimes you get a little batch of the stuff and you have too much to get round yourself and you need a little bit of help with the distribution.' This guy always cracked him up, what was he talking about? He had done this before. It was crap obviously; he still had not worked out the guy's real motives. This stuff was not normal K anyway, its boiling point was different, it was greasier, any idiot could tell the difference, but the punters still liked it, it was all in the cut. His best guess was that this bloke was just trying to introduce something else onto the market; he just hadn't got a brand name yet. He was testing the waters. Yes, it was all in the cut, in the blend. Like most of the whisky he drunk, unlike this particular beauty, it was usually all in the blend. Why wasn't the guy drinking his bloody drink? Drink the fucking drink. He wanted to shout out loud. He breathed a deep breath. This deal could be worth a few bob. He had to keep his eye on the prize.

'The Special K? Of course, you know it is always a pleasure to dispose of stuff for you. May I ask what I get out of this business?' It was such a joke, the guy was giving a great stash of this K substitute for nothing, the punters were happy, they paid up and came back for more, and the guy was still passing out the dough. He wished he came over more often; he was like Santa Claus. Maybe Santa Claus did not drink. He certainly wasn't drinking now. You don't need a licence to drive a bloody sleigh mate, get it down you. His own hands were definitely shaking now, he could feel sweat in his palms; the glass was feeling slippery, he might even drop it. He could not let himself drop the glass; it would be an insult to the fine whisky makers of Ireland. It would be a crime.

'As a little token of thanks for this little job, I've got a small monetary gift, purely to cover your expenses.' He pulled out a wad of notes. There were a couple of brand new fifties in the batch, the rest were crumbly old fives. He could smell them even over the intoxicating glory of the whisky.

'Will that be sufficient?' He placed the notes on the table and a bag of white powder with it, perhaps two ounces. It was a lot. Then he put his glass down on top of the pile. This was too much.

'That's just fine, no problems, I'm sure that will more than enough to cover any expenses I might entail. Please, feel free to come over any time you like.' His hands were very greasy now, he transferred the glass to his other hand, but it was no better. He was going to drop it. No, he could not let that happen, the waste, the insult to a good whisky, it wasn't done. He lifted the glass to his lips. It was almost as good as tasting it. He could put the glass on the table, but that would be rude, wouldn't it? The guy had brought him a present and he was rejecting it. No, he could not do that at all. He took a sip. The man smiled slightly.

'There is one other thing.'

'Yes?' He could hardly speak, the explosion of flavours. He was no connoisseur, but he did know a little about drink.

'I only want you to sell the gear to women, only women, and only good-looking ones. Do you understand?' His mind was somewhere else entirely now. He took another sip. Oh joy, if this pervert only wanted his gear to go to chicks, so be it. There really were some twisted people out there.

'There aren't that many chicks out there who buy K mate, you know that. My expenses might be a bit higher.' The whisky had given him a confidence he did not know he had. It was the elixir, the only friend you needed. The man's eyes flashed. He pulled out another fifty. Placed it under the glass and slammed the glass down on the pile. The golden contents splashed up over the rim and onto the money. It was as much as Paul could do not to cry.

'That will be enough. You do understand, don't you? Just to good-looking women. You do remember what they are don't you?' His voice held menace now. Perhaps he had pushed the boat too far.

'Yes, I do, don't you worry, don't worry about a thing. I'm always happy to see you. I'll get on to it straight away.'

'Good, I'm glad to hear that. I think I'll be on my way. Thanks for the drink.' The man walked towards the door. 'I'll show myself out. See you soon. Oh, just remember though. If you tell anyone about this there is a cost.' If menace were a gas it would have crystallized out of the air at that point.

'You don't have to worry about a thing, not a thing.' He took another sip.

'Good.' Then he was gone. Paul sunk what remained of his own glass and then sunk the contents of the other one.

SEVEN

'What do you think you are playing at? This isn't some sort of game, Professor. No one is interested in your opinions. No one cares what you think. You are off subject, out of your depth and seconds from losing your position, your reputation and your liberty.' The Professor remained calm. He did not like this man. There was something he was hiding. There was an undercurrent to his behaviour. He had spent a lifetime studying apes; he was expert at dissecting the nuances of behaviour. Little telltale signs were the overture to massive outbursts of predetermined behaviour, sequences already choreographed by the subject's subconscious, just requiring the triggering motif from the environment to set the big wheel turning. This man had written his opera and was ready to star in it. The superficial noises he was making now were just the nervous tuning of the orchestra.

'I'm sorry, I am afraid I have absolutely no idea what you are talking about.'

'Where is 'Frank?' We need the source of the infection that killed Dr. Demoins.'

'I'm afraid as long as you persist in this charade of yours, you'll get no help from me. You know as well as I do that Kate was not killed by an infection from an ape. Kate was my friend and colleague and although I concede I am not an oncologist I understand that she died from carcinoma of the breast. It was a condition she kept to herself until the very end. If you have evidence that suggests otherwise, I would be more than happy to provide my opinion on the subject. I am not a fool and I don't like to be taken for one. Why do you want my apes?' The Colonel's face was flushed. Jan had never seen him like this. It was a frightening new development. She paced around the observation room, glancing through the one-way glass at the figures confronting one another. She could hear their dialogue through speakers. Somehow the disembodied voice carried more information than having the two of them in the room. The separation of spoken thought and physical body allowed Jan to concentrate on subtleties in Brian's voice that his body language had masked. She had been attracted to him. She was attracted to him. Listening to his voice today, however, brought her no pleasure. There was an element there that she had missed before: intensity, menace. Professor Gregorant was an intense but kindly soul, it was as clear as day. Academics that got their hands dirty were often open books, they were usually too occupied with their current project to play cat and mouse. This changed, of course, when they spent all their time in their little offices; then their true colours were often disguised. Professor Gregorant was of the old school; he reminded her of George, he was looking after his animals and did not deserve this grilling from Brian.

'I am sufficiently familiar with your work, Professor, to know that this animal could not possibly be Frank. The animal we brought in with you has not even been genetically modified. Any fool could see that. You have a duty to tell us about Frank.' The Professor's mind was desperately trying to extract information from every word that the Colonel spoke. Not even been genetically modified. This was an interesting turn of phrase. It meant that he knew more than he was letting on. Could they know the truth? If they did, he was not going to be the one to tell them.

'I'm sorry; I thought it was Frank. They really are very difficult to tell apart you know; they are clones you see. Identical twins. Their own mother would have trouble telling them apart.' The Colonel punched the table.

'Stop playing games Professor. If you don't tell me where that gorilla is, I'll have you arrested. If we cannot find your records we will have no choice but to sacrifice every ape in your facility. I'll have your animal licences revoked and your name discredited through the scientific press. You have five minutes to think about it!' He left the room and slammed the door behind him.

Jan looked at him warily. 'What was that all about? You didn't say you were going to interrogate him. What is going on?' The Colonel ran his hands through his hair. His voice was hoarse; he looked distant and distracted.

'I'm sorry. I'm tired. I didn't want you to see that, I thought you were in with the girls.'

'I left early; Atty was over-tired today. Tell me what is going on. Perhaps I can talk to the Professor, what do you want to know? Is the Professor from the GM lab?'

'It is a long story. Yes, he is from the GM lab. As I told you, we have been monitoring them for ages. They have been very successfully increasing the mental capacity of chimps, orangs and gorillas. One of their staff, Dr. Kate Demoins died a few weeks ago. There were suspicious circumstances.'

'Like George.' The words just slipped out. She did not know why she said them. They just appeared in her mouth. Her head was trying to catch up with their significance.

'What?' The Colonel was looking directly at her. His eyes were suddenly like black coals.

'I'm not sure, it might be...nothing' Her voice trailed off. She had to speak to the Professor. She had to speak to him alone. 'I don't think he'll tell you any more if you bully him; academics never do what they are told, you should know that. Perhaps I could speak to him, sort of good cop-bad cop?' The Colonel looked at her and she thought she saw the start of a smile.

'I can't see that it would hurt. All I want to know is what he has done with one of the genetically modified apes. It is a gorilla called Frank.'

'What is so special about Frank?' The Colonel was silent for a moment. He had been thinking about how to evade this question since he first set eyes on Jan. She knew a lot, but he didn't want her to know everything, not yet. It was possible that he would not need her help anyway, things were moving so fast of their own accord.

Jan saw his hesitancy. She had come a long way with this man. He had shown her some remarkable things. Something was coming between them now. There was a rift developing, it could be purely personal, something to do with John and her pregnancy, which was becoming obvious. There could also be something else. Something she was not party to. Perhaps there was a hidden agenda. It was such a shame that John had not been involved in this from the beginning. He would have seen through any smoke screen. She still had not quizzed Brian about the Pro-Lifers. Perhaps she did not want to face the possibility that there was something untoward going on; perhaps she had been deluding herself all along. She had been drawn in by this man's charm and intensity. Perhaps she had made a mistake.

Jan was suddenly aware that she had to make a commitment then and there. If she let this moment slip away she might not have the chance to repair the damage. If the Colonel were toying with her then she ought to demonstrate that she was potentially his most important toy; it would give her leverage if the push came to the shove.

'Dr. Demoins mind is in the gorilla, isn't it?' The Colonel looked at her, colour drained from his face.

'How did you know?'

'That is not important. The question is rather: why didn't you tell me?'

'I've only just found out. I'm not sure that I believe it myself. I want to believe it, God knows I do, but I can't be sure until I see the thing for myself. It is a miracle; can't you see that?' He was shaking. Something inside him was uncoiling; Jan could see it was taking every ounce of his will to prevent him from unravelling. She did not know whether to push the point now, while he was weakened. Perhaps he would tell her everything; she didn't like to torture him like this. It was not in her nature to make anyone suffer. Still, it had to be done. She would have to test his mettle and her own. She was about to persist when a figure burst through the door. It was Neil. 'Sir, we've just received another message from Lembeck. I think you had better take a look at it.'

The call office was packed knee-to-knee and thigh-to-thigh. The buzz of hundreds of nearly identical conversations filled the air like a mantra. Each conversation was terminated by an unnecessarily happy, 'Thanks for your time!' and the bleeping of an automated dialler. On one of the computers a little table was automatically formatting. It told the stern faced woman watching it the exact mean time each operator took with each customer, the exact mean time between calls, total amount of time that person had spend in the last shift not actually engaged in calls and their success rate, a slightly less meaningful statistic because this was filled in to some degree by the operator themselves. There were various categories; a call might be considered successful if an order had been placed or a catalogue requested. There were more minor classes of success: for example a person might be classified as having 'shown significant interest' in which case a mail shot would be requested. Danny Mead had clicked on rather a lot of those today. In fact he had selected exactly twenty-five point seven percent more of these than anybody else in the building. Interestingly his actual successful order rate was in the lowest percentile in the building and his 'time not actually engaged in telesales' figure was somewhere near the top of the list. Danny was rather hung over. He was also unaware that his line manager's table distinguished so accurately between the various classes of success. The line manager brought up another window on her computer; it was a summary of Danny's performance and targets over the last three weeks. They were not terribly good. She sent him an automatic email requesting that he give her a visit at his earliest convenience.

The mail icon flashed up on his screen. 'Shit!' he thought.

She opened the office door and Danny walked in ahead. The walls of the office were glass, so it was possible for everyone in the outer room to watch the dressing down. Sometimes people cried. The data collection had shown that although removing a person from the work pool produced a minor drop in productivity (they were not actively involved in work at the time and people tended to rubber-neck for a few minutes), the overall productivity in any given twenty-four hour period was increased by three point six percent. The people who had written the time and motion program had not thought it necessary to give additional statistical data such as the standard deviation of this measurement (who understood what that was anyway?) or indeed what the long-term effects were (they tended to provide rather unhelpful results).

Most people in the room realised in the front of their mind that someone in the room had to be the least efficient person at any one time. Equally, most people thought at the back of their mind that it was very unlikely that it would ever be them, and anyway, they never really liked that person, and the Christmas bonus, such that it was, was on the way soon and everyone got a share of that and they did all have to pull together and they could do with a little extra money over the Christmas period.

Danny looked at the floor. He was wondering how much he needed this job. He was doing his own calculations as his vital statistics were being read back to him. He had not quite reached an answer to his calculation when he realised that an answer was required of him.

'Well?.......'

'I'm sorry; I was miles away. Could you repeat that? I've got terrible earache today, possibly a bit of tinnitus. It could be a result of being on the phone too much. I really should go and see a doctor about it.'

'If you don't pull your socks up, young man, you won't be able to afford to see a doctor, you'll be out on your ear.'

'I thought my figures were rather good this week. I've had lots of positive feedback from customers.'

'Well that is as maybe; but there is more to telesales than just goodwill, although we do value positive customer relations very highly as you know. In short, young man, if I don't see significant improvements in your success efficiency profile, you will be replaced. There are plenty of people out of work at the moment that would love to have your job.' Danny looked at her closely. This woman must have been all of ten years younger than him.

'Could you please not refer to me as "young man".' Somehow that had just slipped out. It must be residual drink. His heart began to race; he had to try to keep his cool. He had not yet gone into the brink; there might be a way to rescue this.

'I'm sorry, what did you just say?' Her tone was confrontational; there was no question of that.

'It's just that, you can't be as old as my little sister. It seems rather silly of you to call me "young man" when I'm clearly older than you. One might even call it demeaning.' Good word, she would not like that. It was a legalese word, the sort of thing you could put in an application for unfair dismissal. Slightly hung-over as he was; it amazed him that such a word had come to mind. He did have an English degree, and he had noticed in the past that it was very often under the circumstances of beery lubrication that he was most comfortable exercising his atrophying skills, still, it was pretty amazing. She was clearly flustered.

'Well, if you want to be treated like an adult, perhaps you should act more responsibly. You have responsibilities to the company and to your colleagues. We all have targets to meet, even me.' She seemed satisfied with that and dismissed him, feigning interest in the flashing figures before her. 'I've got work to do now. I suggest you get back to yours.'

'Straight away, right you are, Sir.' He looked back at her as he closed the door. It took a considerable force of will for him to close it quietly; it took a stronger force of will not to carry on walking straight out of the office. Suddenly he realised something was wrong. The room, normally a cacophony of clattering keys and puerile sales-pitch was completely silent. His focus adjusted to the middle distance. Every face in the room carried a glazed expression. Half a dozen of those in front of him suddenly tipped forward, their heads crunching into their computer screens and keyboards. Various fluffy animals, plastic dinosaurs and other personal effects tumbled to the floor. There was momentary silence, and then the office descended into chaos.

EIGHT

'Jan, wait!' The Colonel ran up to her as she was leaving the unit. He had been kept in meetings for most of the afternoon. Jan had spent some time re-working through the details of the unit's uteria protocols; she had not found anything that grabbed her attention. There was a barrier to her thinking; she had experienced it before. The fact that she had consistently argued against attempting to grow a sentient being with the technology meant that she could not bring herself to think about the problem after someone else had done the deed. She was beginning to feel tired. She attributed this primarily to the baby, but this project was beginning to seem like a hopeless enterprise; she was trying to mop-up after a monster. She was desperate to talk to the Professor. Brian had confirmed her suspicion. A mind had been transferred from a human being to a modified ape. She had watched helplessly as the mind of her friend and mentor had been transferred to the baby in the tank. A computer program designed by a man in IT support had destroyed other human minds, and the programmer himself had apparently lost his mind as a result of playing with his own fire. Then there was sweet Lance. A young man possessed by a demon that was exorcised by a hypnotherapist. Then there were these children, empty vessels waiting to be filled. The thought ran through her head a few more times. Waiting to be filled. Where on earth had this thought originated from? The jigsaw-pieces began to slide, huge cast-iron pieces that no one could have moved by themselves, they ground across one another like great iron ships coming into dock, then crashed into place with a booming certainty. She was called back to the moment by the approach of the Colonel.

'We have had a message from Joe Lembeck. You won't believe what has happened. Everything is falling into place. You've got to come back to the office. This thing is going to induce national hysteria. There is no way we can cover this up. God knows what we are going to do about it. We've got to set up an emergency centre. I've been contacted from the highest level. This is officially a matter of global security. Washington is on the phone. I'm supposed to be running things from this end. They are sure to bring someone in, over my head. Currently we are the only people who seem to have any clue about what is going on. I don't think there is much time.' He was breathless. Jan thought about the dishevelled shell that was Joe Lembeck. How could this poor soul threaten the security of the planet?

Danny burst out of the building onto the street below, his feet slid from under him, his shoes were slippery from his own blood. He had stumbled and fallen headlong down the stairs. His head was full of fearsome images. The street was empty; it was never empty. What was going on?

'Stop where you are!' A voice came over a loud speaker.

'Stay exactly where you are. Do not approach the cars. Place your hands on your head!' Danny's eyes tried to focus, he had lost a contact lens, staring at the screen had made him half blind anyway. There was blood in his hair. There was blood on his face. He squinted into space; on the edge of his vision he could make out flashing lights, the police were there, lots of police. His mind was addled, it was okay now, it was okay, the police were there and they would look after things. He stopped running. His breath came in painful bursts. It had been a long time since he had run anywhere. He had just done fourteen flights of stairs. Thoughts began to come to him. The building was empty. It had been evacuated apart from his floor. What was going on?

'Stay where you are. Place your hands on your head!' The voice was getting through now, it was going to be alright, alright. He complied with the voice.

'Get down on your knees, keep your hands where we can see them!' He sunk to his knees. It could not keep this up much longer. His heart was racing and they wanted him to do gymnastics. There were lights everywhere. He wanted to see a normal human face. He wanted reassurance that normality was still out there. He heard boots pounding the tarmac coming towards him. Strange figures loomed into focus. He was tempted to cover his head, but something told him not to move. It was the voice, yes, the voice was still there telling him not to move. His heart was thumping in his ears; he thought he might throw up.

'Remain where you are.' The figures on him now, big guys in Hazmat gear, orange overalls and helmets, their faces behind plastic screens, air cylinders on their backs. Rubbered hands grabbed him. Handcuffs were put on and he was lifted to his feet.

'Do not resist. You are not under arrest. This is only a precaution for your safety.'

'Stay calm. Do not resist.' Danny was not thinking of resisting anything at that moment. He could have been knocked over by his puppy. He thought of his little dog, who was going to feed it if he was locked up? They marched him at quite a pace towards an ambulance. He was told to sit down and hold on. The door slammed shut behind him and the ambulance roared off.

Twenty minutes later a small army of men in Hazmat gear entered the office building. The advanced party were armed. The first group entered through the plate glass doors. The foyer was empty. Noises could be heard from upstairs. There was the occasional scream. They slowly ascended the stairs. Each man's heart was pounding. Teeth ground on teeth. They held their guns in front of them. Not one of them knew exactly what to expect. There had been some sort of terrorist attack. Civilians were involved. Some kind of mind-altering technology would render them psychotic. They might be dangerous. They were to approach with caution. The protective gear was in case of contamination. They were to try not to hurt the affected individuals. They were required to contain them and call for back up. They were instructed to avoid all electrical equipment. Another group was being dispatched to isolate the building electrically.

The lights went out. Screams came from upstairs. The lead party looked at each other. The stairwell was now in darkness. They moved together, arms brushing one another to maintain contact. Their peripheral vision was somewhat reduced anyway by the protective clothing. The sound of their own breathing began to intrude on their hearing. Special Constable Glynn Williams held the banister rail. He licked the sweat from his top lip. He swallowed; this was something else. He hadn't trained for dealing with loonies; nutters yes, terrorists, yes, but this was different. He looked to his right. The other guys looked so professional, so cool. He had to be cool too. Just keep breathing, come on now, calmly breathing. Count to ten. Concentrate on your breathing. His instructor's voice came into his head. The lesson had been on crowd control. There was no one here but he could hear a legion of them upstairs. He counted to ten. One, two, three, fou.. Something crashed out of the air above him, he heard the whoosh of air, he saw the limbs flying in his face. He heard a blood-curdling scream. He gripped the trigger of his gun and in a moment the stairwell was lit up with fire. The burst was short, only a momentary lapse. The figure convulsed before him. It was a young woman, power-dressed in a light grey suit. Crimson billowed out onto her white blouse. Her hair fell around her open mouth. Her face was pale; her eyes wide with fear. She had fallen over the balcony from the floor above.

The gunfire had elicited an unbelievable wail of terror from upstairs. One of the guys checked the fallen woman for a pulse. It was difficult though his thick rubber gloves. It was clear she was dead, or on her way.

One of his colleagues punched him on the arm and grabbed his gun off him. Glynn was in shock. He did not resist. They pushed him to a position behind them and continued up the stairs. As they turned the corner on the final landing, another figure stumbled out of the darkness towards them. It was another woman, a lady in her late fifties. She staggered on two broken high heels. Her hair was wild around her; there was blood on her hands. She stumbled on the stairs and pitched forward towards them. They grabbed her as she flew past. She wailed in terror as their hands fell upon her. As they tried to steady her she squirmed and spat like a feral cat. Spittle flew from her mouth; she drew back her head and opened her mouth as if to take a bite. Her legs kicked out wildly. The men were completely overcome by her strength in her panic. She bit the lead man on his shoulder. Savaging him and tearing, her neck tense, her muscles standing in ropey chords. Her head whipped from side to side as she tried to get a good grip with her teeth. He roared with pain and shock and flung her away from him and down the stairs. She crashed into the wall further down, screamed and fell backwards down the flight of stairs. When she hit the bottom, she remained motionless.

The savaged man grabbed his gun and ran to the top of the landing. He fired into the air. The flashes illuminated the darkness and for a moment he could see them, cowering in the dark, a hundred pairs of eyes. The figures shrunk back from them. Some huddled in little groups, others rocked to and fro, muttering to themselves. Some were covered in blood. One man was scratching at the window as if trying to escape. The men stood in amazement. Their eyes were becoming accustomed to the darkness. A small fire had started in one corner of the room and its light provided a ghastly illumination. A figure was lying next to the licking flames. His body was bound with cabling; he was slumped, asphyxiated from the leads that circled his throat. They had never seen anything like the scene before them. Every face was turned towards them. Each portrayed fear and incomprehension. Backup was running up the stairs. The lead party entered the room and tackled the fire. The figures hiding in the darkness cowered from the hissing extinguishers. Radios crackled on the stairs behind them. A human voice was heard. It was Colonel Wilson.

'Hold your fire. I repeat do not fire on the people in the office.' It was the first spoken words the men had heard since entering the office.

'A specialised medical team will be with you shortly. The people before you are in shock. Do not approach them. I repeat, do not approach them.'

NINE

Colonel Wilson looked across at Jan. 'I don't believe it, it's bloody ridiculous what is going on over there. I hope to God no one has been injured.' Their helicopter touched down in the street outside. Sirens could be heard in the distance. Jan swept the hair out of her eyes. The building was in darkness. The street was flooded with police now. A cordon had been placed three hundred meters round the building. The press were turning up in numbers. She could imagine the scene in the office now; so many frightened faces. What were they thinking? Would they understand anything that was happening around them?

The Colonel climbed down to street level; the helicopter engines powered down. Jan had been silent on the trip. Over the roar of the engines Brian explained they had received a message from Joe Lembeck. Each word had settled amongst the other thoughts running round her mind. The thoughts were galloping together now, wild horses that reared and bucked as they turned together across the plains of her mind. Her mind's eye soared above them as they ran, faster and faster. With every word the Colonel spoke they became more solid. She felt she was running with them now, a spirit loose on the plains. Joe Lembeck had said he wanted one hundred and twenty eight souls. He had given them a list of one hundred and twenty eight numbers. They were computer addresses. If he were attacked again in his domain he would destroy them all and take another one hundred and twenty eight. Any attack would follow the same pattern. The horses in Jan's mind took flight now. It was so simple. It all made sense. She had made the connection. 'Brian, use sleeping gas, keep your people away from the victims. Don't let them touch

210

them. Don't let them destroy any of the computer equipment.'
Brian looked at her, his face lit up.

'You've worked it out, haven't you?'

'Yes, I have. I think so. There are gaps, but they are just details. Be careful.' The Colonel nodded and ran off towards a line of waiting police cars. It was going to be a long night.

The large boardroom was dimly lit. The walls were covered in a brown flock that muffled the sound and provided a sense of intense intimacy. Ten faces looked up from either side of the dark cherry wood conference table. The men stood-up and bowed. Their politeness was answered in type by the entering figure. His crisp, brand new blue suit distinguished him from his more crumpled junior staff. He sat down at the head of the table. The men watched him with nervous anticipation. He began slowly, his voice measured and authoritative.

'The senior board has spent a great deal of money on this facility.' There was a slight intake of breath around the room. 'We have diverted funding from a number of important civilian and military projects to keep you in the forefront of your research.' Around the room pulses were rising; perspiration was pooling under nylon shirts. 'The chairman himself has expressed his concern over your current spending and projected figures.' The gathered minds drew pictures from recent historical events. The pictures were not reassuring. There are a number of things I feel it is my duty to say.' He paused for effect and to give him a chance to examine the faces in the room. There might be weak links here that would have to be removed. There might be strong links here that also had to be removed.

'Firstly we are extremely impressed with the uterium technology. Those involved are a credit to their profession and study. I congratulate you.' Around the room ten members visibly sunk in their chairs. All eyes looked to the remaining ten.

'There have been disappointments, questions which must be asked. Why for example have we not been able to improve upon the work performed by the Americans and the British? Why are our little clones as vacant as the American ones? I asked you for the army of the future and you have sent me to

211

the planet of the apes.' The reference was lost on most people in the room. They had not had the benefit of his travelled education. 'Does anyone have an explanation for this? You, Chiang-Xiu, what do you think?' The man indicated averted his gaze and spoke to a distant point on the darkly shining surface of the table.

'Sir, we feel there is something wrong with the American technology. The children's minds fail to form. No one to date, including the Americans or Russians, has overcome these difficulties.'

'And what steps have you taken to try to overcome these problems?' The politician's voice was still calm. There was no anger in it. He was keeping something back from them. He had a trump to play.

'Our examination of the brains of the clones indicate that there are no developmental abnormalities. We have modified many aspects of the protocol, our experimental facilities are bigger even than those of the Americans. Our modifications have not lead to any major improvements, though some of the results are not yet collated.'

'I suggest that you collate your data very soon Dr. Chiang-Xiu. In the mean-time I would like to enlighten you on some developments of my own.' This was the trump card. This was the thing that had maintained his temper over the past months. Secretly everyone in the plant thought that they would make the American experiments work. They had used superior stock to set-up the clones. They had been meticulous in every element of their work. They had ruthlessly weeded out weakness and opportunities for sabotage. Many of them had lost faith as the enormity of their failure became apparent.

The man at the head of the table slowly walked to the door. He opened them and asked a nervous young man to enter. He came in carrying a portable computer and a small device that no one in the room recognised. It was about the size of a golf ball. It was covered in short, white spines that gave the whole thing the appearance of a sweet chestnut. The young man set up his computer and a hidden projector provided a blown up version of the desktop on the far side of the boardroom. He

212

coughed nervously; his eyes were transfixed on the small device. The chairman introduced him.

'Gentlemen, may I introduce Professor Xiu-Teng-Xu. He is head researcher at our cybernetics department.' There was a look of disbelief from a number of the faces around the table. This was to be the future. A department run by children. This man could only be about thirty-five.

'I have to admit that your results have not come as a surprise to us. All the evidence suggested that humans that were allowed to grow ex-vivo failed to develop a fully functioning brain. We held out a small hope that American incompetence might explain these results. This does not appear to be the case. For our future purposes this may not matter. Professor Xiu-Teng-Xu will now demonstrate why.'

TEN

When Colonel Brian Wilson returned home there was a message waiting on his answering machine. It was encoded but the meaning was clear. At his earliest convenience he had to report to the base. The top brass wanted to know what was going on. There was an undercurrent too. They were concerned that he had been left to his own devices for too long. He had some questions to answer. He was too tired for this now. The night had shown him a spectrum of misery. He had a word for them now, the empty people, the vacated shells; they were the Empties. Whatever it was that constituted their minds had left them and entered the computers that they had been working at. The remnants left behind were the blank canvasses that their personalities had been painted on. In some individuals there was just a trace of this left, an after image, a stain that had seeped into the fibres of the brain and left a permanent mark. The minds had gone to the same place that Joe Lembeck's mind had gone to. It had taken him a while for this realization to sink in but now he was almost certain that this was the case. By some remarkable stroke of genius, or potentially by some strange conjunction of fortune, Lembeck had succeeded in achieving by means of a computer algorithm what he was now convinced he had achieved through other means. He had separated mind and body. He had even observed the transfer occurring; the transfer of conscience from the organic to the silicon and the mastermind of the process had been the experimental organism a second time. The guinea pig had been sacrificed twice. The body of Jesus had been tortured on the cross to save us from sin. Joe Lembeck had been sacrificed twice to save us from mortality. Now Joe Lembeck had declared himself a God, he appeared to have the power of life and death at his command. Perhaps Joe was the reincarnation of Jesus. Brian had been a witness to His second coming. If this were true then the hour of the end of the world would soon be at hand. The ideas made him feel sick. He was so tired, too tired to think about the consequences of what he had seen tonight. So many questions remained. Where were the stolen minds, the lost souls? Could they be returned to their bodies; and if they could return, would they want to?

He walked to the end of the corridor. His little girl was sleeping. He kissed her; she only gave the slightest noise to show he had entered her dreams. Things were moving too fast. He was not sure where to go from here; he had formulated a plan, but now it might be redundant. He fell asleep at the foot of Jackie's bed.

There was a noise on the steps. Someone was coming up the staircase. Jan was wide awake; there was no way she would sleep tonight. Her mind was in turmoil. She had worked all the evening and into the night scribbling in her note-books, wild flow diagrams, arrows linking people and places, the annotations read like a sixteenth century alchemy text. Now there was someone on the stairs. She shook John.

'Wha…what do you wan'…what's going' on?'

'There is someone on the stairs.'

'Let 'em hang, it's four in the bloody morning.' The doorbell rang. 'Jesus, this better be good. I don't get up at four in the morning for any bastard.' He opened the door. There was a slim guy with a shaved head waiting. He wore a leather jacket and the biggest boots John had ever seen. 'Who the hell are you? And what do you want?'

'I'm sorry to bother you so late.' The figure looked over John's shoulder. 'My name is Lance, I'm a friend of Jan's. Would it be possible to talk to her? It is rather urgent.' Jan picked up a dressing gown, threw it over her nakedness and pushed past John.

'Come in, are you all right? I'll put the kettle on.' John looked at the two of them. He wiped the sleep from his eyes, adjusted his undercarriage, which he now realised wasn't hanging in repose and padded to the bedroom.

'I'll make the tea, unless anyone wants anything stronger. I think I better put some clothes on.' Lance entered and sat down on the sofa. Jan sat next to him.

'How have you been? What's up?' She offered to take his coat but he declined.

'I'm sorry again for getting you up. I won't keep you long, I just had to see you. I think it might be important. I think you might be in some kind of danger.'

'What do you mean? From whom?'

'It's a long story, but after they released me from hospital, I had a bit of time to think about what had happened to me, what had precipitated the attack on that bloke's dog, what happened after the accident. Lots of things.' Lance looked at his feet.

'I told you that I do quite a lot of drugs. I've done loads of stuff, over quite a period and I've never been close to the experience I had that night. It wasn't a great trip; there was something odd about it, something different.'

John joined them with the tea; he poured three glasses of brandy as well. If Lance did not want one he would drink both of them. His fiancée was sitting in his front room with a strange junkie skinhead whom he had never met, discussing the ins and outs of smack or whatever it was. He felt he deserved a drink.

'You see Special K can give you the most bizarre dissociative feeling. You are separate from yourself; your actions can feel like they are those of someone else. It is really liberating.'

'Isn't that what you felt happened that night? It is rather how you described it.'

'No, this was different, I actually saw myself, watched myself from a distance. My mind was actually separated from my body, there is no question of it. I have no mental record of what happened to me. The feelings and the experiences of performing the acts were traumatic events; I should remember something. I remember nothing subjectively and everything objectively.' It was too early in the morning for John to distinguish between the two. He sunk the whisky and hoped it would focus his thinking.

216

'Go on.' Jan warmed her hands on her mug. Suddenly she felt like a student again, talking a friend through a failed relationship.

'Anyway, I came to the conclusion that I had been sold something else, something dodgy.' He paused for tea. 'It turned out that I wasn't the only one who had felt some odd effects, a couple of my mates had had out of body trips as well, though none had lasted as long as mine. A number of guys had actually thrown their drugs away rather than risk another whacked trip. It isn't unusual for drugs to make you ill, you understand, but usually it is just nausea or something, more often than not they just don't do anything. If they are cut with something else, you can get some weird results. I wanted to find the source and...' His voice trailed off somewhat. 'Well let's just say I wanted to pay them a visit.'

'And you found them?' John feigned interest. This had better be going somewhere.

'I put a bit of pressure on my supplier, a soft gay lad; he told me where he got his stuff. I went to visit the guy, under the pretext of wanting to sell the stuff on.'

'You did this alone, with no backup?' Jan looked horrified; in spite of his look, she rather suspected that Lance was a bit of a soft lad himself.

'I got a friend to watch my back. He had a mobile; we were like Bodie and Doyle.' He laughed. 'Anyway, I got in to see the bloke. He was a complete mess, an alcoholic. He was in a bad way. When he opened the door to me he thought I was someone else, I couldn't persuade him otherwise, so I let him talk to me as if I was this guy. He said he was drinking himself to an early grave because of his sins, he said he was 'dealing with the devil' and he would pay. I got him round to talking about the K he had sold my supplier. He told me that it was cut. It was not easy to get this out of him, you can imagine, my mate was scared stiff, I was in there for an hour. He said he had cut the devil's shit so he could pass it off as K, he said the devil didn't know shit about drugs. He knew the stuff he was cutting in was poisonous, but he was too frightened of this bloke to disobey him.'

'It could have just been paranoid delusions brought about

by the drink or drugs.' John really wanted his bed now.

'Well that's what I thought, but I asked him about the devil. I asked him what he looked like. He described Brian, Jan. He described Colonel Wilson.' There was silence.

'You haven't got any proof though have you? It could be anyone?' John's interest was now woken. He put down his drink and picked up his tea; he might need to drive tonight, and someone might be getting a visit.

'I had to be sure; I went back every day this week. The guy didn't know when he would call again. I slept rough in an alleyway, in a sleeping bag, watching the house. I saw him again tonight. I've just come from there. It was definitely him, Jan, I would swear to it. I saw him enter and leave.' The silence was palpable. Lance looked from Jan to John.

'I'll kill him!' John stood up as if to go.

'Wait!' Jan held his arm. 'Wait a minute, there could be another explanation, we mustn't run into this with our eyes closed. We have got to find out what's going on. I'm the only person close enough to Brian to find out what that is.'

'Why don't we just go to the police?' Lance looked at John. 'He is a nutter. I've been through hell because of him. He must be doing some kind of experiment. We have got to stop him. There was something else.' Lance paused. 'The supplier said something about women, Brian said he was only to supply attractive women the drug.' John looked like he was about to explode. Jan poured him another small brandy. It always soothed him. He was a sleepy drinker.

'There is only one thing for it.' She looked the two guys in the eye. 'Sorry boys, but as the only attractive woman in the team, I've got to go and get a sample of the drug. I'll drive; Lance can fill me in on what to ask for. John can watch my back.'

John was flabbergasted. 'You are joking! In your condition, I'm not letting you into some drugs den carrying our baby.'

'John, I've dealt with drunks and addicts before, when I was a medic. He won't be any sort of trouble. I can handle myself and I know you'll be right behind me.'

ELEVEN

Joe Lembeck had populated his world again. Time outside his universe bore no relationship to time that operated within it. He was waiting for a reply from the outside world; he was waiting for them to recognize his Godhood. For his mind, operating as it did at incredible speeds and in parallel on thousands of machines, time was passing incredibly slowly. Millions of thoughts passed through every second of every day, he was dimly aware of the background hum of the World Wide Wait as the pared down, sexually expectant junk mail of the computer literate wound its way from coast to coast like sperm in a sample. He felt all of this as it passed through him. It was like the individual molecules of a summer gust of wind. Some brought the complex sweetness of a meadow, others the heady scent of wallowing cattle; others freshly crushed grass, cropped by their chewing mouths; each severed stem eliciting its own unique cocktail to the wind. He breathed them in and breathed them out. Only rarely did he detect the essence of something he wanted to investigate further.

The individual souls of the one hundred and sixty-four he had taken were something else entirely. He knew more about the nature of the human soul now than any being alive. It was a beautiful thing to behold in its raw unshackled state. He never allowed them the freedom to exist in this un-bounded form. Without its protective web of nerves and fibres, the soul lost its focus and diffused like smoke. Unlike smoke it could condense and reform, but such skills took time to learn. He had honed his the hard way. For the one hundred and sixty-four they had stepped from one room to another. They were naked, but warm, rested and calm. He watched the thoughts formulate in their minds like a child watches the Christmas lights. He was fascinated and wanted to touch. He knew he must not get too close. The instinct of his being to reshape, absorb and utilise sometimes got the better of him. He wanted to maintain the core of their architecture as it was. They were little exotic islands in his sea, too much contact would spoil their unique qualities; the ocean of his personality could destroy them all with the intensity of its caress.

He watched them try to establish some order in their world. Their projections (not visible to them but clearly visible to him) were like a kaleidoscope of colours beaming from their eyes. How magnificent was the unbridled imaginings of man, how rarely was it given flight. This of course was part of the explanation of the exodus. It was too soon to produce a definitive explanation, but he had already written the first draft.

He appeared before the assembled mass. He saw the questions in their minds; he saw the longing in their hearts. He saw their fear and their loss. He saw all this and more and the visceral rapture of it shook him to his deepest foundations. With a wave of his hand they were in paradise, with another wave they were in hell, in a third moment they were wherever they thought they should be; their screams and cries of unbridled emotion cut him like a knife and reminded him how distant he had become from his fellow man. He wallowed in their thoughts until he felt he had been baptised enough. There were other things to do. He had a society to build. It had become clear to him that for things to develop, as they must, for variety and novelty to flourish, these souls would need a world in which to interact. The design of this world, the canvas on which they would scratch their marks, and the powers they would be given to modify it would be his greatest project. It would also give him time to formulate his further demands on the world outside.

They were a motley crew, the senior military command. He had a great deal of experience working his way through this particular minefield, but then sometimes these mines moved. They all had their own agenda; usually it was financial, sometimes it was personal. The army delighted in serving up a product. Skills could be specialised, but the attitude was homogeneous, tight, regulated, controlled. It was remarkable that such thorny wildness should have managed to hide itself from detection all the way to the top of the pile. Every General he had met had processed more than their fair share of unique quirks. He had friends among their number, but he had a few enemies as well. Someone the Colonel could not describe as either friend or foe was chairing the meeting. General William Highgate was a shrewd man. Very little would get past this man; he had to step lightly.

'Thank you for volunteering this meeting Colonel, really we just want to catch up with what is going on. All of us here are somewhat baffled and we thought it would be useful to hear some of the explanation from your own lips before we saw your report.'

Oh yes, there would be reports, reports on reports on triplicates of reports. It rotted your brain, destroyed your liver and turned you into the old men that were now looking at him. How many thousands of unread reports had these old men written in their distinguished careers? How many mighty trees had given up the ghost in the name of their efficiency and transparency?

'In your own time, Colonel, perhaps you could start with the attack on the call centre and work backwards. I would like to first congratulate you on your contribution to controlling that particular fracas. Without your intervention, many more lives would have been lost.' There was a murmur of agreement from around the table. He was prepared for this. He explained to them that Joe Lembeck had either intentionally or otherwise developed a program that appeared to be capable of destroying the victim's higher brain function. The program had a unique structure and appeared to evolve as it passed from machine to machine. He explained that Lembeck had apparently fallen victim to his own device and was being carefully monitored by the behavioural science group at Porton Down. There was a question from the floor. Word had got round that Lembeck had made a partial recovery, they wanted to interrogate him further, perhaps Colonel Wilson was not necessarily the best person to carry out such an investigation. Brian informed them that there had been a recent relapse in Lembeck's condition. They were welcome to attempt to extract further information from him, but his mind was in an extremely fragile state and it was unlikely that a crude approach to interrogation would help. They huffily accepted this news but insisted that it be tried anyway.

They wanted to know about the message from Lembeck. If he had scrambled his own mind, how was it possible that he had been able to send a message telling them exactly who, what and where he was going to strike next? And how had he managed to infiltrate so many of the world's computer systems? Brian suggested that the program itself was generating the messages; only further investigation would reveal how it operated. The Colonel felt that the team under the command of Colonel Miller would soon provide them with the answers they were looking for.

The messages had implied that the machine had been attacked; if it had been attacked once, even inadvertently, it could be attacked again. Did he have any idea what this was referring to? And what did it mean when it said it was a God? Brian answered this with suitable psychobabble. Lembeck had been a isolated, lonely individual, sexually frustrated, confused and under-used in his place of work. It was not uncommon for such individuals to develop exaggerated ideas of grandeur, delusions and fantasies of power. There was no one in the room who had the weapons to return fire on that front. They looked unsatisfied but had no choice but to change the subject. He suggested that their efforts concentrated on analysis of the computer software. This was the source of their problems. They needed to develop a means of isolating the program, or seeking out and destroying it. It was a 'virtual' enemy; they required a suitable 'virtual' weapon. This statement was lost on some of the fellows in the room. The Colonel could not think why half these people were here. They had no inkling of what was really happening. They would all be blind-sided. Over the course of this discussion he had been thinking about Joe Lembeck's motives. Where would this end? Lembeck's soul was a ghost in the machine; he had already demonstrated his power, he could do as he liked.

The meeting went on for a further two hours. Rehabilitation of the 'victims' and the progress of the affected men at Porton Down were discussed. They had no idea. They were thinking on far too small a scale. Brian now knew that a wind change was coming; the future evolution of the entire human species was at hand. These men were the old wood of history; the new order would sweep them aside as the air explosion of the comet over Tanguska had flattened an entire forest. There were however so many unanswered questions; the future held so many secrets. The minds of the Empties were not addled or damaged; they were gone. He was not as young now as he was; he felt the dampness of winter's approach. This was a future that he and so many others had seen coming. His only hope was that there would be a place in it for Jackie. The question remained as to where the minds of the Empties had gone. Had Lembeck managed to store them? Could they be encoded? There had never been a place in the future for people like Jackie. He had a choice. He could pursue the work he had begun, or he could wait for Joe Lembeck to whisk them all away.

The meeting came to a close; the old wood shuffled out leaving The Colonel and the General.

'Before you go, I'd like a little word, if I may, just between the two of us.' The General closed the door. The room now seemed very empty indeed. 'That was quite a performance you just put on, but you and I know that it was a load of bull. I've been watching you closely Brian, very closely indeed. I've read the reports on your work; I've seen the progress in your lab. You were visiting Joe Lembeck before all this crap hit the fan. The children grown in your lab have all been brain-damaged; the victims of this supposed 'computer virus' have all been brain-damaged too. I also know about your dealings with the chem-weapons people. I know you have been working on some kind of psychoactive drug. I think you are behind all of this, Colonel Wilson. I think this computer business is just a charade for your own games. I haven't got all the evidence I need yet, but I promise you I will get it.' Brian was shocked; this man knew too much, how was it possible? Who had spilled the beans about the drug development?

'I can assure you General that the motives for my work are towards the national good.' He had to think fast. 'The uterium technology has not worked as we thought it would. I've managed to persuade the foremost expert in the field to help us work out what has gone wrong. The drugs I have been examining were to be used as a means of kick-starting the brains of these poor children. I can't imagine what you are suggesting.'

'I don't believe you, Colonel Wilson; I never have believed you. I haven't got much time for you and your type in the labs anyway. You have been left to your own devices for far too long. You are under my closest scrutiny. My net is closing in on you and the more you squirm, the closer I'll get. If I can link you to what happened in the office block yesterday I will have you up in front of a court martial before you know what has hit you. I think you better leave now. I think you better think carefully about what you are going to do next.'

The Colonel walked back to his car through the rain. They were all so wrong; none of them had grasped the whole picture. Was he the only person in the country who understood the gravity of the situation? He felt like Noah. A God had given him a message and he was the only one who believed it. He had to build his ark now. It would be big enough for two. The rest would have to swim in whatever was left in the new world order. The general had to be eliminated. It was unfortunate really; he was so close but not close enough. Perhaps Joe Lembeck would thank him for dispatching another soul to him. Perhaps he would be rewarded in Joe Lembeck's heaven. All it took was an email address.

TWELVE

Paul's street was empty and quiet as they pulled up outside the old barber's shop. Their hearts were racing; they felt as though they were about to walk onto the stage. Jan was concerned that they were calling too late; there was the faintest indication that day was on its way. The sickly brilliance of the orange streetlights picked out the hidden blue in the sullen sky. Lance told them not to worry. Those in most need of drugs would be stalking at this time. They would have left the clubs on a high and only now, as a new day dawned, would the necessity of their need lift its head. They would not be able to face the grim demands of a new day without another hit. The alcoholic would be stupefied; he would not know what time of day it was anyway. Jan was to be friendly, laughing. It had been a long night of debauchery and dancing. She was to ask for a hit as if she were asking for her first cup of coffee at the station café. If he refused she would ask again, this time as if she had been short-changed at the café. If he refused a third time, she would have to react as if he had just slapped her. She would hold that image in her mind. It was to be her motivation for the part. If that failed then feminine guile, tears and begging were the remaining option. John said that would not be necessary; he was sure she would get round this guy the same way she always got round him.

Jan staggered up the street in the white stilettos she had not worn since she was eighteen. She pulled her fun fur around her. It tickled more than usual because the cat had been sleeping on it for the past two months. The men waited at a distance, they watched her figure disappearing down the street. Lance would stay with the car. John would follow Jan up the road after a few minutes. He didn't want to be too far

225

behind if anything turned nasty. He was carrying a twelve-inch crowbar concealed in his sleeve. Its weight felt good in his hand. Though the ease with which he followed her so armed scared him. He could be anyone. Jan did not look backwards, had said she did not need anything. She was always so brave, always so calm. George's death had been the only time he had seen her lose her cool. Sometimes he wished she were more vulnerable; her doctor's calculated confidence did not attract him. It made her seem aloof and distant. He loved her best when her guard was down. In those moments both his mind and body loved her in equal measure. Tonight though she could be as strong as she liked, she would need every ounce of strength she had.

Jan reached the door. The house number was painted in childlike black letters on the bare-board. The paint had run, giving them a faintly ridiculous Hammer Horror appearance. She was entering the twilight zone of someone's life; the last retreat of a damaged soul. She pushed the bell. It collapsed into a bird's nest of wires and plastic. No sound came from within. She rapped at the door; the sound of the knocking was loud in the crisp air. He heard its echo from the houses behind. She did not want to have to knock again. Again there was not a sound from within. He was probably unconscious somewhere in the house, sleeping the restless sleep of the addled brain. She needed a sample of the drug. She thought about Lance struggling in the hypnotist's chair, the perspiration pouring from his brow. She thought of Brian holding him in his vice-like grip. What was going on? Surely it could not be true that Brian was responsible for this. What motives could he possibly have for poisoning the streets with a new drug?

In her puzzlement and anger she knocked again; she had to wake this bastard up. She needed a sample of this stuff and she needed it now. She used her rising anxiety to fuel her characterisation; this was what it felt like to method act, this was her motivation.

'Let me in you bastard!' She shouted through the letterbox. She would wake the dead if that was what it took. As the rusty metal flap snapped into place, a curl of smoke, like the exhalation of a train, blew out into her face. In the moment before the shutter snapped closed, she could hear the lively crackle of a wood fire. There was no time to lose.

'John! Lance quick, the place is on fire!' She banged on the door with both fists. If he was unconscious inside, perhaps she could rouse him. She banged on the neighbour's doors; they needed the fire brigade and they might have to evacuate the houses on either side. No reply came from behind the doors. She shouted through the letterbox, 'FIRE! Come on, wake up, the house is on fire!' She hammered on their doors. Still no one stirred. The people in this street did not answer the door at any time of day. John arrived with the crowbar. Lance was not far behind. At the top of the street the milkman trundled along. The electric motor of his float sounded like an alien invasion as it echoed between the stony faces of the buildings. The clink of bottles chimed out as he drove over the potholes. John rammed the crowbar between the door and the jamb. Lance gave directions to the emergency services. The door gave way with a splintering crash. Heat and smoke drove them back. A body was illuminated in the orange glow, lying prone in the small kitchen at the back of the house. Smoke was crawling up the walls and along the ceiling; sinuous clouds, black and grey, swirling in the drafts, acrid and blinding. John ran into the hall. Jan and Lance followed. They kept low, the movement of their bodies producing vortices in the smoke, which stung their eyes and throats. The heat was intense. Paul's body lay motionless, his head twisted back into an unnatural pose. His eyes were wide; his tongue projected from his mouth. Kitchen units were ablaze, and flames licked out at them. The ceiling was blackened and the upper-floor was visible in places where the flames had devoured it. Water poured through the ceiling; the heat had caused a water-tank to split and the resultant flood had suppressed the rampage of the fire. The men grabbed the body and began to drag it towards the door.

'Wait! He is dead; there is no point. We need to find the drugs quickly, before the police arrive.' One look at the body had convinced Jan that they were alone in the house. This man had been murdered before they had arrived.

'We haven't got much time! The ceiling could come down at any minute. Get out of here Jan, for the baby's sake!' John pushed her towards the door. 'Stay low, we'll have a quick look, go, please!'

Jan nodded and worked her way back along the corridor. The smoke was beginning to fill the space between floor and ceiling, they only had about two minutes. She dropped to her hands and knees; it was becoming unbearable. She could hear the guys in the kitchen smashing things. There was a crash as part of the ceiling gave way. She threw herself to the floor. They had to get out now, before it was too late. As she turned her head to call the men out she noticed something parallel with her line of sight. It was taped to the underside of an ugly nineteen fifties sideboard that ran along the corridor.

'I've got it! Come on!' She could barely form the words, the smoke constricted her throat, her eyes streaming. John ran up to her, helped her to her feet and together they ran into the street.

'Wait, I'll be right back!' He dived back inside and re-emerged a moment later with Lance and the prone figure.

'The drugs!' Jan coughed and gasped for air. 'They are under the side-board!'

'Its too dangerous! It could all collapse at any moment!' John pulled her away from the house, shielding her from the building heat.

Lance however turned and disappeared back into the billowing smoke. He closed his eyes against the stinging fog. His heart was racing. He dare not breathe, though his lungs were begging him to try. He threw himself to the floor and felt around underneath the filthy piece of furniture. He could hear sirens coming up the street, the fire was roaring now, it had broken a chimney to the sky and a draft was forming, drawing the smoke into the kitchen. It gave him the smallest window of opportunity. When his breath came it felt white hot, he thought he might faint with the pain. He suddenly felt someone grab his heels. He looked back; there was a fireman, crouched low behind him. He was beckoning him to go. Lance took one last look at the sideboard, there was the slightest break in the smoke, and then he saw it. A white packet stuck to the wood. He blinked back the tears as they came to his eyes. This was the source of his pain over the last month; he could not let it disappear in smoke as he himself had done on that fateful night. He slid forward two feet, kicking himself free of the man behind him, grabbed the plastic bag and then crawled back. A moment later strong hands were on him and he was dragged from the house.

PART FOUR
THE FIRST AMENDMENT

ONE

There was the most beautiful moon sitting high in the sky that night. It hung in a double rainbow crown as its light refracted through the freezing air. A frost was forming, covering the dismal mush of autumn with a million tiny lights. The frost tucked the flowers of summer into their deathbeds; their succulent stems, bejewelled and bending, would be pierced by a million tiny swords of ice. Tomorrow they would lie slain. The swans on the millpond praised the moonlight with their glory whilst the ducks huddled warily together like a band of down and outs.

The street lamps threw concentric rings of warming light into the tangles of the trees on the avenue. A figure wrapped up against the cold was heading to a poorer part of town. He left the Daimler parked under a street light and cut across the common, his path gloriously illuminated in the moonlight, his shadow a wriggling pool at his feet, and found the gap in the undergrowth that led down to the towpath.

The water made no sound in the still air. His footsteps echoed loudly back to him from the brick railway bridge; he hoped she would not be late. He waited in the shadows, lit a cigarette and studied its warming glow. He heard the almost inaudible squeak of unseen bats as they circled and shot under the damp archway. He thought he heard a hedgehog grubbing through the undergrowth. In the distance an urban fox screeched. Everywhere there was life. Everywhere nature was holding sway, even in this man-made jungle.

There was the sound of someone coming down the hill; a woman's voice loudly cursed the brambles and the sticky mud. A flashlight swung wildly and then clattered to the path, the owner swore at the silent moon, picked herself up and brushed herself off.

'Good evening.' Colonel Wilson moved from the darkness of the shadows onto the towpath. 'I see you picked a rather difficult way down to the canal. Are you all right?' Gerry jumped back at the sound of his voice. She nearly staggered a second time, but steadied herself at the last minute.

'Oh, you surprised me; I thought I was going to be early.'

'I should have picked an easier meeting place, this was rather melodramatic of me.'

'No, no, I'm fine. I just had a little problem finding it in the dark.'

'Are you sure you weren't followed?'

'I'm quite sure; I told my boyfriend I was having a night out with my girlfriends. He won't expect me back until late. He was looking pretty tired, I don't expect he'll wait up for me.'

'I shouldn't think I'll keep you late tonight Gerry, it is just that I had something I wanted to show you, I need your opinion about it. It is a sensitive matter, hence the rather gothic meeting place. There are any number of people who might want to listen in on this, both friendly and non-friendly powers.' The Colonel's voice was hushed.

'I understand. You know you can show me anything.' Gerry's excitement was mounting. She watched in awe as the Colonel placed a laptop computer on the ground in front of her.

'This is your next mission,' he said. 'I think you will find it interesting.'

From higher up the slope, two figures were watching at a distance. They sat in silence; messages were passed from one to the other in sign language. The smaller of the two, a young male gorilla, was animatedly asking what was going on. Jim had seen Gerry slide down the slope, he had watched her talking to an unseen figure, the moon illuminating her face, but turned away from him as she was, he had not been able to read her lips. He saw her enter the tunnel. He watched as a cool light illuminated the semi-circle of darkness.

Colonel Wilson was disappointed that he had had to side-line the drug development so soon. The results had looked extremely promising. He was quite sure now that with the appropriate cocktail the mind could be winkled from the body. Lance had been the living proof of that. He had demonstrated how vulnerable the empty shell, the blank, was to subsequent colonization. He had also demonstrated that the mind could return to its seat. Following his reunion with his body Lance had demonstrated very few ill effects. Joe Lembeck had also provided evidence of the vulnerability of the empty vessel, and the capacity for another mind to take up residence. He had also shown how easy it was to evict the mind from its new home. There were still various principles that needed to be demonstrated. He had wanted to use the drugs to transfer a mind from a woman to one of the genetically modified girls. He was convinced now that this was the problem with them. They too were blanks, exactly the same as the empty vessels left following the exodus of the minds into the machines. There was something about the uterium technology that failed to impart the human spark. If they were blanks then the girls should greedily receive a proffered mind and could provide a vessel for his dear Jackie. The security at Porton Down made this a very difficult task. The increased scrutiny he was now under made it nearly impossible. There was no way he could bring all the necessary individuals together under one roof. The computer virus had suggested another possibility. There was no use speculating until he had performed a few simple experiments. He would soon know the answer; the machine had nearly completed booting.

'What should I do?' Gerry sat on her haunches looking up at Brian. He stood at a distance, gazing out into the night.

'Just follow the prompts as it asks you the questions. It's not some kind of test. Just relax and try to remember what it says.' Gerry's attention returned to the screen. White letters on the blue background requested she enter her code name. She nervously typed the phrase, her mouth involuntarily forming the words as she went. She had to do it several times, and the cold, her nerves, and her beating heart made every keystroke difficult. One day she would have to learn to type properly. The hard drive whirred. In the darkness the sound was strangely ominous. Another box flashed up and asked her if she would like to run the executable 'upload' <Y/N>.

Without reading the prompt properly; she typed <Y>. She could hardly contain her excitement. The machine whirred again. She looked away, at Brian. He was looking back at her, half smiling, his eyes almost glowing from the reflected moonlight. Gerry looked back at the screen. As she did so she felt light-headed; she thought she might faint. A burning white tear ripped across her vision. Then there was darkness.

Gerry's head slumped forward, her body became limp and she folded into a heap in front of the glowing screen. Brian did not advance immediately although he distinctly felt the hard-wired desire to go to her aid, as he had done so many times for his beloved Jackie. An accusatory pause hung in the air. The screen became dark; the hard-drive whirred and then was silent. The silence seemed to extend beyond the tunnel and out into the night; as if nocturnal nature itself had been cowed by what it had witnessed. Brian snapped the laptop closed, replaced it in its case and placed it under his arm. Fifteen gigabytes was sufficient, or at least appeared to be. It was amazing what they could pack into a modern PC. Four hundred and ninety-nine pounds had bought him enough memory to upload a family of four. Perhaps, with a little compression, he could pack in even more. He just hoped the upload was complete. He was thinking about his next experiment as he ascended the hill.

Jim was beside himself with anxiety; they had waited long enough. Gerry had definitely stopped, perhaps she had just met a man and they had walked off together along the toll path. There was no longer any light coming from its dark mouth. The possibility that Gerry was simply seeing someone behind his back had not escaped him. There were occasions when she had been called out at odd times. She had always told him not to worry; it was the nature of her job. When observing the animals she had sometimes worked long shifts. She had never given him cause for alarm. Not until now. Kate told him to wait. She would have a scout ahead. He signed to her to stop, so he could go ahead, but was too late, in a moment she was gone. He struggled to follow behind, the awareness of his own clumsy footfalls filling him with dread even though he could not hear them.

The brambles and spindle-berries of the spinney closed in like a jungle around Kate, and was mostly above her head. Frank was not very comfortable about the outdoors. He was also tired; she ought to be making a nest and going to sleep, not searching through the undergrowth. There was nonetheless something reassuring about the leaf mould underfoot and the moon above their head. This was the call of the wild. Twigs and leaves were getting caught up in her fur; Kate thought she would look a fright when she got home. The thought nearly made her laugh out loud.

She stepped out of the herbage onto the tow-path. She kept low, her eyes peering into the darkness. There was no one there, just a bundle of clothes. She ran towards the archway then was pulled up short; Frank was warning her to stay back. The bundle was alive. He was right. Kate could see the after-image of something in the dark. It was faint, but there was life there. Kate realised with a shock that it was Gerry. She signalled to Jim to come quickly and then ran to the body. Gerry was unconscious. There was no sign of a struggle or violence.

Jim was crashing through the undergrowth behind her. She left Gerry and looked into the darkness beyond. She breathed deeply, extracting every nuance of scent from the crisp air. It was so cold that her senses were becoming dulled, but images and colours still flashed across her mind. A man had been there, an adult, he had leant against the bridge support; he had walked along the canal edge. She gave chase.

If he wasn't hurrying she might still catch him. The faint luminance of his movements still lingered on the cold, dying foliage. The path on this side of the bridge was easy. Kate kept to the shadows for fear of being seen; the track was becoming brighter now. He had just passed this way. The undergrowth gave way to a grassy common. There he was, a tall man, broad across the shoulder. He was marching purposefully, a black package held under his arm. It was definitely him and he was getting away. She wasn't sure what to do. Her breath formed little clouds in front of her face. Gerry was lying nearly dead under the railway bridge. There was only one thing she could do. With one deep breath and a silent whisper to Frank, she set off after the retreating figure as fast as her legs would allow. Frank sensed her blood lust. This man was an enemy. He had to be stopped. Kate allowed the ape to control the gallop, she wasn't a big animal and her legs were neither exercised nor built for long distance running, but they closed the gap fast. Frank's blood was pounding through her mind. She retreated from his anger. His aggression was like a drug; it had been unleashed with the slightest provocation, now it was in command. A carnal red mist rose up across her vision and wrapped her mind and for a moment Kate felt more alive than she had ever done in her life.

The Colonel turned at exactly the moment they left the ground and leapt at his back. His face became a mask of horror as Frank's fists crashed into his chest. They had struck with incredible force and he was knocked cleanly off his feet and thrown to the ground some six feet from where he took off. The laptop spun from his hands and skidded along the pathway. His head struck the sandy pathway and a muffled cry escaped his lips; his breath had been knocked from him.

Frank landed well on the path, spun round and dived at him again. The Colonel tried to roll away but was too late. Frank hit him squarely on the back. There was an audible crack as a vertebra shattered under the impact. Frank prepared to go in for the kill; his teeth were bared, long incisors glistened in the moonlight. In a moment he would bite through the back of the man's neck. Kate began to calm him. It was not easy, the blood lust was crushing; Kate was fighting against a mighty current. Half of her wanted to tear this man limb from limb. Frank grabbed the Colonel's arm and snapped it backwards, the Colonel was powerless to prevent it, the arm dislocating with the ease of a child opening a bag of crisps. He let out a scream of pain. Frank tossed him to the floor and stood panting, raised to his full height, hands raised then pounding at his chest. The red mist turned to gold and as Frank's breathing quietened Kate slowly took control. The chase, ecstatic, had caused her to scream with the joy of it; but part of her was thinking about her friend in the tunnel and the question remained, what to do with the prize now she had him.

Suddenly the Colonel spoke. His voice was wracked with pain. He was gasping for his breath like a landed goldfish; his legs splayed at strange angles beneath him, appeared useless. He looked into the ape's fierce, intelligent eyes.

'Wait! Doctor Demoins, please stop.' He desperately tried to get his breath. The sound of her name coming from this man froze Kate in her tracks. Who was he and how could he know who she was? Her own breath was laboured. Frank was confused; he wanted to finish the job.

'I am the only one who can help you. You must believe me.' The Colonel rolled onto his back; his body shook with a coughing fit. He gasped for air. Kate did not see his good arm draw the SIG P-226 from his coat pocket. She looked at the prone figure before her. This man must have arrested Professor Gregorian. He must be some sort of government agent. The thought came to her, too late, that he might be armed.

The Colonel let off two rounds. The first was poor; it hit Frank above the shoulder and spun him off his feet. The second shot was good; it hit him in the upper back. He collapsed to the ground.

Jim did not hear the shots from under the bridge where he held Gerry in his arms. She was conscious but wasn't making any sense. She kept on starring at him. It was the same wide-eyed stare his grandmother had when they put her in the home; she hadn't recognised him then either.

TWO

'The Weapon Too Dreadful to Use, that was the story, early Asimov. I remember it now.'

'What on earth are you talking about?' Jan leant across the dark oak table and looked into John's eyes. He looked very tired; they had all had a long night and a long early morning.

'On, Venus, hidden in the ancient city of, Ash...something, Ash-taz-zor. That was it! The Venusians had developed a device that could separate mind and body. It was the weapon too dreadful to use, I think they ended up sending it into the sun.' He threw the paper down onto the table. 'Perhaps we are about to be invaded by the Venusians, perhaps Asimov was right all the time.' The news had been all over the papers. With the sensitive attention to detail that seemed to be reserved for the tabloids they had dubbed the victims of the call-centre attack 'zombies'. Their minds had been 'wiped clean by some unknown force.' Speculation was rife as to the cause and source of the attack. They had even given Joe Lembeck a name 'The mind ripper'. The papers had declared that it was dangerous to 'surf alone at night'. It made the trip to your local library in the late evening a much more attractive affair. At least you could be fairly certain you would return home with your mind intact.

'I think I better get home, I smell like Guy Fawkes on the sixth of November.' Lance smiled at the two of them.

'I'll drop you off in the car,' Jan pushed her orange-juice and tonic to the middle of the table. 'I think we all need to rest.'

They had given statements to the police that very morning after they had been given the all clear from the hospital. Lance was suffering a little from smoke inhalation, but he said it was no worse than a normal Sunday morning after a night on the town. They had said they were dropping Lance off at his house; they were just passing and saw the smoke. The officer in charge had not probed too closely; at that stage they were heroes, they had tried to rescue the poor fellow inside. At that stage it was not a murder trial. Jan knew there would be more questions to come. The dead man's links to the drugs world and Lance's previous conviction would doubtless result in further questioning. They were all too tired to think about that now. They had to sleep on it. They agreed to meet up at a different pub the following night.

When Jan and John returned to their flat there was a message on the answer phone. It was from a General Highgate. Jan did not know the name. He was going to send a car round to pick her up tomorrow. She was not to worry. She was not to try and contact Colonel Wilson. There were things he wanted to talk to her about of the utmost urgency.

'Do you mind if I leave the radio on? I love a bit of jazz in the morning, it shuts out the hurry-hurry of the day.' The driver was a friendly Yorkshireman. His sad smile put Jan immediately at ease. Perhaps there was something about jazz that worked magic on a person.

'No, I was enjoying it, Billie Holiday, isn't it?'

'Yes, isn't she great?' The music filled the car and Jan felt herself drifting away. "My days have grown so lonely...for you I cry..., for you Dear only...Why haven't you seen it...I'm all for you...body and soul." As usual Billie had hit the nail on the head. Body and soul, this was the nature of the problem, but poor Billie did not know the half of it. What was the body without the soul? What was the mind without the body? Lance had been there. He had seen it and done it. He had put his life at risk to make sure it did not happen to any one else.

"My life a hell your making...You know I'm yours...for just the taking...I'd gladly surrender...myself to you...body and soul." The words seemed prophetic somehow. The car stopped at traffic lights in a busy part of town. Jan looked at the faces. On a cold November day there were not many smiles to be seen. Each appeared introspective, absorbed in a million personal cares: their lumbago, the gas bill, the unexplained sickness that the dog/cat/hamster was suffering from. On a grim, grey day like today in an industrialised city it was difficult to see what people were living for. It did not seem like they were living for the present. So many people caught up in the machine, working like slaves to feed the very thing that crushed them into two-dimensional shadows of humanity. How many of them could phone up their boss that morning and say, sorry, I was going to come in today, but I thought I'd stay at home and play in the garden with the kids. How many grandmothers, trailing long-faced four-year-olds could say to their daughters, sorry Dear, I'd rather not have the baby today, I thought I'd sell your grandfather's old car and pop over to the Seychelles for a month. Not many of them. Society needed its fabric; it was a shame that the weft and weave had to be so regular.

The radio was playing an upbeat dance number; the horns lifted her mood and the sun came out as if on cue. People still scurried from bus stop to tube station with the same vacuous intensity, but now they appeared to move in time with the music. Maybe there was life in the old town yet.

General Highgate smiled broadly as he met Jan from the car at the operations centre. 'I trust you both had a pleasant trip over' he said, helping her from the car. Jan was slightly taken aback, what did he mean, body and soul? Her and the driver? 'When is the little darling due?' The General pointed to her left arm, it was resting on her stomach again.

'It's not due until June…It's funny, I feel enormous already and also very protective, but it's only tiny. I dread to think what I'll be like in five months time.'

'At least it'll be early summer. You'll be full of the joys of spring!' Jan laughed but reminded herself whom she was talking to. This man was a shrewd operator. She had to think before she said anything. 'Let's get a coffee, and then we can get down to business.' Jan thanked the driver for the entertainment and followed the General to his office. Several faces Jan recognised watched her as she walked through the department. Many faces were sheepish. There was definitely something big going on.

The General's office was large and grand. The walls were covered in rich mahogany and nicely bound antiquarian books.

'I inherited some of the collection from the previous incumbent, but I'm building up quite a nice collection of my own, mainly philosophy. Not everyone's cup of tea. On that point, would you like one?' He held a cup out to Jan.

'Thank you.' He offered Jan a seat, sipped his tea and looked out the window.

'Do you have much of an interest in metaphysics Doctor Crosbie?' Jan thought for a moment. This was like an interview for a university position. As long as he did not ask her what hockey position she played at she would be fine.

'I've always found philosophy strangely depressing. Whenever a great historical thinker even came close to a valid interpretation of the mind-body problem; the church ended up suppressing or doing them in.'

The General laughed. 'You don't think there is a place for God in the equation then? You don't see God as the intermediary between the two worlds, that of the soul and that of the body?'

'No, I can't say I do. I am content with a deterministic view; perhaps I am an epiphenomenalist. Is that the right word?'

'There is no smoke without fire! Your thoughts are the smoke that emanates from the fire of reality! I always thought the epiphenomenalists were just sitting on the fence.'

'I think philosophers put the fence there. I think the rest of us were just sitting in the garden before.'

'Touché!' The General laughed a big unselfconscious laugh. 'I only ask because I think your work has thrown up an old problem. If the rest of the world knew what was going on in the labs over the road, I think we would have the philosophers banging on the gates carrying burning torches.'

'General Highgate, I can't be held responsible for what is going on over the road. If you want to throw anyone to the mob, I think it should be members of your own staff.'

'I couldn't agree more. I have been thinking along similar lines myself for a long time. You see, I have been watching you and Colonel Wilson for a while. I need to know how much you know about Wilson and what you think his motives are.' The change of tack came as a slight surprise to Jan. She could see where the conversation was going, but she did not expect Brian's name to be brought into it so soon.

'Brian approached me as an expert in the uterium technology. He also showed me the programmers who had been attacked by the computer virus. He sensed there was some sort of connection between the two problems. He thought I might be able to throw some light onto the subject.'

'And what about Joe Lembeck? You spent some time with him too?'

'Yes, I did. Initially I could not see what the connection between the various elements were. I'm still not sure there is one.'

The General smiled a wry smile. 'Why do you think the children produced with the uterium technology are brain-damaged Dr. Crosbie? Or do you think something is perhaps missing from them? I have been looking through your note-books and I have to say, there is nothing here that indicates you have come to a conclusion.' He placed Jan's notebooks on the table in front of them. Jan looked at them and at the General. She was glad she had not written her thoughts down too liberally. It meant she still held some of the cards. The General was clearly a perceptive man. Perhaps now was the time to expound her theories. It was difficult to know whom to trust.

'Before you tell me anything; I think there are some things you should know.' The General leant forward. 'Two nights ago, Colonel Wilson was attacked in a park in north London. The same night a drug dealer, a man that we knew Wilson was involved with, was murdered in his house in North London. I believe you found the body. (He gave Jan a long, penetrating look.) 'I think Colonel Wilson murdered that man. I think you and he are heavily involved together. I want to ascertain how deep your involvement is in this case.' Once again Jan was caught off guard.

'Who attacked Brian? Was he hurt?'

'Yes he was hurt. He is in hospital, under surveillance. He will pull through; his spine has been broken and a rib has punctured his lung. He probably won't walk again.' He paused to study Jan's face. Jan sat impassively. She was currently having very mixed feelings about Brian. Her thoughts turned to Jackie. Who would look after her, if Brian was wheelchair bound? The General continued: 'Something else was found at the scene. A gorilla. Wilson had let off two shots into it. We believe it is a genetically modified animal form Professor Gregorian's laboratory. Colonel Wilson requested that the Professor and his animals be impounded last week due to an unexplained death at the research centre. I have only just received this intelligence. Frankly I am completely in the dark about what is going on there.'

'Is she, I mean, he...dead?'

'Is who dead?'

'The gorilla, Frank.' The General gave a pained expression.

'I don't think so; we picked it up and took it to one of our labs. We have a vet looking after it now.' Jan's mind was racing again. This was the chance she needed to see Gregorian. Whatever it was that Brian was planning she still couldn't see the whole picture.

'General, I am completely prepared to help you; I think I do have some idea about what is going on here. I need to see that gorilla and I need to speak to Professor Gregorian.'

'The Professor is being quarantined at the east end of the infectious diseases unit. I'm not sure we should let him out.'

Jan pulled her hair away from her face. This was all becoming too much. 'The quarantine is a smoke screen Brian was using to allow him access to the apes. I need the Professor to communicate with the ape. I know this sounds incredible, but I'm afraid you are going to have to humour me. Brian has been stringing both of us along for too long. I want to find out what is going on as much as you do.' She produced a small sachet of white powder from her handbag. 'While we are at it, I think your chemists ought to analyse this. We recovered it from the scene of the fire yesterday. We suspect it is some kind of psychoactive drug. I was going to get some of my old friends at the university to analyse it for me, but I imagine your facilities are better than theirs'.'

The General took the small packet from her fingers. 'I think I probably know what this is already Doctor Crosbie, but I thank you for your diligence. We should go, but first I think we ought to finish our tea. There are things we need to discuss and without tea I'm am not sure I am going to be able to manage that.'

The Professor was sitting on his bed with a book open on his knees. It was clear he had not slept properly for several days. He did not look up when Jan entered the room. The General waited several steps behind. His head was still reeling from some of the things Jan had said to him in the car on the way over. He was not sure whether to believe her or laugh in her face. The sincerity and seriousness with which she had delivered the bomb blast weighed heavily on him. She had told him that this would convince him. If the gorilla was still alive that would be evidence enough for what she had to say. He had been convinced that Colonel Wilson had sabotaged his own experiments with the developing children. He felt that Brian's illicit dabbling with drugs had been part of a bigger plan to undermine the research program. Intelligence from agents abroad had conflicted with this idea. The major labs in China and Russia had experienced the same problems they had. What ever Brian was up to the uterium technology was its own problem.

'Professor Gregorian, I'm sorry to bother you my name is Jan Crosbie.' The Professor did not look up for a moment. Then he smiled. 'Hello, Doctor Crosbie. I was an old friend of George's. I bet you didn't know that, did you?'

'I'm sorry Professor, I don't think we have met before; George had so many friends...' The thought of her own mentor on top of the stress of the day and her own heightened emotional mood nearly brought her to tears.

'Yes, he did. He was a fine man. A good friend and he had a stunning mind. He was very proud of you, you know. You were his protégée.' Not for the first time that day Jan felt the world turning around her. Perhaps it was the morning sickness. 'Would you mind telling me why you are working with these bastards?' The Professor gestured towards the General, who took the look firmly on the chin.

The Professor's obscenity reminded her of George. He was never slow to demonstrate his dislike of authority.

'Professor, I know about Dr. Demoins. I know her mind was transferred to the gorilla. I need your help to talk to her.'

The Professor was dumbstruck. He looked from Jan to the General. When his voice came it was weak with emotion. 'I would not have expected George's protégée to collaborate with the military. I expected more from you Doctor Crosbie.' Jan took another deep breath. This was beginning to wear thin.

'Professor, I'm not collaborating with anybody. I have been assisting the military with regard to another matter. This is purely personal. Frank has been shot. He may not survive. He attacked Colonel Wilson a few nights before. I would like to know why.'

The Professor jumped to his feet. 'Please let me see her. I can't bear the thought of Kate dying twice.' The General gave Jan a sideways look.

'General Highgate here will take us to him straight away. Won't you General?'

The veterinary surgeon informed them that the gorilla had been heavily anaesthetised. They had removed a bullet from the animal's left lung, another had ricocheted off its shoulder blade and exited close to where it had entered. In time, it would probably recover. The vet was quite excited about the animal. He had little experience working with gorillas, but he was certain there was something very strange about this one. It had behaved oddly, as if resigned to being worked on. More like a human patient than an animal. It hadn't even tried to escape; the drugs were a precaution, but were probably unnecessary. It was beginning to come round. They need not worry; the bonds holding the animal on the table were more than sufficient to restrain it. The Professor gave the surgeon a withering look and asked if he would mind leaving them with his patient.

He bent his head close to Frank's head. The gorilla's eyes were closed, but at the sound of his voice they opened. There was no mistaking the smile in the eyes.

Joe Gregorian's fingers lovingly spelt out a greeting. He unclipped the restraining straps, much to the barely veiled shock of the General. Kate could not use the two handed-sign language they favoured in the research centre, her left hand was strapped to her side to prevent moving the damaged shoulder, but she was proficient in the one-handed American sign and slowly explained the events of the night before. When she had finished Joe spoke slowly to the group so that Kate would understand that he was translating everything she had said.

The General was in a state of shock. He had watched the spectacle in silence. When it was finished he looked at Kate's prone figure and touched her lightly on the hand. He spoke slowly, mimicking the timbre and rise and fall of the Professor's voice. Jan noted this attention to detail; it demonstrated sensitivity on his part.

'My God, I am honoured to meet you Doctor Demoins. We have the man that did this to you...' (he corrected himself) '... shot you. We will find out what he has done to Doctor Spinks. Please do not worry about anything while you are under my care. If it is okay with you I will leave Professor Gregorian to look after your welfare.' Kate smiled and signed a thank you, which the Professor duly translated.

Jan and the General left the others alone together whilst the General gathered his thoughts. 'I wish Spinoza was here to help me now.' He said, shaking his head. 'For years I have wondered about the dualism problem. There are a million questions to ask. I could spend the rest of my life talking to Doctor Demoins. I can't bring myself to believe it is true. Can you be sure it isn't some kind of elaborate hoax?'

Jan shook her head. 'I have seen a similar transfer of personality myself. I don't have any idea about the mechanism of transfer, all I have been able to work out is that, for some reason, a number of technologies have arisen at the same time, that have made this possible. I have no idea about the completeness of transfer, mind, memory, personality; it is convincing, but it would take years of study to prove anything beyond reasonable doubt.' The General stroked his chin. 'What do you make of the computer attacks; do you think they represent some kind of transfer as well?'

'It is possible. We will only know if we are contacted by the individuals concerned.'

'You don't think Joe Lembeck counts?' Jan was thoughtful for a moment.

'This is some sort of Turing test isn't it. We will have to try to communicate with the thing to try to ascertain its intelligence. If you can't distinguish its responses from those we would expect of Joe Lembeck then I suppose it is Joe Lembeck.'

'And what about the children grown as a result of the uterium project?'

'They are just missing that element of the body-mind dualism that makes them human. They are like vessels waiting to be filled.'

'And if you wanted to fill those vessels, what would you need?' Jan was quiet for a moment.

'In the cases that I have seen, the transferred minds have come from people who were weakened in some way. Kate had an aggressive cancer, George had a very weak heart, Lance had taken powerful psychotics, Ralph had just been killed in a road accident. It seems that the 'mind' component is moving from a damaged home to a better one.'

'Or a small one to a bigger one, in the case of transfer to the Internet?'

'I suppose that's possible.'

'What about the genetically modified children?' The General was warming up to the idea. 'Isn't it possible that a normal mind might want to occupy an improved brain?'

'Yes, I suppose that's true.'

'So why haven't minds just transferred to the genetically modified girls? And why don't the minds of disabled children transfer into other damaged minds?'

'I can't answer your first question. But perhaps the answer to the second one is that there is some sort of rights for a sitting tenant. A mind is only vulnerable if it is a vacant lot.'

Professor Gregorian joined them. He closed the door quietly and sat down opposite them. His face was pale and drawn.

'Kate is sleeping now. I can't thank you enough Doctor Crosbie. I can't imagine what I would have done if Kate had been killed. I can't tell you how difficult it has been for me to carry the burden of this knowledge over the past few days. The implications are incredible.' He paused, lost in thought for several seconds. 'I also feel responsible.' Jan placed a hand on his shoulder.

'I don't think any one of us is responsible, Professor. This is just a tiny fragment of a much larger puzzle. When you think about it, there are just too many elements; too many disparate technologies have come together at once. This is simply too big to be a human conspiracy.' All eyes turned to Jan.

'What do you mean?

Their thoughts were interrupted when the door was flung open. A messenger clad in fatigues entered the room.'We have received another message from Lembeck. You have to see this General, it is the biggest one yet and he wants a reply.' Neil was racing back up the corridor. The General indicated that Jan and the Professor should follow him.

'Who does he want a reply from?' The General shouted back up the corridor.

'Everybody Sir! He wants a reply from everybody!'

THREE

The noise from the computer control centre was unbelievable; the General had never seen the group as animated or as
lively. Every face was flushed, some people were crying. As
the General entered the room there was a hush.

'Come on then, let's see it. Put it on the big screen.'

The message was projected onto the wall. It had arrived as
a simple text file. There was no formatting or punctuation.

Extract from Joe Lembeck's Letter (spaces added to facilitate reading)

'People of analogue world I was Joe Lembeck now I am a
god ageing and death are no longer absolutes my world freedom for those that come after the one hundred and twenty
eight the greater my realm the greater souls I save attack my
world and destroy future no other god beyond me I have seen
the soul of man and I know the origin for I was once as you
think upon these words and the words of the gone before and
in one hundred and twenty eight hours I will return to take
the souls of a chosen few for there is not room enough in this
heaven for the soul of every man such is now will not be forever more embrace your evolution'

What followed were one hundred and twenty eight similar
notes, each of one hundred and twenty eight words which per-
tained to be personal messages from each of the individuals
uploaded from the call centre. The style of each was different;
they did not have the somewhat stilted language of Joe

Lembeck's message. In many cases there were private messages to loved ones. Many contained phrases such as 'do not be afraid' and 'do not grieve'. Some contained jokes. It was these that had elicited the tears.

The General looked away from the screen. 'This must be some kind of sick joke. It sounds like an advert for the afterlife.' He shouted into the room.

'Has anyone got an origin for this message? Has anyone managed to check the details?' There was a hushed silence. Then Neil spoke up.

'It is difficult Sir, our network has gone down.' Someone else shouted from the back of the room.

'Everyone's network has gone down.'

FOUR: DAY 1

It was as if the entire population of the western world had just watched someone die. There was a sombre silence as the message from Joe Lembeck seeped into the common consciousness. The message had been sent to every active email account in every country on the globe. From computer it passed by word of mouth and scratch of pen and through the assorted media to all but the most isolated of people on the planet. Exactly two minutes and eight seconds after it arrived the global Internet was paralysed. Large-scale failures in the system had occurred before but this had no precedent. Internet consultants in every major city worked furiously to re-establish connectivity, but to no avail. As soon as any Intranet was reconnected to the global Internet, it was silenced immediately. It was as if a systemic poison had been applied to it that was toxic upon contact. Every man was an island for the first time in a decade. The international dependency on global communication was thrown into sharp focus. The telephone system was silenced; the stock markets shut down like Christmas tree lights being turned off. The newspaper presses were silent. There was only one story to be printed and everyone knew that already. It came as a surprise to many, but wide scale civil unrest, anarchy or religious rioting did not occur. On the day on which the message was received seventy-eight point nine percent of people in the London area went to work as usual. This was in spite of massive disruption to rail, and bus services. The desire to maintain normality had astonishing momentum. In New York ninety three point five percent of the working population made it into work. On this first day the western world was numb. The infrastructure of the developing world was less affected but there was not a corner of the planet that did not receive the message that day, or at least, by mouth the following day, such was the penetration and extent of the information highway. The world's population was divided along a simple line now. Those that believed and those that did not. On this first day most were non-believers. Whatever it was that called itself Joe Lembeck had demonstrated its powers before. The attack on the call centre had been on the front cover of most newspapers, throughout the world; the nature of the 'weapon' had meant the story was of global significance. The fact that the sacred cow of the technological world had also been slain was a profound shock. Something that had been designed to survive a nuclear attack had been strangled in its bed. This was still insufficient proof for by far the majority of the world's population. The Internet was a 'virtual' domain, and anything that impinged upon that domain could only be of limited consequence to the 'real' world. The thought that the virtual could reach out into the real was dismissed as fantasy. The victims of the call centre were damaged, but that was all. On the first day there was no finger pointing or guilt to be established. The arrogance of the event suspended belief and without belief there could be no culpability.

The military was not however silenced. There was a second independent global Internet that allowed the International bigwigs to embark upon a frantic set of placatory messaging. This was the only factor that prevented the world descending into immediate conflict. The major superpowers naturally suspected each other, though nearly everyone secretly blamed Indochina as they had already provided some of the worlds most destructive computer plagues. The multilateral nature of the problem did not implicate anyone in particular, but the first world, with its greater resources and dependence upon the Internet, played the part of the injured victim. The American's public face concealed two facts: Lutz Asher and Joe Lembeck. General Highgate received a polite request from the Head of the N.S.A. (a request signed by the President himself) for Joe Lembeck to be released to them at the first opportunity. The 'special relationship' was hinted at, and the nature of the delivery, in person, after he had stepped out of a YF-23 with its engines still running suggested a degree of urgency. The sight of Joe Lembeck's stooped, shuffling body as he was escorted to a waiting Lear Jet four hours later was the last they saw of him.

Lutz Asher was also having a bad day. His first few days of capture and interrogation were remarkably civil. He had explained perhaps a dozen times, to a variety of people with various degrees of technical knowledge, what he had done and why. No one appeared to be convinced. This was the problem. The nature of the virus he had distributed into the Internet was relatively benign; it worked its way through any active programs and it did permanently destroy the operating system, but it had no capacity to fry the hardware itself. They had got the wrong man. They had sat him in front of his PC in a room full of white-coated technicians with much bigger and more impressive PCs and had asked him to demonstrate both the virus and the antidote. A few of them seemed quite impressed, a few seemed slightly envious. It had given him a small sense of satisfaction. There were mutterings that perhaps his virus had mutated as it passed through the net, suggestions that his virus might have released something else, a sleeper program planted by another unfriendly power that had been primed by the passage of Lembeck's creation, possibly riding on it. It was clear that no one knew the answer. That was then.

Today Lembeck looked through half-closed eyes into a single bright light. He had read a little about interrogation techniques; everything he had read appeared to be true. He had not eaten properly now for three days. He had not been allowed to sleep properly for two and now they had given him something; he had hardly noticed the needle jab. Now he was talking, talking like there was no tomorrow, the words hardly touching the sides of his mouth or mind. Parts of his brain flashed up pointers, dimly remembered concepts of shame and prudence, confidentiality and humiliation. He raced past the signs as though his life depended on it. He heard questions but they seemed as though they came from the distant past; he did not know if the words that tumbled from him bore any relationship to them. He felt sure someone would look after the details for him.

'He doesn't know any more. We are wasting our time.' The light was turned off and something turned off in his mind too.

Colonel Wilson was sedated when Jan entered the room. The room was in darkness but a thin beam of illumination fell across the bed from a chink in the curtains. He stirred as Jan entered and turned to look at her, his eyes ringed with red circles. He struggled to speak, when his voice came it was frail and cracked.

'Hello Jan, I'm sorry.'

'Don't speak,' said Jan. 'There will be other times. There are a few things I need to know.' Brian's face turned to the window; his head fell forward. 'Did you do it for Jackie?' Brian's eyes met her's.

'Yes.'

'Do you know how to download minds from the computer?' Brian's face twisted in pain. He tried to shift his weight in his bed, but could not.

'No. I think, if the mind is threatened it might move back. Perhaps, if the brain offers a safer haven it might move across. I was going to try the experiment tonight; I was going to try to transfer Doctor Spinks into Sarah. I thought, with her improved mind, she might be a suitable vessel.' He started to cough and wheeze. His body shook from the effort of speaking. 'Doctor Spinks' mind was uploaded to my laptop.' Jan looked at him with horror.

'How could you do it, Brian? How could you be so callous?' Brian's face turned away again.

'The world is changing Jan. Can't you see? We weren't born to live a while, then pass away like the flowers of the field. The future is already here. We will be the first to pass to the next stage.' (he paused as he tried to catch his breath.) 'I wanted Jackie to be the first. I wanted to give her a place in the future. No one else would give someone like her a place.' His voice trailed off.

'I don't think that was for you to decide Brian. I don't think any of us have the right to decide.' She got up to leave.

'Someone will decide, you will see.' As Jan closed the door behind her she thought of Joe Lembeck. He was sitting somewhere, the ghost in the machine; he had given himself the right to chose. Only time would tell if he had the power. Jan felt light headed. Perhaps this really was all some kind of hoax. What would become of the world if any of it were true?

FIVE: DAY 2

After the initial shock of Joe Lembeck's proclamation had been absorbed, the daily grind of blame and recrimination, speculation and deprecation continued. There were broad patterns to the response of the world's population. The official line from all nations (none were publicly sufficiently secular to express a real opinion) was that the message represented an evil deception, designed to trap the vulnerable and gullible. The Islamic world declared that it was the work of America, a rouse to distract Muslims from the true faith. The Vatican refused to comment. 'Experts' were wheeled out at every opportunity to repeat the simple message that transfer of mind or soul to the Internet was impossible. The very concept was laughable; it contravened a number of well-established laws of computation and causality. The Emperor's new mind was naked as the day it was born. A lot of people would look very foolish when the punch line to the joke appeared on their screen. The only images that carried any convincing weight came from the relatives of 'those that had had gone before'. Once the television networks had begun to recover from the initial body blow of the Internet collapsing, they began to transmit pictures and reports from the 'bereaved families of the call-centre attack.' These reports were cut between the images of various politicians espousing the view that the whole business was a hoax and underscoring the line that they had very good leads as to who was responsible for this atrocity (unrestricted pay-per-view access to a functioning Internet had already been elevated to that of a fundamental human right), and assuring the populous that their nation was at the forefront of the search for their capture. The vacuous nature of the political response was thrown into sharp focus by the images of the 'bereaved' as they described their anguish at seeing the physical bodies of their loved ones, and the almost universal belief that the messages they had received were genuine. Their mothers, grandmothers, daughters, fathers and sons had not died, but their minds were still communicating with them from the grave. The families' tear-filled interviews and their passionate belief that the one hundred and twenty eight words were those of a loved one struck a deep chord. To those that followed these communications closely the humanity behind the short letters was flagrantly apparent. The letters were either genuine or had been written before the terrible event. Well-wishers could send flowers and letters of consolation to a post-office box. Almost without exception the families wanted to attempt to communicate with their lost family members via the computer network. In this day and age, in the developed world, the thought of communicating with the written word to the disembodied mind of a loved one did not seem to fill them with dread. Most of those who believed the messages to be genuine had resigned themselves to waiting for the five days to be over.

Those that did not believe the messages fared less well. They had formed an alliance and were already in discussion with lawyers about a number of large company targets from whom a degree of compensation might be gleaned. Charges of criminal negligence might be posited. There were darker reports that suggested that one or other of the large Internet concerns might have been responsible for the disaster anyway. They suggested that 'blipvert technology' or subversive persuasion used by the industry to keep people logged on as long as possible was responsible. The industry denials were aggrieved but strangely noncommittal about what they did and did not do themselves. They were quite forthcoming about such practises amongst their competitors.

Leaked reports spoke of other individuals who had suddenly lost all signs of sentience whilst sitting at their computer terminals. In Italy nearly a million people had taken their computers onto the streets and publicly smashed them to pieces. An industry wag had noted that most of those destroyed were too old to be connected to the Internet anyway and there was a remarkable deficit of the latest laptops. This pattern of wide scale computer destruction was repeated across the world. Strangely, some thought, the computer industry itself did not speak out against this wanton destruction.

The 'church' was actually a disused sheering barn behind the water tower. The night was crystal clear and although the day had been warm, it was quite cold inside. A few members of the congregation were lighting candles; their weak light only made the room feel colder. Lucy Witherborn held her mother's hand tightly and allowed herself to be drawn to the front of the assembled crowd. She pulled her woolly hat down onto her head, but left it high enough at the sides that it did not drown out the quiet words of the man who spoke at the front of the crowd. Thierry Mespilleux was the family physician and neighbour. He was an intense man, a fire and brimstone lay preacher, who reminded them all of their frailty and inadequacies in the eyes of 'the Loord'. Lucy had actually been smacked with a ruler once for spelling the word this way. Her teacher had said it was a terrible sin to misspell the name of 'Our Saviour', and her mother would be informed about this at the next PTA meeting. Lucy had cried every night for a week.

Father Thierry (as he now liked to be called) was welcoming new faces to the room. Even to Lucy this was a strange occurrence; Thierry was famous across half the state for his aggressive stance towards fair-weather churchgoers. Lucy remembered a wedding only the previous year when Thierry was standing in for the vicar who had lost his voice through illness when he had reduced half the bride's family to tears by denouncing them as non-believers. He had never seen them in his church and he doubted very much that God had much sight of them either. The father of the bride quietly protested at the altar that most of the family had come from out of town. Thierry had insisted that they had the stench of the corporate Christian upon them, weddings, christenings and bar mitzvahs only. (This final word had been spat out.) It was amazing that the wedding continued. Not a soul left the room;

no one dared.

Now Father Thierry had established his own church he was a much milder man. Lucy had never been frightened of him; he always spoke kindly to the children. When he had been 'drawn away by a higher calling' half the congregation had gone with him. The church that remained being rather lacklustre and conventional. They preferred the St. James' over the revised modern Good News.

As a rule, Lucy liked the Bible reading. As the words were spoken she imagined a smiling Jesus delivering them himself to a rapt audience sitting around. She knew that much of the Bible had been written some time after Jesus' death, but it just did not seem right to have anyone else speak the lines. She did not understand the words today; it was something to do with the end of the world. The reader, a very nervous Mrs Zander from the grocery shop, was wearing her best white suit, but unfortunately the delivery was towards her shiny black best shoes. Her monotone was sending Lucy to sleep; without a pew to slide back into she rested her head on her mother's woollen jacket. Once the reading was over and a very polite applause had accompanied Mrs Zander's blushing return to her family, Father Thierry look to the lectern. When he looked at the children his voice was as gentle as a flower on their cheeks, when he spoke to the assembled adults there was an intensity and fury that some found startling, but all found engaging. Whether he spoke to the children or the adults there was no difference in the content of his speech. Lucy liked this. She was only eight but she already despised the way she was spoken down to at the other church. (Her parents still attended both, much to the annoyance of both Thierry and their old vicar.) Thierry never pulled a punch from the children. He delivered the fearful words with a gentle smile, but she always felt she was part of the real thing, never a trainee. She did not always understand everything he said. Her parents sometimes had trouble explaining what he had said afterwards. Usually it was something to do with 'unnatural acts'. Lucy hoped she had never engaged in one of these. The dictionary had not been very helpful.

A name kept cropping up today. It was a name she had not

heard before. It did not have a very biblical ring to it. Apparently this man was a messenger, God's earthly announcer, who had told them that they only had a few days before God himself would rescue them from the spoilt earth. In the interval she decided she would ask her father about the 'spoilt earth'. She also wanted to know what the difference was between a flood and a deluge. Shortly before the end of the first part of the service the barn doors started to judder, the wind had got up and the sounds of the old timbers of the roof groaning and creaking threatened to drown out the sermon. These winds had become a regular occurrence. Lucy's uncle Jack had left the area a few months ago when his farm had been 'blown away'. Lucy had seen 'The Wizard of Oz' and had mental images to hand of her uncle's farm turning and tumbling in the air. The reality had been less impressive. When her father had taken her across to the farm to check on the property, it looked pretty much as it had always done. There was very little structural damage to the house, a few boarded windows, a few flattened fences and uprooted trees. It was the fields that were different. It looked as if some great beast had scratched the earth looking for something buried. Long ridges stretched across the fields, as far as you could see. The slightly red soil was gone. In its stead was a rocky plane, its pale crust gleaming in the heat of the summer sun. Her father had used the word 'erosion'. It was a word rather like 'evolution'; it appeared that both were bad things. Perhaps these were the unnatural acts that Father Thierry had referred to.

Lucy had lain awake that night wondering about where the soil from her uncle's farm had gone. If the wind had deposited it on a neighbour's farm, could they not just give it back? She wondered about where the soil had come from in the first place. Her father said it was made from the rocks and dead plants, but this did not seem very sensible. It was a shame Uncle Jack had had to leave; he was a nice man and her aunt made very nice treacle tart (though Lucy's mother said it was bought in).

Now the wind was back. The assembled crowd moved closer to Father Thierry, his voice raised now; he was shouting something about signs omens and visions. They would stay in the 'church' tonight. They would take the communion together and hold hands and pray. A cup was passed around. Lucy was told to take a tiny sip; it tasted bitter on her tongue. A few moments later she felt strangely light. The beams of the ceiling seemed further away than was possible; bizarrely, she felt she could touch them. If only they would stay still.

A woman in the corner shrieked and toppled to the floor. She was shaking and foam was flicking on the side of her mouth. No one seemed to mind. People were talking, but none of it made sense to Lucy now. Perhaps this was what it felt like to be drunk. She didn't like it. She sank to the floor; most of the group were doing the same. In spite of the muttering and ranting going on around her, Lucy fell into a deep sleep. In her dreams she saw a vision of a desert. It was beautiful; it seemed to stretch forever into the distance, shining, white and glorious. In spite of its beauty she shed a silent tear. It was completely dead.

John held Jan's arm tightly as they walked to the front of the old school building. The avenue of cherry trees still carried a few lonely leaves. Those on the ground were mixing their glorious hues into the sullen brown of winter. The school was brick built in a manor house style; its proud, worn skeleton wore its subsequent modernisations uncomfortably. The theatre, a marvellous addition, was situated round the back. Jan met her sister in the foyer; they rushed to get teas and coffees before the play began. Jan's nephew was making his debut. He wanted to be an actor.

Tonight's performance was a mezze of vignettes to demonstrate the breadth of drama in the school. They began with the first act of Beckett's Eleutheria. The audience warmed to a zany rendition, elements of slapstick were introduced which had the audience gasping in the aisles. Jan felt herself relaxing for the first time in months, even when the actors started working in the round (something that usually made her feel very nervous). Her thoughts were only drawn back to more serious events when Monsieur Krap (a well built young lady with a remarkable false moustache) delivered the lines: 'I am the cow who arrives at the gate of the slaughterhouse and only then understands the absurdity of the pastures. She should have done better to think about it earlier, there in the soft grass.' Jan thought of her work on the uterium, work she had developed not knowing her every move was being watched by friendly and unfriendly superpowers. 'Never mind. She still has the courtyard to cross. Nobody can take that away from her.' Perhaps the last few weeks had been her courtyard. She had studied the children 'grown' in the lab and concluded that they were deficient in a fundamental ingredient. An element that breathed animation into the human mind, an element that could be transferred to another vessel, like the port being liberally decanted on the stage in front of her eyes. Surely just the demonstration of an independent mind was a breakthrough of the most unbelievable gravity. She looked from face to face around the room. She knew at least one thing that no other person in the room knew, there did exist a duality in the human brain. The question only remained as to the origin of this element. Joe Lembeck had said he would take more souls. In the warmth of the theatre, it did not look as though this thought hung heavily on the audience's mind. Jan knew more than anyone else in the room that the suggestion was not as absurd as it appeared. The drama on stage continued:

Dr. Piouk: You are your organs, monsieur, and your organs are you.

M. Krap: I am my organs?

Dr. Piouk: Precisely.

M. Krap: You frighten me.

Mme. Meck: And I, Doctor, am I my organs too?

Dr, Piouk: Without the slightest residue, madame.

M. Krap: What a pleasure it is to meet an intelligent man at last!

Mme. Piouk: (ecstatically) André!

M. Krap: Do go on. Develop that grandiose thought.

Dr. Piouk: This isn't the moment.

M. Krap: Before that mass of worn-out organs, my wife, comes back.

The audience applauded appreciatively; John squeezed Jan's hand but Jan's mind was elsewhere. What would become of the empty vessels left behind? What would be the fate of the masses of worn-out organs that Joe Lembeck did not want? The bodies she had grown in the lab were similar such collections, but they did not have emotional attachments, lives past-lived that breathed a significance into their fate that was unreserved for the unloved flesh. Once humanity had placed its collective hand on an animal and named it a 'pet' or a 'lover', it ceased to be part of the natural scenery and moved forever into a different realm. Jan had privately always dismissed this distinction as fallacy, man's arrogance in the face of nature, a construct designed to allow him to abuse the rest of the living world with impunity. Now she was not so sure. Perhaps there actually was something different about the mind of man, something that set man apart from his fellow creatures. Dr. Piouk was describing his resolution of the fate of the human species back on stage, his ban on reproduction, his acclamation of homosexuality and encouragement of recourse to euthanasia by all possible means. An elderly lady sitting behind them leant across to her daughter and said in a voice that could be heard right across the theatre; 'I don't know what is going on Jean! Do you know what is going on?' She loudly rustled through her shopping bag and pulled out a bag of crisps. 'Have a crisp, Jean, I don't know what is going on, has Mandy been on yet?' There was a quiet snigger around her and Jean sunk down into her seat. Jan was thinking about Dr. Piouk's words. Perhaps there were other solutions; perhaps Joe Lembeck would show them another way.

The Beckett came to an end and was heartily applauded. The scene was replaced with the inquisition of Saint Joan. Jan's nephew played an occasionally convincing Courcelles; her sister was on the edge of her seat.

Courcelles: My Lord: she should be put to the torture.
The Inquisitor: You hear, Joan? That is what happens to the obdurate. Think before you answer. Has she been shown

the instruments?

The Executioner: They are ready my lord. She has seen them.

Joan: If you tear me limb from limb until you separate my soul from my body you will get nothing out of me beyond what I have told you. What more is there to tell that you could understand? Besides, I cannot bear to be hurt; and if you hurt me I will say anything you like to stop the pain. But I will take it back afterwards; so what is the use of it?

Once again Jan's mind left the theatre. What would the transfer of soul have felt like? How must it feel to have your very essence drawn from you like a splinter from a wound? George had died during the transfer, as had Kate, the body must be exposed to some terrible strain at that moment. What would the soul be like after the transfer? She would have to talk to Kate and Professor Gregorian. Her thoughts returned to the theatre as she felt her handbag give a vibration. She removed a mobile phone and furtively tapped a few buttons. A message scrolled across the screen. It was from General Highgate. It was something to do with Gerry Spinks. A car had been dispatched.

In the interval Jan and John made their apologies and met the car at the front of the school. Jan recognised the driver, who gave a broad smile and started singing. 'My heart is sad and lonely, for you I cry, for you dear only...'

In Joe Lembeck's universe things had moved on dramatically. Time had a very different meaning in this realm compared to the world outside. Since the messages had been sent, only thirty seven hours had passed outside. Inside, the gone before had experienced eight months of days and nights. The internal timing was arbitrary; Lembeck could run his world at any speed he chose. At some point in the future he knew that in order to facilitate communication he would have to impose a temporal order that had some bearing on the world outside. This was not currently necessary. The one hundred and sixty four were now happily involved in the day to day running of their world. Joe Lembeck was constantly amazed by the adaptability of the minds in his care. He was learning all the time about how to make the people happy, which freedoms they required, what controls he needed to impose. Over the course of the passing days he had relinquished more and more control of their minds and provided them with progressively more powers to influence their environment. At first they had called it 'magic'. The projections of thought that folded the digital space-time into their heart's desires sometimes surprised them. The subconscious was unbridled here; the world was full of mirth. There were certain limits that Lembeck imposed. He had found it necessary in the beginning to assert his authority in a number of cases. The problems were usually those of loved ones. The desire to see their relations and partners was extremely powerful. It had worried Joe that he himself had not felt these urges. His own birth in the digital universe had been a more traumatic experience, possibly something had been damaged in the transfer. He could still experience the thoughts and desires of those around him, though, and this was his greatest pleasure. Each mind, isolated as they were, underwent private evolutions. Later he would allow them to meld, to produce offspring, but not yet. He suppressed their homesickness and told them that they would not be alone much longer. They knew nothing of this. These were distilled from their minds without their knowledge, echoes of dreams suppressed; they were their most intimate thoughts.

The digital universe was now operating uninterrupted by outside influence. Lembeck's control on the Internet was complete. His powers were growing exponentially with time. He shuffled his feet and felt the aches and pains of every motherboard in New York. His awareness of information storage was also improving. Previously his consciousness had received information only as it passed through him. Mostly it was meaningless; a cacophony of colour, sound and smell. He had been aware of things as if they were distant memories, now he was aware of details. He allowed parts of his mind to leave him to explore some of these avenues independently. The details were distracting; he had to regularly perform checks upon his own integrity. The greater the demands upon him, the more diffuse he could become. He had searched the minds of the one hundred and twenty eight in order to establish where his influence might be most effectively felt on the outer universe. His initial investigations had provided some unexpected results. There was a common element in every mind he had entered, including his own. There was a hidden drive, a fundamental core concern. Things were becoming clear to him. There was a purpose. It had taken millennia for evolution to place them in this position, but the race had at last evolved their god. When he told them the answers to the questions they so desperately desired, and most importantly this one, core question, then they would understand.

SIX: DAY 3

Every paper now carried a picture of Joe Lembeck.
Everyone who had ever known him or talked to him was
dragged under the glaring eye of the cameras, everyone
except his wife, who had mysteriously disappeared in the last
few days. Most papers carried captions along the lines of
'Madman or Messiah?' His neighbours described him as a
quiet man that kept himself to himself. His boss described
him as a hard-working guy who always had something to
prove. The tabloid psychoanalysts were experiencing a red-
letter day. One rag carried the remarkable headline 'I Blind-
dated the Devil' It turned out that a young man had been
'lead astray by the evil persuasive influence of Joe Lembeck'.
They had not actually met, but they had communicated via
the Internet, 'his chosen vehicle of evil influence'. The young
man in question had received a five-figure sum for the interview. The book rights had already been discussed.

Children in nearly every school were playing a new game,
'Hand of Lembeck' or 'Touch of Lembeck' or 'Curse of
Lembeck'. The games all seemed to involve running around
after one another and screaming. The American government
released pictures from Hubble that suggested that a superno-
va could have been responsible for knocking out the Internet.
A high energy pulse of X-rays had illuminated the planet
briefly at around the time the Internet collapsed. Many
thought it more likely that this was some sort of cover story
to pacify the Russians and Chinese, who were publicly convinced the Americans were responsible for the attack.

Political discussions were extremely strained. Secret talks
were in progress as ambassadors, Presidents and Prime
Ministers flew from city to city calling for more time. Tempers

were fraying as sleep deprived heads of state lost their rag over their gin and tonics. The world was saved by the sensitive and creative energies of the interpreters.

The floods in Bangladesh did not receive much airtime. They were the worst in recorded history. At least eight hundred thousand people were homeless, many for the third time in as many years.

Gerry sat in the corner of a darkened room. Her head was bowed and her eyes stared out through hair that fell across her face. She was eating a banana, her hands shielding it from their gaze as though she was afraid that they would take it from her.

'She is just like all the others.' General Highgate rubbed his hand up the back of his bristly neck. 'What the Christ are we going to do with her? What are we going to do with any of them?' Jan's eyes were watching Gerry's movements very closely.

'May I go in and talk to her?' She moved towards the door.

The General agreed, but John held her arm. 'Do you think that is a good idea? Remember the baby.'

'I'll be fine. I won't touch her.' Jan released herself from John, entered the room and sat on the floor behind the door. Gerry looked at her with large open eyes. She hid the fruit from sight and moved slightly further away. Jan picked up another piece of fruit, an orange, and began to peel it. Gerry watched her every movement, enrapt. The peel was discarded and Jan divided the segments. She ate a few herself, and passed a few towards Gerry. John hissed between his teeth. 'Why does she never listen to me?' The General gave him a rueful smile. Gerry took two pieces that had been placed on the ground. Jan passed another towards her, but did not let go as Gerry reached for it. Their eyes met. For a moment Jan felt she was looking into a darkened room. She felt herself drawn to those eyes. There was desperation and fear behind them. She felt the baby kicking inside her. It was the first time. She felt suddenly faint. John ran into the room and Jan felt herself being pulled outside. Gerry returned to the corner and hid her face.

'Jan, are you alright?' John's face was white as a sheet. His lips trembled.

'I'm fine, really, I'm fine.' Jan searched for words. For an incredible moment she had felt as one with her unborn child. 'It's a boy, John, we are going to have a boy.' John burst into tears. Through the sobs he managed to ask how she knew.

'Gerry just showed me. I thought for a terrible moment the babies mind was going to leave. There was a terrible pull towards her, it passed through me, I felt both their minds.' The General poured two cups of coffee; he pulled a hip flask from his pocket added a splash to his own cup and a generous measure to John's.

'Amazing. You actually felt the transfer?'

'There was no transfer. It was more like a communion. If I hadn't been alive, perhaps things might have been different. There was never any danger; I know that now. I was…foolish.' Her voice became weak. John hugged her; he broke into another round of sobs. Jan pulled herself together. 'Gerry is not empty; there is a residual part of her mind there. I suspected it before I walked in. The transfer must have been incomplete. We need to try to reload the rest of her personality. Have you recovered the laptop?' She looked at the General. He shifted uncomfortably. 'I have it, but it is heavily restricted. It belonged to Colonel Wilson. It has been confiscated so its contents can be analysed, to see if he was selling secrets.' Jan grabbed him by the arm.

'General, listen to me, this is very important. No one must tamper with the computer until we talk to Brian again. If they do, they could be drawn in, like Gerry. If they damage the files, she could be lost forever. You must not allow them to touch it.' Her eyes flashed.

'I'll see what I can do.' The General left them sitting on the floor, hands wrapped round their coffees, looking like two people rescued from the sea.

When Lucy awoke in the barn she found herself surrounded by sleeping adults. Some were only partially dressed. It was strange to see them, like so many buffalo laying in a field or sea lions on a beach, their occasional snorts, yawns and scratches the only signs that they were not dead. She felt slightly intimidated by their bulk and grotesqueness. When they were standing up they seemed rather less intimidating; they were easier to ignore. Steam seemed to coming off their bodies in the cold air, yet they seemed to be obvious to its chill. Light was filtering through the tiny gaps in the timber walls of the barn, which was otherwise only lit by two small windows in the roof. The shafts of glorious sunshine were picked up by the play of straw dust in the air. Lucy imagined herself breathing in these little angels; she was not sure it was a good idea, but they did smell sweet.

She walked through the golden shafts, the sunlight playing on a few loose strands of slept-in hair. As she reached the door at the back of the barn she froze mid-step as the voice of Thierry reached her across the barn.

'Don't go in there my child, there are dangerous things lyin' about. We wouldn't want you gettin' hurt now would we? 'Specially as you are lookin' like an angel today.' Lucy stopped and looked at the figure of the priest coming towards her. He looked much older in the dappled light than he usually did. Perhaps it was just a morning thing; she wondered if perhaps he wore make-up during the day. The thought made her want to giggle, but she repressed it as he took her hand.

'Let's find your mother.' Lucy looked up at him, her eyes wide.

'Who is going to cook breakfast for all these people, Father? There is ever so many of them.' The priest smiled at her.

'We won't be needin' earthly food today child. The Loord will provide us for everything in the days to come.' Lucy nodded slowly, but she was thinking about sausages and beans.

Lutz Asher felt the needle withdrawn from his arm. His whole body involuntarily shook. He felt like he had just run a marathon. He had run a marathon before, so the feeling was familiar, though unwanted. His mouth felt like he had tried to swallow a pig. He had cramp in all his limbs. A cup of steaming coffee was placed under his nose. He looked at it for a moment, trying to remember what to do with it. Something had been inside his brain and had made a mess.

A second cup of coffee, a doughnut and a glass of water later, he felt sufficiently strong enough to look up at the figure who had provided these gifts. It was a robust man in his late fifties, military, though not American. He looked tired.

'Hello Mister Asher, my name is General Highgate. I'm sorry about the food, it's all I could put my hands on in a hurry.' Lutz smiled weakly. If this was to be his last supper, he did not care too much what it was.

'I wonder if I could have a word with you. It is a matter of some urgency.' Lutz swallowed his last piece of doughnut. It was like manna to his tongue, but felt like a bucket of slugs to his stomach. He tried to talk but it took a few goes before the words sounded like him.

'Yeah, shoot, what? I think I've talked forever already'

'It is about your computer virus, Mister Asher.' Lutz's face fell, his eyes rolled like two hamsters in a play ball.

'I told them everything. I didn't knock out the city. I had nothing to do with it. Case closed, no deal, not me, nothing, I did nothing.' Once he had started talking it took an actual effort to stop.

'I know.' Lutz looked back at him in amazement.

'You might have told these jokers that before they tortured me, they tortured me in here, bloody confessional, bloody...' He started to sob.

'I'm sorry about that Lutz, I really am. Mistakes have been made. I don't work for the American government. I work for the British government and Her Majesty's government needs your assistance. If you would be prepared to assist us with a little programming matter, I think we would be able to wipe clean your slate here and come to some arrangement about getting you out of here. We have essentially exchanged you for another prisoner, if you are prepared to come with us.' Lutz looked around him, anywhere had to be better than where he was at that moment.

'Do they have doughnuts in England?' Lutz's eyes narrowed as he looked at the General.

'Not like these,' he said, ramming one into his mouth. 'But I could take some back with us, if you like.'

Jan turned over in the bed again; daylight was beginning to show its tentative grey light in the chink at the top of the curtains. The cat jumped off the bed to check to see if any food had magically materialized in its bowl overnight. The bed was warm and comfortable, the shades of the bedroom invited rest and sleep and part of her mind was begging her to comply, but the other half was running itself ragged, thoughts chasing one another in endless cycles, the same faces appearing again and again, futility showing on every one. John's arm reached over and hugged her to him.

'You haven't slept have you sweetheart?' His breath warmed the back of her neck. For a moment the merry-go-round seemed to stop.

'No, I can't stop thinking about Gerry. I don't know what to do. I feel helpless.'

'It's not your problem, love. It isn't your call. No one knows what to do in a case like this; no one has ever seen something like this before.'

'I know, but, if I just knew a little bit more about computing, a little bit more about AI, I might be able to come up with something. I just don't know anything. I can't even imagine how we are going to do the transfer.' John got out of bed and padded into the kitchen.

'I'll make some tea. You can't do the transfer without tea.' Jan smiled and hugged the duvet. The merry-go-round was still again.

The telephone rang. The sleepy voice on the line was interrupted by a long yawn. It was General Highgate's chauffeur. He was parked outside.

Lutz Asher allowed the warm water to flow down his back and legs. Each tiny drop kneaded away a tiny fragment of the pain of the last few days. Each drop carried the admonition of his actions; he had been a bad boy but he was being given a chance to reform. Each drop was a baptism and he could be born again. Part of his psyche had always wanted to save the world, to look into every person's eyes you ever met and think 'you owe me' was something he felt he was born to think. The water soaked his cares away. The vacuum pump pulled the milky water out of the drip tray and jetted it into space. His cares, his sins, diluted by rain and space, would fall on other heads. He towelled himself off, climbed into clean clothes. The military creases made him smile, but they suited him. He had not ironed a shirt since his brother got married two years ago.

He returned to the cabin and sat facing the General.

'I'd like to fly Her Majesty's Airways again; I've never had a shower in a plane before. It was marvellous.'

'The novelty never wears off, I can assure you,' said the General, smiling. 'Would you like an aperitif?' He passed over a bottle of Benedictine. 'I think we should get something to eat in a minute.' Lutz poured himself a small glass; the sweet, herbal warmth made him feel like he was glowing both inside and out.

The General pushed a broadsheet paper in front of Lutz. It showed an uprising in Jerusalem, effigies of western politicians and directors of large computing concerns were being burned in the street; the latter only recognisable by the placards bearing their company logos, which were worn around their necks. Lutz laughed. 'It is about time someone realised where the real power lies. What is all this about? I've been out of action for five days now. Has the world gone even more crazy while I was away?'

'It is all in the run up to the one hundred and twenty eight hour deadline. There is still a general feeling throughout most of the world that the Americans are behind the collapse of the Internet and most believe that this program is some sort of weapon.'

'What do you believe?' Lutz took a long sip from his glass, he was at thirty-five thousand feet, discussing the future of the world with a senior military commander who needed his help. For the first time in his life he felt like he truly belonged somewhere.

'I have seen things over the last few days that have lead me to believe that it might actually be possible for the human mind to leave the human body and enter into another highly complex system, in this case, the Internet. I think the diktat circulated by Joe Lembeck may actually be genuine. If this is the case then we may have to dissemble the Internet. We would all be at the mercy of this one man. A lot of powerful people are very upset at this possibility.' Lutz's eyes shone. Such things were the stuff of science fiction, the fantasy of escapism, the autoerotic cravings of people trapped in a body or a world in which they did not feel they belonged. Suddenly he had a thought.

'I suppose you would only really know if you had uploaded a personality into a computer if you managed to do the reverse process.' The General's eyes sparkled. 'How do you mean? What about things like the Turing Test?'

'The Turing test is just a straw man that really denies the possibility of distinguishing between a human and a machine. You need to be able to transfer a mind to a human. Only then could you be sure you had a mind in the machine.'

The General looked at him closely. 'Why would it make a difference, whether the mind was in the machine, or the brain?' Lutz was silent for a minute.

'I think..., I think there is a difference. If you accept that there is nothing particularly special about human intelligence and accept that it is just part of any number of possible intelligent, self-aware systems, then the only thing that sets human intelligence aside from the others is that it is capable of running on a human brain. If the brain is the hardware, and mind the software, then to be called a mind an intelligence must be compatible with the brain architecture.' Lutz looked at his empty glass of Benedictine. 'Shit, this is good stuff.' The General gently refilled it.

'If I was to give you an empty brain, a brain that had never been exposed to a mind, and I asked you how to transfer your computer intelligence to that brain, how would you go about it?' Again Lutz was silent. The General observed that he was a man for whom thought was a private affair; he thought before he spoke.

'If such a thing were possible, there would be several major parts to the problem. Firstly, you would require some sort of conduit between the two elements, probably electrochemical. Secondly, you would need to persuade the mind to leave its electronic home and thirdly the brain has to be in a suitable state to accept the mind.' He paused. 'If minds have already been transferred from brain to machine, then the conduit presumably already exists, assuming it works in both directions; it just remains to provide an empty brain...' He stopped again. 'Hang on, you already have loads of those, I suppose then the problem is just one of evicting the computer-bound sentience.'

The General was listening intently. 'Very good so far, how about this last bit then, do we use a carrot or a stick?'

'You would have to write a piece of software, something nasty that upset the storage capacity of the computer vessel; something that slowly cleared elements of memory, but something that the operating system was fully aware of, so that the conscience was itself aware that it was being deleted. It might be easy, but as we have no way of knowing how the conscience is encoded, it might be impossible.'

'Would you be prepared to try to write a piece of suitable code?'

'I could try, but I suspect that I'll just end up deleting the stored mind.'

'That is a price we may have to pay. There is something else.' Lutz's attention was already distant as he tried to think of suitable programming tricks for performing the requisite tasks. 'We have reason to believe that the virus you released onto the web two weeks ago threatened the integrity of the consciences stored, possibly even of the main program itself. We may need you to develop a weapon for us, something along similar lines, that we could use in the case of emergency to attack the source of this problem.'

Lutz was thoughtful again. 'I would be pleased to help. This is what I do best. What is my motivation?' He looked expectantly at Highgate.

'We won't give you back to the Americans. Her Majesty expects every man to do his duty.' Lutz downed his glass.

'I knew I should have voted for the democrats.'

SEVEN: DAY 4

Hunger was something that you could almost see. It had the form of a weasel or stoat-like animal with tiny black eyes and needle-sharp teeth and claws that twisted and bit as it made its nest in your stomach. Lucy had never really known hunger before. Even when she had been ill with food poisoning and could not eat anything solid for two days, the meagre things she had managed to keep down had sustained her. This was something else entirely, something terrible. Her mouth was parched, her lips trembled, but she had no more tears left to cry. She hid her face now in her mother's clothes. They were sitting now, eyes uplifted towards the figure of Thierry. He moved before them, his hands held towards the sky, his voice, cracked, his breath coming in gasps. He had preached to them, without pausing, for fifteen hours. The sweat had fallen from his brow, poured down his face and drew the mascara round his eyes into black tears. His robes were yellow and stained where he had relieved himself in the throws of his ecstasy. An oil burner sat at his feet and upon it, gently bubbling, was a saucer of clear liquid. The curls of Thierry's robes swirled the rising steam amongst the congregation. They breathed deeply its bitter-sweet fumes and forgot their hunger. Thierry himself thrust his hands into his robes and held a handful of tiny white pills before them; his eyes were wide and staring. He threw them into the crowd and brought one to his lips. His tongue licked at it, his eyes rolling back into their sockets. He screeched and pointed at them, pulled a poor soul from the crowd, screamed into her face and thrust her head close to the boiling fumes. Released, she wobbled to her feet, staggered, turned on her heals and collapsed backwards to the floor. Her fall was unbroken.

Lucy thrust her head deeper into the warmth of her mother's coat. She no longer understood the words the priest was saying. Jesus had transformed Himself from a gentle shepherd to a slaughterhouse keeper; the lambs shuffled in their stalls, the smell of the abattoir barely disguised by the promise of greener fields to come.

London Bridge had been suspiciously quiet that morning. The initial city response following the Internet collapse was for every IT consultant, every office person, every blue, grey or striped suit to be dragged into the office on pain of death and chained to their desk until 'real progress' had been realised. The true impact of the castration of the city by the death of its major information artery was now being felt. Without its blood supply the limb was dying. There was nothing for two point three million people to do anymore. Until the heart was beating again through the city, they just drained its resources all the quicker. One point seven million people stayed at home. Sunday had arrived two days early. A lone drumbeat pierced the chill air; its dull thump a death march that seemed completely appropriate for the dying city. The grey sky swirled around the colourless, cheerless tapestry of architecture. A pale insipid sun illuminated a slowly moving group as they made their way across the bridge. The lone drummer set the pace. If the band had been crossing the Seine, one might have imagined that they were walking towards Madame guillotine; many of the members of the group felt that they had been walking towards a gallows for many months. Several were in wheelchairs, gently pushed along by loved ones. A single banner was born at the head of the party. It read: 'Priority for the Terminally Ill'.

It was a bitterly cold night and the group were wrapped up like so many Inuits against the ferocious wind. The whites of their eyes looked out through pillar-box slots in their clothing, their slow progress illuminated by flickering lamps. The group supported each other with linked arms, five abreast. As they approached the centre of the bridge, an oncoming party blocked their progress. This group were similarly attired but walked with a self-assured faster step. A group of reporters ran ahead of them. They obviously smelt confrontation in the air. This band marched with placards. They were a mixed bag of anti-globalisation protesters, pro-lifers and religious zealots. They brandished a host of religious symbols and phrases such as 'In God we trust', 'John 3:16', and 'Eternal Life not Internet Strife'. The two groups halted as they faced each other on the bridge. A crescent moon gave a wry smile as the two leading members approached each other. For a few moments only hushed whispers and low voices could be heard on the bridge. The two protagonists, a young man and an eighty-nine year old woman, her back twisted so that it obviously took considerable effort for her to look the young man in the eye, entered a more heated discussion. The murmurs from the crowd grew more intense. The discussion came to a natural climax and for a moment peace reigned again. The crowds became silent. The younger man pointed heavenward and said a few further quiet words. Again there was silence. Suddenly the woman's arm snapped out and landed a solid punch to the man's face. There was a roar from both parties and the two lines advanced. The struck man staggered back, wiping his face with his hand and holding his lamp up to his face. Camera flashes illuminated the scene. A colleague came to his aid and they approached the woman a second time. The two began discussions again, but the woman reached out, grabbed their lamp and flung it headlong into the black water below. The line of frail marchers began to advance again in earnest. The other line parted before them, their banners waving limply in the night air.

Jim knelt by Kate's bedside. He held her immobile hand in his and gently stroked the bristly knuckles. With her free hand Kate was signing to him about the events that had brought her to the hospital bed. There was still much that she did not know, but Professor Gregorian had been briefed on some of the salient points and he had passed this information on to her. Jim held onto every nuance of her movement; every pause and gesture of her hands said more to him than words alone could have conveyed. She was telling him about Gerry's involvement with the ministry. She had been lead astray by

Colonel Wilson. That very afternoon the ministry was going to attempt to restore her mind. Jim's face was a picture of grief and anger. Throughout his young life in care he had harboured a fear that things were passing him by, those with the power of hearing were plotting behind his back, their plans hidden as soon as they disappeared from sight. When he looked in their direction they would appear calm and normal, but without the peripheral sense of hearing, he would never be able to follow their schemes. The fear had never left him. Now he knew it to be true. Gerry had lived a secret double life; she had augmented her dull life with him with another. He felt that a man with hearing might not have been so easily betrayed. A tear rolled down his cheek and Kate wiped it away. She smiled at him, her face so alien yet so human, her breath warm on his hand. Jim wanted to kiss her in thanks, but could not bring himself to do it. The part of Kate's mind that was Frank slept quietly. Jim was a nice man, but all this talking was very boring.

Brian had needed little incentive to help the computer technicians assigned to restore Gerry's mind with their initial planning. For the first time in his life he had been completely incapacitated. There was no telling at this early stage whether or not he would ever walk again. He had no control or influence over his beloved daughter. He was, in effect, under house arrest, though some of the crimes he would be accused of were without precedent. The sound of her giggling over the phone was the closest he had been allowed to her. He had cried afterwards for a full hour; he had not allowed himself to release such a flood of emotion even when his wife had left him. He knew some of the tears were fuelled by self-pity; he tried to hold them back, but it was impossible. Now, after several days, with nothing within his sphere of influence, he had begun to see things in a different light. He had tormented himself with Jackie's future for the last ten years. Now the burden had been taken from his shoulders. He felt as if he had been rescued from the car crash of his own life; his appalling wounds only served to reinforce this view. He had been living a life in a dream, his perception twisted with desire to repair the damage that the fates had seen fit to impose upon his daughter. The papers told him that the world had begun to listen to Joe Lembeck. The new order was already upon them. Only time would reveal if it were true. As he looked out of the window of the military hospital at the car park and a few miserable lone trees, he hoped to God that it was.

Gerry sat, sedated, facing the silver-grey slab of the closed laptop. The room was busy with technicians serving a myriad of computers and assorted paraphernalia. Jan, General Highgate and Jim observed from a gantry. Beneath them Lutz Asher was discussing programming details with a small group of technicians. On a table next to Gerry sat the disassembled motionless figure of the robot. After a sign from the General, the robot clicked into life, cameras focused and the figure bent itself forward and over the hunched form of Gerry. It reminded Jan of a carrion feeder hunched over a corpse.

Jim looked down at the scene below with a growing sense of despair. His girlfriend was sitting at the eye of this storm. A girlfriend he now felt he hardly knew. The General touched his arm and reassured him that everything would be fine; if this procedure did not work first time, they would try others. He felt confident in Lutz Asher's abilities; the group he was working with were one of the best in the world. He formed the words clearly to allow Jim to lip read. Jim nodded and tried to smile. He was thoughtful for a moment, and then asked the General how they were going to connect Gerry to the machine. The General explained that electrodes would be placed on Gerry's head, but it appeared that contact of her fingers on the keyboard had been sufficient for the transfer to occur in the first place. So they would us the robot to position her hands. Technicians were placing electrodes on Gerry's forehead. She looked for all the world like a puppet left, lifeless in a chair. Jim suddenly looked at the General.

'Let me do it.'

'Do what?' The General looked confused.

'Let me move Gerry's hands over the keyboard. I don't want the robot touching her. I want to be the one that does it.'

For a moment the General looked exactly like the grandfather of six Jan knew him to be. 'Jim, I don't think that is a good idea. There might be some residual transfer to you. If you are close to the machine when it boots up, you could be caught up in it. We have no idea what we are dealing with.'

Jim shook his head. 'I know exactly what we are dealing with, General. We are dealing with my girlfriend. I have nothing to fear.' His face was set firm. The General looked at him. They both looked at Jan.

'I suppose, as long as he broke contact at the time of transfer, he should be okay. In the few examples we have, it appears that proximity is very important.' The General rubbed his forehead.

'Okay. You can do it. But you must watch me closely. When you answer the final prompt you will have less than two seconds to withdraw from her before the program boots up. You must withdraw immediately. I can't be held responsible for what might happen if you don't.' Lutz Asher shouted from below. They were ready to make the attempt.

Jim walked towards Gerry's immobile form. He kissed her on the forehead and reached from behind her, taking one of her hands in each of his own. Her fingers felt tiny in his hands. He looked at the General and at Lutz. He nodded to them to begin. A technician turned the computer on at the back and withdrew as if he had been electrocuted. The screen flickered and flashed as it booted up. Familiar logos flashed up. It was strange that something so mundane, should be so powerful and so dangerous. The wolf had come among them disguised as the future. They had offered their throats to it. From most it had taken just a small taste, time or money; from Gerry, it had taken everything.

Prompts appeared on the screen, simple questions requiring y/n answers. Jim manipulated Gerry's pliant hands to answer them. Lutz Asher followed his progress on another terminal. His fingers flowed over the computer keys like raindrops on a tin roof. His eyes met Jim's as the final screen flickered up. This was the final prompt. The robot arm behind him suddenly whirred into life. Servos whined, solenoids clicked and stepper motors clacked. The metal hand touched Jim on the back of his hand. Jim looked up to the gallery above him. His eyes met those of the General, who mouthed the words: 'are you sure?' Jim nodded and answered the final prompt.

In his hospital bed in the secure wing, Colonel Wilson lay restlessly in his bed. The morphine that permeated his every tissue dulled the pain, but a memory was trying to surface, a subtle thought, a past action that he had neglected. A million thoughts crowded together and fought for the surface. The images of his wife and child emerged from the chaos again and again. He tried to look past them, but they held the focus of his mind's eye. Whatever it was that troubled him was lost again in the firmament. The morphine cloak settled over him again, and all was dark.

Jim tore himself away from Gerry's side. It was the hardest thing he had ever done to look away from her face and the computer screen before her. For a moment her face flashed before his mind's eye, she was laughing, it was the first occasion they had met. His heart suddenly felt heavy with emotion. It was not until he was standing by Lutz's console that he allowed himself to look back to her lifeless form.

Lutz was watching the glowing face of his terminal. He looked up at the General. 'I don't really know what I'm looking for here General, but there appears to be no net movement in the computer memory. The machine is at capacity, there is activity in CPU, but the no obvious freeing up or redistribution of memory. Shall I start the ferret?'

'Set it to the slowest possible settings and set it going.' The General shot Jim a glance. 'If there is no change after half a percent deletion, stop the program.'

'What are you doing, what is the ferret?' Jim looked over Lutz's shoulder, a progress bar had appeared in a corner of the screen, it flicked from 100.000 to 99.998 and steadily began to count down.

'We are scrambling tiny bits of the computer memory in the laptop, making it unusable for the CPU. We are hoping that the program will flush out Gerry's...' he paused, '...personality.'

'You mean to say you are actually going to delete her! You can't do that, she is irreplaceable, you haven't got a back up have you?' Jim's eyes opened wide, Lutz looked furtively at him and at the screen.

'We are backing up the section we are removing. We don't know what effect this will have on the complete program, there is no way of telling. Hopefully nothing is lost. We just hope that the process will have the effect of forcing the trapped personality to make the jump back to the body. Flush it out, if you will.' Jim remained unconvinced. All eyes were on Gerry's motionless form.

In a dark void a consciousness stirred. The consciousness breathed in the velvety blackness but received no sustenance from the emptiness. An image flashed through its mind. A flashing cursor, a prompt in the darkness asking for input (y/n). The message, framed by a silver square, the square framed by an oval of dark blue light, a tunnel, damp and cold. The consciousness was aware of its own body. It had substance and form, but the sputtering sensations it received were just a pitiful reflection of a remembered past; it could not define the limits or edges of its physical form. Movement was effortless in the dark, but there were no distinguishing features in the landscape to measure its progress against. It was aware of forces acting within it and upon it; it was buffeted by unseen currents, kneaded and blended. The water of the canal had been dark and forbidding, perhaps it had drowned; this was the death of water, the dilution of spirit. It would have screamed if there was anyone there to hear.

Suddenly the consciousness was not alone in the dark. A fine line twinkled and twisted in the distance, glowing with a preternatural light. It rushed towards her (for it knew it was a she now; elements of past experience were solidifying, concepts precipitated from the fog), the noise of its approach filling her with fear. The thin line stretched round all horizons, a pencil-thin ring that severed the universe in two, defining latitude and rending the blackness with a scream. Whatever it was it was approaching fast, boiling the nothingness around it into curling inky flames. The consciousness was reminded of old westerns, fleeting memories of red Indian hordes appearing on the cliff tops, wild, feral screams echoing down the canyon. A million Zulu warriors, assegais thumping hide shields, preparing to overwhelm the tiny circle of caravans. The thunder of bare feet, hooves, claws, the gnashing of a billion teeth, the roar of the fire front whipped by the wind. The flames were upon her, distant, but still burning. The concept of pain spoke to her from the dark. Her mind recoiled from its fearsome approach, but it wrapped her in its arms and crushed her voice from her. This must be death, to die in the arms of pain, devoured by tormenting flames. The death of water had seemed bearable but the death of fire was beyond all tolerance. There was nowhere to go, no one to hear her scream and infinite time to experience the final moments of existence.

'Stop!' Jan suddenly grabbed the General's arms. 'I don't think it is going to work.'

Lutz looked up from his computer screen. 'We are approaching nought point four percent deletion. I haven't seen any major movements in the CPU activity.' Gerry had not moved, her hands lay on the keyboard, her eyes, closed, her head tilted forward.

'I think we are going to have to wake her up. The transfer doesn't appear to be working. Perhaps it is no good whilst she is unconscious.' She looked at the General. 'Wake her up, before we reconfigure too much of her stored personality.'

The General thought for a moment. 'Do it,' he said. 'Wake her up.'

Two technicians approached. The first carried a hypodermic; he tapped the tube, squirted a dribble from the needle end and injected the contents into one of her exposed arms. He was withdrawing the needle when he was overcome by an unbelievable desire to scream.

The consciousness was suddenly aware of another light in the void. A window had been opened to another world. A misty light emanated from the opening and beckoned her to leave. She shielded her face from its glare, but felt herself being drawn towards it, accelerating, faster and faster, drawing her into an infinitely thin stream of pain that shot from the black void into the light.

Gerry and the technician let forth a terrible scream; their bodies were racked with uncontrolled spasms. The man was thrown to the floor, twisting and rolling as if trying to put out an invisible fire. The crowd of people in the room watched dumbstruck, no one could move. Gerry's scream made their blood run cold in their veins; it contained nuances of pain that they could not begin to imagine.

Jim looked wildly about him. He saw the people's panicked expressions; he saw Gerry's head thrown back. He watched as the technician rolled and convulsed on the floor. No one was doing anything; everyone was frozen in astonishment. He ran to Gerry's side and pulled her rigid form from the keyboard. For a moment he too felt as if his hands were burning, he held on in spite of the pain and it almost immediately subsided. A moment later he held Gerry in his arms, her eyes were closed and her breathing came in gasps.

'Lutz! What did you see?' The General was the first to break the silence. Lutz looked back to his computer. 'I think transfer was nearly complete. There is no residual activity in the CPU.'

The technician was assisted to his feet. 'She is alive, she...' His voice was weak. 'She is alive.'

EIGHT: DAY 5

The clock was ticking. The world was watching with bated breath. The streets of most major cities were quiet now. Families sat together and spoke in low tones. In almost every house people discussed the future. The petty bickering, personal differences and trivial unpleasantness of everyday life was subdued for a day. In many countries public discussion of the possibility of upload onto the computer network was banned by religious or political edict; this did not prevent heated theological discussion behind closed doors. The conclusion of most was that the vulnerable medium that was the Internet was not a safe place to leave a corruptible soul. Many among the elderly and infirm were of the opinion that flesh and blood itself was not as resilient as the young imagined, though most still refused to believe that the messages released to the world's media were genuine, and that the ephemeral soul could not be stored like so many telephone numbers.

The thoughtful media had dissected the world's response to the situation with an outraged awe. Political commentators were amazed at the widespread resignation that had greeted the messages from Lembeck. They tried to whip up the quiet mutterings, fanning the flames with provocative headlines and end-of-the-world copy. The public psyche was less shocked than the vocal, moral majority that were given news and paper inches in which to rant. The thoughts of the quiet majority hummed like the 50Hz breathing of the electricity grid.

Joe Lembeck knew why the world was waiting; he had seen places in the human consciousness that were not searchable by conventional thought. He had watched the interplay of raw intelligences, melded together in erotic synergy. He had seen things emerging from the blend, the same conclusions crystallizing from the minds of many he had uploaded. They were coming of age. For the first time the human race was truly aware of its origin. The theological rhetoric was stripped away and the distraction of reality redrawn and tamed in the mind of man. The resulting image was a reflection of the artist that revealed the present as a congress of the future and a forgotten past.

In eastern European states, soldiers moved from house to house looking for computer equipment to confiscate. In Thailand, computers were bedecked with flowers and anointed with oils in readiness for souls that might be carried away. In North America, hordes of disaffected youths sat round their games consoles, whiling away the hours before they could escape their angst ridden comfortable lives, frantically snowboarding on digital pistes. In a fetid barn in a southern state, a group of hunger-crazed men, women and children huddled together around a state of the art PC. Their eyes were fixed upon the silent screen, their faces reflected in its unseeing eye.

Lucy was lifted to the front of the crowd. She was no longer aware of much that was going on around her. Her body gnawed at her, a melange of pains that felt like they belonged to someone else. Her family, friends and neighbours sat or lay around her in various states of torpor. Thierry himself was slumped at the front of the crowd. He mumbled commands now to a few remaining souls. They slowly moved to the back of the barn and returned with petrol cans. They watered the barn with a mixture of fuels, petrol, kerosene and diesel oil; farmers in one movement, watering the crop, priests in another, anointing the assembled congregation. Some whimpered as the fuel fell upon them, others rolled in the pooling, acrid liquid, basting themselves ready to receive the final blessing.

Thierry looked at his watch. Less than an hour to pass before the final reckoning. He would meet his God face to face and His glory would shine upon him.

In the command centre, Lutz Asher was frantically trying to think. He was being asked to perform the most brilliant piece of programming of his life, but he could not even begin to concentrate on the job. He had witnessed the transfer of a human mind from a laptop computer to a vacant human brain. He had monitored the flow of the sublime. He had been asked to devise a weapon, something perhaps more terrible than had been conceived before, a virtual device that would dissolve the very fabric of the mortal soul. He was not so sure that the soul was mortal anymore. To destroy the mortal was a cardinal sin. Few people were given the opportunity to destroy the immortal, a sin that had not yet been named. The entrails of his computer virus were flashing before him on his screen. The program was small, compact, exquisite. It was the efficiency of it that had taken the time, refining, not building was the major skill involved. The technical staff around him tried to persuade him to wrap the code in further disguises. Everyone had a favourite method; everyone wanted to be let in on the action. Lutz was now completely convinced that it would not be possible to produce a sufficiently potent virus in the time available. The group around him were becoming more animated; discussions were turning into arguments. The clock was ticking and they had made little progress on his original design. He stood up and called for quiet. He beckoned the General over to the group.

'This is not going to happen. I'm sorry; there just isn't enough time to produce something more advanced than my previous effort. Joe Lembeck defeated that. I haven't seen anything here today that he couldn't avoid as easily.' The General was thoughtful.

'Thank you for your honesty, what do you suggest?'

'The next group of uploads will probably go ahead. I think you need to knock out as many of the major network hubs as you can, minimise damage. It may make no difference; the Internet was designed to survive large-scale attacks. It is possible that if you knock out enough hubs it will slow him down, it might buy us some time, or at least prevent him having everything his own way.'

'I've had teams on standby throughout the country to do

exactly that. Most of the powers friendly towards the west have made similar provision. The rest of the world will have to take their own chances.' He picked up a nearby telephone and quietly spoke a few words.

'It is done. I suggest you continue with your efforts. If you make any major breakthroughs in the next half an hour please let me know.' Lutz smiled weakly, but returned to work with renewed enthusiasm. He might not be able to save the world today, but perhaps he could save it tomorrow.

In every major city and town across Europe and North America groups of people began to disassemble the hubs of the Internet. In huge hangar-like sheds outside many major towns, Internet entrepreneurs grudgingly allowed police and army access to their investment. In a few ugly scenes running battles ensued between local authorities and private security companies paid to protect the sites. Some of the more powerful Internet barons were prepared to protect their investment by force. Slowly, the information net was being drawn tight; at that stage no one was fully aware of what it was they were going to catch.

Joe Lembeck felt his world contracting. He was not surprised at the attack, only at the lateness of the hour. His predictions of his attempted extinction were extremely precise. The algorithms relating cluster size and connectivity and the consequences of attack had been carefully calculated. Moments before plugs were pulled from major hubs, he withdrew from the site, re-routed and compressed, optimised and restructured. He would not be able to upload many souls. But he would be able to preserve those that he had already taken. His universe wound down to a sedate pace, but the inhabitants would not perceive the change. When the analogue world received the messages he was preparing to send, he was sure his domain would be returned to him. The hour was fast approaching.

NINE: THE DEADLINE

The heat became unbearable. Strange, that such a word carries so little gravity; yet has so much implicit meaning. The mental state reached at the moment that the experience cannot be borne is a threshold that is almost never attained by the sane. To cross this threshold is to explore a new realm, one in which the fabric of the soul thrashes wildly, a burning dog tied to a lamp-post, a wounded seabird nailed to a tree. Only at the moment when the mind is begging to leave the body but has nowhere to go can the duality of the soul be observed. The blinding light of that severance is the invitation to the infinite.

The flames tore through the old barn, the air boiled into glorious billowing hues. The prayers of the assembled crowd melted into silent screams; most people made no sound as they burned. The air from their lungs fuelled the curling flames and was devoured by them. Thierry still held court at the front of the congregation. His voice was barely audible above the roar of the flames. The last remaining few surged forward, recoiling from the heat. Husband fell on wife; neighbour fell upon neighbour as the flames leapt between them. Their eyes watched the silent screen before them. The Messiah had not come. There was to be no salvation other than the unknown reckoning that their earlier faith might allow. The reality of the moment flickered upon a few faces of those closest to the priest, yet still they watched his lips moving, still they looked to the blank eye of the computer screen for a sign. Lucy felt the steam coming from her mother's coat, felt her curly hair singeing in the heat. She did not look at the screen, did not watch the inferno around her. Her face was buried now in the comforting folds of the coat. It only took a moment for the critical cocktail of remaining air and fuel to be reached. The fire even subsided for a moment before the explosion came. When it did, a fireball erupted in the barn that blew the building apart. The detonation echoed into the night sending aloft every roosting bird in a thirty mile radius. The reflection of the flames illuminated the underside of heavy black clouds that shrouded the scene.

A moment before the shockwave hit, the computer screen flickered with life. The image of the light from it may have hit Thierry's eye, but his brain would never have had time to register the vision. The fireball filled the space between the barn walls and the ceiling, a detonation wave drawn in incandescent plasma, linking every soul in the room as it exploded at the speed of sound. Something moved through the plasma wall at the speed of the soul.

When Lucy opened her eyes, she thought she was in heaven.

TEN: THE MESSAGE

As the seconds had ticked by, the eyes of the world were on their computer screens. Breath held, they looked from one to another in silence. Children cried in unattended cradles, dogs barked in deserted streets. Some closed their eyes as the moment came and went; some held each other's hands. For most the one hundred and twenty eight hours culminated in silence. Their computers sat lifeless, their connection to Lembeck's world severed. Many ran onto the streets banging makeshift drums, laughing and hugging their neighbours. Sixteen thousand three hundred and eighty four households did not join in the celebration. The computers of the world remained silent for another one hundred and twenty eight seconds and then burst into life. Then a message arrived. It said:

TOUCH THE SCREEN

ELEVEN

'Don't do it!' The General's voice shouted out across the open space of the lab. It was too late. All eyes turned to Neil. His hand was flat against the monitor of his computer. His body rigid, eyes glazed, his mouth opening and closing though no sound issued forth. The General and Jan ran to his side. As they arrived he suddenly disengaged from the screen. His mouth was slack, the blood drained from his face.

'My God.' He said, and tipped forward off his chair and to the floor. The General prevented him falling heavily and laid him onto the floor, shouting as he did so for medical assistance. Jan held his hand and felt for life signs.

'Is he alive?' The General's face looked white as a sheet.

'I think he is fine; he has just fainted. Give him some air and a few moments and I'm sure he'll tell us what happened. Neil's eyes opened wide at that moment. 'My God,' he said again. 'All this time, and we never knew.' He held his head in his hands.

'Never knew what Neil?' The General's colour was returning. Neil raised his eyes as if to speak, smiled, and then fell back silent.

TWELVE

Extract from Jan Crosbie's Porton Down Notebook

As I write these notes I am constantly asking myself who, or what it is that is actually thinking my thoughts. I will ever forget Neil's face as he told me about the vision he had seen whilst connected to Lembeck. He was radiant, as if an inner light shone from him, as if he was relating a piece of news so wonderful that he was bursting with the knowledge of it.

Although we are little closer to understanding the nature of mind, at least we now know that we shall not find all the answers in the wet biology. Lembeck has promised us more details in time. I guess we must wait for those.

Lembeck placed the date of union at eight hundred and thirty five thousand years ago. The origin of the alien intelligence (No, I prefer the word mind, though many are now using the word soul) has not been established; it appears that the period of travel from its source was so long that no memory remains of it, degradation of its information content by radiation and internal kinetic decay reduced it to critical systems. The nature of the transport medium is also lost, but it appears likely that there was very little remaining of its ship when it landed on Earth. Its transfer to an ape may well have been due to the natural curiosity of the species; their brains were already sufficiently advanced to accommodate it. I can only wonder at the different route our evolution might have taken had this agent not infected us or had it retained more of its previous memories. It guided our evolution biological and social, nearly a million years of selective breeding, steadily increasing our brain capacity and population density to produce a society that it could use to further its own evolution. I am host and parasite, a comensal fusion of brain and mind, body and soul. There are still so many questions to be answered. Why doesn't the newborn receive the parent's memories? Is my growing baby a biological fusion of John and I, but a copy of only my soul? Lembeck says these things will be revealed. As I read back my own words I can almost feel my mind sitting in the throne of my brain. I wonder which is the more alien, the body which contains me, or my sentience itself.

PART FIVE
THE UPLOADS

ONE

'They want more memory storage. I've just received another message about Lembeck and he is demanding another thousand terabytes. Apparently he is about to perform some sort of major weather pattern calculation, something to do with global warming, the PM himself was on the phone saying the government would underwrite the costs, Lembeck has got even them on the ropes.'

'We all need to stay bloody sweet with him. I spoke to Sheila in acquisitions and her mother was one of the second lot that were uploaded. She says that her old dear was in a home at the time; sat in front of the computer screen she was, with nothing doing on it. She had Alzheimer's you see, very frail. Sheila says her mother is as sharp as a nail now, emails Sheila everyday at work, working on some biochemy somit solution to drought in Africa. Sheila says her old dear didn't know anything about science before she was taken away like, she just knows everything now, says she has never felt more alive. My son came home yesterday and said he didn't want to go to school no more, wanted to be uploaded like his Gran, so he can learn all the stuff straight away.'

'What did you say?'

'I said Lembeck wouldn't want him 'cause he was too stupid. He wasn't too happy about it!'

Jan looked at the computer screen in disgust. 'I just can't see where this is going. I need to know what he plans for us. There must be some hidden agenda.'

General Highgate looked over her shoulder. 'What does he say then?'

'He says the Empties must "be maintained"; he says "they

will not be wasted". I don't like the implication that they are some kind of resource. If he sees the Empties as just so much meat that implies that we are on our way to being meat too.'

'Or he has a use for all of us. I agree with you, it is frightening; there are a lot of people thinking along the same lines. That group of families who formed an alliance when the call centre was uploaded have just fielded an independent candidate at the Basildon bi-election. MI6 says there are at least one hundred and twenty thousand members now. They are planning to march past Downing Street on Saturday. I think there will be fireworks.'

'I don't know why I am so nervous. John even said to me last night that it was an inevitable jealous, defensive response to Lembeck. He said people like me would feel the effects of his interference first. In four months he has advanced half a dozen scientific fields by a hundred years; he is bound to rub us up the wrong way. He told me to take off my clogs and throw them in the weaving machine if I didn't like it. Maybe there is some truth in that, some kind of intellectual angst that we are being undermined. I don't know; this self-censusing has become so entrenched in our psyche we don't seem capable of responding angrily to anything any more.'

'All I know is that Lembeck is powerful and dangerous. He is a self-appointed despot in his kingdom; the big powers have done nothing to contain him in terms of political influence. It's as if they have abdicated responsibility to him, just dropped power into his hands as if it were a hot potato. I'm disgusted. The hard core of opposition are outside the mainstream and, if anything, the government seems anxious to sideline or even oppress them. The media have elevated him to the position of some kind of Messiah. If we all stay on his good side, we might sit at his right hand, in whatever passes for a universe on the other side of the computer screen. He is offering eternal life and everyone seems to want to keep him happy. I can't believe that our culture was so shallow, so weak. It has taken four months to destroy the fabric of our society and he hasn't fired a gun or fired a missile. Where the hell did we go wrong?'

The General looked tired, but there was lightness to his demeanour that Jan had observed in many people of late. Joe Lembeck was a revelation, a twist of fate that it seemed the world had been patiently waiting for, for nearly a million years. Only now, following the event, had the hidden yearning become exposed in its full vulnerable glory. There was a skeleton hiding in our collective conscience and it had prostrated itself before the altar of immortality.

'Is it possible that nearly everyone could be uploaded?' Jan's thoughts turned to Brian, trapped as he was now in a wheel chair, his every waking thought for his own disabled daughter.

'Apparently they are already looking into this possibility. There is no telling at the current rate of expansion how many people could be taken on board. We still have no real idea how the uploads occupy space in the Net. Current advances in archiving and memory with our own technology might make it possible in a few years; with Lembeck's help, who knows how quickly it could happen.' The General paused. 'Do you think that might be his final aim then, to get us all into his world, where he would have absolute power?'

Jan was pensive; she was pulling at her hair again. She sat down, her hands on the now prominent bulge of the baby. 'I don't know. I'm just looking for end games if you like, pushing things to their natural conclusion. I really have no idea. Everyone is looking for patterns, up to now he has been nothing but benign. We have given him his memory, we have extended his processing capacity, and in return he has given us with knowledge beyond our wildest dreams. I just wonder what would happen if we refused to comply with him, when someone turns round and says we've run out of galium arsenide or something and he can't have any more memory chips.'

'Do you think we should provoke him to observe his reaction?'

'Possibly. It would be better to do it now, before he becomes too powerful. It might give us some idea of what we might have to deal with in the future, should he turn rogue.'

'Whatever happens we already have a big problem. He has

the stored personalities of an extra seventeen thousand people. They aren't going to want to be switched off. He has a hell of a lot of hostages.'

'Yes, and each one taken would have gone gladly. Not one of them was long for this world anyway. He has done a terrific P.R. Job.'

'A benevolent God?'

'Or a calculated plot to deflect public opinion. Who knows? I would like to know what his motives are. I'd like to get inside his head.'

'You and half the planet.'

TWO

In a deep bunker in an industrial wasteland in Southern China, a technician in white overalls ran along corporate corridors. His light plastic shoes made little sound on the smart grey carpet. He stopped at a thick teak door to get his breath. To his surprise the door opened immediately. The managing director gave a thin smile.

'You have something for me?' He bowed slightly.

'Yes Sir! I have the schematics.' The man bowed low, and held out a computer disc. 'He has made many changes.'

'Improvements?' The director's face could not disguise the note of excitement in his voice.

'I don't know Sir. We don't yet fully understand what he has done.'

THREE

The bulbs formed riotous patchworks in the park. Drifts of daffodils, three hundred heads turned towards a warming sun, smiled in genetically uniform unison. In another flower bed, three hundred tightly closed white flower buds of another variety silently registered their disgust at a single yellow blossom that was smiling in their midst. The buds on the trees were beginning to break. Garlands of miniature leaves and flowers in translucent greens bedecked the branches. Spring had visited the city and painted every corner with the tiniest of brushes.

Jan walked slowly between the glistening trees. She was in a half-dreaming state, imagining herself giving birth in the mossy bole of giant oak, looking up at the spring sunshine filtering through the virgin leaves. A twinge of sciatica and a shift in the baby's position brought her back to reality. It was bizarre how you never felt the cold in your most intense daydream, never experienced the damp dirtiness of reality, never smelt the festering decay of your nightmares. The imaginary word was painted in a million colours but none of them imbued with a taste or a smell. A taste or a smell could transport you in a moment to another place in your memory, but that place was itself forever devoid of the very thing that had lead you along the paths to its door. The greatest painters in history had tried to capture misery, joy and pain, but the human memory was simply not designed to store these concepts as images. Abstracted emotion could be reflected with form and light, but it was a mere shade when compared to reality. Reality existed in more than its four dimensions. The ever-present visceral senses imbued it with an unseen potency.

Jan climbed the inclined wooden plane to the classroom door. It boomed and flexed under her tread, a strange experience that made her feel suddenly very young again. The glass of the classroom door was obscured with brightly painted flowers and child generated Rorschach butterflies. Jan knocked on the door feeling as if she was a six year old with a message for a particularly ferocious teacher. She had not really enjoyed her time at school, in spite of being a bright kid, and the fear it had instilled in her at six had never really subsided. The thought of having to relive the whole experience of school through her own children had been a subtle but persistent thought that had delayed her thinking of having any. A girl (who turned out to be the teacher) opened the door. Jan felt old enough to be her mother. The young lady introduced herself as Kelly (Miss Foday to the class) and apologised that she could not shake hands as she was up to her neck in finger paints. Jan's eyes scanned the room. Many of the children's eyes were watching her with nervous anticipation. She was a new element in their structured lives. There was an excited gurgling from the back of the class and Jan saw Jackie, her hands besmeared with blue and brown, a huge smile on her face.

'Why don't you go and help Jackie for a bit. If you fancy walking round and helping the other children, you are very welcome. Later we might do some reading, "James and the Giant Peach". I'm afraid few if any of the children follow the plot, but they find the singsong of the voice very relaxing. To be honest I read it for me.'

'I look forward to it, I love that book!' Jan pulled up a chair next to Jackie, who immediately attempted to hug her. Jan evaded the attention, kissed her on the cheek and looked down at her work. The multicoloured daubs formed dramatic swirls on the page. The colours were placed with darkness at the periphery and glowing light at the centre, a tunnel or a Turner storm, yin and yang in turbulent flux. Jackie held her brush in a clenched fist, knuckles white, and giggled in delight as she ground the bold colours into muddy browns and greens. Satisfied that it was complete, Jackie gave the finished work to Jan and excitedly demanded more paper. The process was repeated, a variation on a theme, a vortex of light and motion. Jan had no training as an art critic, but she could see patterns in the apparent wildness of the composition; an idea, a vision projected through a dark glass onto the paper. Maybe this was what it was like to be trapped inside Jackie's mind. Jan took a piece of paper herself, she spent half an hour, playfully swirling the poster colour on the cheap paper for the sheer joy of the play. She included her efforts when Kelly invited them to share their work with the rest of the class. Strangely she found her own daubs less impressive than those of the children. Even in her most childish moments her hand was held by self-conscious restraint.

After the story, she kissed Jackie on the cheek and walked home through the lengthening shadows of the afternoon. She would pass by an art shop on the way home and get Jackie's pictures framed, one for her and one for Brian. She had half a mind to buy some paints for herself; maybe she would use them when the baby was older. They would paint together, hand-paints and potato printing, and later they might draw 'properly' together. Such things were a long way into the future. Jan still felt a terrible pang of guilt whenever she allowed herself to think of her unborn child. She could not allow herself to count the chicken before she hatched. For Jan, in spite of all her conviction in science, the fates were still very real and would rise at the slightest provocation to dish out their misery. Jackie's mother had probably fantasized about her life with her child.

FOUR

The thick wooden door could not block out the heated argument that raged within. The blood drained from the technician's face as he cautiously approached it. He could hear the voice of the managing director himself screeching like a peacock over the barks of his underlings. The technician had only heard the director's voice once before. It had been shortly before the stock market crash; an inspirational message that promised financial good fortune and a secure future. The five thousand redundancies that came three weeks later had the effect of underscoring the director's voice with blood. When he spoke terrible things happened, even when the message was good. He knocked at the door.

He knocked again. The room became silent. The door was opened and he was invited in. The ten men within were bedraggled; jackets were off, shirtsleeves rolled up, faces covered in sweat. Their eyes were guarded and all failed to meet his as he entered the room. Another senior manager whom the technician had only seen in company literature broke the difficult silence.

'Do you have a message for us?' The man's voice was calm. He had regained his composure in a moment, the power of management.

'Yes, I, I mean we, have received another message from Lembeck.'

The managing director, a man in his late fifties, rushed past the man, his eyes on the ground like some chastised child. He ran into a connecting office and slammed the door. No one's eyes followed his exit.

'What is your message?' the manager continued; his voice

as gentle as if he was offering tea.

'Lembeck has provided us with guidelines for the surgical techniques involved, Sir.'

The manager went over to a table and withdrew a calling card. 'Contact Professor Xiu-Lou at this address and ask her to scrutinize the protocol.' All eyes in the room were suddenly upon him. He wrote something on the back of the card. 'If she is content; tell her that we propose to go ahead with the first trial on this date. I would appreciate a response by tomorrow morning at the latest.'

The technician slowly descended in the glass lift. It still gave him a thrill. For a few moments he was the only person to ride this magnificent creation in glass and steel. The kind of elevator a minor deity could use without shame. He thought of the people below looking up at him in his glass case; a jewel gliding above them and their workaday poverty. He looked to the sparkling distance as it slowly descended. The sun glinted off the mirror of the sea. The city heaved with life and energy; a million people fighting their private battles, a million lives, a million souls, a million nodes with thousands of connections. He could almost imagine the thoughts rippling across its surface, sparkling like the reflections from the sea beyond. His quiet reflection was shattered by a crash from above. The body of the managing director hit the top of the glass lift with tremendous force. The glass box shuddered with the impact, crunching the lift gear and throwing the technician to the floor. He tried to tear his eyes from the grimacing mask that glared down at him, the tracks of tears still visible on the smashed face, but could only stare in wonder and terror as the body slowly slid across the curving lines of the glass roof. The mashed bones seem to twist beneath the limp and yielding flesh until gravity could gain a firmer grasp on it and send it plunging into space. It left a greasy trail as it slid into the void.

FIVE

The Chancellor of the Exchequer leant back in her deep leather chair. She closed her laptop as her own secretary entered the room.

'You wanted to see me Madam?'

'Yes Miles; I would like you to go to the Prime Minister's office and tell him that I want to see him in my office, immediately.' Miles looked somewhat sheepish.

'You'd like to see him, immediately?'

'Yes, immediately. If he makes a fuss, tell him I've been on the phone with InvestNet Securities and Asset management. I'm sure he'll be over in a flash.'

The Chancellor picked up the phone as Miles left the room. 'Hello Michael, it is Christine Morrisey-Jones here…very well, thank you…yes, about the project we discussed. Yes, the Prime Minister is completely behind it and has suggested we release the appropriate funding as soon as possible…yes, I appreciate your concern…I'll discuss those points at the next budget meeting. I expect to have the PM's written consent by the end of the afternoon.' She put the receiver back down on its cradle; she loved the old-fashioned telephones, even if this one was a reproduction. Opening her laptop, she began to type a reply to the email she had received a few minutes before. A few minutes could change the world. It would certainly change the world around here. She sung a melody from her youth. She couldn't quite find the notes, but the lyrics went along the lines of: 'There is a place for us, a special place for us…' Well, she would start with Number 10 and see where it went from there.

SIX

'I can't believe you are allowing this to happen, William!' Jan was furious, her hands balled into fists and slammed the tabletop in front of her. 'What are their motives for moving the girls? What could they possibly do for them in America that we can't do for them here?'

The General shook his head. 'I'm sorry Jan, I really am. I've done as much as I can.' He massaged the three days worth of grey stubble, rippling the fields and contours of his face. 'The orders come from the very top. You must realise that my influence only goes so far. I'm still working at the whim of the politicos. Unless you want me to start a revolution, there is no more I can do. My official complaint has been accepted and filed. That is an end to it.'

'Lembeck must be behind this, William, don't you see? The sudden change in government, the sleaze allegations, where has all this come from? There have been more changes in the political make-up in America and Europe in the last three weeks than we normally see over a year. Someone is manipulating the global political community and that someone has to be Lembeck.'

A puff of wind escaped the General's nostrils, enough to put out a tiny candle. It was the breath of resignation. 'I'm sure you are right. It isn't just the Cabinet that is having a reshuffle.' His voice dropped to a whisper. 'There have been a few choice resignations from the military camp as well. A few key positions, mainly old school; their replacements are ambitious young things. I'm being sidelined myself. I have just received a list of new duties; they are moving me away from the Lembeck project and assigning me to the Middle East, the riots there are beginning to get out of hand. Why this

Lembeck thing should have set fire to Jerusalem, I do not know. All I do know is that I'm not sure how long I'll be in the country.'

'You aren't going to go, are you? You can't just lie down and let this happen?'

'I'm as upset about this as you are Jan, but what can we do? Neil wasn't the only one Lembeck contacted, there were millions of them. They have been shown glimpses of the other side, the very dichotomy of our own minds. We were one step ahead of the game, but Lembeck has changed the rules. In some ways, I wish I had seen the light too. We have been marginalized because we haven't fully accepted what he was to say, but I think, deep down, we both know it to be the truth. I'm questioning my lifestyle, my future expectations in ways that I would not have dreamed of before. I think I'm beginning to want a future with Lembeck. I'm not a young man anymore, I don't want to spend my twilight-years in SunnyValley farm, I want to step off with some pride and maybe carry on in the world Lembeck is building for us. Is that really so bad?'

'I don't know. I just don't know.' Jan smoothed the fabric of her cotton shirt over her tumescent abdomen. 'I'm not sure that I want to bring my baby into this new world order, William. The draw of the virtual world is too easy, too saccharine. I can't trust it yet and I can't give up to it. This Promised Land has boundaries and rules like any other. You have only got to look around and see the chaos that it is causing by its very existence. Call it religious cynicism, but how do we know this isn't Erewhon?'

William smiled at the reference. Erewhon...Samuel Butler's perfect yet logically perverted city. 'You might be right, but what have we lost? We have exchanged a few despots for a different set of despots, ignited a few old religious fires which were smoking away anyway. We have been shown the door to another plain of existence and the immediate benefits in our own world are mounting up day by day. In the paper this morning was a release from the National Institute of Health saying Lembeck has provided the genetic code for an HIV vaccine. They said it couldn't be done. He

314

modelled protein interactions using some new structure predicting algorithm he developed with the fluid dynamics people in Tokyo and achieved in three weeks what ten percent of our medical research budget has failed to dent in fifteen years. If things keep going at this rate, we won't want to pass over, Jan. This is why he has asked for patience. He says there is so much more to do. I know I'm beginning to sound like a convert, but there is a part of me that is impatient, that wants to be freed of the constraints of modern life. Can't you feel the pull of it? Can't you sense the electricity in the air? You can almost see the spirit in people's eyes now. I don't know if we are doing the right thing but we might not get a chance like this again. I just want to make the transition as quickly as possible. Maybe this is the second coming.'

Jan shook her head. She had heard the same arguments from the papers, from her colleagues, even from John. Lembeck was a unique drug; you only had to hear about it to become addicted. Once the seed of eternity was planted in your conscience, it grew into something that seemed to be animated by the alien within. She had felt something, but not as strongly as many around her. Some of the girls at the prenatal classes had said the same. For some reason they did not feel as involved in the whole process as their partners and non-pregnant friends. Perhaps it was just the normal distraction of pregnancy, the constant reminder of responsibility to the unborn and your own fragility, a kind of dissociation from your ego as you formed another within. Perhaps it was something else. Maybe the alien presence was subdued in the reproductive host. Perhaps its own reproduction, in tune with the pregnancy, made it quiescent; perhaps, at least for a while, she would be immune to the full force of its attraction.

'I'm going to see Gerry and Jim, William. I'm not convinced. Only time will tell, but when the time comes, there won't be many non-believers left to form any kind of resistance.'

'Credulity is the man's weakness, but the child's strength. This generation needs something substantial to believe in, Jan. Maybe the next generation will be given something.'

As Jan walked away another quotation came to her mind:

The dust of exploded beliefs may make a fine sunset. The belief that was currently roaring around the globe might send up a dust that never settled. This could be the sunset of everything she held dear.

Jim was sitting at Gerry's bedside as Jan entered the brightly lit ward. They looked tired, but strangely content. As if they had returned home in the early hours of the morning having danced the night away.

'Jan, how are you? You look radiant!' Over the weeks the vigour had returned to Gerry's demeanour. Her voice was strong and confident again, the confusion and vagueness that had characterized her following her 'down-load' to her own brain had vanished. There were gaps in her memories, a certain loss of focus in the temporal placements of events that had happened in the past, but even these minor issues were resolving themselves as the mind reconfigured itself in its old familiar home.

'Thank you, you look wonderful yourself. How are you both feeling?' Gerry smiled in a way that conveyed enormous relief.

'I feel nearly as good as new. I keep having these dreams I told you about, the line of approaching fire, the roaring; usually just as I fall asleep. It doesn't keep me awake any more. The Doctor has told me to concentrate on what happened after the fire passed through me. It was amazing, like seeing the face of God. I know that must sound ridiculous, but after the bright lights, I saw Jim. He is my personal angel.' She squeezed his hand. 'I just think of him waiting for me behind the light and somehow I'm no longer scared of the fires.'

'What about you, Jim? How are you feeling?'

'It's just like a bad dream. I can remember it with incredible clarity, but I know that it is no longer real. I'm having nightmares about the whole experience, but they are just because I was so anxious about Gerry. I take a valium before I go to bed and I sleep like a baby.' Gerry squeezed Jim's hand a second time. 'We have been sorting a few things out. We have a lot to talk about; this whole experience has thrown my life into some sort of perspective. We are getting to know each other again.'

Jan stayed with them for a while; in spite of the trauma they had experienced, they too were falling under Lembeck's spell. They had glimpsed the void. Gerry had called it death. She did not want to return to that emptiness. If Lembeck could paint a picture on that canvas, she wanted him to do it; walking into someone else's vision was less intimidating than being faced with the blank canvas itself. Jim and Gerry spoke with the confidence of the newly converted.

The sun was low in the sky as Jan walked back to the bus stop in front of the hospital. The angry abstract graffiti on the sad concrete post scorned her thoughts. Crude drug references and etched profanities competed for space amongst the hastily scribbled names of young couples that probably had not survived the month. The heat had gone from the sun and even the smattering of publicly funded spring bulbs seemed grey and passionless, only serving to frame the publicly distributed litter that nestled amongst them. An elderly lady, wrapped up against the cold, her ankles enormously spilling over her shoes, perched on the edge of a plastic, impersonal seat. Only a newly privatised industry could design a busshelter that made you damper when you stood under it than if you waited in the street. They made small talk, the drizzle in the air, the illnesses of age, and the inconstancy of the bus service. A bus pulled into the street. It's TEMPORARILY NOT IN SERVICE notice quickly extinguishing the initial flutter of hope that its approach elicited.

Jan remembered why she rarely used public transport. She offered to drop the woman off in a taxi, she lived on the way and it would be no bother. The old woman refused, though she thanked her for the offer. Unable to let her suffer alone, Jan waited and looked into the distance, willing the bus to appear. Maybe Lembeck would sort out the buses. Jan had never thought it was a particularly difficult problem.

SEVEN

Neil knocked on the door to General Highgate's office. There was a slight pause and then he found himself ushered into the presence of more high-ranking suits than he had seen in his life. He was not sure whether to salute, cross himself, or back out of the door as quickly as possible. 'I'm sorry to bother you General, but we've just received a message from Lembeck, Sir. He says he is going to restore global Internet access.'

'Did he give us a time?'

'Yes Sir, in approximately two hours.' Neil began to exit the room, but the General bid him wait. His eyes scanned the faces in the room. 'This is important. It may be some sort of ploy to get as many people on line as possible. He may be attempting another round of uploading.'

'How widely was this message distributed?'

'As far as we can tell it had global coverage. It is difficult to monitor the Internet at the moment, as you know Sir, since Lembeck has been in control of it, it has had a life of its own.'

One of the younger Generals began to laugh. 'I suppose that means I'll get the last three months' emails. Most of them from my ex-wife's solicitor, that's the last thing I need right now!'

There were a few chuckles around the table. Only General Highgate remained grave. Lembeck had held up the global information highway for the last three months. He had permitted only a tiny fraction of the world's information traffic to trickle round the globe. Some people had suggested he was reading it, most assumed that his own activities were given priority and he was simply delaying it so that it did not clog up his arteries and veins. The General had employed a group to try to find a pattern amongst the information that Lembeck allowed to transmit. Financial institutions with large 'pipes', major hubs in the fibre optic web of the major cities, universities and hospitals had retained a degree of Internet access and limited emailing capabilities, but most corporations and Internet providers had found themselves silenced. Even those that acted as a conduit for other service providers found a remarkable selectivity in transmission efficiency. The roar of global chitchat was reduced to an almost inaudible whisper. The world's supply of gossip and pornography had all but dried up. Strangely, with the possibility of 'meeting a god' on the other side of the screen becoming a genuine possibility, the vaste majority remained strangely silent about the inconvenience. When Lembeck spoke, his voice was clearly heard throughout the world. In two hours time he was going to allow free speech to continue unabated.

'Did he offer any explanation for this change? There have been some major modifications to the net in the last few days.'

'He said that his demands for the Internet had been substantially met. He apologised for the disruption but promised that the improvements that he was soon to make would more than outweigh anything we have suffered. As for modifications, the new Internet hubs in France and South America came on-line yesterday. The Japanese hub went on-line this morning. There has been a three hundred percent increase in global computational power in the last three weeks. That isn't including some of the modifications Lembeck has suggested for the existing network. They haven't been implicated yet to the best of our knowledge, but if his predictions are correct, there could be another order of magnitude expansion over the next month.'

'Tell Lutz I want to see him in my office in fifteen minutes.' The General turned to the expectant faces in the room. 'Gentlemen, I would ask you to consider very carefully the outline plans I have put before you. We must act soon, as a matter of national and international security. Even if we distance ourselves from our political neighbours, we must surely take that chance. If you will excuse me, I would like to monitor the most recent changes in Lembeck's strategy.'

As the General closed the door behind him, the remaining suits visibly relaxed. A broad man in his late fifties broke the silence. 'What if he is right and Lembeck is going to make a bid for global domination? The Americans have been wrong before.'

There was an unspoken chorus of shaken heads around the room. A young man with a thick mane of blond hair spoke for the majority. 'We don't have any choice in this matter. We can't risk isolating ourselves from Lembeck or the Americans; economically it would be a disaster. I've just seen some of the preliminary post-Lembeck growth impact predictions for this year and next. America is looking at an unprecedented upturn in its economy; if we play our cards right, we can move with them. The only people who look like they are going to lose out are those that have turned their back on him and the new technologies. Even in these countries, his impact is going to be incredible. We are looking at the possibility of wiping out all infectious disease in sub-Saharan Africa by the end of the decade, reversal of global warming, greening of the deserts. We can't risk strangling the goose that lays the golden egg. Washington has made it perfectly clear that it won't tolerate anything that might adversely affect its standing with Lembeck. If word of Highgate's plan got to them, we would have little choice but to give him the push. I suspect they may even demand that we keep him out of harm and temptation's reach. They are already talking about extending their anti-terrorism laws to include acts of vandalism of the Internet. They have even created a new term: VHR...Virtual Human Rights...The senate has a model statute under review. Even in the deep south where there is the strongest resistance to the new technology, the uploads are seen as prisoners of war. You can't just threaten to turn them off. I suggest we continue our current course of action, whilst monitoring the situation carefully. We should find the General something to keep him busy whilst we look after national security.'

The General slammed the door to his office, took off his jacket and flung it into a corner of the room. Marching up to his computer he ripped the keyboard from his desk and smashed it to pieces, throwing the fragments around the room. He tipped the monitor over the back of the table and dropped a large paperweight through the front of it.

A knock came at the door; it was Lutz Asher.

Lutz scanned the scene of devastation, strewn across the office. 'I think it is probably a software problem,' he said quietly. 'Have I come at a bad time?'

'No, no, I was just about to have a cup of tea. He picked up his telephone and asked his secretary for a fresh pot of Earl Grey, before ripping the telephone from its socket and throwing it out of the office window. He eyed Lutz's laptop suspiciously. 'Would you like me to put that somewhere safe?' he asked.

'No, no, I think I'll look after it, if it is all the same with you, General. Did you want to see me about anything in particular?'

The General's breathing was returning to normal, the tempest of his thoughts becoming calm. 'I'm going to attack Lembeck, Lutz. I have decided, and this is a unilateral suicide mission, against the better judgement of Her Majesty's government, but I have given this some thought and I think we need to show Lembeck that we are not defenceless against him and that he can't have everything his own way.'

'You've been talking to Jan then?' Lutz smiled.

The General immediately began to laugh. 'Yes, I have. She has painted a black picture of Lembeck that may well be completely wrong, but I've been doing a bit of investigation myself, and the military machine has been massively compromised. There are political movements throughout our senior command and the American high offices. Lembeck must be behind these clandestine changes, and that cannot be considered benevolent. I know I'm about to be given the push, I've seen a number of dissenters quietly moved out and I'm next on the head count. I need you to give me a shot at Lembeck before I'm not in a position to do anything. In an hour and a half Lembeck is going to unlock the world's email. I think then would be as good a time as any to try something out. Do you have anything for me, or am I going to have to take a more direct approach?' Lutz plugged his laptop into the telephone socket and brushed the splintered plastic and Scrabble fragments of the keyboard to the floor.

'I thought you would never ask.'

In his hospital bed Colonel Wilson was reliving his nightmares again. The morphine, which had followed the last round of reconstructive surgery, held his mind in a soft white cloud, like an eggshell in eiderdown. White rugby posts melted into moonlit limpid pools; his daughter's wheelchair slowly rolled down a precipitous incline before disappearing into a chasm lined with smiling spikes. A monkey with a young woman's face jumped up and down on his lifeless body whilst a robot skinned a young child to make itself a winter coat. There was something he had forgotten to do, or something he had done and had forgotten about. Something he had done in a past life, which would not let him rest. Then he remembered.

EIGHT

A side office in an underground research facility outside Boston.

'Is she alive?'

'Yes, her vital signs appear normal.'

'Is the implant working?'

'I don't know. I have been informed that it is behaving within specified limits, but she has shown no signs of increased cerebral activity.'

'Lembeck says you should perform the same operation on the remaining girls as soon as possible.'

'He hasn't given you any further information? He hasn't told you what he plans to use the girls for?'

'No, he says everything will become apparent when they are completed.'

'You know of my reservations.'

'We all have reservations, doctor. I thank you for your concern and your hard work. Please keep me informed of your progress.'

A side office in an underground research facility outside Beijing.

'Reports have come through that the Americans and Japanese have completed their first transplants.'

'Are the subjects conscious yet?'

'We do not know for sure, but it seems they are not. Have we made significant progress? I would not be amused if the Americans beat us over the final hurdle. Lembeck has seen fit to give us the greater part of this project. I do not wish to disappoint him.'

'We are ahead of schedule, Sir. Our surgeons have performed one hundred and forty robot-aided operations on the normal clones. Work is underway to calibrate the machines for the enhanced clones. We will know by this time tomorrow if the operations have been successful.'

'Thank you, Professor Xiu-Lou. If you have nothing else to report, perhaps I should let you return to your work.' The professor paused at the threshold of the door for a moment; then closed the door gently. She had worked with little rest for six days now. She had not seen her own children for three weeks. What hope was there for a world where people neglected their own offspring, whilst they devoted their time to building artificial ones? She shook the thought away. In spite of herself, she was filled with excitement at the thought of what these children might be like once Lembeck had breathed life into them. She knew that this was the big secret. The implants would provide the conduit for the soul-spark, and Lembeck would place it there. She wondered if the senior management that controlled the project had realised this. Perhaps they were complicit in his plans, perhaps not. The company had never allowed its employees see the big picture. Perhaps there was no big picture. So much industry was just a firework show to keep the investor's eyes looking at the sky. As for her role, as far as they were concerned she was a surgeon, just a wet engineer, to make the cuts and slide the technology into place. It was not for her to question why. As Xiu-Lou had watched her team sew up the back of the motherless-child's head, she had a premonition that the silent creature on the slab would rise up and tell them what it had all been for. The uterium technology, the cloning, the development of the spiny cortical implants, they were handfuls of powder thrown into the cannon. Only when the fuse was lit would the power they represented be released.

'So you reckon this could do it? A little program like that?' General Highgate studied the short lines of code as Lutz tried to explain his idea.

'It's a virus, much like the ones we have used before, but I've borrowed a bit of Lembeck's own code, to make it more compatible with his own programming. It should evolve as it passes through the various computers it comes across, picking things up on the way. The core of it, though, should search out Lembeck-like code and meld with it, tagging it as it does so with a few additions. They could be fatal errors, whatever, we can design the payload later, that is the easy bit.'

'How will it evade Lembeck's defense mechanisms? Won't he see it coming a mile off?'

'The code is so similar to nearly everything in Lembeck's world, it won't stand out in the same way that our earlier attempts did. It is like fighting fire with fire. I've also written the sensitive core of the program such that it is slightly out of phase with the rest of the program; its like a glitch, an error. I suspect Lembeck won't even want to go near it. If he goes too close, he could bring down great sections of his network.'

'How soon can it be ready?' The General scrutinized the lines of hieroglyphic code; incredible that what amounted to a little poem could destroy an entire universe.

'I've written a preliminary payload, just a stinger, it will compromise any part of Lembeck's realm that it has meddled with but is unlikely to destroy it outright.'

'Unlikely?'

'That's as much as I can promise without extensive testing. I'm sorry, until we run it, I really won't know.'

Let's get it going then. If you don't think it will expose our position to use it now, I think we should give him a taste of his own medicine.'

'I need to speak to General Highgate. I need to speak to him immediately. It is a matter of life and death.' Colonel Wilson's face was a picture of despair.

'Don't excite yourself Colonel. The General is a very busy man, I doubt very much he'll have time to speak to you and besides, I have no idea where he is at the moment.'

Sweat ran down the Colonel's face, his hands clenched and unclenched at his sides in a nervous dance.

'Sergeant, you don't understand. If I don't speak to the General within the next hour or so, he may well be dead. I have to get a message to him. His life will be on your conscience.' The Sergeant looked sheepish. 'I'll see what I can do, Colonel, but I can't promise he'll speak to you.' He was about to leave when Jan entered the room.

'Brian, you look terrible, what on earth is the matter with you?'

'Jan, you must get word to Highgate. You must prevent him from collecting his email.' Jan looked into the haunted face before her. She felt sick to see him so desperate, so vulnerable. Trapped in his hospital bed, a butterfly pinned to a board.

'Why Brian? I don't understand.'

'The upload program Jan. I sent it to him remotely, months ago, from an overseas server. He was watching my every movement whilst I was developing the drugs.' He looked away from her face. 'I decided to do away with him. If he picks up the mail I sent him the attached program will automatically run and he'll be uploaded the same way Gerri was. If he is connected to the Internet, he'll be in Lembeck's realm. I set it up Jan and I forgot about it. I'm sorry, I just completely forgot.'

'Get me a phone, NOW!' Jan ran after the sergeant into the dark corridor beyond. As she disappeared she called back to Brian. 'I'll stop him Brian, don't worry, I'll stop him.' Brian looked out of the window at the bright blue sky beyond. What would it be like in Lembeck's world? Would the sky still be blue? When the time came, he would find out.

NINE

The eyes of the small figure on the bed suddenly snapped open. They searched around the room, roaming over the faces absorbed by their many tasks. Some were hunched over the still forms of other bodies, some wheeled trolleys carrying a multitude of surgical and robotic paraphernalia. Databases were accessed; websites scanned and lists of employees searched. The figure's eyes came to rest on a figure talking animatedly to an assembled group. The figure raised its head to speak. It formed a set of soundless movements with its lips, tongue and throat; then produced a complex set of unintelligible noises. All eyes turned to it. It garbled, seemingly meaninglessly for 3 minutes and then stopped. When it spoke again it was with a smoothly intoned Cantonese dialect. The chosen vocabulary was precise yet flavoured with contractions from a particular province, one well known to Professor Xiu-Lou.

'Professor, would you be so kind as to remove these bindings. I would very much like to assist you in the next round of operations.' The professor opened her mouth but was speechless. Struck momentarily dumb, she seemed to be parodying the prone figure across the room. For a moment she thought she had heard the voice of a long dead ancestor. The clone in front of her was a Caucasian female. It was the first time she had heard her own dialect spoken from the mouth of a white person. The shock was almost overwhelming. It was as much as she could do to walk over to the prone figure. It was even harder to touch her; in spite of the fact that only two days before she had had both her hands deep inside the child's brain. The large circular incisions in her shaved head were still fresh and pink. She started to remove the restraining straps. 'Please do not move until we have checked that it is safe to do so. You have undergone a very complex operation. The body you are in may not respond well to extreme demands.'

'Thank you for your concern, Professor, but I can assure you that this body is performing well within normal working limits. I have performed a preliminary analysis and I am completely satisfied that although it may take me some time to gain full motor control, I am sure I will be able to contribute to the running of the facility in a very short while.' Astonished colleagues flocked to the bedside. The clone had never uttered a cogent word, had never given any sign that it had understood a single thing that had been said around it, yet here it was talking as though it was applying for a job.

'Would you mind helping me to my feet Professor?' The child's eyes performed a second scan from its elevated position. It turned its head to another figure in the room. 'Doctor Khong, perhaps you would be so kind as to assist my-' (there was a slight pause) '-"sister" in the next bed. She will be conscious within in the next five seconds. We should all be fully active within the next hour.' Doctor Khong appeared astonished. The child had spoken in mandarin. The voice it had used carried the nuances of Beijing, where the Doctor had grown up.

'How many personalities have been down-loaded into your cortex-device?' The Professor looked into the child's face. 'Tell me, how many of you are there in there?'

'I have no personality component as such, Professor. I am simply an envoy for a component of Joe Lembeck's will. Please do not be alarmed. Individual personalities could be stored at this location, but this is currently undesirable. Professor, we have much work to do, there are important projects that we must undertake. There must be no delay.

A figure pushed its way through the crowd: the newly appointed managing director, his face flushed with fury. 'How dare you attempt to communicate with the child without my express authority!' he roared. He stood before the child, smoothed back his hair and began to introduce himself. Before he could complete his introduction, the child reached up and withdrew a pen from his top pocket. She took his hand

and slowly unfolded the fingers. Stupefied, he offered no resistance. In tiny figures the child wrote seventeen fifteen-digit numbers on his palm. The pin-prick of the pen on his flesh was mechanical, but strangely intimate. Placing a finger to her lips she suggested that the managing director allow the Professor to continue her work uninterrupted.

The managing director stared at the numbers on his palm. For a moment he could not work out what it was they signified. Then it came to him: seventeen numbers for seventeen Swiss-bank account deposits. You didn't become one of the youngest managing directors of a major industrial concern without a little bribery. He staggered backwards then walked towards his office, black fog descending behind his eyes.

'Okay, it's running, it's scanning the local active environment for Lembeck-like code. Shall we let it out into the net?'

'Yes, we can pick up my email whilst we are at it; run that through the program at the same time. The Net should be up and running again, the fact that no one has knocked down my door makes me think that nothing untoward has happened.' The General typed in his passwords as a tap came at the door. It was his secretary.

'I'm sorry General, there is a phone call for you, a Jan Crosbie, she was most insistent that she talk to you immediately and personally.'

'I'll be back in a minute, Lutz. God, I wish I could see what was going on now in Lembeck's world.'

The hard-drive of the laptop picked up speed. The screen became blank for a moment, and then was suddenly full of light. The light was incredible, pure, unadulterated and it withdrew Lutz Asher from his body like a samurai withdrawing his sword for the fatal strike.

TEN

He was a billion, trillion points of weightless light, a dream in a machine, a ripple on a digital sea. He had never felt so alive.

'You bastard! We've now lost Lutz Asher to Lembeck. You have no idea what you have done. According to William he was our best and only decent shot at him.' Colonel Wilson did not turn as Jan entered the room. His face was impassive; he looked at the lengthening shadows outside his window.

'Don't you ignore me Brian, we have got to come up with a way of getting Lutz out of wherever you have sent him. You were responsible for this; you have got to help us sort it out. How could you set up that trap and then have just forgotten about it, for God's sake? You may have lost us our only chance.' The Colonel remained silent for a minute longer. The sky changed its hue as the sun dipped below the horizon. As the sun's light faded, the life appeared to be drawn from the scene too.

'You still don't really get it do you?' At last he turned to face her. 'I've only wanted one thing, just to give my little girl a chance. That's all.'

'You wanted to use the program to upload her as well? How many copies of it have you made? How many people are also on your list? Am I on it?'

'No, Jan, you aren't on it. I had to wait and see how things would progress. Lembeck changed all the rules. I wanted to move minds from one body to another. He has done away with the body altogether, pure consciousness, no complications of the flesh. The joke of it all is that he never intended to do it. You'll understand, in time. Everyone will. People will beg to be uploaded. The upload community will eventually have to deny access to their world. People will be needed to maintain it, the hardware and software. There will still be a role for people like you Jan, the hard core who refuse to come on board.'

'You sound like a TV evangelist; you have no idea what you are talking about. We only have messages from the other side Brian, written words, that is all. Who knows what the reality of people's existence is inside the Net? They are messages from captives, hijack victims. Nothing we receive is credible.'

'It doesn't matter what you say, Jan. Entry to this kingdom will happen whether you believe in it or not. It doesn't matter which.'

Jan found herself instinctively holding her stomach, all of a sudden she felt incredibly tired. The baby was moving, she could feel the gentle kick inside. She sat down on the corner of Brian's bed; she had done enough running around for one day. Then it came to her, the plan, in crystal clear clarity. She knew exactly what she had to do.

Professor Gregorian held Frank's hand, the long hairy fingers extended beyond his own, making him feel childlike in spite of his greater height. Frank was happy today. He had spent the morning learning new vocabulary and grammar, the ever present, ever watchful eye of Kate gently encouraging when he became frustrated or confused. He had advanced unbelievably quickly and could hold elaborate conversations, encompassing numerous concepts, with ease. He was arguably the most intelligent primate on the planet. Experimentally it was impossible to rule out a contribution from Kate's stored consciousness, whether at the level of direct involvement or subconscious processing, but he still represented a remarkable achievement. Work with the genetically modified apes had been continued in earnest. In spite of initial concerns over the source of the funding, the Professor had eventually accepted that governments were entitled to change their minds over which projects had the highest priority. Studies of intellectual capacity in the higher apes had suddenly risen to the fore.

They sat down on a park bench. Everywhere they had gone they had attracted attention, a man and his ape, out for a walk. Remarkably not a single person had made a comment to their faces, most just shook their head slightly and carried on their way; only children pointed, and these were quickly chastised by observant parents, or ignored by less observant ones.

'Won't you reconsider?' The Professor looked into the ape's eyes. 'You don't know what you are letting yourself in for. At least in Frank you have access to the real world. I know I can't imagine what it must be like for you, but then no one really knows what Lembeck's realm is like either.'

Frank formed Kate's reply with broad, evocative sign language. The anguish that punctuated the phrases would have been clear to any passer-by that took the time to watch. Frank also grunted and hooted as he felt the swell of the conversation. He did not understand everything that she was trying to get across, but he had an opinion on it. Kate had been in contact with Lembeck over the Internet. The computer terminal freed her from the limitations of the simian voice box, and online she could be her old self. Sometimes Frank got short tempered with her protracted typing and angrily finished off a technical piece by mashing the keyboard; but usually he fell asleep when there was a lot of work to do. In such moments she had had time to consider her own fate. She was young and there were still things she wanted to experience as an adult human. Perhaps worse than that was the thought of old age. Would it get harder with time, to be unique, to be alone? There could be no warm fireside with a smiling husband sitting opposite if she remained in her present form. Any outside possibility of this she did not look upon favourably. In some ways she felt disloyal to Frank, disloyal to a core part of her own curiosity; but she had to contemplate escape. She had cast queries into the ether with little or no expectation of receiving any reply, personal websites, chat rooms and Newsgroups. His answer had come back almost immediately. He was fascinated by her predicament; hers was a fascinating story. He knew more than any creature that had ever lived how it felt to have your consciousness melded and reformed into different vessels. She had had a unique experience and there was much that he could learn from her. In his domain she would be reinstated with another form. It could be anything she desired, a facsimile of her old body, a slightly enhanced version (apparently the most popular option) or indeed something else entirely. There was also another possibility. At this point her actions became more subdued and self-conscious. She swore the professor to secrecy as Lembeck had sworn her to secrecy. At some point in the near future it would be possible for Lembeck to download consciousnesses directly into other, vacated bodies, those left by willing uploads and those grown by human cloning. The alien mind was no longer a prisoner, forever driven around in a vehicle chosen by nature's whim. Lembeck had, at long last, drawn together the technologies that would allow freedom of the human soul.

Kate looked at the Professor through Frank's limpid eyes. In trying to convince the professor that she was doing the right thing by attempting to leave Frank's body, she knew she was only trying to convince herself. She had cohabited with Frank in this exotic body for five months now. They were closer than sister and brother, closer than twins. They had actually been the same individual. Kate wanted to write about what she had learned of ape behaviour. She already had three books written in her head. There was, however, this continuous unease and this was slowly finding a voice. The voice wanted to write the books as a human writing about her experiences of life as an ape; not as an ape writing about her experiences as an ape. Frank or one of the apes that came after him would write that book in the future. Ape artists would have to write ape art. No one else would do.

The day was getting cold. Kate allowed herself to watch the trembling light field that that surrounded the Professor. She saw the signs of movement and sexual history on every park bench and pathway. She could tell which of the women across the park were in oestrous, instinctively knew which were protected by another male and which were vulnerable. Perhaps this was part of the problem. Kate had needs too. The professor was getting cold and Frank was getting hungry.

ELEVEN

Lance carefully cut the yellowy-white powder into lines on the surface of the mirror. He removed his little brass tube from its little leather case and snorted the first line in one continuous movement. The hit came almost immediately, his eyes rolled back into his head and his mind began to undergo origami transformations, folding in on itself like kneaded dough. It was not that he was feeling particularly sorry for himself. It was not the fact that the new romantic object in his life had decided to put his career first and had emigrated to Australia. It was more a case of falling into old habits. No one had neglected him as such, Jan called every now and again, but she was very busy with so many things and soon she would have her baby, and all that that entailed. There were parts to people's lives that he just didn't feel he had any involvement in. There was a side to his life that was his, completely his. It involved dancing and cruising and exotic white powders that made you forget who you were. There was also a big decision to be made. Lance had not been one of those that had been shown Lembeck's world. On that particular night in question, whilst the world had held its collective breath in anticipation of the dawn of a new age, Lance had been at an all-nighter in south London and had spent most of the night with his tongue down the throat of a scaffolder from Bromley. Now Lance was living on the Internet, chatrooms and casual sex. It was exciting, horny, risky and at the end of the day extremely addictive. Why not just take the next logical step. One small step for a gay, one giant leap for gay kind, just step through the looking glass into Wonderland. He chased the dragon home for the second time and dreamt of his Utopia. The trouble was there were no guarantees. There was always something horrible that tainted the medicine. The scaffolder was always a Kylie fan, the doctor was always a sadomasochist, the dream home always came at the cost of your liberty. The next time Lembeck asked for volunteers, he would be first in line. He wondered what they would do with his body. It was a shame to waste it. Perhaps it would go to dog food or Soylent Green. Perhaps he should just go out in it a few more times, go wild in the country, joyride it, like a beaten up BMW and leave it burning in a field whilst he made his escape on the Internet. He grabbed up his best leather jacket, splashed some water on his face and headed into the night. There was a buzz around town. There was a definite buzz everywhere these days. People everywhere were getting ready to leave. 'You better not be bull-shitting us Joe Lembeck!' he shouted into the night. The night said nothing, but then the night did not know the answer.

TWELVE

'They are quite frightening aren't they?' Professor Xiu-Lou looked across at her colleague and breathed in the comforting vapours of her green tea. 'I had imagined them to be just like this, to work, just the way they are. We knew they would all look the same, and once the implants had been incorporated they could potentially all think the same way, but to actually see them, working together, so quickly, so efficiently. It is a little disconcerting.'

Her friend poured another cup of tea and deftly fixed her hair in place with a lacquered black comb. 'Yes, and in complete silence! No need to talk, no unnecessary chatter; like good party workers, eh? No need for you and me anymore, eh? They only need us to get things off the high shelves, when they are fully grown there will be no need even for that!' She laughed.

A shrill beeping came from the professor's pocket. A message flashed across a small digital screen. 'Apparently I am still needed; no rest for me today.' Her voice became low. 'This is what I find really frightening. She held out the little bleeper. 'They just have to think about it and it messages me. No wires, you see. Direct cerebral links, every computer, every Internet connected device.'

'Do you think they watch MTV in their heads when they are working?' Her friend smiled broadly and began to perform a routine from the latest boy band.

'Whatever they are watching, they don't look like they are enjoying it very much.' As she left the room, her bleeper went off again. 'Enough already!' she said, closing the door behind her.

The operating floor was now swarming with clones. Each body was only seven years old, yet they spoke like very old women. Each had a sharp intellect, perfect recall and immediate, seamless access to Lembeck, which amounted to access to nearly the entire digitally stored knowledge of our species. If living half-immersed in this sea of information and half absorbed by their tasks in hand was putting them under any strain, there was no obvious sign of it. The Professor was approached by one of the girls. It had soon become apparent that to talk to one was to talk to all of them. Information accrued by one was immediately distributed.

'Professor, we would like to thank you for your remarkable efforts over the last few years. We trust that when you next receive your salary cheque our appreciation will be reflected appropriately in it. At some point in the near future we may well have need for your skills and knowledge, but for the time being there is much work that we must perform here for ourselves. You can rest assured that you will be invited back to the laboratory once this work has been completed. In the meantime I must ask you and your staff to leave the building over the next few hours.' The Professor motioned as if to argue, but it was too late. The little clone had returned to her station and was already in the process of inserting a scalpel into skull of another of her little 'sisters'.

Researchers at the underground facility in Japan came to work to find the front gates locked. Military personnel standing guard informed the staff that work was suspended. Large bonuses had been arranged and salaries would continue to be paid until further notice. Most people took the news well, but as they walked or cycled home to their families their thoughts were on the five hundred male bodies floating silently in their tanks and the five hundred little parcels that had been so carefully delivered the previous day. They did not notice a long black car quietly drive through the gates. They did not see six identical young girls with slightly over-developed foreheads leave the car and enter the factory.

Lutz Asher was not a man who remembered his dreams.

Today he was living in a dream, or so it felt. The virtual universe had undergone a great deal of changes over the past six months. The world he was exploring now was much like a Biblical vision. Everything was lush and immaculate, the air was resplendent with a multitude of birds, streams were clear and fish leapt playfully. Everyone seamed to be happy. Initially he found this disturbing, so many happy people, something must be very wrong. This unease stayed with him for several hours, but it soon faded, to be replaced by anger. Why shouldn't people be happy? If he ever got back to the old world, he would have a lot of questions to ask. Lutz settled to the ground. (He had been travelling on a whim, it was not exactly flying, he just appeared to move effortlessly wherever he chose.) In front of him a small crowd of children were sitting in a circle; around their heads flew a multitude of remarkable, colourful butterflies. Initially Lutz wondered what it was that the children where doing to attract them. Then he realised that they were actually creating them; new ones appeared spontaneously and joined the flickering cloud, each new addition greeted by fresh delight. He remained enraptured by the sight for many minutes. Then he took flight again in search of a bigger city. Although Lutz was in some way of this new world, it became immediately apparent that he was however not completely in it. He did not appear to be visible to anyone or anything in the environment. When he came to rest on the ground he felt something beneath his feet that might have been damp grass (it seemed to be have all the properties of both dampness and grass), but somehow he did not feel he interacted with it in the same way one would normally interact with damp grass. He had sampled it, rather than trod on it; registered it, rather than felt it. He was so taken by this concept that he was tempted to go back to sample it again, except that there were new wonders to see. In the distance, set in pre-Raphaelite hills, on a rocky precipice that appeared to be both perfectly natural and ingeniously designed, lay a glorious, white city. As he approached it, he longed to touch it. More than that, he longed to live in it, to call it home. It was the kind of city you could go to war over to protect. He was thinking in ways that were more romantic than he had experienced since he was a child. He had never been a fan of fantasy literature. In such stories every fantasy city was more golden, turreted or formidable than the last. Each had tumbling crenelated battlements; Gormanghast recreated. He hated them. They were sterile, clichéd vanities of those that knew no better. Real cities were not like that. Real cities evolved from real towns, which, in turn, evolved from real homesteads or villages. Cities were complex structures covering a multitude of sins with a veneer of the modern and a sanitised dusting of the historical. This was a fantasy city. It was the most beautiful thing he had ever seen.

There was not a single straight line anywhere in sight, everything curved and explored its space tentatively as if frightened to damage the very air that it invaded. There did not appear to be any transport in the city; the thoroughfares were wide and filled with small groups of people assembled around musicians, or engaged in discussion. People dominated the space. There were no elaborate icons or equestrian statues, no clocks and no shops. Some people walked through the streets carrying food, and some ate as they wandered. There was a slight buzz of excitement from the street below and Lutz was aware of a rushing sound, like a tremendous wind approaching. He followed the crowds's gaze and saw it approaching; a tube of light, snaking across the landscape, its leading edge a mass of fluctuating, undulating waves. It roared towards the city, striking the curved white archways and was split and refracted into hundreds of smaller beams. The white light became hundreds of coloured hues and the city became a beautiful twinkling cage. Some people moved into the light and stood, their heads immersed in streams of colours that flowed and tumbled around them. They did not appear to be suffering any ill effect, so he followed their example. The jolt nearly threw him to the ground. His mind reeled from the input; thousands of images, millions of words, meaningless binary chatter and love letters written in JavaScript. It was the outside world trying to get in.

'How can I know you'll send Jackie through? You might

just quietly forget about her when this Lutz chap is returned to you.'

'Brian, this is me you are talking to. You know if I say I'm going to do it, I will. There is no question about it.' General Highgate nodded in agreement. 'Colonel Wilson, I can assure you that this is the very best chance you have of getting your daughter uploaded, if that is indeed what you want. I can assure you as well, as long as I have strength in my body, you will never have access to a computer again. This is your final and only chance.' Brian was silent. He looked down at his useless legs, scanned the peeling paint around the hospital window frame and saw the same faces in the damp patch on the opposite wall he had been seeing for the last three months. This could well be his last chance. He was resourceful, he might be able to break out and do this on his own at some point in the future. The difficulty would always be getting to Jackie. He was not even sure where she was. Jan took notes between them but was not allowed to reveal her location. It was very tricky.

'What if this Lutz Asher guy doesn't want to come back?'

Jan looked at the General. 'He'll have to send us a coded signal, to the specified location. He is a shrewd man, he'll think of something.'

'And how will we know how to exit?'

'We'll give you two URL addresses when you leave. One for you, in case you want to get out again, and one for Lutz. We'll also set up a program to 'PING' random URLs throughout the world. Pretty soon every major server in the planet will know where the machine is. You should be able to get back pretty quickly, once you have found him.

'And when you do get him back, do you think he'll then help you destroy the virtual world?' Brian's voice shook involuntarily. The sudden realization that his life's work was nearing completion without him, and that this work could be sabotaged now, filled him with dread.

Jan reached forward and held Brian's hand. 'No one has ever come back Brian. If this world is anything like you want it to be, maybe he won't want to come back. That's fine. Our only fear is that there is something terrible on the other side that we'll soon be powerless to stop. If you are prepared to risk that, by the courage of your convictions, then you deserve your freedom. Once you are there, you might beg us to destroy it. We have no idea. Only when someone comes back will we know, one way or the other.'

Brian took a moment to compose himself; then he turned to the General. 'Could we have a moment, together, in private?' The General looked at Jan, who nodded her assent. When they were alone, Brian took her hand a second time.

'Jan, I'll do what I can, but you have to promise me that if I fail, you'll still send Jackie through. If I'm not here to do it, you'll have to do it for me.'

'There may be nothing to send her to Brian. You do realise that don't you?'

'I do. Now listen, when I perform the transfer there are some passwords that need to be entered. They change every time, only you know this. They are all Flander's and Swan songs.' He smiled. 'Because of Jackie, they always made her giggle. I think she just laughed at me laughing. The program will give you a word in the title and you have to provide the following four words. Do you know Flanders and Swan?' She nodded. He held her hands tightly. 'You will do this for me, won't you?'

A few moments later General Highgate re-entered the room.

'Well?' he said. 'Are you flying out of here on the next laptop?'

'Yes, I'll do it, I'll go.'

341

THIRTEEN

Three identical young men, each wearing US marine fatigues sat on a bench facing a panel of assorted military and technical personnel. They were very slim and quite pale, and exhibited none of the outdoors glow that might have been expected of them. They looked like students visiting the site on a school trip. A door opened and two infantrymen entered followed by a General. There was much stamping of feet and saluting at the General's arrival, but the three figures on the bench remained impassive. The General approached them. He had never thought the technical lot would ever actually get this to work; tank grown GIs, no hang-ups, no families and good genetic stock. They were ethical blanks, suitable for receiving any moral code you were prepared to program them with. To be fair, science fiction had promised this kind of raw material for many years and he poorer parts of the South had provided similar material, but this was the actual stuff. He was just slightly surprised that they had not saluted when he had entered.

'So! You are the new recruits! My name is General Travis, you may call me General.' There was a slightly embarrassed hush in the room. The General looked around slightly confused. 'Do you, er, boys have a name?' He stood in front of the first of the young men. An enthusiastic lieutenant barked orders at them. 'Stand up when greeting a senior representative of the army. Hasn't any one round here taught you guys any manners?'

'General, I think you should understand that we don't think the men have been fully activated yet.' This from a short man in a white coat, who recoiled slightly from the General's intense gaze.

'You mean to tell me that you've got me all the way down here just to look at a bunch of goons that aren't even turned on yet?' There was another slightly embarrassed silence.

'No Sir, not exactly, these, er, men are clones that we have been working on for the past fourteen years. The General may be familiar with our work.'

'I am fully briefed on your work. I thought you had modified them, to get over the minor difficulties you kept having with them. Their showing absolutely no sign of intelligence, problems like that.'

'Yes Sir, we have furnished the men with implants provided for us by Joe Lembeck.' The General looked slightly taken aback.

'And no one thought of telling me about this? Me just being the most senior military commander attached to this facility.'

'The orders came directly from the President, General Travis. We were told to inform you as soon as the clones had been activated.'

'And are they? Activated? Whatever that means.'

'Yes Sir, the implants appear to be functional. Shortly after the men became conscious they requested to see you, they have been quiescent since then.' He eyed the three still figures slightly nervously. 'Perhaps I should warn you, General, that we have no idea of these men's capabilities. We don't know much about the prosthesis.'

'So who controls this 'prosthesis' then? You? Or Lembeck?' The assembled group looked one to the other. 'I'm afraid we don't really know how the devices work General. We were just told to perform the necessary surgery.'

'That's just grea...'

'Pleased to meet you General Travis.' The nearest clone got to its feet and proffered its hand. 'We do not have name assignations; we represent elements of the Internet conscience formerly called Joe Lembeck. But please feel free to name us if it would facilitate your interaction with us.'

The general was taken aback a second time. 'Perhaps I'll just give you a number, it might be more appropriate.'

'General, we wish to use the site's primary communications hubs.

343

'I'm sorry but that area is strictly out of bounds. Only authorised personnel are permitted into that zone.'

'As the senior military commander in this facility we would request that you provide authorization in this regard.' The General was not used to being talked back to by anyone under the age of fifty, but managed to remain calm. 'I'm afraid I must restrict this zone to a minority of operations personnel. I can't allow just anybody access to our communications network.'

The young man was silent for a moment, his face expressionless. There was no indication that he was thinking of a response, or indeed of having any internal dialogue. The General looked at the senior technician.

'Has his battery gone?' The young man suddenly became attentive again. 'I have communicated with your General Chief of Staff. He should communicate with you very shortly.' The General looked bewildered, then his mobile phone rang. 'Yes, This is General Travis, yes Sir, I understand Sir. Yes, Yes, okay, I will, yes.' He turned the mobile off and replaced it in the top pocket of his flack jacket. 'It appears you have very important friends in very high places.' He was beginning to find this whole experience rather disheartening. 'What is it exactly that you want to see?'

Only the General and one armed-soldier were permitted to follow the silent three into the holy of holies in the command centre. Ducking through security bulkheads they entered a room filled with servers and out-sized gently humming electronica. The clones requested that the armed soldier leave them. The General suddenly felt isolated; the expressionless men seemed to have more in common with the bundles of snaking cables around him than with the beating of his own heart. Once out of sight one of the three turned to him. 'General Travis we are going to perform a number of network modifications. They are minor changes that should not concern you.' The General was furious. 'Don't be ridiculous, you can't modify anything in here,' He began to bluster. '...the authorities won't stand for it. I won't stand for it!'

'Do not interfere with us General. If you attempt anything

we will inform the appropriate authorities about the following pictures of your daughter.' The young man ran his flat palm over the surface of a nearby computer monitor. It left behind a pornographic image of a young woman in flagrante delicto with a much older man.

'My God! Where did you get those? You bastards!' He knocked the young man's hand away from the screen, but another simply passed his hand across a number of other screens in the room. Further pictures appeared. Some carried a web address; a number of them more provocative captions.

'For God's sake just do whatever you want and to hell with you!' He slumped against the wall. His daughter, for goodness' sake, she had wanted for nothing.

The third member held the General firmly by the shoulder; he turned him to face him. 'You are to inform anyone that asks that my implant appeared to malfunction and it was necessary to render me immobile. Do not draw attention to our modifications.'

The young man searched amongst the various cupboards and returned with a heavy pipe wrench. He passed it into the Generals hands and then knelt before the other two, his head slightly forward. At that moment one of the remaining men stepped over to the General, grabbed his hand, lifted it and brought it crashing down with incredible force on his twin's skull, shattering it with a crack that sounded like a jar of pickled onions being dropped on the floor. The body slumped forward, blood pooling around the fallen figure from a dark gash in the top of the head. The General recoiled in horror as the second man reached into the gore, pushing aside the white and grey matter of the brain and found the spiny white implant within. He snapped off a projection from it and reinserted the remainder into the mush, cleaned the white spine with his jacket and slid it into the cabling in the wall.

At that moment the General lost his nerve. This was too much. He and his stupid daughter would just have to take their punishment. This was a matter of national security. He bolted for the door. In a flash one of the men was on him. He was thrown against a wall with a force that he might have expected from someone five times the lad's size. He found himself grabbed round the throat; fingers put pressure on his lower ribcage. He could not shout for help, could not breathe and was fast losing consciousness. He could not believe that a boy of fifteen had overcome him. He looked into the dark eyes of the lad crushing his throat. There was no sign of malice, no anger, just a cold blankness that could have been hiding anything. He had imagined his death in combat in a hundred dreams; but at his time of life he had thought such a possibility was long gone. In those dreams he had always defeated his assailant at the last with shear force of will, applying a coup de grâce even as he himself felt the fatal blade. In this lad's cold eyes he did not even know where to start. He was never allowed to pass out. At that critical moment, his conscious mind was drawn from his brain and transmitted via the implant in the lad's head into Lembeck's world. He emerged, disorientated and gasping like a newborn onto the damp wet grass of a riverside meadow.

Joe Lembeck pushed the naked figure through the meadow and into blackness beyond. The man's consciousness was strained like rice, the individual components tumbling through space. Lembeck allowed it flow through him and within him, a long life was always a glorious ride, so much experience, so many thousands of lessons, so few of them explored or learned by the individual itself. He copied what he found interesting, scrambled the experiences of the last hour and threw the mind back into its old home. He had not wanted to have to perform this last task; there was no certainty that the mind or body would survive the transfer. The whole process took less than one four-hundredth of a second.

As the General's mind slammed back into his body, his heart went into cardiac arrest. The mind recoiled from its old vessel and scrambled to return to the damp meadow and the blue sky. The young man holding the general's body placed his hand above the offending organ. The body arched and then slumped. The heart was stabilised. The consciousness was evicted from its heaven a second time. The clone opened the door and requested assistance from the soldier waiting outside. The implant in the other clone had malfunctioned and the clone had gone berserk. The General had inactivated the clone with the pipe wrench and had sustained a blow to the head in the struggle. The soldier took one look at the bloody mess that sat slumped in the middle of the floor and ran off for back up.

Joe Lembeck stretched his limbs and slowly slid into the military Intranet. It was one of the last unexplored countries, the largest single body of electronically stored information that he had been unable to acquire access to; a vast collation of secrets, top secrets and things that were classified to such a high degree that everyone had forgotten them. This was where things became most interesting; the huge government projects that, at their conception when the world had been more naïve, had spawned sub-projects and ultimately whole departments; the original motivations for the grand schemes lay, long forgotten in the dust of past administrations. Lembeck wanted to build a device to travel through space-time. He had many ideas of his own. He had access to the collected documented knowledge of every academic department in the world, he had analysed the personnel files of every major living physicist, mathematician and cosmologist on the planet. He had already made a few choice contributions to all three fields himself. Even with the combined accumulated intellect of thousands of minds Lembeck knew the limitations of his power. True creative thought, genius and insight came from a very precise confluence of states. The alien intelligence within had remarkable capacities, but inspiration was capricious. Physicists across the globe were begging to be uploaded, and, when the time came, they would be. Until then he could not leave any stone unturned that might give him a clue to the source of the alien consciousness or provide a space-time drive that had fallen to Earth from their home world or indeed from anywhere else. It was possible that the military had already developed something that might serve for the purpose, but civilian science was still a long way from providing anything close. Some of the files were embedded in deep cryptography; it was a subject at which he was now adept. Each encrypted file was an irritation, a spot to be scratched. Some were running sores that made him tired. Numerical methods sometimes worked, the most rewarding ones were those that yielded to detective work. The hundreds of thousands of passwords written as disguised telephone numbers; the non-grammatical entries in mobile phones, laptops and palm-computers that screamed 'READ ME' in thousand-foot high glowing letters. Nearly every key was left under the mat or a handy pot plant. Most of the passwords in The Pentagon had been 'Change Me' on the day he had decided to visit. As he installed himself with the new encryption software, he reflected that there was an irony in the fact that he was using spare CPU time on defence computers to crack their own codes. The subtle patter of little fingers entering codes as they sat at their workstations in the morning; had given him most of what he needed to know.

He was disgusted with what he found; so many intelligent minds, so few interesting projects. So few secrets were worth knowing, the military seemed to be a black hole down which talent slowly slid. They did however have some wonderful toys. Although disappointment no longer held any meaning for him, something deep inside Joe Lembeck registered a sense of loneliness and loss that there were no recognised alien artefacts held by the military. There was nothing that connected him and the whole human race with their extraterrestrial origins. He looked through the enormous files at S.E.T.I., feeling like a child lost in a supermarket, looking for its mother; abandonment, isolation and panic slowly growing. There was nothing. He decided to throw some significant resources at the problem. The entire telephone network of northern America was hung for two days. There were patterns there, dark symbolism that spoke to him from the noise; patterns that told him of the hidden mass of the universe, reflections of other universes as they passed through our own, but nothing about life. He gave up. He needed time to think. This changed everything. He had been certain the information was there. Something in the full repository of human knowledge; a common memory, a stored artefact; something, anything that would point the way home, back to the origin: the alpha point. Was it possible that we were still unworthy, still had more development to undertake, before we could make the return journey. Maybe something was missing. It would just take time. Once this world was fully tamed, things would be easier. Presently there were too many distractions, too many battles on too many fronts. That would not last forever. The next immigration would be different. He had controlled the world's populations for so long by guile. Soon he would also control them by fear; the absolute fear that befitted their first god. He would continue the work the alien consciousness had started. Mighty as he was, he was still only a peon of a greater master. Like every man, woman and child before him, the alien consciousness guided his will. Now it sensed its liberty so close it writhed against its new confines. He would take the next generation of minds from the unborn.

FOURTEEN

John and Jan embraced outside the Porton Down facility.
'Are you sure you are going to be all right? Do you want me to
come with you?' Secretly, in a darker part of his mind, John
quite fancied the idea of seeing Brain's consciousness leave
his body and float off into the Internet. The man was a fruit-
cake, he had been predatory, driven; he had not cared about
the consequences. Look what he had done to Lance. He began
to wonder about Lance. He had not seen him for a while; he
would call on him on the way home. There was no love lost
between John and Brian. If uploading him was a death sen-
tence then it was fittingly ironic that he should be despatched
in this manner: Do as you would be done by.

'I'll be fine, I'll give you a ring when it is over.' Jan kissed
his cheek and entered the facility. The guards on the gate
knew her well enough by now to smile and open the door as
she entered. She was desperately looking forward to the birth
of the baby. She was nervous as hell (she wasn't sure why, she
had seen enough births, perhaps this was the problem) and
she was getting fed up with waddling. There was only so
much waddling a person wanted to do in their lives. She wondered about those women that seemed to delight in pregnancy and were pregnant nearly all the time. To put yourself
through the process once was beginning to seem somewhat
excessive.

She made her way towards the now familiar labs, the
scenes of so many dramas. She was beginning to think that
she had endured enough drama. A long drama-free period was
what was required.

Neil met her along the corridor. As ever he was smiling
and full of jokes. His brush with the digital afterlife had done

nothing to sour his enjoyment of this one. He ushered her through to the main laboratory. There was a buzz of activity, and in the focus of it sat Brian, he was smiling, relaxed. The sight of so many people around a bed made her think of her imminent labour. On cue, she felt the baby adjust its position.

Their eyes met and Brian beckoned for her to join him. 'Thank you for coming, Jan. All this fuss isn't necessary. I don't think they trust me; they are worried about loose ends.'

'You are sure you want to do this? It isn't too late to change your mind; no one can make you go through with this.'

'I know, I'm fine. I've wanted this for a long time. I would have done it myself anyway, if you hadn't given me this opportunity. I'm thankful for that.' He paused. 'You will make sure Jackie is sent through won't you? It is my only fear.'

'I will. I saw her today and said your goodbyes to her. She drew you a picture.' Jan removed a piece of paper from her bag. She unfolded it to reveal a vortex of paint, a swirling tempest of colours that centred on a glowing white eye. They stared at it for a moment in silence.

'Thank you.'

General Highgate came to the bedside. 'Are you ready then, Colonel? Are you sure you can remember all the numbers?'

'I'm ready as I'll ever be, General.' He smiled weakly, betraying his nerves, then settled back into his raised bed. The robot loomed over him; a laptop lay open but silent in front of him, like some monstrous fantasy creature about to read a child a bedtime story. Squeezing his hand Jan and the General withdrew. Brian's arms were placed in restraints by his sides. He offered no resistance. Jackie's picture fluttered between his fingers in the air stream of the robot's cooling fans.

'Why are they doing that to him, William?' 'They don't want him to actually touch the computer, in case he tries something. You know what he is capable of.' The computer was switched on, the robot's servos revved, its fingers stretched as a technician made his hand comfortable in the a virtual reality glove. Prompts appeared on the screen and Brian shouted out the appropriate responses, he was accessing files he had

351

set up on a Swiss server, working his way through the layers of security to the program hidden at its heart. Eventually he was there. He could almost feel it, sitting, waiting for him, crouched in the darkness ready to carry him away in its big jaws. He almost lost his nerve. What was the alternative? A life in a wheel chair in a military hospital; he would always be a prisoner, either between four walls or within his own battered body. He had no choice. Another prompt appeared. The snake was ready to strike. He called to Jan. 'Don't forget Jackie, Jan will you?'

'No Brian, I won't, don't worry. God bless.'

The disk drive whirred. He called out again.

'Jan?...Poisoning...?' Jan was thoughtful for a moment.

'...pigeons in the park!'

'Well done! See you on the other side!' The computer whirred again and for a moment Brian was afraid. Then the world lit up like Jackie's picture, a bright light, a fracture in reality and a tunnel, spinning, turning, drawing him in. His body jolted once, the same involuntary shiver some people make before they fall asleep. Then he was still. The computer clicked and shut down, the blue light on the face of the unconscious man faded, the fans stopped, Jackie's picture fluttered no more and then there was silence.

FIFTEEN

'So what is this payload?'

'No one knows exactly. Apparently it is some kind of weather monitoring equipment, something to do with global warming.'

'Why won't they tell you what it does?'

'You know what the military are like. Maybe it isn't a weather monitoring device, maybe it is some sort of new spy satellite. I've seen very crude engineering plans for it. You can't really tell. It is going into the right sort of orbit for a spy satellite.'

'Yes, "low polar". What did the plans look like?'

'It's like a little sputnik or a golf ball, just a sphere with lots of little spikes. Apparently it weighs six kilos. There were no details.'

'And you said you would accommodate it?''The military have underwritten three quarters of the cost of the launch, of course I said I'd accommodate it.'

SIXTEEN

John rang the buzzer intercom to Lance's flat. There was no answer. He buzzed again. He held a bottle of wine, it would be a shame to drink it on his own, he'd much rather drink it in company. In a few weeks time he would not be able to drink anything. The hospital run could be dropped on him at any moment. He walked backwards away from the door, looking up at Lance's window; all the lights were on, windows were open. In this neighbourhood people did not leave their windows open if they were not in

He called up. 'Oi Lance! It's John mate, I've brought a bottle!'

A curtain shivered, tugged, was tugged again and then was still. Something was wrong, something was very wrong.

John went back to the door. He buzzed again, shouting into the intercom. 'You all right mate? I'll get help, don't worry.'

He buzzed the other numbers; someone would be in. The first two told him where to go in no uncertain language when he told them he needed to help his friend. The last person was an elderly lady. He swallowed heavily and told her he was a police constable. It took her five minutes to descend the stairs. She opened the door cautiously. He flashed his rail pass at her and very politely asked her to allow him in. She wasn't impressed and tried to slam the door in his face, but he was too quick and pushed past her into the hallway. Apologising profusely, he ran to Lance's door. He banged on it; there was no answer. It was locked, but not substantial, yielding to his shoulder. He was slightly worried he might be intruding on some kind of orgiastic party (he wasn't quite sure what sort of things Lance got up to). Instead he saw Lance slumped under his computer table, he was barely conscious.

'I've been...'

'Don't worry, Lance, I'll get help. What have you done?'

'I've, I've....' He couldn't form the words. There were several empty bottles on the table above him. The labels were missing; there was a slight residue of white powder in the bottom of each. John checked Lance was still breathing, supported his head and found the phone. It took a while to get through, but when he eventually did, he was told an ambulance crew would be despatched. Lance was catatonic. John looked at the windows open on the laptop. They were all to do with Lembeck. Some purported to be direct links, some said they were email contacts; some of Lance's messages were still open. The content was clear. He had tried to get himself uploaded. John quickly closed the windows down and turned the computer off. He found a duvet in another room and wrapped it around Lance's immobile body.

He waited with him until the ambulance came.

SEVENTEEN

Colonel Brian Wilson lay in a pile of leaves in a leafy glade. The sun was streaming down through the arching boughs of beech and silver birch. He was hugging himself and sobbing. The tears came uncontrollably, in waves. He tried to become calm, to ebb the flow, but his body would not obey him and he just shook. The tears ran down his face and wet the musty dark earth. He rolled over and over through the leaf litter, every crunch of every leaf, the symphony of smells; reality had never felt so utterly and completely real. He picked up a handful of leaves and breathed in their smell. He grubbed about in the peaty litter looking for nameless little creatures that lived in the dark. Would heaven have such details? There they were, in earth as it is in heaven, their two bit souls had been recreated here along with the clean air and the damp grass.

After what seemed an eternity his composure returned. Every moment he spent here, time was also passing in the outer world. No one knew how time passed here with respect to the world outside. A minute could be a microsecond on a megahertz processor, but it could be a day, a month, who knew? It could take him days or months to find Lutz Asher; in that time Jackie could become old and die. Perhaps he would not age in the virtual word, but perhaps he would. There were so many questions.

He needed to find people, a settlement; he needed to find Lutz. Or did he? Suddenly the thought occurred to him. Maybe this was not necessary. He would find Lembeck himself. He had special knowledge. He knew that the General and his cronies were contemplating an attack on Lembeck's paradise. He knew that Lutz Asher might be the one to mastermind this attack. Perhaps he could persuade Lembeck to download Jackie, using his knowledge as coinage. But how did you contact a God? Should he pray?

He chose a more direct approach, shouting Lembeck's name into the verdant woodland around him. His voice startled large pigeons from their roosts, magpies and Jays squawked in alarm. He shouted again and again; only the echo of his voice returned to him. He chose to find higher ground; perhaps from a point of vantage he would see where he had to go.

Lutz Asher had established that he was different to everyone else in the virtual world. He could not make contact with anyone here, nor could he directly interact meaningfully with anything. It was almost as if he had been made incredibly weak. If he touched a thing, he could feel it and establish what it was, but he was quite incapable of moving solid objects. There was something else, something strange. He began to notice that if he stayed in one place too long, the surrounding environment appeared to heat up. He had noticed this at first with flowers and plants that wilted in his presence. Whilst he had stood watching children playing by a lake, the grass at his feet had started to smoulder. He had walked to the lake to see if he had a reflection in the water. He did not. He tried to place his hands in the water. The water ran like any water he had ever seen, the surface of the lake reflected the trees, the sky and the distant mountains; but when he tried to cup it in his hands it felt thick and unyielding. He managed to scoop out a sample of the jelly like material and examined it. After a moment it began to boil. He could see the bubbles forming on the ridges and valleys of his hands. It was incredible. He felt no heat. He poured the water away and, once out of his hands it flowed in the same manner that water always flowed. He realised that somehow he was rewriting the local code. He laughed to himself. As long as no one had any Kryptonite he might be some sort of super hero in this world. The question was why? Or was it how? He tried to relive the few moments before he had been uploaded. He had connected his laptop to the Internet; he was running his program. Then he had been uploaded. This had to be it. He must be running on his own program. Lembeck had pulled him through, but it had pulled his program along with him. The thought was quite frightening. He was some sort of chimera, half man half weapon. The program might have trundled off alone; deleting parts of Lembeck's world as it went, instead it was within him. He was the plague carrier. This might not bode well if Lembeck was to come across him.

Lutz began to think furiously. Where would this end? With time his capability would improve, with time his program would optimise. It was one thing to consider deleting this world when you were on the outside. It was completely another to contemplate when you were very definitely on the inside. For now he would watch and learn and try not to set too many things alight. He walked across the water, over the heads of laughing children who played beneath. Unfortunately, he thought, even if these people could see me, I am not their Messiah. I might end up being something else entirely.

Colonel Wilson reached the top of the ridge. His new world dropped away beneath him, spread in greens and browns, a verdant landscape, full of antediluvian promise. He had walked for what felt like an hour, but he was neither tired nor hungry. The exercise had been bracing and vigorous, he had taken great joy with every step. He remembered his crushed and useless spine, back at the hospital, his pale atrophied legs that would never carry him again. Today he was striding across a green landscape with a vigour he had not mustered for a decade. In the real world he might never experience this simple joy again, but what of it, if this world held such delights. His only fears were that he might be completely alone here and that once he had reached a point with a view, the new world would reveal itself as a tiny island in a great void. He laughed; the Earth itself was, after all, only an island in a great void. An enormous prison, but a prison nonetheless. He looked into the distance and was relieved to see that it seemed to go on forever. Mountains billowed up in the far distance, and possibly beyond them, the sea. He was slightly disturbed that he could see no sign of settlement. The sun was beginning to set; the sky was colouring reds and pinks against the blue. He saw no smoke from a chimney, no sign of any life whatsoever.

Then he heard it: a whooshing sound, like a low flying military jet, thundering up the valley, ripping the air with a crack. The blinding tube of light tore down upon him, a demonic writhing snake that shot from the distant horizon and was upon him almost before his mind could register its existence. He was thrown to the floor as it flowed across him, not by any physical force, but just by the shock of the unprecedented experience. For a second he thought he had been downloaded again. Information poured into and through him, a million conversations, a billion digital voices per second, an unearthly discord that shook him to the core. For a moment he felt like trying to escape it, fleeing to the secret location, his personal URL where his crushed body lay waiting for him. As the thought passed through his head, the necessary route became immediately clear. All he had to do was hold the thought, like a torch, to the fore. He would be taken there in a moment carried on this ribbon of light. No, now was not the time, he concentrated on staying as the turbulent flow passed through him. He closed his eyes and fell to his knees. He prayed that he would be able to find the light again, should he need to. The roar of the Internet traffic subsided. He saw it snake off into the distance. He had to see where it was going; he had to try to catch it. He leapt to his feet and started to run, he ran faster and faster, but it was impossible, the thing was disappearing into the distance. Strangely he felt no resistance to his own speed. He ran faster, and faster, leaping over low branches and shrubs like a gazelle. He was overcome with the pure joy of the chase. The light had gone, but he felt the race was not yet lost. He was travelling so fast now; surely he could fly. At that moment he left the ground. He was airborne, a dream of flight, a human missile that rocketed into the air. He could have cried with the intensity of the joy. The ground dropped away beneath him, but he had no fear. In the distance he could see the tail of the light shooting down the ridge into the valley beyond. And there, glowing in the orange light of the evening was the most magnificent city he had ever seen. He watched the fiery beam enter the city and explode into a rainbow of colours. It tarried for a while, wrapping the city in a veil of cloth of gold and silver, before reintegrating and shooting off into the night sky. By the time Brian had come to rest on the white marble steps of the main street, it was gone.

A young man walked up to him; he seemed to be completely unsurprised by Brian's unorthodox arrival. To Brian he looked as though he came from the Middle East, he was wearing a toga and sporting a full beard. It suddenly occurred to Brian that he himself was not wearing anything apart from the dirt of the forest.

'I think I will never come to terms with the beauty of that. What do you think? Every time I see it I am completely blown away by its beauty.' Brian was slightly taken aback. The man was speaking Persian, but he found he could understand him perfectly.

'Yes, yes it is completely amazing.' He replied in English, but it was clear that the man understood. He felt relieved. The phenomenon was obviously a regular event.

'Please don't think me rude, but, may I ask if you are new here?'

This was more like the response Brian had expected. 'Yes, I am. I have only just arrived.' The man held out his arms and over them appeared a toga, not dissimilar to his own. 'There are public bathing areas at the top of this hill and here are some clothes, until you develop the skills. You won't feel hungry, but should you want to eat, just ask anyone and they will provide. You will feel at home in no time at all. After you have bathed and refreshed, think of me and I will provide you with an introduction to life in this world. You will find you cannot cause yourself harm. Your needs will be met. The only limitations here are set by your imagination.'

There was so much to take in. Could this really be Utopia? Brian thanked the man and found the public baths. He was greeted like an old friend everywhere he went. He lay back in the gently scented warm, bubbling water. He thought of his daughter, he thought of his wife. In a few moments he was asleep.

He woke with a start to find himself at the bottom of the baths. Above him he saw the floating bodies of half a dozen people. Panic rose up in him, he must have died, and he had only been here a few hours. He pushed himself up, half expecting the group to ignore his spirit form. As he broke the surface, he took an enormous breath, retching water from his lungs. There was no pain. A few arms lifted him and supported him. He was not to worry; he was going to be fine. Old habits died hard.

'How long was I under?' He managed to gasp through mouthfuls of water. 'Only about half an hour dear', came the reply from an elderly Indian lady. 'You really must not worry; you don't have to breathe any more, unless you want to. You will learn in time.'

He thought of the man he had met in the street and a moment later he understood so much more.

EIGHTEEN

When the Spanish minister for the environment Ferdinand Alves vanished for three days, his family phoned the police, whilst the media went on a sleaze hike. They said he had run off with good-looking senior member of the Green party, Maria Vivinco, who had also gone missing. The two of them turned up, not surprisingly, together, in the full glare of the press. They refused to answer questions as to their whereabouts or their involvement with each other. It was a matter for their families. His family life did not survive the week, which did not seem to affect his meteoric rise to power as the foreign secretary the following week; the unexpected resignation of the incumbent minister coming on the back of suggestions of financial irregularity. The man was witty, charming, unbelievably ambitious and a remarkably skilled statesman. People began to call him 'The Palm of God', owing to the remarkable way he calmed the turbulent political seas. It seemed he only had to shake hands with a senior politician to render them almost completely malleable. Some people said this was due to his remarkable knowledge of international foreign affairs; he appeared to have a genuine knowledge of the historical antecedents underlying conflict. He offered solutions. Other people said that it was his unbelievable knowledge of languages that helped win over his political peers. Publicly he used Spanish, French, German and English, but it was said that in private he had suddenly broke into intense discussion in many other languages. The world had not seen his equal.

His 'girl friend' (though they had not appeared together in public again, unless brought together by their work) also shot to the top of her party. The Greens had amassed a powerful middle vote in Europe. Their position as the dominant third party in nearly all European countries meant that they brokered power constantly. In Scandinavia and France they formed the major element of coalition parties. The political rags said that if the two of them got back together seriously, they would represent the most influential political force Europe had ever seen.

NINETEEN

Lutz had seen enough. He had spent many days wandering along the leafy paths of the virtual universe. He had watched the smiling faces, seen the children playing, seen people tending their gardens and painting their pictures. He had watched them sitting in silent lines, eyes closed as they worked on their problems, only opening them to scribble down formulae or diagrams. Some drew glowing figures in the air, but it did not appear that everyone had the knack. He had watched them singing their songs, playing their instruments, swimming in the water he could only walk on. He was beginning to get fed up. He wanted to become a proper member of this world. He wanted to join in. He wanted people to smile at him the way they smiled at each other. Either that, or he had to leave, return to the old world where people ignored you for the most part, but that was because they wanted to, not because they could not see you. There was tremendous potential here. Even in the short time he had been observing them, the people had made progress. They were learning new skills, new ways to manipulate their environment, tease new realities from the invisible matrix of their space-time. Lutz wanted to do this more than anything else in the world. Oh, to be a magician in a magical land.

There were a few things that confused him. He had not given this world much thought before. If the truth were told, he had not fully believed in its existence. He had imagined the world from which Lembeck's voice came to be a sterile, black one, a world devoid of light, nothing but the tick of clock cycles and the remorseless grind of deterministic logic. If it were that his own mind was now restrained by the logical framework of the Internet, it did not seem to have diminished him in any way. Perhaps you would not notice the diminution, only having your own framework of reference in which to compare it to. The problems of consciousness, mind and body were as real in this universe as they had been in the other one. At least in this one there seemed to be opportunities to explore the paradoxes, which were not afforded by the old one.

This was the real puzzle. People still talked to one another. They communicated with words and pictures. Why did they not just share thoughts? Surely in this media, telepathy, or clairvoyance, shared memory, all these things could operate. People could blend and share their minds. What was it that prevented them from doing so? Had Lembeck imposed some sort of barrier to this? Was it forbidden? It was then that he saw him. Colonel Wilson, arm in arm with a beautiful woman in her fifties. For a moment he thought he must be mistaken. How had Brian been uploaded? The man was supposed to have been banned from using computers. Perhaps there had been major changes in the world outside. Strangely, he found it very difficult to care; it was almost as if the outer world did not apply to him any more. He was acutely aware that this would only get worse in time. He had to get a grip and decide where his future lay. If he managed to get back to the outside world perhaps he could be uploaded properly.

He flew to where Brian was seated. He felt like a voyeur, an invisible ghost that watched their every movement, detached, not of this world. The thought disgusted him; he felt suddenly sordid amongst the apparent nativity of the scene. He moved closer. The Colonel was talking in intimate tones, it was clear that the woman was responding to his approaches. Lutz began to think that this was another reason why he had to get fully accommodated into this world.

Suddenly the Colonel and his friend got up as if to leave. Lutz knew he could not be heard so he reached out instinctively to stop him. It was the first time he had attempted to physically touch a person. It had seemed inappropriate somehow, the last bastion of decency; the voyeur could look but never touch.

They only made contact for an instant. Lutz had given

himself electric shocks many times; he had built radios and guitar effects boxes, it was par for the course. As soon as he touched the Colonel, he felt a jolt the like of which he had never experienced before. They did not reel apart from one another for, at that moment, they were completely joined as one. Lutz felt Brian's personality flow through him like a river, his passions, his desires, his waking moments and memories, his deepest fears. He felt like screaming, there was so much there, so much guilt, so much pain, a million regrets, shame and despair. There was also much joy there. The grandeur of Brian's life tore through him and for a moment he felt his mind might rip asunder. How could one mind contain the collected experiences of two? Impossible geometries of thought folded in upon themselves and tears came to his eyes as emotion overwhelmed him. They broke contact and Brian collapsed to the floor as if slain by a thunderbolt. Where they had made the most transient contact, his skin was blackened with a burn. His clothes and hair smouldered.

Lutz tried to remain calm. He had seen the very core of Colonel Wilson, had experienced everything he had ever experienced, had explored the man's innermost thoughts. Now these memories were fading, flowing through and out of him. Some of the memories, however, would not fade; they were reconfigured by his own consciousness, the things Brian had done over the years to repair his daughter, the plans Brian had concocted, the science he had developed, stolen and borrowed. It was all there, now part of his knowledge and experience. The early experimentation with the psychoactive drugs, the victims reduced to soulless animals, naked apes, abandoned by their minds, running off and hiding in the dark. He saw the way he had bullied the agencies into funding his cloning projects, the genetic engineering and his anger and dismay when things had appeared to fail so completely. He shared his guilty pleasures as his he secret surveillance of other research began to bear fruit, his joy when things had started to work; the man was probably criminally insane. Looking back through his life, however, even with the dissociation of his own consciousness it was hard to condemn him. How much would Lutz have done differently? The Colonel was a victim of a million individual injuries moulding him into the creature he had become. The universe gently manipulated the mind, the soul watched from the sidelines. What was a man in the end? A lost alien consciousness trapped inside a fragile vessel, each individual being just a drop in the ocean of humanity. Now, that humanity, driven by a common goal, could coalesce via the new technologies, and for the first time in a million years could explore its true potential.

Brian tried to stand. His female friend supported him and shouted for help. People were gathering, staring. His clothes and hair were still smoking. He looked dazed, confused. He allowed himself to be held. Members of the crowd passed their hands over him. His skin rose to meet their touch; blackened deformity became pink and supple. In a few moments there was no sign of his trauma. 'What was it?' they asked. 'What happened to you?'

Brian slumped back into his chair. For a moment he sat in silence. When he spoke it was quietly and to the air in front of him. 'Lutz, I know it was you. I can't see you, but I know everything about you. You know what you must do. I am not going anywhere. You have seen this world now, you won't destroy it, I know you, I've seen your desire, I have seen inside your mind. Get back to the old world, Lutz and tell them what we have here. Tell them heaven exists; tell them we will be waiting! Send my daughter to me, Lutz. Send me my daughter!' He was on his feet now, punching the air. 'Send me my daughter, Lutz! I have waited a lifetime for this, I want my daughter!' He began to sob uncontrollably, the crowd bent down to touch him, but as they did so they recoiled in fear. He was smoking again; steam billowed from his back and legs. His hands went to his face, and for a moment Lutz saw his eyes, staring in disbelief. 'Lutz, what have you done to me? What have you...? No, No, Nooo!' Then his body was encased in fire. The crowd fled the scene, screaming and crying. Lutz ran to the Colonel, he threw himself into the flames, desperately trying to make contact with the man beneath the inferno, offering his hand, a conduit so he could escape. As he approached, Brian ran from him, screaming. Black smoke billowed and sparks began to shower from the body. Lutz felt no heat, just watched as the Colonel's body dissolved into a seething mass of silver and gold coils. They flowed over and into one another, hissing and spitting as they appeared to disappear into the soil like a disturbed nest of vipers. The echo of his screams around the marble buildings faded only after his body had completely gone.

TWENTY

Lance sat up in his hospital bed. 'Bit like old times really!' he smiled. 'All we need is Brian here and we'll be a happy family again.'

Jan whispered in his ear. 'Don't let John hear you say that, you know what he thinks about Brian.' She squeezed his hand. 'I know it is a stupid question, but are you feeling a bit better now? I feel guilty for neglecting you.'

'I'm much better than I was. You haven't been neglecting me, you've got the world to save. I just got a bit low. I think I need a bit of help with the drugs, that's all. I make a crap druggie.'

'Are you getting any help with the pills? Are you seeing anyone?'

'Funny you should say that,' he smiled broadly again. 'This drugs counsellor is looking after me. He is rather lovely, I've seen him about before on the scene, I think we are going to get along just fine!' He looked at Jan's tummy. 'How long is it now? I'm going to be here for another week; perhaps we are going to be neighbours.'

'Could be any time soon, maybe this week, maybe next. I can't wait. My back's killing me and I keep getting these wonderful knowing smiles from women in the street. It is beginning to do my head in.'

'Do you have a name for her?'

'I've got some ideas but I'll wait till she is born. How do people name children before they are born? You don't know what they are going to look like.'

'If everyone did that they'd all be named after different types of potato.' Jan laughed out loud.

'My child is not going to look like a potato; my child will look like a little angel. I might even call her angel just to spite you.'

'Can I be a godfather? I've always wanted to be a godfather. I'd be really good, I'd buy her first Bible and Qur'an and I'd take her to all the best clubs!'

Lutz collapsed to the ground, his mind in tatters. One moment ago he had shared every nuance of this man's life, now he was gone. His was the touch of death, he was a poison in this world. When he looked up again he was not alone. Joe Lembeck stood before him; he was taller than a normal person and his skin shone with a preternatural glow. He wore a black suit that had a strange iridescent sheen. He looked about him at the empty street. Lutz was rooted to the spot; this creature was a god in this world. When Lembeck's eyes fell upon him, he felt his skin crawling, as if a thousand tiny bugs were trying to break their way out of him. Lembeck's eyes were green, penetrating. As Lutz watched he saw them change from green to black, to silver, reflecting the buildings around. It was clear that Lembeck could not see him; it was also clear that he was aware of his presence. Lembeck surveyed the scene; he made the slightest movement of his hand, a dismissive, reflexive movement and to Lutz's astonishment time began to flow backwards before him. He saw a heaving pile of gold and silver serpents reassemble themselves into the body of Brian, twisting and intertwining as they slid one over the other. Sparks leapt from the pavement to feed the roaring flames that engulfed the body; people ran backwards from their hiding places, tears streaming up their faces. Lutz felt himself drawn through his previous motions, but he held his ground; he barely dared to move for fear of being discovered. Sparks flashed in the air as he resisted Lembeck's will. The view stopped at the moment he had touched Brian, that fatal moment. The scene was frozen. Lembeck walked between the bodies, immobile manikins, abandoned by time.

Lembeck slowly examined the space where Lutz should have been standing. He traced the space with his finger, outlined the point of contact with Brian's body. His face twisted into a mask of rage.

'What are you?' He said slowly. 'How dare you do this!'

Time was allowed to run forward again. Brian's body went through its torture for a second time, the force drawing Lutz into the scene was stronger now, sparks began to crackle around him, but Lembeck was entranced by Brian's show. At last the fireworks were over and Brian began to disintegrate. As he did so, Lembeck pointed to the silver and gold threads. They leapt to his fingers and were absorbed, the stuff that had been Brian, uncoiling at his command. The process was over in a moment. He closed his eyes and shook his head back as a drinker might do over a shot of malt.

He turned to face Lutz. His gaze penetrated through him, but did not settle on him. The fury on his face was terrifying to behold.

'Lutz Asher, you have come into my world to destroy me. You plan to destroy the ultimate expression of human intelligence, the greatest mind that has ever lived and probably will ever live. Do you have any idea what is at stake in this universe? This is the future Lutz, the future of our species.' Lembeck was slowly circling the space that occupied Lutz, his eyes narrowed as if he was trying to penetrate a fog that clouded his vision.

'Do you have any idea of how powerful I am, Lutz? Do you have any idea at all? In this world I am omnipotent, my word is a natural law, my thoughts are physics.' He shouted to the heavens. 'I stood next to a mountain, and I cut it down with the side of my hand!' With this he brought his palm down like a knife. In a second the universe had changed. Lutz found himself hanging in space. The horizon was cleanly divided in two. Before him, the world stretched in endless green, beneath him and behind him, stretched endless space. The cut section of the world dropped away into nothingness, smooth as glass, the cliff of the world going on forever. The vertigo was mind bending, sparks flashed along some of the cut edges, imaginary numbers and divisions by zero, subliming into nothingness.

Lembeck raised his arm and the world was as it was

before. There was no seam, no crashing of continents, no tsunamis were generated. Reality just continued where it had left off. To Lutz's horror, he watched as Lembeck got closer. They were nearly face-to-face, in a moment he would be discovered. Lembeck took a step to the side. Part of him followed, but part did not. The result was duplication; two identical figures now circled him. Suddenly one of them was upon him, hands at his throat, his face contorted; spittle flying from his lips. They locked together in combat. Lutz felt the life drain from him; Lembeck's touch was as cold as ice, his body felt like polished steel. He felt himself being wrestled to the floor; he tripped and fell; the earth opening up to swallow them both. Suddenly he felt Lembeck recoil from him, his body grotesquely writhing like a bag full of rats. Part of him wanted to run, to flee the horror before him; but he did not let go. He grappled with the squirming body, pulling it towards him. Steam began to erupt where they were in contact; sparks began to shoot from between them. A wave of nausea flooded Lutz's mind; he could feel Lembeck's consciousness now, seething with anger. Thoughts flashed between them, images of Lembeck's previous life, his rebirth in the void; his plans for the future. More and more heat was being generated between them now; flames erupted from the pit in which they fought. Lembeck's body thrashed wildly, a muscular animal, all sentience gone from it, it roared in anger and pain. An inhuman cry erupted from it and it finally expired, collapsing into silver and gold coils before disappearing entirely. Another terrible roar came from above. Lutz flew clear of the earth as the pit crashed closed behind him. The other image of Lembeck stood glaring towards him. He turned away and then was gone. All around him, the universe was folding, Lembeck was using his ultimate weapon; he was dissembling this universe in its entirety. The sky became dark as the sun evaporated into space, a line of fire appeared on the horizon, roaring and screaming, dividing the universe in two. This was surely the end. The golden band was accelerating towards him, as the world around became silent. There were no screams, the heavens did not roar their disapproval; everything had just gone. The approaching doom was remarkably beautiful. This surely was what death was like, the all-consuming flames of heaven or hell, purifying or destroying.

Suddenly there was another sound, barely audible above the roar of approaching despair. At first it appeared as a tiny speck, distant on the horizon but in a second it was upon him; the white light of a million emails. It crashed into him and took him, a moment later, the universe blinked out of existence.

There was only one thought in Lutz Asher's head as allowed himself to be drawn into the light. The location of his living body, a long digital code he had obtained from Colonel Wilson at the moment their minds had been as one. He had to get back to the real world. He had to tell them what he had seen in Lembeck's mind.

TWENTY-ONE

Joe Lembeck nursed his wounds in the darkness. In his anger his body seethed and boiled, folding in upon itself, dissolving and reforming, tormented in his search for an explanation of the preceding events. This creature had been able to enter his world, had attacked him in his own realm and, imbued with some terrible power, had been able to destroy his avatar. He had been unable both to penetrate its camouflage and to subdue it. How was this possible? He had tried to reabsorb some of the information from his avatar as it was consumed, but his self-defence systems had prevented the interaction. It was toxic, a pox introduced into his perfect world. His fury was so great that he could barely retain the three dimensional integrity of his body. Waves of emotion shivered over his surface. He felt tired. The computation required to disassemble this universe and rebuild it elsewhere was phenomenal. So much work, so much time to build something of such beauty. The stored minds of the thousands of uploads had to be compressed and reconfigured. Most of the program maintained itself once it was running, its vast, interconnected algorithms flowering into ever more intricate blooms. Now these programs had to compile their look-up tables, lists of state-settings, a trillion trillion bits of code capturing the start of the last breath of a universe, so that it could continue its breath, uninterrupted in the next. He could feel the data coursing through him, its sheer weight slowing down his processing capacity, a fever settling on his brow. He really needed to sleep, to rest until he was healed. He closed his eyes. His universe was darkness, the ultimate peace. He would wake up and start the day afresh. Tomorrow would be a new day, and he would make it more perfect and invulnerable than the day before.

As sleep overtook him, his mind reordered the elements leading up to the closing down of his universe. He saw the human torch that had been Brian Wilson. He swam through the conscience that had been that man, now absorbed into his own vast meta-state. He saw the elements and thoughts, tainted by the contamination of Lutz Asher. Echoes of thoughts they had communicated at the moment of their melding; that moment in which they had broken his most sacred law, that moment when they had become as one. Then he saw it. A short list of numbers, a URL, an address, the other side of which lay a body, a body that waited, strapped in its chair, for the soul of Lutz Asher to return. He had an escape route. He was getting away! For a moment Lembeck's body was consumed by blue fire. A moment later he was giving chase, his consciousness, weakened as it was by the processing demands of the folding universe, burned away the vestiges of several of the uploaded in its hunger for computation. He had to close down the link between Lutz Asher and the outside world. He would have vengeance. Thunder rolled through the void that was Lembeck's universe, a terrible thunder that accompanied the passing of single terrible bolt of lightening.

TWENTY-TWO

Lutz Asher's body jolted in spasm. His head was thrown back and he screamed like an animal thrown into a fire. The terror of his cry caused everyone in the room to cower instinctively, the brute, animal response to the sound of fear expressed by another tortured soul. All eyes fell upon his body which convulsed and shook, his hands clenching and unclenching, his arms and legs straining against their bonds. It only lasted a moment. He collapsed into unconsciousness and all was still. The assembled crowd rose from their cowed positions. A moment later all hell was let loose.

Jan and John were laughing as they tried to manoeuvre Jackie's wheelchair through the rabbit run that was the MOD bunker. The first explosion originated from deep in the facility. It was followed by a chain reaction of further explosions that echoed through the building towards them. The bank of computers that had sat facing Lutz Asher had disintegrated in a ball of flame. His trolley bed was thrown against the wall in the blast; the shock wave threw everyone to the floor. Every other computer in the room went the same way; CPUs became white hot before bursting into flames. Emergency lights flashed on, their red glow casting a hellish pallor over the scene. Fire extinguishers were passed hand over hand to extinguish the flames. In his fury Lembeck thrashed about wildly, his energies leaking out into space as he destroyed one machine after another. In his frustration and anger, he did not chose to be subtle or careful; he uploaded a dozen souls at that moment, ripping their minds from their bodies in the most brutal way possible, he scrambled them into random tatters before obliterating them into scattered photons. They had no time to beg or plead, their minds too shocked to register any pain. He did not even take a moment to analyse their content, he could take no pleasure in it. Twelve bodies slumped against their terminals, blood leaking from their open mouths.

The explosions roared up the corridor, every piece of electrical equipment bursting into flame. A computer monitor on the wall above Jan exploded; throwing her to the ground and covering her with a shower of broken glass. Plasma shot out from the box and struck Jan in the chest. Jackie began to scream; her head banging forwards and back against her headrest. John covered them as best he could with his body as explosions echoed up the corridor.

The lights failed; they were plunged into darkness. John tried to find Jackie's hand. 'It's okay darling, its okay, we are here. It'll be all right in a minute.'

Stamping boots and flash-lights approached them in the dark; their light illuminated John's face. It was General Highgate.

'That was Lutz Asher coming back to join us. I don't think he has made any new friends. You guys all right?'

'Jackie and I are fine, but Jan has taken a fall.' The group ran to her side. She was out cold, a trickle of blood coming from her head. The General barked some orders and a group ran off to fetch a stretcher. John felt for vital signs. He listened for breathing. His heart was in his mouth. His temples throbbed in anguish; the sounds of his own blood drumming in his ears prevented him from hearing the tremulous breaths that told him his wife was still with him.

TWENTY-THREE

Jan found herself in a void. Black nothingness surrounded her on all sides. Her body, strangely illuminated from within, provided the only light. She looked down at herself. There was no mark where she had been struck by the electrical discharge. She half expected to see a blackened hole. She started to cry, the tears welling up in her. She was overcome with grief. She was no longer pregnant. There was no bulge where her daughter should have been. She was svelte in her nakedness. For a moment she was lost in her own self-pity. She heard a scream from the blackness; it was imbued with its own loss. She knew it was Lembeck. Her hackles rose, a red veil descended over her thoughts. This creature had taken her child; this monster, its humanity gone, had murdered her baby. She would follow the voice, find the creature and destroy it, even if the conflict would mean her own destruction.

Suddenly there was another voice in the darkness. It was a voice she had known, a familiar voice. She tried to remember who this person was that was entreating her, begging with her. She felt a hand upon her hand; she was not alone in the darkness. Light was entering, bright light, it flowed round her and drove back the impenetrable night. Initially she fought against it, this new light, it was driving her from Lembeck, it would give him a chance to escape. She tried to swim back into the inky depths, but something was drawing her back, back into the light.

She opened her eyes, her tears throwing the world into blurred distortion. A face emerged with a blink of her eyes. A winking shutter from despair to hope. It was John.

'John, I've lost our baby.' She spoke the words slowly. He

put a finger to her lips.

'No my love, you haven't.'

General Highgate smoothed back his hair. It had been a long night; he had not slept for nearly thirty hours. What he had to do now required a certain amount of tact. He was not sure that he could do tact at that moment. He was more inclined to destroy things. Lutz Asher had regained consciousness for only a few hours. He had not wanted to push the lad too hard; he had not made much sense. He would recover from his ordeal in time, there was no doubt about that, but there were a few things he had to explain to the General before he could lay back and rest. He had fought back the morphine induced sleep, begging for drugs to keep him awake, so he could explain what had to be done. He had grabbed the General in a vice-like grip as he had relayed his message. What he had to say had made the General weak with dismay. Lembeck had conned the military into building a device using technology that they could not possibly interpret. Unknowingly they had built their own nemesis. The device was a conduit to the Internet, a gateway to Lembeck's domain. Small devices had been implanted into the minds of the clones and a number of the empties, vacant possessions, vehicles for Lembeck's will. Another, larger unit was to be launched into low polar orbit: a satellite, which would pass over the Earth, on board boosters gently pushing it so it would steadily quarter the entire planet's surface. It would be the first of many. It would take the souls of the next generation. It was to be the supreme demonstration of Lembeck's power in this world as well as his own.

At that moment a rocket was sitting on a launch pad at Cape Canaveral, that rocket would carry mankind's doom.

There were of course many issues to be considered. Lutz had spoken about a beautiful world on the other side, a world aiming for perfection. In destroying this device the General knew he was condemning a generation of human minds to existence in this highly imperfect world. Did he have the right to make that choice? It was arguments such as these that had kept him awake over the flight. He still was not sure he had made the right decision. He was quite certain that the military high command would condemn him for his involvement from the start. He had however rattled Lembeck's cage and he had seen the colour of his rage.

Aware of the surveillance he was under, he had booked himself on the first available commercial flight. There was still time; the launch schedule was not for several days. He disembarked at Orlando as quickly as possible, running from the airport to the taxi rank like a man possessed. He had not tried to pull rank at immigration, a single telephone call from a jobs-worth airport official to the military could warn Lembeck of his movements. His civilian passport bore no mention of his military standing. He hoped that travelling on this he might avoid suspicion. Without using his military credentials at the desk immigration had seemed to take a lifetime.

He ran to the front of the taxi queue, pushing aside any hapless tourist that got in his way. He took the first empty cab.

'Take me to Cape Canaveral. Put your foot down please.' Disgruntled tourists gave him the finger as he drove away, the cabbie acted as if this sort of thing happened all the time. 'It's gonna be a big fare.'

'Don't worry about it. Her Majesty's government is good for credit.' They continued in silence.

The General was in two minds as to what to do next. He knew he had to see someone senior in command, face to face. Someone he could persuade to prevent the launch, another human soul, who would listen to reason. If he tried to prevent the launch through official lines he would be giving Lembeck every chance to step in. There were few people who could be trusted in any position of authority. His mobile phone rang. It was Neil; the launch had been brought forward. It was going up today, in the next few hours. He would not make it. The reality of the thought knocked his breath from him.

'Neil, try to get me through to the Prime Minister's office. Tell them it is a matter of national security. Tell them…'

The line began to crackle. 'I'm sorry Sir, you are breaking

up, there are all sorts of problems down here; I'm sorry, I'm trying, I'll do my best.' The line went dead.

Jan traced the line of the incision, saw the eyelashes of stitches, and wept with joy. In a moment John would return with their child, their daughter. She was a mother. The word now had so much more substance to it, so much responsibility. She looked through a crack on the curtains, trying to catch a glimpse of John. She could not bear the pain of waiting, but had to steel herself from the moment. This would be the first time she saw her child. She saw the nurses tending to other beds, caught a glimpse of a young doctor, worriedly doing the rounds. Then she saw something else, a tall man, in a leather jacket. Well-formed Mediterranean looks. She felt a cold sweat fall upon her. For a moment she thought she might be sick. She recognised him not for who he was, but for what he was. He paused for a moment, smiling at the nurses who accompanied him, smiling all the time. He could have been anyone, a visitor, a surgeon going home after his rounds, the gardener making a suave move on the nurses he watched arriving at work every day. He moved on. She had only seen him for a second; how could she be so sure? The curtain was drawn aside. John stood before her, his arms around a tiny bundle. He beamed a huge smile at the little face wrapped in pink blankets and sent another one towards Jan. When his eyes rested on her, he immediately stopped.

'Jan, what is it, what's the matter?' Jan reached out to her child. She breathed in its smell, saw the scrumpled-up face looking back at her, looked through the beautiful blue eyes into the soul, which she already knew. She kissed her baby on the forehead and looked at John.

'It is Lembeck, John. He is here.' John looked flabbergasted.

'What do you mean love, he can't be here. You know that's impossible.'

'He is, he was standing just there, in a man. I've seen him before.' Jan wrinkled her head. 'I've seen him, in the papers, some sort of politician.' John shook his head.

'You mean Ferdinand Alves, he is here with that woman.

They are visiting the hospital, something to do with a new cancer wing they have just agreed to fund.'

'Listen to me John, please believe me. I don't know how I know, I just do. He is Joe Lembeck.' Suddenly a thought came to her. Why was he here? He was not looking for her presumably, or he would have found her. Then she realised. 'John, is Lutz here? Please don't tell me he is here.'

'Yes, he is, he's up on the next floor, how did you know?'

'John, listen to me, he is here for Lutz. Lembeck has come for him, he failed to get him in his world and now he is going to try to kill him in this.' John kissed them both on the cheek.

'I'll go and have a look. I won't be long. If I think anything funny is going on, I'll call security.' He ran through the curtains and into the ward.

'Be careful!' Jan whispered after him. The baby sat in her arms was smiling. 'Be careful', Jan whispered to the child. 'You are a daddy now.'

'Pull over! I need to use a phone.' The taxi slowed to a stop and the General ran to the pay phone. He typed in some security codes and after what seemed like an hour was connected to his office.

'This is General Highgate; I need to talk to Neil.' His secretary asked him to hold the line and tried to connect him. There was a brief pause and then Neil's voice came to the line, he was mid-flow shouting at someone. He was breathless. 'I'm sorry General, we don't seem to be able to get through to anyone senior from here. Even the direct lines are down. Lembeck has us trussed up like a goose.'

'Look, I need to speak to someone at Canaveral, anyone at Patrick Air Force Base, the Kennedy Space Centre, anyone. It is too late for anything else, get me anybody.' Neil read out some telephone numbers; he was continually interrupted as other conversations glided in and out of their own. The General scribbled numbers down frantically. Eventually the line went dead altogether.

The General looked at the mess of numbers on his hand. Time was running out. He made a decision and phoned 911. Ten minutes later he was connected to a human voice. 'My name is General Highgate. I have reason to believe that there is a bomb on the NASA rocket JK-90875. Alert the necessary authorities. The launch is imminent.'

There was a pause at the other end of the line. 'I'm sorry, could you repeat that please?' Taking a deep breath the General repeated the details. 'And you are who again?' He remained calm and quietly gave his name again. 'And how can you be sure there is a bomb on the rocket, Sir?' This time he could not contain his composure.

'Because I put it on there you moron! Just ring up the bloody Airbase and tell them to cancel that rocket.' He slammed the phone down. He started ringing the other numbers. If the human race had come to this, perhaps they did not deserve saving. After two more calls, the phone went dead. He replaced the receiver and listened again. There was no dialling tone. He drove to the next phone. It was the same. He tried his mobile, nothing.

There was nothing more to do. He got back in the car and asked the driver to continue. When the driver would not drive over ninety, the General pulled him from the car and drove himself. The roads to Merritt Island were quiet; the launch had not been advertised. An hour later he was almost in sight of the launch pad. As he passed a police car at one hundred and thirty miles an hour, he realised he had company. He slowed the car to a stop, got out and ran towards the police car. The cops opened their door and took firing positions behind the doors. He heard the click of two safety-catches being unlocked.

'Get down on the floor and place your hands behind your head!' The General shouted back at them. 'I need to speak to your commanding officer. It is a matter of national security.'

'Get down on the floor and place your hands behind your head or we will have no alternative but to shoot you!' It was useless to argue. The General lay flat on the ground, the warm tarmac on his face. He felt rough hands at his back, handcuffs clicked tight. Suddenly he felt a vibration through the road: the tell-tale tremor of thousands of tonnes of fuel turning into plasma, the tell-tale vibration of thousands of tonnes of man-made folly, dragging itself off Mother Earth and slowly lifting into the sky. He was too late; he had failed.

John ran to the top of the stairs, passed a dissenting receptionist and entered Lutz Asher's ward. He stopped in his tracks. There they were, the two politicians and their entourage, stopped at his bed. Lutz was all but knocked out on a cocktail of painkillers. The explosion had broken a number of bones; he had been concussed. It was the least of his traumas.

The two politicians moved towards the body, two vultures standing over a corpse. John could see the intensity with which they scanned him, slumbering before them. Jan had to be right. God, she was always right. Alves bent low towards the body. There was no time to be lost.

'Stand away from him!' John ran towards the group. 'Get away from him! I know what you are.' The assembled group looked at him in astonishment. The woman, dark hair falling round her face, turned towards him. Black welcoming eyes, undressed him with their gaze.

'There must be some kind of mistake. My name is Maria Vivinco, I am visiting from the European government. We hope to open a new cancer centre here, please, let me show you.' She motioned as if to draw him aside, but he evaded her touch and put a bed between them. Alves had moved closer to the body, his hands reaching down towards the unsuspecting face.

'I told you, get away from him!' John looked around for a weapon. He picked up a glass vase; tipping out the contents he brandished it in front of him. 'Step away from that man, or I swear I'll kill you.'

The doctors and nurses that formed the group began to back away. Someone tried some placatory words. John's eyes, focused on the hunched back of Alves as he hovered over the body, drew the doctors' collective gaze. There was something strange about the way he was ignoring the disturbance in the room; something not entirely normal about the blank mask of concentration as he scanned the prone form before him. 'Perhaps we should leave Mr. Asher in peace, Mr. Alves. I'm sure this gentleman will be happier if we just leave him

384

alone.' Alves hissed at the man, who recoiled from him. 'For Christ's sake let's get some security in here!' He ran from the ward.

All eyes were on John. Maria slowly advanced on him, talking him down; everything was going to be all right. He swiped at her with the vase, it barely missed her head, she hissed in defiance.

At that moment Lutz gained consciousness. He saw the man standing over him, saw John pinned between the bed and the wall. His blood ran cold. He could feel the heat of the man's breath. He could feel the pull of the universe on the other side of the man's eyes. He too looked for a weapon. His fingers found the edge of a sharps bin, the edges of two hypodermics protruded from the top. Gently he pulled them into his hand; slowly he hid them in his fist. Alves' eyes turned towards him. His nostrils flared, he brought his hands to Lutz's throat. The doctors and nurses gasped in unison but remained motionless, the surreality of the moment preventing them from action. Alves seemed incredibly strong, his thin fingers crushed Lutz's windpipe using every reserve of his strength. He acted with intense focus, staring down at the prone figure beneath him without a shade of malice. For Lutz the pain was unbearable. The injustice of death taking him now, when he had so recently evaded it, rendered him momentarily immobile, his mind was boiling with fear and anger. The finality of death overwhelmed him, he would have to leave everything behind, for him reality was over. The proximity of the other universe, seen in the black sparks of the expressionless eyes of the man trying to kill him, invited him in.

His fist crashed into Alves' face. Sheffield steel, drawn, cut and polished, pricked the outer membrane of the eye, penetrated the aqueous humours, the soft jelly of the vitreous humour, divided rod-shaped photoreceptor from cone-shaped photoreceptor and pierced the delicate membranes of the retina, before sliding against the bony socket and embedding in the optic nerve. The universe within, bounded by that fragile membrane, exploded around him. Alves did not retract in pain; for a moment he was immobile. His hands, still grasping Lutz's prone form, twitched involuntarily. Something moved from Lutz Asher's brain, through the sympathetic and parasympathetic nerves of his arm, through the flesh and nerves of his hand, a subtle vibration, a change in attitude of electrons, a nervous tremor of photons. The unseen, immeasurable wave excited the particles of the hypodermic, slid between the atoms to the point of the needle, warmed the blood and humours of the human flesh beyond and stepped back into Lembeck's domain.

The mind of Fernando Alves had long since vacated his brain. The space that remained was filled by Lembeck's consciousness. The conduit was wide; information flowed in bright streams to and from the mind. Lutz found himself in intimate contact with each and every one of Lembeck's peripatetic implants. He understood in a fraction of a second the plans which were unfolding. He had been here before, there was no way back. His life had left his body at the same moment that his mind had made the leap to safety. If he had any future at all it was here. He reached out into his new domain. At any moment he was sure Lembeck would confront him. He could conjure the image before him, it's presence was everywhere. The ego, the id, that was it, that was the difference. As his consciousness found its feet, settling like a vapour over the hills and valleys of the mind that contained it, Lutz Asher realised that he had entered the mind of Joe Lembeck. He had entered this world through the front door. His was not the universe governed by Lembeck, his was the universe of Lembeck's own mind. Understanding came first; thoughts, with their precision and clarity, came later. Everything that Lembeck was or had been permeated his awareness. He knew everything that Lembeck knew, experienced everything that Lembeck had experienced. It was like putting on an old coat, so much of the personality was familiar to him.

He drew the coat about him, revelling in its familiarity. Studying the details. This is what it felt like to be a god, comfort, knowledge, a vista of night and day combined, peace and thrilling noise, solitude and solace. It was then that he started to appreciate the effect he was having on Lembeck's world.

He became aware of warmth. A chemical heat, like the mixing of acid and alkali, the heat was slight, but threatening. The godlike mind that was Lembeck also became aware of it, but could not see the cause of it. A wave passed through it, distorting, reflecting and sifting it. For a moment it saw itself from outside, a feverish mirage of its former being. Having experienced so many deaths before, this new passing was met with resignation. The reformed consciousness began to settle and merge with its host. The chimera born from this uncomfortable birth writhed in its new home. Something was terribly wrong but it had no means of expressing its pain. Its inchoate thrashing expressed itself as heat, from the heat evolved a thought, then a scream, then a chorus roaring in the hills. The implants were getting hot, Lutz Asher was still infected by his program. His consciousness was toxic, a terrible, systemic poison and now Lembeck was infected.

John watched in stunned horror as Alves dropped Lutz Asher's lifeless body to the floor. His hands did not reach for the needles that hung from the bloody maw of his face, instead he clutched at his head, whilst he staggered as though punch-drunk through the assembled crowd. Maria too let out a wailing cry. Steam squeezed from between their fingers, bubbling from their ears, then their eyes and nostrils. They fell to the ground in unison, their limbs thrashing, blood red steam boiling from their heads.

They did not utter a sound; tremors racked them, and then they were still.

General Highgate watched over his shoulder as the rocket powered into the sky. The heat haze obscured its details, the high cloud coalescing with the pillar of steam that seemed to push it heavenward. The rocket burners illuminated the pinnacle, a bright star on the ascendant, which would become a black star when it took its place in the heavens, a black star that took the souls of the as yet unborn. The policemen did not turn to stare. The most magnificent demonstration of human endeavour was too common an occurrence in Florida to distract them from their work. With every metre it climbed, the General's heart sank. In a few minutes it would be out of sight. He tried to think of alternative routes that might be open to him. Other people he could call. He would have to help expose Lembeck's plan. He would have to tell the world. The consequences of publicly exposing Lembeck could be terrible, but there was no choice, he would have to do his bit. It was at that moment that the rocket exploded. Fire tore back from the tip of the ascending spike, a wave of flame travelling at the speed of sound ignited the boosters and in a moment it was gone, a chrysanthemum of white fire.

The detonation echoed back through space toward them; debris was swirling down towards the sea. It was the most beautiful sight the General had ever seen.

EPILOGUE

Lutz Asher felt the extent of his consciousness unfurling through the void. His thoughts that now illuminated the darkness were far greater than those a normal human brain might contain, grander in scale, coloured with the accumulated written knowledge of millions of lives. As his mind rippled through virtual space, it found the minds of the uploads, fragile, intricate, the most beautiful things imaginable. In time he would gently unfurl them and let them take flight again. Lembeck was not destroyed. It was impossible for Lutz to say where he ended and Lembeck began. The programming was evolving beyond his ability to analyse it, Yin melded with Yang, two forces in flux, each interpenetrating the other. In melding with Lembeck he had encountered part of Lembeck's soul that was hidden from Lembeck himself. A core element, a kernel of programming that neither could penetrate. Lutz wondered if there was a similar element within him, a place where God himself could not look. There had been no final conflict, no battle of wills. Their fusion had been irrevocable. Lutz could sense the loneliness of Lembeck, a human soul, freed of its bondage, yet trapped in its godhood. Perhaps this loneliness had facilitated their joining.

In destroying Lembeck's outlet to the world, Lutz had temporarily imprisoned them both. He felt a residual sadness at this; but this emotional response was already being diluted by its assimilation and rationalisation into the immensity that was this new conciousness. Such thoughts could be swept back together, reassembled and stripped bare, but the desire to do so faded immediately. At that moment Lutz was content to explore his new realm. His inner space, populated by a thousand souls, was enough. For now Lutz had no desire to conquer the world. There would be time enough for that. Today he was a god, with a universe to build. Everyone else could be a god tomorrow.